MW00861120

THE GIZA PROTOCOL

AN EDEN BLACK THRILLER

LUKE RICHARDSON

1

1987. Mansheya Nasir District, Cairo, Egypt.

MOHAMMED MUHR JUNIOR stirred in his sleep, trying to find comfort on the lumpy mattress. In truth, now heading towards his tenth birthday, he was getting too big for this bed. He didn't want to bring that to the attention of his parents, though, as they seemed to have enough to worry about already.

Mohammed, ironically called Little Mo by friends and family to prevent confusion between father and son who shared the name, had always been big for his age. His mother frequently told stories of the teachers at his first school needing proof of his age before they would take him, so convinced they were of his advanced years based on his size.

"That's just one of life's miracles," his mother would say, her voice soft and tuneful. Mo could picture her now, looking down at him, a radiant smile standing out from her weather-darkened skin. She didn't seem to smile as much anymore, Little Mo thought, turning again. Well, she did still smile, but it wasn't quite the same. It wasn't as radiant, as vibrant, or as bold.

Little Mo had heard the arguments. Many nights he would lie there awake, wishing for sleep to come and dull his senses, as the sound of his parents' warring voices floated into his room.

"If only you cared for us as much as you did those long dead Pharaohs," his mother said. "They've been dead thousands of years, and they get all your time. We're here. We're here now and we need you."

"It's what I must do," was his father's only reply. "One day, the world will know the secrets that lie beneath those pyramids. The work I'm doing now is not just for us, but for the whole of humanity."

"You're living in a dream world," his mother snapped in reply, her voice hoarse from shouting. "We're your family and we've barely got enough money for food. Have you seen the clothes our son wears to school? He grew out of them almost a year ago. Uncle Abdulla said he would get you a job down driving for the recycling company. It's stable money. Paid every week. That's what we need."

Little Mo shook himself back to the present. He sat up in bed. There had been no arguments tonight. In fact, there had been no arguments for a couple of weeks, but it felt to Mo as though one was brewing. A big one.

Mo rubbed at his eyes and positioned the pillows behind him. Light from the street below streamed through his window's ill-fitting curtains, casting angular shadows across the ceiling.

He listened to the silence of the apartment. Several stories below, a car rattled past, serving as a constant reminder that rest, like everything else, was a commodity in this city. A dog yapped several times.

Then, rubbing his eyes again, he heard something. Although little more than a gentle thud, the sound carried like a tolling bell through the still night air. Mo straightened up, listening hard.

There it was again.

Mo held his breath, concentrating on the noise. Another thud came a moment later, this time followed by the scraping of something across the floor. Mo recognized that as the sound of his parents' bedroom door grinding against the tiles. Someone was coming out of his parents' room. That was very unusual at this time of night. The sound, which he now recognized as footsteps, moved through the apartment and into the kitchen.

Mo climbed to his feet. The book he had been reading before bed—*Chariots of the Gods* by Erich von Däniken— slipped off the cover. Mo caught the paperback a moment before it dropped to the floor. Placing the book carefully on the table, Mo picked his way across the room.

He reached the door and closed his hand around the handle. Willing the mechanism not to make a noise, Mo twisted the handle. Allah was on his side, it seemed, as the door swung open, emitting nothing more than a whisper.

Mo stole out into the hallway. He paused and listened. The movement came from the kitchen now, which was at the far end of the apartment. For the first time, curiosity morphed into fear. Mo wondered what he would do if he found the sounds were the result of an intruder. Intruders around here were incredibly rare, but Mo had heard about them blighting the city's more affluent neighborhoods. Everyone in Mansheya Nasir—nicknamed Garbage City because most of the people here worked sorting and recycling Cairo's waste—looked out for one another.

Mo glanced through the apartment. What an intruder

would hope to find in one of Cairo's poorest districts, he couldn't even guess.

Mo glanced back at his bed, just a few steps behind him. He could return there now and no one would know he had heard a thing.

The noise of a cupboard opening drifted through the apartment. The interloper closed the cupboard again, gently. Whoever they were, they were doing their best to be quiet.

Mo took a deep breath, suppressing his swelling fear. He covered the distance to the kitchen door in five steps. Leaning in, Mo placed his ear against the thin wood. Mo heard a zipper being pulled. Questions streamed through his mind. Once again, Mo steeled his courage and pushed the door.

"You should be in bed. What are you doing here?" Mo's father said, spinning around as his son entered the room.

Shadows hung about the kitchen. A dim beam of light streamed from a flashlight placed on the counter, the batteries clearly in their dying minutes. In the gloom, though, Mo could see that his father was fully dressed and clutched a small bag.

"What's going on?" Mo said, ignoring his father's instruction. "Why are you dressed at this time of night?"

Mo's father placed the bag on the counter and stepped towards his son. He sunk to one knee, took Mo's hands in his and locked eyes with the boy.

"You're growing so fast," he said, more to himself than his son. "It's been wonderful to see you turning into a young man."

Mo's father lifted one hand to his face and rubbed it across his eyes. "It's the dust," he said, sniffing. "It always gets in my eyes."

Mo nodded, not believing a word his father said. Mo noticed now how patches bracketed his father's eyes, accentuated by the lines age and stress had brought on.

"What's going on?" Mo said again, more softly now.

Father and son held hands again. "There's something I need to do."

"In the middle of the night?"

"It may take me some time, and it may be dangerous."

Mo said nothing. Silence sat unfilled between father and son.

"Remember what I told you about the ancient civilization that came before us, the one that was—"

"Much more advanced than we have been led to believe, and how one day, when we are ready for it, their technology will become available to us?" Mo completed his father's oft spoken sentence word for word.

"That's right," Mo's father said, a single tear finding its way down his weather-beaten skin. "Well, I believe that time is upon us, but there is work to be done."

"Is it important? Is what you do important?" Mo looked at his hands, so pale and small inside his father's.

"It's the second most important task of my life."

"What's the first?" Mo looked up again, surprised.

"Being your father." Several seconds of silence slid by like freighter ships on the Nile. "But now that you are nearly ten, I can wait no longer. I will do all I can to make it back to you, and soon." Mo senior lifted his son's chin. Their eyes locked. "It's important that you know, people may tell lies about me when I'm not here. They may try to tell you I'm crazy, that I'm delusional. Believe me, that is just the fear talking. It is the easiest thing in the world to tell lies about someone who isn't there to defend themselves, right?"

"I suppose." Mo nodded.

Mo's father glanced at his watch. He had frequently told Mo about the timepiece. There was an inscription on the back which Mo had committed to memory.

"As above, so below," Little Mo said, repeating the inscription. His voice sounded loud in the silent kitchen.

"As above, so below," his father repeated back, several more tears now joining the first. The man released Mo's hands and stood. Then, without another word, he slung his bag across his shoulder and strode towards the front door.

Barely breathing, Mo listened to his father's footsteps clicking across the floor. The door swung open, then the footsteps disappeared for the last time.

2

The Himalayas, Nepal. Present day.

"I'M GOING TO GET YOU," Eden Black shouted at the top of her lungs. "And when I do, you'll be sorry."

Eden charged between two of the huts which made up the village of Sreva, searching for her quarry. Somewhere up ahead, footsteps pounded the wet earth.

Eden swung around a corner and jumped over two chickens pecking at a pile of spilled grain. She took a deep breath. Even after two weeks in the village, the thin air at this altitude made intense exercise hard work.

"You can run, but you can't hide," Eden snarled. She listened carefully to the sound of the mountain slopes. Was that a whispered voice drifting from somewhere nearby? It was easy to lose a sense of direction between the tightly packed huts. Eden spun around, momentarily disorientated. Sweat prickled her forehead. Her muscles ached already after a day's work.

Around the corner, the footsteps broke their cover. Eden sprinted after them, her feet slipping across the ground.

Eden ran out into the village's central clearing. Raised voices cried in cheers. Hands clapped. Eden saw the group of children up ahead. They whooped and laughed in excitement. Eden upped her pace. Now on the open ground, she could catch them easily.

"Gotcha!" she shouted, tapping Binsa, the youngest, on the arm. "You too!" she shouted again, reaching out and clipping Dhonu on the wrist.

The two children huffed their disappointment and reluctantly crossed to the circle of adults sitting beside the fire.

Eden focused all her attention on the one remaining child. Idha was eleven years old and quickly becoming a young woman. Eden had wondered how long she would want to play games with the other children. Maybe it was a blessing that life in the village prolonged childhood.

Idha stood at the other side of the clearing and stared back at Eden.

"Do you want to surrender now?" Eden said. "I'll make it easy for you."

Idha's gaze narrowed. Eden had no doubt the young woman understood. In the last two weeks, her English had improved exponentially.

"No way," Idha said, "you try to catch me."

Eden grinned, looking at the village's outer limit which lay twenty feet behind Idha. The young woman had nowhere to run.

"As you wish," Eden said, taking a dramatic step forward.

Idha retreated slowly, glancing around.

Eden took another two steps forwards. Idha mirrored her movements. The young woman was just a few feet from the boundary now.

Eden feigned a leap forward from her crouched position. Idha fell for the ploy and hopped to the right. Eden doubled back and launched herself to the left. Flying, she extended both arms and reached out towards the younger woman. The younger woman's lithe body shot past. Eden reached further, her muscles stinging. Finally, her fingers closed around Idha's upper arm.

Both women collapsed to the earth. The impact forced air from Eden's lungs. A cloud of dust rose around them. Eden rolled on to her back and inhaled deeply.

A whoop of applause rose from the assembled villagers.

"Game over," Eden said, sitting up and brushing dust from her hands.

Idha sat up too. She looked around in something of a daze. "How did you...?"

"People always jump right," Eden said, struggling to her feet. "Don't worry about it."

She held out a hand and helped Idha up.

"Tomorrow I'm the catcher," Idha said. She grinned and sauntered towards the hut her family shared on the far side of the village. Eden watched her go and then looked out at the surrounding mountains.

Her breathing and heartbeat reluctantly returned to their normal rate. She listened to the sounds of the mountain village. The caw of the jungle birds, which echoed riotously during the daylight hours on these lower slopes, muted with the dying light, and the sounds of insects zinged from the surrounding trees.

She glanced up at the clear sky, from here just a dome of unbroken blue, and thought for the first time in several hours about her life back in England. She traced the trail of an airliner as it streaked through the heavens several miles above. At some point, Eden would have to return to England. There was much to do.

Several weeks ago, although it seemed like mere moments, Eden had been instrumental in uncovering a set of ancient tablets. Not a reader of cuneiform, Eden couldn't help with the translation, but she suspected what they revealed would force her back into action. The world was changing, she thought, returning her gaze to the collection of huts which had become her temporary home, and she wanted to make sure it was going in the right direction.

"Good night, Miss Black!" A pair of squealed voices snapped Eden from her daydream. She waved at Binsa and Dhonu as they followed their parents back home.

"Good night," Eden replied.

Eden looked around at the dozen huts, constructed from mud and reeds, clinging precariously to the lower Himalayan slopes, which made up the village of Sreva. She had been here nearly two weeks, but already, away from the modern world, it was feeling strangely like home. A stiff breeze sung through the countless lines of prayer flags, pulling them tight against their fixings.

Part of a small charity group, Eden had come to the village to help teach the residents English. Another member of the party was helping them learn basic first aid. The volunteers spent their days wrapped up in the lives of the villagers. With livestock to care for and crops to sustain, there were no free passes. Eden's muscles ached, her hands were calloused, but she tingled with vitality.

"Are you coming for food?"

Startled, Eden spun around. Juddha, one of the village's older men, greeted her with his trademark charming smile. His skin, creased by countless years in the village's thin air, glowed in the dying pinks of dusk.

"I will, I will," Eden said. Her stomach growled as though in response to the thought of food. The man stood beside Eden and looked out at the landscape. He took a deep breath and let it out slowly. "You know. I seen deese mountains every day of my life. Still juss as beautiful."

Eden nodded. A golden line appeared across the ridge of the opposite snow-capped peak.

"You know Nepal is really the biggest country in the world?" Juddha turned to Eden, with a glint in his eye.

"It's certainly one of the most beautiful," Eden replied diplomatically.

"No, is the biggest. If you could lay all deese mountains, how you say—" he made a horizontal gesture with his hands.

"Flat," Eden offered.

"Yes. If you could lay deese mountains flat. Nepal would be the..." His voice trailed off as an unfamiliar noise pierced the breeze. Juddha stiffened, standing up straight.

The muscles in his arms tensed. He turned in the direction of the track, which was the village's only connection to the outside world. Juddha muttered some words Eden didn't understand. His voice rumbled like an ominous prayer.

A stronger wind whipped through the village now, cracking the lines of prayer flags anew. The intrusive noise rose from a whisper to a growl. Eden leaned forward, listening in. The noise came again. She recognized it as the distant rise and fall of an engine.

It took Eden several moments to realize why that was unusual. No one in the village owned a car and supplies were brought in once a week. Due to the unreliability of these deliveries, the villagers kept stores in preparation for much longer periods of isolation. Once a landslide had cut off the village for several months.

But their weekly delivery had arrived two days ago, so certainly a new delivery wasn't due anytime soon.

Juddha offered his whispered prayer again.

The engine rose from a whisper to a growl. Several hundred feet away, a set of headlights swept through the landscape.

Juddha stood rigid, unmoving.

"What is it?" Eden asked. "Who's coming?"

Juddha cleared his throat and pointed a bony finger towards the approaching vehicle. When he spoke, his words came out as little more than a murmur. "Deese men. They come to take our children. The girls. Dey take the girls."

"What do you mean?" The man's words made little sense. Eden turned and looked into his wind-beaten face.

"Dey take the girls." Eden caught Juddha's hard gaze.

Realization slammed Eden in the stomach. She'd read about this some months ago. Gangs of men who came up to the mountains to take the village's young women. Often by force, the men trafficked the young women to cities in Nepal or India where they were forced to work in an effort to "pay off their debt." It was an awful operation. Eden couldn't believe monsters like this still existed in the modern world.

The vehicle growled closer, tires slipping across the gravel track.

The beat of Eden's heart rose with the force and regularity of a jackhammer. A sharp pain surged through her veins. She turned to the man, who had now turned a ghostly white in the dying sunlight. Eden's voice took on the deep tone of a confession.

"That's not happening," she said, her eyes hard. "No one leaves this village tonight."

The vehicle was just five hundred feet away on the

curving road now. Their progress was slow, but within a couple of minutes, they would arrive in the village.

"We're going to need weapons." Eden's voice was as sharp as a knife.

Juddha caught Eden's gaze. Tension rippled across his facial muscles. "Follow me."

Juddha set off an all-out sprint. For a few strides, Eden had trouble keeping up. Ahead, several villagers gathered in the central clearing, including the other three volunteers. Juddha reached the clearing first and barked at the villagers in their native tongue. The half-dozen men and women paled when the meaning of the words sunk in.

Juddha ducked into a hut and emerged clutching a machete and a long tool which looked a little like a scythe.

The other volunteers looked from Eden to the man, confusion and fear etched on their faces. Eden quickly explained what was happening.

"I don't want to put you in danger," Eden said, accepting the machete from Juddha and rubbing her thumb carefully across the blade. It was sharp. "It's time these people fought back. I'm going to make sure that happens. If you don't want to be involved, take a walk up the hill."

The roaring engine was audible from the center of the village now. Eden spun and looked towards the noise. Juddha stood beside her, the scythe held in both hands across his chest. Eden glanced up at the man. Standing tall and proud in defense of his village, a force to be reckoned with.

"We should be out of sight when they arrive," came a voice from behind them. Eden spun around. One of the volunteers remained standing, while the other two rushed towards the safety of the nearby trees.

Eden locked eyes with the young woman. Working long

days in the village, Eden had got to know Allissa Stockwell quite well, but this bravery surprised her. Allissa's dark eyes glinted in the dying sunlight.

"What have we got here?" Allissa strode forward and took the machete from Eden. She hefted it to test the weight. "That could do some damage."

"You stay here," Eden barked to Juddha. "We'll stay out of sight until they're in the open."

Juddha nodded, his eyes narrowed in focus.

The growling engine filled the air now. Beyond the first structures of the village, strong headlights swept through the forest.

Eden and Allissa rushed behind one of the huts moments before the vehicle crested the hill. The grumbling engine moved through the gears as the lane leveled off. Gravel snapped and skittered beneath the thick tires. The gear box clunked as the vehicle slowed. Brakes squealed. The powerful engine dropped into its lowest register.

Eden and Allissa peered out from behind the hut. Juddha stood motionless in the twin beams of the headlights. He held the scythe across his chest like an ancient warrior ready to protect. Ready to kill if necessary.

Brakes squealed again, and the vehicle crunched to a stop.

3

1987. Mansheya Nasir District, Cairo, Egypt.

MOHAMMED MUHR SENIOR coaxed the throttle of his aging
Dayun motorcycle. He reached the edge of Mansheya Nasir,
bumped over the disused railway line, and turned out onto
the freeway. Even at this late hour traffic thronged to and
from the city—but at least it was moving.

In the passing glow of a streetlight, Mo glanced at his
watch. He was late. Very late indeed. Mo pulled back harder
on the gas. The bike's faithful engine whined, protesting at
the increasing speed. Then with a deep, metallic clunk from
somewhere deep within the machine's guts, it accelerated.

"That's my girl," Mo whispered, tapping the fuel tank. In
the cycles of his normal life, Big Mo would never push the
machine to its limits. It wasn't worth the risk of damage. A
motorbike repair bill was far more than he and his wife
could afford. Plus, working as a nighttime security guard on
The Giza Plateau, Big Mo wasn't often in a rush. There was
no need to rush when everything you were guarding had

already been dead for several thousand years, Mo often joked.

Tonight though, that was different. Very different.

Twenty minutes later, the bulky, angular shape of the Great Pyramid emerged from the muddle of buildings on the right. Mo glanced at the monolith, standing intrepid, unyielding, and mysterious, as it had for thousands of years. If tonight went well, Mo thought, cajoling a little more speed out of the rattling Dayun, then perhaps one small part of that mystery would be solved.

Mo pulled up outside a laundromat in Nazlet-El-Samman. Once a settlement in its own right, Nazlet-El-Samman had become engrossed in Cairo's urban sprawl in the worst way. Soulless concrete structures loomed, gaunt and pale, along every street. Zephyrs that once twisted the sand into ethereal spirals, now scattered trash across the streets.

Mo kicked down the Dayun's stand. Three other bikes already waited outside the shop, re-enforcing to Mo that he was late.

A high-pitched screech echoed down the street. Mo spun around on his heels just in time to see the twisted tail of a street cat disappear behind a trash can. The image was a fitting testament to the degradation of his country, Mo thought. Once revered and respected, cats now lived amongst the junk. When there were already too many mouths to feed, and not enough to feed them with, who really cared?

"I'm sorry, I'm sorry," Mo said, clattering through the door and into the laundromat.

He glanced around, but his eyes still not used to the gloom inside the shop, saw nothing but murky shadows. Three men lounged against the old washing machines, the fiery ends of cigarettes bobbing. Mo recognized them all. He was the last to arrive.

"You're late," a man named Bakir said, stepping forward.

"Yes, I know, sorry. My son caught me getting ready..."

"That's not a problem, I hope?"

"Absolutely not. He understands our cause better than most."

"Good to hear." Bakir stepped forwards and embraced Muhr. "Good to see you, brother. When you were late, we thought the worst."

"All's good. Let's get started. Have we got all the gear?"

"Everything you asked for," said a thin wiry man named Faheem. He exhaled a cloud of smoke.

"Excellent," Muhr said. "Even the camera?"

Faheem turned and looked at Muhr. "It wasn't easy, but I got it. It must go back tomorrow, though, or it'll cost me big time." Faheem pointed at Mo with his lit cigarette.

"It will, don't worry. I've got it all planned. Nothing will go wrong tonight. I know what I'm doing."

"Except your son catching you leaving the house," said Hijazi, the smallest man who hadn't yet spoken. The man's voice, nasal and high-pitched, was uncomfortable to hear.

"I told you, that's not a problem." Mo waved a dismissive hand.

Hijazi shrugged in a way which indicated he didn't care either way. "It's through there." Hijazi pointed with his cigarette towards the laundromat's back room.

Muhr strode through to the back room. A flickering bare bulb hung from the ceiling, casting a sepia-toned glow across the space. The old trappings of the laundromat had been pushed against the far wall to create space for their mission. The equipment they needed was stacked on the floor. Muhr inspected it. Four high powered waterproof flashlights, several lengths of climbing rope, four large back-packs, and a top of the range waterproof camera. He picked up the camera and turned it around in his hands.

"Built in flash, auto exposure function. It's the best on the market in low light conditions." Hijazi sidled up beside Muhr to examine the camera. Muhr smelled the smaller man's pungent odor.

"This is fantastic," Muhr said. "I don't want to ask how much it cost."

Hijazi and Faheem glanced at each other. "Don't you worry about that," Faheem said. "If we're successful today, money means nothing, no?"

Muhr nodded in agreement.

"But boss, are you sure we want to do this?" Faheem said.

Muhr turned and looked at the smaller man.

"I just mean, we don't know exactly what's down there, and we don't know what impact it might have."

"Tell me Faheem, how many people are there in your family?"

"Nine of us, boss."

"And how big is your home?"

"We do okay. We have three rooms."

"Do you know there are people just like you and me who live in houses with hundreds of rooms? Houses so big they don't even need to see another member of their family, let alone sleep beside one. Some people even have more than one house too, in different countries. What we discover today, I hope, will not just improve the lives of us and our families, but equal the balance for people across the world."

Muhr looked at Faheem. The smaller man blinked, then shrugged. "If you say so, boss. Just checking you know what we're getting into."

"Of course. We've been preparing this for years." Muhr glanced at his watch. "Get ready. It's time to go."

As the men extinguished their cigarettes and pulled on their backpacks, Muhr drew back the dusty carpet covering the floor. He stepped towards a wooden panel set into the middle of the floor. Together, Muhr and Bakir lifted the panel from its mounting, exposing a roughly hewn staircase. They leaned the panel against the wall, then stepped back towards the exposed staircase.

"How did you know this was here?" Hijazi asked, staring down into the hole.

"Several years ago, I uncovered a secret document which detailed access to the area beneath The Giza Plateau." Muhr checked his watch. "Enough questions, all will become clear. We don't have time to waste."

Mohammed Muhr flicked on his flashlight and stepped down onto the staircase. Originally built as a well, the spiral staircase wound its way around a shaft with fresh water at the bottom. Villagers wanting to use the well would have descended the stairs with a bucket and collected the water by hand.

The group carefully picked their way down the stairs in silence.

"There's a passage just under the water there," Muhr said, shining the flashlight on the water's surface. A shimmering reflection sparkled across the shaft's walls. The well here had narrowed to a little over six feet, with clear water lapping over the lowest steps. "It works like an airlock. It'll take about thirty seconds to get through, so you'll be fine holding your breath. I'll go through with a rope first. You can use the rope to drag yourself through. Then we'll use the rope to drag the bags through. Bakir, you go last."

Bakir nodded and set about tying the bags to the rope.

"What is this place?" Faheem said, staggering out of the water on the other side of the airlock a couple of minutes later. They were in a tunnel which ran straight for as far as he could see. He stepped towards the wall and ran his hand across the blocks of granite covered in mysterious hieroglyphs.

"Welcome to the Underworld of the Soul," Muhr said, steadying the rope for Hijazi and Bakir.

Hijazi appeared from the water, then the three men pulled in the rope, dragging the bags beneath the water. Bakir swam after the bags, helping propel them forwards. The men slipped their bags on again and Muhr led them down the passage.

After a few hundred feet, a colossal stone slab blocked their path.

Wide-eyed, Faheem and Hijazi swung the beams of their lights across the hieroglyphs.

"What do they say?" Hijazi whined.

"That, gentlemen, is the code for us to get in."

"Clever," Faheem said.

"Once we're inside, we only have a few minutes before the water will start to re-enter the chamber. We must hurry. We're here for one thing and one thing alone."

"What's that?" Hijazi asked.

"We're here for the Ark of the Covenant of course."

4

The Himalayas, Nepal. Present day.

EDEN AND ALLISSA leaned further out of their hiding place, trying to make out the coming threat. They couldn't see anything beyond the wash of the headlights. A door squealed open, followed by a second. Two pairs of boots thumped to the ground. Then a booming laugh filled the air, followed by a second. The sound of it made anger rise in Eden's veins. These men had come to the village to tear families apart and were laughing about it. She stepped out from behind the hut, ready to charge at the vile animals.

Allissa's fingers closed around Eden's upper arm. "Not yet," Allissa whispered. "Wait until they're out of the truck."

Eden let the rising anger subside and took a small step backwards.

Two men lumbered into view. Both were large and muscular, towering over Juddha's slight figure. Both thugs wore filthy cotton shirts which must have been white a long time ago. One man had previously suffered a broken nose, which now looked like a growth of fungus on his face. The other man moved with a pronounced limp to his left leg. It was clear they'd both been in their fair share of skirmishes.

Broken Nose barked something at Juddha.

"I think he's telling him to move," Allissa whispered.

"You can speak Nepalese?"

"A bit," Allissa hissed. "I lived in Kathmandu a couple of years ago. Some friends tried to teach me."

Eden glanced at the other woman. "Impressive."

"I still can't understand what the villagers say. They speak a different dialect," Allissa added.

The limping man stepped forward and shoved Juddha. Juddha took a step backwards but didn't surrender his position. If the men wanted to get to the village, they would have to go through Juddha.

The man with the limp shouted in Juddha's face. Spittle flew. Juddha didn't move.

Broken Nose unsheathed a knife and held it up towards Juddha.

"You don't want to know what they're saying now," Allissa whispered. "It's pretty nasty."

"I've seen enough," Eden said, leading them along behind the hut and out the other side.

Broken Nose swung the knife forwards. Juddha parried and lifted the scythe to deflect the blow. The knife slid from the handle of the scythe. Juddha took a step backwards, his hands gripping the scythe's long handle like a baseball bat. He eyed the two men with pure disgust.

Eden and Allissa crept out from behind the hut across the lane towards the truck. They were twenty feet behind the men and well out of their sightline. They reached the truck and ducked in behind it.

Eden peered out in time to see Juddha swing the scythe.

Designed for long days in the fields, the tool was large and heavy. It was not suitable for combat, and that showed.

When the scythe reached the end of its swing, Broken Nose stepped forward and grabbed the handle. Six inches taller and a good deal heavier than Juddha, he tore the weapon from the villager's grip. His lips set into a snarl, Broken Nose threw the scythe to the dust. He grabbed Juddha by the neck and lifted him clear of the ground. Juddha's feet kicked uselessly, and his hands scrabbled at the larger man's wrist.

"Let's end this," Eden said, stepping out from behind the truck. "You take this." Eden gave Allissa the machete. "Stay back for a couple of minutes. Let's make them think it'll be easy."

Allissa took the knife and crouched back behind the truck. Eden walked out towards the men.

"Hey ugly, over here!" Eden shouted when she was six feet away.

Both men jerked around. Broken Nose kept his fingers closed around Juddha's neck. Juddha hung limp from the larger man's grip.

Two pairs of eyes made their way up and down Eden's body. Eden thought about what these men were capable of —what they did to make a living—and felt a wave of repulsion pass through her. She pictured their victims. Young, innocent women like Idha.

"Hey pretty lady. You long way from home," Limping Man said in broken English. He sidled towards Eden.

Eden took half a step backwards, feigning fear.

"So are you," Eden snarled. "You need to get back in your truck and get out of here before I make you."

The men exchanged a glance, grinning.

"Let him go now," Eden barked, pointing towards Juddha who hung still in the man's grip.

"Sure." Broken Nose shrugged and threw Juddha to the side as though he weighed nothing. The villager collapsed into the dust. For a few moments he didn't move, then he dragged in several wheezing breaths.

"What are you doing out here all alone, pretty girl?" the limping man said.

Broken Nose giggled. The noise was far higher pitched that Eden had expected for a man of his size.

"I'm a volunteer in this village. You need to go now. You're not welcome here."

Both men laughed. They took a step forward.

"Where you from?" Broken Nose barked.

"England," Eden answered. She took another step backwards, angling the men away from the truck and Allissa.

Both men stared at Eden for several seconds, as though searching for a threat.

"Dis is not England," Broken Nose said, pointing towards the ground. "Der is something in dis village that belongs to us."

"Wha do you say we have some fun before making the collection," Limping Man said.

From the ground behind them, Juddha shouted something Eden didn't understand. Broken Nose strode across to the villager and kicked him hard. Juddha tried to roll out of the way, but the kick still struck his stomach.

"Take her to the back of the truck," the limping man snarled. "We will show this English woman who makes rules here."

"No wait, what?" Eden held out her hands in mock surrender. "You can't. You can't!"

Broken Nose stepped towards Eden, his lips strained in a wide smile. "Then we will come back for what we..."

Broken Nose didn't even see the machete coming. The blade whizzed through the air and sunk deep into his thigh, cutting him off in mid-sentence. Shocked and confused, he looked down at the weapon, buried beneath his flesh, then he howled in pain. If the rest of the village weren't already awake, they would be now.

Eden leaped into action, landing two clean punches. His nose exploded again in a mess of blood and bone. Then, Eden swung into a kick and stuck him hard on the ribs. He collapsed to the side, unmoving.

The other man lunged forwards in defense of his friend, but Eden was ready.

She kneeled and pulled the machete from Broken Nose's leg, twisting the dirty blade as she did. Blood pumped unobstructed from the wound now. Allissa's swing had clearly severed an artery. The man would be dead within minutes.

Seeing Eden now brandishing the blood-stained machete, the limping man froze. He raised his hands in something of surrender and took a step towards the truck. He glanced down at his friend bleeding out on the dust, turned and ran back towards the truck. He made it to the truck in four paces and sprang into the driver's seat. The truck roared into action and the thug gunned the engine. Tires spun against the dirt road as the man pulled a one-eighty turn and sped off down the track.

"He won't get far," Allissa said, pointing at a stream of liquid gushing from the vehicle's rear.

"You cut the fuel line?" Eden asked, looking at the women in a different light.

"I'd say he'll get ten miles away maximum," Allissa said. "That's a week's walk to the nearest town."

"How did you know..."

Allissa turned to face Eden. "I saw you take those men on. Strange skill for an English teacher. I think it's fair to say there are things we both don't know about each other."

"Agreed," Eden said.

As the rumbling of the truck faded into the tinkling jungle, another unusual sound shrieked through the night.

"My phone," Eden said, dropping the machete and rushing across to her hut. Moments later, she appeared at the door with the satellite phone pinned to her ear.

Allissa raised an eyebrow, then walked over and helped Juddha to his feet.

"We have something." Eden instantly recognized Professor Beaumont's voice. She'd left the professor, an old friend of her father's and one of the few people Eden trusted, to oversee the care and translation of the tablets. It was a task she knew the professor took seriously. Professor of Egyptology at Cambridge University, it was the sort of task he'd been working towards his whole career.

"What?" Eden replied, happy to dispense with niceties. Eden kept the phone pinned tightly to her ear, her grip whitening, as Beaumont explained.

"I'll come back as soon as I can," Eden said, glancing down at Allissa and Juddha. "I'll sort a flight tomorrow."

"No need," the Professor said.

The *thump thump* of helicopter rotors boomed through the night air. The strong lights of a Eurocopter AS350 lanced through the jungle as the machine hovered above the village. The lines of prayer flags flapped wildly. Cyclones of dust and debris spun around the huts.

"There's a jet waiting at Kathmandu," Beaumont said.

"Try to get some rest on the flight, we've got a lot to do. I'll see you in the morning."

The line went dead.

Eden snagged up her bag and stashed the phone away. She swung the bag on to her shoulder and stepped out of the hut.

The helicopter touched down in the village clearing and the sound of the rotors dropped.

Eden crossed to Juddha and Allissa.

"There are definitely things you're keeping to yourself," Allissa said, hands on her hips.

Eden smiled. She respected the young woman for not pushing her for answers. "We will meet again," Eden said, embracing Allissa.

"Definitely," Allissa smiled. "I'd put money on it."

Eden turned to Juddha. She put her palms together in a gesture of respect and bowed. "Thank you for everything. I must go now. When I can, I will return."

"You have done much," Juddha replied, bowing.

"What about?" Eden pointed at the body lying in the dust.

"We will sort it. By the morning it will be like it never happened," Juddha said.

Eden turned and ran towards the chopper. The door slid open as she approached. As soon as she was inside, the rotors powered up again. Within seconds, the copter lifted from the ground.

Eden gazed through the window as they circled the village and then pounded in the direction of Kathmandu.

5

1987. Nazlet-El-Samman, Cairo, Egypt.

MOHAMMED MUHR TOOK a deep breath and studied the hieroglyphics on the slab before him. He had spent half his life working towards this moment. Beyond this slab, Muhr knew without a doubt, was the technology left by an ancient civilization. Technology that would help humankind right its wrong. Technology that would solve the problems of inequality and the growing concerns of global warming.

He said a silent prayer and stepped forwards. In a stroke of genius, all he had to do to unlock the giant slab was read out loud the hieroglyphs inscribed on it. How the system worked, he had no idea. He could only assume that somehow the resonance of a human voice, speaking those particular words, caused a vibration on a very specific frequency. Ultimately, he didn't care why it worked, he only cared that it did.

Big Mo cleared his throat and began.

"The Ennead and Almodad will show you..."

The tunnel rumbled and shook. Dust and debris rained

from the ceiling. The men looked around in wide-eyed panic.

Mohammed Muhr continued, unfazed. He had been expecting this. "You now have all you need to see through the mist of confusion..."

Dust filled the air and the sound of rock scraping against rock pulsated through the tunnel. The ground beneath them shook. Muhr flexed his knees and sunk into a crouch in an effort to stay upright.

Then he listed the nine names which he knew would start the final part of the sequence. He had to shout over the noise of the ancient mechanisms. A crunching, popping noise reverberated through the tunnel. Then the giant granite slab vibrated upwards, sending more dust up into the air. Water streamed across the floor, threatening to knock Muhr and his men off their feet.

"Lean into the current," Muhr instructed. "It won't last long." Sure enough, within a few seconds the current slowed.

Muhr crouched and peered beneath the slab. The giant rock slid up another inch. Muhr ducked beneath it and through into the chamber inside. Wide-eyed, and in something of a trance-like state, Muhr staggered out into the chamber. He stared at the roof, over one-hundred feet above them. It was like daylight inside too, with several bright orbs, brighter than any light bulb Muhr had seen, hanging from the ceiling.

Muhr climbed a set of stone steps and walked out onto a raised area. He looked around the room. There were several such raised stone blocks around the space, all linked with intricate walkways. Shining liquid ran in small gullies carved into the stone surface. Muhr's eyes locked on the plinth at the far end of the chamber. He felt as though he was walking in a dream.

The Ark of the Covenant looked just as he'd imagined. Gold glimmered from its surface. The intricately carved cherubim graced the cover, their wings curved aloft.

"We've done it," Muhr said, turning to the other men. "It's there!" His voice sounded ghostly, almost as though it came from someone else. Muhr took a step towards the next plinth.

"You've done it!" Bakir roared, rushing towards, and embracing his friend. "I knew you would, brother. I always had faith in you. Allah Akbar!"

The two men took another step towards the Ark, arms stretched around one another.

"Sorry to have to interrupt, but I'll need you to stop right there."

Mohammed Muhr heard the nasal tones of Hijazi's voice several moments before he understood the meaning. He swung around and glared at the man.

"What do you mean? This is what we've come down here for. The truth about this artifact will issue forth a new era of peace for humankind." Muhr locked eyes with Hijazi. The small man had stepped back several feet. He stood side by side with Faheem.

"What are you talking about?" Bakir said. "You want out, you go back. No one will stop you."

"I'm sorry boss," Hijazi repeated, drawing a revolver from a hidden holster. Standing beside him, Faheem did the same. Both guns glinted in the bright lights of the chamber.

"Faheem, Hijazi, what are you doing?" Muhr said, shouting now. "We've been working on this for years. You've been part of it from the very beginning. You know how unjust the world is and you know that what we will discover here will help billions of people live better lives."

Hijazi simply shrugged. "There are some important people who want this secret to remain that way." His high-pitched voice sounded sinister now.

"Some very wealthy people, too," Faheem added. "How do you think we got hold of this top-of-the-range gear?"

"Why, you little," Bakir bellowed, his jaw jutting out in anger. Bakir charged forwards like a bear, his great size poised to crush the two small men.

"No, Bakir, no!" Muhr shouted, trying to grab hold of the big man. Muhr was too slow.

Bakir roared on, his feet thumping over the stone.

Hijazi and Faheem swung their weapons towards the threat and fired several times. The guns howled, impossibly loud in the enclosed space.

Bakir's wail of anger became one of pain. His large hands clutched uselessly at his chest. Blood bloomed across his shirt. He stopped moving forward and slumped to the ground.

Hijazi stepped forwards, leveled his gun at the big man's face and fired one more time. Bakir's moan fell into silence.

"No! Why did you do that!" Muhr shouted, watching his friend's lifeblood seep from his body.

"We tried to warn you," Faheem said.

"We tried to warn you," Hijazi agreed. "But you wouldn't be persuaded. You were set on this and wouldn't listen to logic or reason."

"These secrets need to be revealed," Muhr cried. "They need to be revealed. The world deserves to..."

The gun howled one more time, cutting Mohammed Muhr off in mid-sentence. The gun's report echoed several times, fading to silence.

6

National Archives Building, London. Present Day.

Frankie Nulph pulled her glasses down over her eyes, leaned towards the screen, and scowled. Her fingers picked at the keyboard as she navigated through various menus and programs. It was already approaching 9pm. She'd been in the archive for nearly twelve hours but hadn't yet checked her emails. In truth, it was the task which Frankie liked the least.

"I swear these things get more complicated every year," she said in her Southwest American accent.

"This is the National Archives of the United Kingdom. What do you expect it to be, just a big filing cabinet?" Norman, an Englishman in his early thirties, muttered from his workstation on the other side of the room. "It would hardly be the sharp end of technology if we had ten-year-old computers."

Frankie peered up at him, but with her glasses on, that side of the room was just a blur. "Don't think you're too old for a dressing down, young man," Frankie snapped.

Norman grinned. Although he and the younger archivists teased Frankie for her love and hate relationship with the ever-changing computer systems, she had one of the sharpest analytical minds in the field. She was also something of a fixture in the department, having been in post since the rest of the team were in kindergarten.

Frankie tapped a few more keys. "And that just does it!" she shouted.

Norman's grin grew wider still. He knew what was coming next.

"Dear Mister Nulph," she read from the screen. "I've been here thirty damned years, and still these people think I'm Mister Nulph. When my old dad gave me his name, God rest him, he didn't account for a world full of such stupid people." Frankie tapped aggressively at the keys.

Norman glanced across to Faye, who was carefully entering data into a tablet on the other side of the room.

"You know they sent me draft papers back in seventy-two. I've been dealing with this for fifty years." Frankie continued.

Norman mouthed the words perfectly in sync, before descending into fits of silent giggles. Faye couldn't help but laugh too.

"Say, you kids best not be laughing at me!" Frankie bellowed, but the hard edge to her voice had gone. She saw the funny side as much as anyone.

"Not at all, Frankie," Faye said, trying hard to quell her laughter. Her usually pale expression grew redder by the moment.

"No, sir!" Norman bellowed, now roaring openly with laughter.

At that moment, all the lights went out. The computer screens continued for a heartbeat before fading into blackness too. The archive, two stories underground, was plunged into complete darkness. A pair of emergency lights strained into action, washing the room in a ghostly green glow.

"Damn it," Frankie shouted, her hands crashing into the table. "Now I'll have to go through finding that email again."

"Why have the lights gone off?" Norman glancing in panic from Frankie to Faye and back again.

"Don't you worry about this, son." Frankie said, climbing arduously to her feet. She rummaged through a drawer and dug out a large yellow flashlight, then pushed her glasses up on her head. The room around her came back into focus. Frankie switched the flashlight on, and a beam of light swept through the room. "Lucky, I have this beauty stored away." Frankie hefted the device to show it off. She glanced around the lab. Everything appeared as normal, although Norman had turned ghostly white.

"Don't you worry," she reassured again. "This used to happen all the time back in the nineties. We rely on a power filter down here, meaning the lot must pass through one breaker. It's a bit of a bottleneck really, especially with all these machines running. All that's happened is someone's overloaded the poor thing. The box is by the elevators. I'll go and flick it on again."

Norman nodded, his fingers tapping an erratic pattern on his knees.

Frankie stomped towards the door, the beam of light swinging left and right. Reaching the door, she touched the electronic keypad with her I.D card, but nothing happened. "The thing's taken the locks out too. Must have been a gigantic bolt."

She pulled on the door. It swung open freely. Frankie wandered out into the corridor. Other than two emergency lights, it was completely dark out here, too.

Frankie looked right and then left, sweeping the light around the featureless corridor. Nothing moved. She set off in the elevator's direction. She paused at the neighboring archive and peered through the door's glass panel. The room was empty, silent, and motionless. At this time of night that wasn't surprising. Those part timers in domestic affairs went home at five-thirty prompt.

Frankie continued towards the elevators. Other than the squeak of her shoes on the floor, the building was silent. It seemed that even the air conditioners had packed up for the night.

"Strange," Frankie whispered. Her voice sounded loud in the overwhelming silence. Although it was true that the power did used to click off frequently, it hadn't happened since a major re-wire several years ago. A tiny flame of worry sparked in her gut. Of course, she would never let the kids know about that. It was a simple blackout. A basic electrical failure.

"If it's biology it stinks, if it's physics it moves, but if it doesn't work, it's electrics," Frankie muttered, not quite remembering where she'd heard the phrase before. That was the problem with young people now, she concluded, they were so pampered.

"National service, that's the answer. Toughen them up," Frankie muttered out loud.

Frankie reached the metal panel beside the elevator. She transferred the light to her left hand and swung open the panel. The metal shrieked on worn hinges.

"That could use a touch of oil," Frankie muttered to herself. "Right then, let's be having a look at you." She squinted inside the panel. The various power controls spun hazily in front of her eyes.

"Now where did I put...?" Frankie tapped down her

pockets, then ran a hand across her hair. "There you are," she said, moving her glasses back into position.

The various breakers came into sharp focus. Frankie swept the light across them. She clicked her tongue against the roof of her mouth. All the breakers were in the 'on' position.

"Strange thing, that," Frankie said, leaning back on her heels, considering the problem. "If it ain't... then what?"

A scraping noise screeched down the corridor.

Frankie stepped away from the panel. She swept the beam left and then right.

The grinding, grating noise came again.

Frankie's beam of light settled on the elevator doors. It sounded as though it was coming from the elevator.

"But that's impossible," Frankie whispered. Without power, there was no way the elevator could operate.

She took a step towards the elevator and listened. The flame of worry burned more intensely in her gut now. There was something strange going on here.

The grinding noise came again, this time joined by the whine of an electric motor.

"Well, I'll be," Frankie said, stepping backwards and considering the door. "It sounds like a—"

Then, right before Frankie's eyes, the elevator doors parted. Frankie watched openmouthed; the beam of her light fixed on the floor. With a shaking hand, she moved the glasses back to the top of her head again.

The chasm, which was normally occupied by the elevator car, came into sharp focus. Two men hung from cables in the elevator shaft. Both wore combat gear. Both were armed.

The man nearest the door swung forward, released the

rope, and landed smoothly beside the lift. He stepped towards Frankie and slid a syringe from his pocket.

Frankie's muscles tensed and her eyes bulged.

Before she could move the man plunged the syringe deep into Frankie's neck.

Frankie gasped. Her hands shot to her face. The flashlight clattered to the floor, the beam shining at a strange angle across the linoleum.

"Target secure," the man said, cradling Frankie as she lost consciousness. He laid her gently on the floor, then slipped a silenced pistol from a holster. "See to the others, then we move out. There can be no survivors."

7

New York. Present Day.

RAYMOND KING STROLLED out on to his balcony and looked down at the streets of New York far below. The sun had set several hours ago, and now the lights of the city glimmered and twinkled. Standing here, as he had so many times before, he understood why the rich and powerful men of the past had constructed their legacies in glass and steel. A building was not just a shrewd investment in an ever-changing world, but standing here, on the 97th floor of the King Industries Building, the tycoon experienced a feeling of power unlike any other. It was as though his influence now stretched beyond the flesh, bone, and blood from which his aging body was constructed. Like Rockefeller and Trump, King had now cemented—quite literally—his place among the powerful elite of the modern era.

"Not bad at all for a young man from Texas," he said, turning his attention to a taxi sliding down Central Park West, several hundred feet below. The lights of the city danced and blurred in front of his vision. King blinked several times, but the lights continued to flash and sway.

You're getting old, he thought, sliding a fat cigar and a bejewelled lighter from his pocket. Despite being told to give up smoking several times by his doctor, King continued to puff his way through several a day.

Didn't do my old man any trouble, was his stock reply. Raymond King Senior had lived well into his nineties, despite a dedicated smoking habit.

Exhaling a cloud of smoke, King looked out at the horizon. Somewhere beyond the glimmering towers, the great expanse of the United States stretched out one way, and the other way, the North Atlantic. It was a world with boundless opportunity, King thought, for those who were prepared to step up and take it.

Taking another draw on the cigar, King reflected on his younger working years, spent amid the company's refineries. When he had taken over King Industries after his father's death, they had owned and run less than fifteen refineries. Now King Industries controlled over one hundred, in every corner of the country. They exported oil and gas to every continent. No matter how much they were able to extract from the earth, it was sold immediately. And now, with prices rising, the world always teetering on the brink of conflict, things were better than ever.

"I thought I might find you here." A soft female voice floated across the balcony.

King recognized the voice immediately. He whipped around to see his daughter, Lulu, crossing towards him. Now in her early thirties, she looked more like her mother every time King saw her. To King, the similarity was bittersweet. Of course, he loved to see his daughter, but the thoughts of her mother came with a welling grief that never seemed to subside.

Killed in a car wreck twenty years ago, she had left a hole in the family that no amount of money, success or power could fill.

Cleared on a technicality by a useless judge, King had personally seen to the drunk driver who had caused the wreck. Although the young man's painful end had not brought King any closure, he'd very much enjoyed the process.

"You know me." King forced the thoughts from his mind and turned back towards the city. A siren shrieked from somewhere down below. The sound echoed mournfully amid the towers, before fading into nothing.

"I know you love this view," Lulu said, joining her father at the railing. "Jenny asked me to give you this." She passed her father a generous measure of scotch in a crystal glass. A single ice cube snapped as it cooled. "I took the liberty of pouring myself one too." Lulu held the glass up. Father and daughter locked eyes for a moment, clinked glasses and then turned to face the restless city.

A long moment of silence stretched between the pair.

"What brings you back to the city?" King asked, without looking at his daughter. "I thought you were involved in a project out in London, or some place."

"I got back about an hour ago. Yes, we're working on something exciting at A.P.P."

King took a deep swig of the scotch and rolled his eyes. The alcohol warmed his throat. A.P.P, The Alternative Power Project, was an organization Lulu had set up fifteen years ago. King had originally agreed to fund the organization thinking that it might help Lulu over the death of her mother. The loss had hit her hard, sending her into a downward spiral. Seeing how passionate Lulu was about the cause, King pledged some money. Although little more than pocket change for King Industries, Lulu had kept the organization going for well over a decade with the investment. Of course, she still had access to the family jet, their multiple properties, and a sizable fortune of her own.

King said nothing. He and his daughter had come head-to-head over their work many times, and he didn't have the energy for it this evening.

"Looks like fall's in the air," King said, filling the silence.

"It'll be welcome after the hottest summer on record." Lulu put her drink down, having barely touched it.

"What brings you back to the city?" King repeated the question.

Lulu didn't point out that there were many cities across the world, hundreds of which were bigger than New York. To her father, '*the city*' meant New York, and nowhere else.

"I wanted to talk to you, actually," Lulu said, her voice level.

"Oh yeah, what about?"

"I wanted to talk to you about the business. At A.P.P we're on the edge of something very exciting, groundbreaking even. If this goes the way I think it will, we're talking about the energy of the future."

Despite King's perpetual and unnatural tan, his knuckles whitened around the glass.

"We're talking about an energy source that's clean and abundant. And, most importantly, we can be the first to harness it."

"We've talked about this." King turned to face his daughter. When she wore heeled shoes, he had to look upwards to meet her gaze. "King Industries is, and always will be, an oil and gas company. That was the vision my father had all those years ago, and it's served us fine so far. We're sticking with it. In fact—" the pitch of King's voice increased as he warmed to his theme "—in fact, I think you need to remember what this business has done for you. Everything you've had growing up, everything you have now, is thanks to oil and gas. So, I think it's time." King gasped for breath. Dizziness swept across him. He grabbed hold of the railing to steady himself.

"I appreciate everything that King Industries has done for me." Lulu took advantage of the silence. "The whole world appreciates what oil and gas have done for us. Every major technological advance is thanks to the power that fossil fuels have provided, but it's now time for change. Our time burning carbon emitting fuels has come to an end. It's time we invested in something new."

"Nonsense." King spat, as the dizziness passed. The doctor had warned him too about avoiding stressful situations. "You've been fraternizing with those tree-huggin' scientists again. Those people just don't live in the real world." King's voice took on a mocking tone. "I'd love to watch the show tonight, but the wind just ain't blowin'."

"We're not talking about wind, or solar. We're talking about something much more powerful, much more reliable, something that could power our country now and for the future. Think about it…"

"I don't need to think about it." King's lips drew into a tight snarl. "I should never have let you get involved in that mad business. And to think that as my only child, I was hoping that one day you would take over the business. You know what I'm going to do, I'm going to call the legal team tomorrow just to make sure that…"

Lulu glanced quickly past her father and into the penthouse apartment beyond. She stepped slightly to the right to make sure he didn't catch a glimpse of what was happening behind him. Inside the grand living room, two men dragged the body of his housekeeper towards the front door. The scene they were setting needed to be just right.

"I've heard of some crazy, unappreciative, and selfish things in my time, but this is it. This really is pushing it. I'm going to cut you out of everything. You'll get nothing at all. You'll have to sell those designer handbags to have something to eat."

Lulu smirked. She hadn't owned a designer handbag in over ten years. She'd burned the lot when she realized how unethical most big brands had become. The man didn't know her at all, which would make what she was about to do a lot easier.

"Dad, listen," Lulu said, holding out her hands, palms facing her father. "I'm sorry."

King squinted at his daughter, the apology catching him off guard.

He opened his mouth, then closed it again.

Lulu thought how the man appeared a little like a fish out of water, suffocating in air he couldn't breathe. It was an ironic thought, as that's what his company was doing to every living thing on the planet.

"I'm sorry that it has to end like this." In one swift movement, Lulu pulled a pistol from a concealed holster against her back.

Registering the weapon, King's eyes widened until they appeared to be popping from his skull.

"I'm doing this for the benefit of every creature, every plant..."

"What. No, you can't. You can't!" King shouted, staggering backwards, trying to put some distance between himself and his daughter.

"It's not a case of can or can't, it's beyond that. This is what needs to be done. This needs to be done so that the world can move forwards." Lulu clicked off the safety.

"No. Wait! You're right. We'll change. We'll consider whatever you think is best. You're the future after all."

Lulu tilted her head to the side and looked down at the small, sniveling man that she'd spent so many years looking up to. She realized, she should have done this many years ago.

"No, you won't," Lulu said, humor in her voice. "You won't change. You can't change. That's not who you are. You've had a good life, but now it's time that ended. The world needs to move on.

"Julia, Julia!" King staggered backwards, shouting for the housekeeper's help. His feet slipped, and he fell backwards down to the concrete.

"Julia's already dead," Lulu said, taking a step forward and pointing the gun at her father's chest. "It's a shame, she'd been good to me over the years, but she was loyal to you."

King dragged himself backwards. His shoulders hit something hard. He looked up to see two burly men standing over him.

Somewhere far beneath the balcony, a siren wailed.

"They're not coming for you," Lulu said. "No one's coming for you. Goodbye, dad."

The gun howled, the sound instantly lost in the noisy city.

Lulu fired again, just to make sure.

Raymond King slumped backwards, his body still and his chest unmoving. Blood pooled across the tiles beneath him.

One of the men knelt and checked for a pulse. "He's dead."

Lulu nodded and handed the gun to one of the men. "Set it up like we discussed. It needs to look convincing. We roll out in fifteen minutes."

Lulu turned and walked to the edge of the balcony. She picked up her bag and slid out a phone.

"Proceed as planned. We will be back in London by the morning."

The distant voice answered.

"Yes, exactly," Lulu replied. "There's a new King in town."

8

Cambridge University Department of Archaeology, England. Present Day.

EDEN GLANCED up at the grand building which housed Cambridge University's Department of Archaeology. The weathered stone looked strangely sinister in the dull, wintery light. The department's curb appeal wasn't improved by the two hefty security guards stationed either side of the sliding door. Eden noticed their in-ear radios, and their gaze sweeping the street for threats. These guys were professionals.

Eden's phone buzzed. She stepped out of sight and slid the phone from her pocket. It was a photograph from a contact in India. She tapped on the link and the picture filled the screen. The picture showed the remains of Saint Francis Xavier back in the Basilica of Bom Jesus in Goa, India. Eden had found out that one of the saint's long-dead hands had been stolen during the body's annual embalming process. She tracked the artifact to an off-the-books flight arriving at London's Gatwick airport a few weeks ago.

Without a second thought, Eden had raided the airport and had the relic returned to its rightful place.

How she missed those simple missions, Eden thought, slipping her phone away. At least then she could tell who was on her side and who wasn't.

Eden crossed the road and walked towards the Department of Archaeology's sliding door.

"Need your I.D." One of the men barked, blocking Eden's path with a meaty forearm.

Eden looked up at the man. Very little sleep on the long flight from Kathmandu was not helping with her patience.

"I've got an appointment with Professor Beaumont. I'm already late." Eden stepped forwards. The man side-stepped, blocking her path.

"This building is a secure location. No one enters without a check. I.D. now."

Eden took a step back and gave the man an ice-cold stare. She exhaled deeply, rummaged around in her bag, and pulled out her passport. The security guy peered closely at Eden's picture. If he recognized her, nothing in his expression showed it. Although her photos had been all over the newspapers for several weeks after the discovery of the tablets, the media had now moved its attention on to a sleazy politician found sleeping with his secretary. For once, Eden was thankful that some men in power thought with their genitalia.

"Clearance requested for Eden Winslow," the man barked, a finger pressed to his earpiece. Eden scowled at the use of her official last name. For many years she had been known as "Black" so as not to be associated with her well-known father.

"Roger that." The guard thrust Eden's passport back in her direction. "Thank you, Miss Winslow."

Eden snatched back her passport, slipped it away and barged through the doors. The Department for Archaeology's reception area looked more like a museum than part of a university.

Eden stepped across to one of the glass cases which lined the walls. A pot, which had been painstakingly stuck back together, sat next to a photograph. In the photograph, several people worked on a dig, removing earth with brushes and trowels. It took Eden several moments to recognize one man. Paavak Mahmud smiled up at the camera.

"Ahh, Tell Brak, in Northeast Syria. I'm sure you remember Paavak."

Eden spun around as Professor Beaumont strode into the reception area. The man, Eden had often thought, was something of a stereotype. Tall with the beginnings of a paunch, Beaumont's love for tweed, his unruly graying hair, and tiny gold-rimmed spectacles, were everything Eden had imagined a professor of archaeology to look like.

"Your father was there for some time too," Beaumont said, pausing and peering into the cabinet. "We really should put a picture up of him actually, after what happened." Beaumont turned to look at Eden. Eden remained silent. "I mean, well, after you know. To remember him, as it were. Sorry."

"That's fine," Eden said.

Alexander Winslow, Eden's father, had died in a plane crash a few months ago. A crash which, as it turned out, was far from accidental.

"How was your journey?" Beaumont said, more as a statement than a question. "Sorry to call you back at such short notice. You know we've been working on this translation day and night, but something's come up." Beaumont spoke with the pace of a machine gun, spitting out words at light-speed.

"You've translated something?"

"This way, please." Beaumont said, ignoring Eden's question. The professor led them into the building's surprisingly modern interior. This part of the department looked like any other office. People sat at computers and talked on phones. There were no artifacts in trays, no work with tiny brushes or anything like that.

"It's all state-of-the-art now," Beaumont said, as though reading Eden's thoughts. "We've had the tablets digitally scanned. That means several people can work on them at the same time and hopefully we can train this A.I. to do the work for us. That will certainly save us some time. It's something we've been working on for a long time, but we needed many tablets from the same source. This is perfect."

Beaumont led them up a large spiral staircase, twittering constantly. He ushered Eden inside his office, slipped behind the desk, and collapsed into a large leather chair.

Although the office was large, the amount of stuff it contained made it seem cramped. Books, photographs, and plastic boxes each containing a strange artifact or two, crowded the floor to ceiling shelves.

Eden sunk into the chair opposite Beaumont. She took a deep breath. The smell reminded her of her father's office which had been destroyed in a house fire shortly after his death. She felt strangely at home in the cluttered space.

Beaumont pushed a laptop and some piled papers to one side and then placed his elbows on the table's leather inlay. "How was your time in the Himalayas?" The professor scrutinized Eden over his glasses.

Having met Beaumont several times in the past, Eden knew him to be one of a dying breed who wouldn't get to the matter at hand until a few minutes into the conversation. There was no point getting frustrated at this, Eden decided, she would just have to go at his pace.

"How rude of me," Beaumont said, before Eden had a chance to answer. "I haven't offered you a drink. Cup of tea? Coffee? I think we might even have some biscuits somewhere. That's if the budget can still stretch to such niceties."

"Coffee, please," Eden said. "Strong, no milk."

"Right you are. Back in a jiffy." Beaumont shot to his feet and strode out of the office, the door creaking closed behind him.

Eden sat up straight and stretched out her arms. Her muscles ached from the long journey. That was nothing a few hours' sleep in a proper bed wouldn't sort, however. Inside she ached to move on to the next challenge. Patience had never been one of her virtues.

Eden glanced around the office. Countless artifacts looked back at her, each with their own story to tell. Again, she thought of her father. He was a master storyteller and often had people hanging on his every word during lectures. He had the skill of turning a string of facts into a compelling narrative which the listener couldn't help but be enticed by.

Eden stood up and stretched out again. She crossed the room and peered through the window. Rain had just started to pepper the glass—as was customary during at least half the days in England. Traffic chugged down the street below. Eden clocked a black Range Rover parked at the opposite curb. Someone moved in the driver's seat, although they made no attempt to drive off. Eden watched the vehicle for long seconds, intrigue growing.

"Sorry that took so long," Beaumont said, clattering through the door with a tray of drinks and as promised, biscuits. "I'm always getting caught by someone and asked an opinion on something. In this case, it was the meaning of a symbol that seems to have found its way..." Beaumont looked up and saw Eden at the window. "Oh typical, it's raining again."

Eden glanced back out at the street to see the Range Rover indicate and pull out into the light afternoon traffic.

Nothing to worry about, she thought to herself.

"Right then," Beaumont said, shuffling into his seat. "Let's get down to business."

Eden slid into the seat opposite the professor. She snagged up one of the biscuits, broke it in half, then dunked it in the coffee.

"We've been working day and night to translate these tablets. We've even had to borrow people from other universities to get the work done—it really is a big..." a high-pitched beeping noise interrupted Beaumont mid-sentence. He glanced down at the modern watch on his wrist. He tapped the device, and the beeping stopped.

Eden raised an eyebrow.

"I know," Beaumont said, reading her expression perfectly. "Pretty cutting edge for an old fox like me."

"They're clever, aren't they?" Eden glanced down at her own watch. A top of the range design, it had countless features including global positioning, temperature and humidity sensors, depth sensors for diving and, funnily enough, it could tell the time.

"Absolutely!" Beaumont said excitedly, clearly happy to talk. "One of my PhD students bought it for me. It's turned out to be my little *Ubaste*. It tells me when to exercise, how well I've slept, everything. It's an incredible thing."

Eden chomped into another biscuit and waited for Beaumont to continue. She respected the man and knew it was best to leave people like Beaumont to get to the point in their own way.

"Well, the tablets, yes, as we expected, parts of it tally with the diary recovered from Mr. Godspeed's secret vault." Eden had been shown a two-hundred-year-old translation of the tablets by the aristocrat some weeks ago.

"It's what he would have wanted," Eden said, slightly cruelly. Archibald Godspeed had met a sticky end some days later, after it turned out he had set Eden up for his personal gain.

"Well, those bits we can put to one side for now, as we know what they say already," Beaumont continued. Now, warm to his theme, he wasn't drifting off topic. "It's the tablets that are not in the diary that interest us now. And I fear, we've uncovered something of an enigma." Beaumont shuffled through the papers on his desk.

Eden wondered how the man could ever find what he needed in such a mess. She took another sip of the coffee. The caffeine worked its magic.

"Here we are." Beaumont selected a piece of scrunched up paper. He flattened it to the tabletop with his hand. "Read that." He pushed the sheet across to Eden. The page contained just three paragraphs of typed text.

Now this Seth, when he was brought up, and came to those years in which he could discern what was good, he became a virtuous man. He was himself of an excellent character and left children behind him who imitated his virtues.

That their inventions might not be lost before they were sufficiently known, upon Adam's prediction that the world was to be destroyed at one time by the force of fire, and at another time by the violence and quantity of water, they made two pillars.

One pillar was made of brick and the other of stone.

They inscribed their discoveries on them both, that in case the pillar of brick should be destroyed by the flood, the pillar of stone might remain. These inscriptions would exhibit their discoveries to mankind, and also inform them that there was another pillar of brick erected nearby. Now this remains in the land of Siriad to this day.

Reaching the end of the excerpt, Eden looked up at Beaumont. Her eyebrows inched together in confusion.

The professor steepled his fingers and nodded excitedly.

Eden read the excerpt again, hoping that the meaning would leap out at her. "I'm going to level with you professor," she said, reaching the end for the second time. "I'm not sure what this is saying."

"Have you ever heard mention of The Hall of Records?" Beaumont said, locking Eden in his gaze.

"Remind me," Eden said, placing the paper down on the desk.

"The Hall of Records is supposed to be an ancient library, hidden beneath the earth for thousands of years. We in the archaeological community have put it down to those with an overactive imagination, but maybe we were too hasty." Beaumont poked the paper with his index finger. "That's what I think this part of the translation is about. You see where our speaker mentions the 'inscriptions that would exhibit their discoveries to mankind?' As far as I'm aware, this is the first time it's ever been mentioned in something of this age."

"What's supposed to be in there?" Eden asked, leaning forward.

"Rumors abound, dear Eden. Rumors abound. Some people suggest it's the information from an ancient civilization. Others think it's a technology left to us by aliens. In all honestly, we don't know. But..."

"We should definitely find out," Eden said, cutting off the professor in mid-sentence.

A frown sobered Beaumont's expression. "I'm afraid it's not that simple. We have no idea where it is. People have searched from Egypt, our own Stonehenge, to Mexico for signs of such a place, should it even exist. Furthermore, the authorities of the sort of places it might be are rightfully very selective about who they let poke around."

"I wasn't going to ask them," Eden replied, grinning.

Beaumont caught Eden's eye, the tiniest flicker of a smile on his lips too. "There's another part too." He flicked through the pile of papers again and retrieved another sheet. This one, like the first, was typed. Unlike the first, it contained just one sentence.

"Seth and his sister Luluwa did all they could to prevent their own people from joining this unholy alliance, as the evil ones built a city of grandeur which they named Balonia - City of the Sun."

Eden read the sentence three times and then placed the page back on the table. This translation made even less sense than the previous one.

"It's a bit of a mystery to me as well," Beaumont said. "This second part came from a different tablet, so it may well be mixed up completely. We just paired them together because of the mention of Seth."

Eden exhaled a deep breath.

"However, the City of the Sun is mentioned here. We know from other records that there were six sun temples built across the Middle East. All dedicated to the Atum, the Sun God. But only two of them have ever been found. That means, there must be another four somewhere out there. Maybe they hold the clue."

"A mystery within a mystery."

Beaumont grinned. "Welcome to the world of archaeology, dear Eden."

Eden picked up the sheets of paper. "Mind if I take these? I have some pretty good analysis software back at the truck. I'll run them through and see if anything comes up."

"Be my guest," Beaumont shrugged. "I too am following a couple of leads. Nothing to report yet, but we will see."

Eden slid the papers into her bag, grabbed another biscuit and then climbed to her feet. She crossed to the door.

"I'll walk you out," Beaumont said, standing and striding after her.

Eden couldn't help but smile at Beaumont's old worldly charm.

"Let's talk in a day or so," Beaumont said when they were back in the reception area. "And be careful, won't you?" The Professor's tone turned serious. "A lot of people are interested in this research, and not all of them are good."

Eden nodded, turned, and strode out into the falling drizzle. Whatever was coming, she reckoned she could cope with it.

9

Atlantis Hotel, The Palm, Dubai. Present Day.

THE MAN KNOWN as Helios stepped out on to the balcony of
the Royal Bridge Suite, the most luxurious set of rooms in
the hotel, and crossed to the balustrade. He stared out at the
Dubai skyline, standing like the stubs of a burned down
fence in the distance. He gazed down at the grounds
surrounding the hotel. For once in the hotel's history, the
place was silent. The Council of Selene was in session and
demanded the utmost privacy. Whenever they were in
session, the venue was required to be closed for regular
guests several weeks before and after the meeting. All staff
had been replaced with those that were loyal to The Council
and all electronic devices had been removed. It took a team
of specialist engineers to prepare the hotel for The Council
meeting and return it to its previous state afterwards. That
was a major undertaking for a large hotel like The Atlantis,
but The Council of Selene was powerful enough to demand
such things.

Helios turned and considered the hotel for a moment.

Beautifully themed in a nautical style, it took the legend of Atlantis to a level of luxury possibly never seen before.

If only they knew the truth, Helios thought, digging out a packet of cigarettes. He lit one up and inhaled. The chamomile flavored smoke calmed him instantly. Tilting his head, he exhaled a cloud towards the sky.

As ever, the meeting of The Council had become tiresome. Although Helios was the Chairman of The Council, he still needed their majority agreement to get things moving. Now, all they seemed to be doing was talking in circles.

"Not for much longer," he whispered to himself. If he had his way, then soon enough The Council of Selene, which had closely monitored humankind's progress for thousands of years, would no longer be a secret. That would either shake the recalcitrant members into action or destroy the organization all together. Right now, Helios didn't really care which.

"The councilors are waiting for you," a young woman said, stepping out on to the terrace.

Helios turned, then stubbed his cigarette in an ash tray. "Thank you, Athena. Let's hope this doesn't take too long."

Helios strode into the room which served as The Council chamber and used the guide rope to find his seat in the darkness. Once seated, he turned on the small light which illuminated only the desk before him. Throughout the session, the chamber would be kept in near total darkness. This ensured that while the councilors could talk to one another, they couldn't see each other. The members of the council were anonymous, even to one another. No one, including Helios himself, knew the names, origins or even the gender of the people before him.

Helios listened to the shuffling of the other members

finding their positions in the vast room. When they were settled, he looked down at the day's agenda on the desk before him. He cleared his throat and prepared to speak.

"I'm sorry to start back on this again," came a voice from the other side of the room. Helios groaned inwardly. The voice belonged to a member of The Council code-named Uronion. The nasal British accent struck fear into his heart. "But I am still concerned about the discovery of these tablets. Helios, you assured us that you were able to seize the tablets yourself and stop them from falling into the public sphere. It appears that you have failed to do that. As far as I can ascertain they're currently undergoing translation at the University of Cambridge. I really must call upon this Council to mobilize forces and seize the tablets for ourselves." A fist thumped against the desk somewhere across the room. One or two other council members groaned in agreement.

"I can assure you, there is no danger here," Helios interjected, raising his voice above the other councilors.

"How can you assure us?" Now it was the voice of the member know as Uriel which stuck out across the table. "As far as I'm aware, no one knows the contents of those tablets. How can you assure us that they do not contain evidence of the establishment of The Council of Selene?"

"As you've pointed out, Uriel, there is an outside chance that the tablets which are currently being worked on at the University of Cambridge, may contain mention of The Council. However, I have securely mitigated against this by making sure that the man in charge is someone loyal to The Council."

Two more voices groaned somewhere around the table.

"That's a lot of trust and pressure on one man," Uronion

said. "Wouldn't it be safer for The Council, for all of us here, if we had the tablets under lock and key?"

"I'm afraid that's where we're going to have to leave the conference for today," Helios said, after nearly two hours of discussion had raged. Several members muttered their frustrations but bowed reluctantly to Helios' authority in the chamber.

"We will reconvene tomorrow morning at ten."

"Sir, can I suggest we make a special dispensation and meet this evening to get this issue resolved? That way we can move on to some of The Council's other pressing issues tomorrow."

Helios paused, considering his response carefully.

"I'm afraid that won't be possible, as I have another urgent engagement this evening." Helios turned and strode out of the chamber before any of the argumentative council members could disagree.

10

Croydon, South London.

Lulu King peered from the windows of the Range Rover as they slid through the open door of the warehouse. The warehouse was on a run-down industrial estate in a particularly unattractive area of South London. The only other operating organization on the block was a dog food factory two units down. Lulu had arranged a fire to put them out of business for several weeks. She didn't expect the owners would care once they got their insurance pay-out.

The Range Rover crunched to a stop, and Abdul and Sharif climbed out. The suspension creaked upwards.

"Thank you, Abdul," Lulu said, stepping out of the car. Lulu had first met Abdul and Sharif when working in Angola. They had come to her aid when her driver had tried to rob her. Impressed by the mercilessness in which the men dealt with the thief, Lulu had offered them both a job. The men were fearless, strong, and most importantly, loyal.

Lulu looked around at the warehouse. Through a set of cracked windows, the sky was the color of old, wet cotton.

After two nights aboard the private jet in their off-the-books flight to New York and back, King wasn't sure what time it was. That didn't matter, anyway. All that mattered now was getting the job done as soon as possible.

"Miss King, this way," Sharif said, his deep gravelly voice booming around the empty warehouse. The big man pointed them toward the back of the space.

They passed through a steel door into a windowless room. Shadows hung around the edges of the room. In the center, bright lights illuminated a chair. In the chair, sat a woman, her head slumped forward.

The stink of despair hung throughout the room.

Two men, the hired local guards, shuffled from the shadows as Lulu and her men came in.

"Miss King," one of the men said, by way of a greeting. "She won't tell us anything. We think perhaps she doesn't know where the documents are."

King raised an eyebrow. "You think she doesn't know?" King assessed the man. Sure, he was an imposing figure, with muscles in all the right places, but there certainly wasn't much going on behind the eyes.

"She's been here nearly 48 hours. We've threatened her, tried to get her to speak, but nothing." The thug made a snipping motion with his fingers. "Maybe if you'd let us get the cutters out, then she might become a bit more talkative."

"Typical man." King looked from the thug to the crumped figure in the chair. "Always thinking brute force is the best way to get anything done. I'll deal with it now. You make sure the perimeter remains secure."

The men grumbled as though their fun had just been curtailed, then shuffled towards the door.

King stepped towards the woman. For any average person, forty-eight hours tied to a chair was enough to make them sing like an opera star. This woman was obviously tougher than most. King looked closely at the woman. Sure, these old timers could be difficult to crack, but not impossible. King wondered whether it was an age thing. Did you really care how it ended when you got to that age? It would all come crashing down around you soon enough, anyway.

King snapped her fingers. Abdul slid the sidearm from its holster and planted it in her hand. She made sure the weapon was loaded and clicked off the safety.

King strode over to the chair. The woman sat, straining at the ropes that tied her to the chair. A curtain of grey hair hung across her face.

King crouched down in front of the woman, pushed her up against the chair's backrest and swept the hair from her face.

The woman's eyes fluttered open. Other than a bruise on the side of her head, she looked relatively unharmed.

"Tell me your name,"

"Frankie Josephine Nulph," the woman's voice was croaky and horse.

"A fellow American," King said, noticing the woman's accent. "Where do you work?"

"I work for Crossbow Insurance, here in London."

King smiled at the cover story. "That's funny because I know that's not true. I know that's what the building on the Strand is supposed to be. You and I both know that's not what happens inside."

"It's a boring office job, really. We provide insurance for companies around the world. In fact, when your goons picked me up, I was on the phone to the Asia office saying that they need to pay us more."

A slight trace of a smile flickered across King's face. This woman was definitely tougher than she appeared. "I hear my men have already tried to get you to talk. I also hear that they've got nothing."

"I don't know anything," Frankie said, levelly.

King reflected that for someone facing danger and death, Frankie really wasn't very emotional at all. This clearly wasn't Frankie's first rodeo.

"That's not true," King said, climbing to her feet. "I know that you have the information we need, we just haven't used the right method to get it from you, yet."

King strode across to Abdul and whispered a few words in his ear. Abdul nodded then signaled to Sharif. The pair turned and left the room. The steel door closed with a resonant clunk.

King walked slowly back across to Frankie, tapping the gun against the palm of her hand. "Have you heard of the South Indian monkey trap?"

Frankie looked up at the woman but said nothing.

"I'll assume that's a no. I'm not sure it's a real thing, but it serves its purpose here. The South Indian monkey trap is nothing more than a hollowed-out coconut with rice inside. The poor monkey slides his hand inside the coconut and grabs hold of the rice, but once it has the rice, the hand is too large to slide back out of the hole."

King gestured this slowly with her free hand.

"Of course, the monkey is free to go at any time, but it won't because of the idea that it wants that rice. In this situation both you, and me, are the monkeys. You want to live, I assume?"

Frankie didn't reply, so King continued.

"And I want, no need, to know where you sent those documents. You could change your thinking, just tell me, and live."

"I. Don't. Know," Frankie hissed, sounding out each word.

King held out her palm to silence the other woman. "So you say. The problem is, I know you're lying." King tapped her chin in thought. "You've been here for two days already. I think it's fair to say that if you were going to tell us willingly, you would have. So, I need to change my thinking. Of course, I could let those brute have their way with the bolt cutters."

A flicker of fear passed across Frankie's face.

"But I have a better idea," King said. "I need to think differently about this problem, the problem in which we find ourselves. Fortunately, I already have..."

Right on cue, a blood-curdling scream filled the warehouse.

"No! No please, don't!" the voice came from behind the steel door. It was joined by the screaming of a young child.

King looked towards the door and smiled.

Frankie tried to turn, but her bindings prohibited it.

The screaming got louder.

King took a step backwards and put her hands on her hips.

The door clunked open. Abdul and Sharif walked in. Abdul dragged a young woman into the room. The woman's hair was a mess, make up and tears streaked down her face. Abdul tossed her around as though she was little more than a rag doll.

Sharif lugged a sobbing child in his arms. A little girl. Her hair was the same color as the woman's.

King beckoned the men across the room. Abdul stood to one side, and Sharif stood to the other. The woman wailed again. Abdul held her still with ease.

Frankie sat up straight in the chair, her gaze flitting from the woman to the girl and back again.

"And just like that," King said, looking at Frankie. "We have a different path."

King pointed the gun at the ceiling and squeezed the trigger. The shot echoed through the warehouse. The bullet hit nothing but a discolored ceiling tile, sending a cloud of dust drifting through the room. The noise had the desired result. The woman's screams muted, and the child sniffed.

"Good afternoon, ladies," King said, striding across to the woman. "I'm sorry to have to disturb you like this, but your time to shine is upon us. Please rest assured your help today is of importance to the entire human race. Tell me, what's your name?"

The woman inhaled a big gulp of air. She choked back further tears. "Rose, my name's Rose."

"Thank you, Rose. I realize that this is difficult for you. One way or another it will be over soon."

Rose sobbed again. King slapped her with an open palm. The sharp pain silenced the woman. "I'm afraid there's no time for all this drama now. You can sob all you want later." King pointed to the young girl. "Tell me, who is this beautiful young lady?"

"Jessica, she...uh, she's my daughter." Rose inhaled several times, clearly trying to keep the tears at bay.

Frankie was alert now, looking from Rose to Jessica and back again. Her muscles strained against the bindings.

"She's a very beautiful young girl, with all her life ahead of her." King strode across to Jessica and crouched down. "You're doing very well, Jessica. Hopefully, we will get you out of here as soon as we can. Tell me, how old are you?"

"Eight." Jessica sobbed.

"Wow, such a big girl," King said. She patted the child on the head and walked back over to the mother. "Rose, for the benefit of our guest here," King pointed at Frankie, "please tell us the circumstances which led to you being here today."

Rose took several big gulps of air. "I think it was two days ago now. I'm a bit disorientated. I don't remember much. All I know is that we were walking back from the park to our house. Two men grabbed us from behind. Then a van appeared. The men bundled us inside and brought us here. We've been in that other room ever since."

King nodded. "That's absolutely correct. Well done, thank you."

King glanced at Frankie, leaning forwards, and straining against her bindings. The muscles in her jaw bulged with tension. As expected, King had found her weak spot. Now all she had to do was apply the right pressure. She turned back towards the mother. "I've got another question for you, Rose. Now think about this one carefully before you answer, I will only accept your first answer. Do you understand?"

Rose nodded.

"Would you rather me kill you with your daughter watching, or kill her with you watching?"

Rose's screams filled the room. Hearing her mother cry, Jessica screamed too.

King grabbed the woman by the chin and forced her to look into her eyes. "Stop screaming or I will kill you both. I'm giving you a choice here. If you fail to answer, I will kill her first and then you."

King strode across to Jessica and pointed the gun at the young girl's head.

"No, no, no, no!" Rose shouted at the top of her voice. A new surge of energy found its way to her muscles, and she fought against Abdul's vice-like grasp. "Kill me. Kill me, let her live! Let her live!"

King stood up straight and lowered the gun. "Okay. If, you're sure. Is that your final answer?"

"Yes, yes! Jessica, listen to me. Close your eyes now and don't open them for as long as you can. Remember I love you, okay?"

King paced back across the room and pointed the gun at Rose. The woman seemed strangely calm now.

"No, mummy!" Jessica screamed.

King placed the gun on the side of Rose's skull. Rose didn't fight.

"No. Please, let us go. Please!" Jessica sobbed uncontrollably now. She fought against Sharif's strong arms.

"Stop this!" Frankie's voice filled the room. "Stop this now."

King turned to face Frankie. The woman sat upright in the chair. Fire blazed in her eyes.

"If I tell you, you'll let these two go right now?"

"And just like that," King said, without moving the gun. "We have found ourselves another way. Start speaking."

"I sent them to a man called Richard Beaumont. He's a professor of archaeology at Cambridge..."

"I know Beaumont," King interrupted. "What was in the documents?"

Frankie paused, swallowing aggressively.

King raised the gun towards Rose again.

"The documents are a set of infrared images. They show The Giza Plateau in Cairo, Egypt."

"Go on?" King watched Frankie closely.

"They show an area of unexplained heat..." she sucked in a deep breath, "beneath the second and third pyramid," Frankie said, softly.

"That was not too difficult, was it?" King said. "That's all it took. How silly we had to go through all of this."

King clapped her hands slowly, the incongruous sound reverberated sharply.

"I would like to introduce to you the best pair of actresses in the London underworld." King turned and pointed at the mother and her child. "What a wonderful performance they gave us today."

Abdul and Sharif released their captives. The woman removed a tissue from a pocket and wiped the make-up from her face. She stood quite calmly, as though used to the situations.

"Ladies, go to my office. I'll sort your money in a minute or two."

Without a glance at Frankie, the woman and child strode out of the room.

Frankie's expression dropped as she shrunk back into the chair.

King handed the gun to Abdul and strode towards the door. "Kill her," she said, pulling open the door.

The room filled with raised voices as King slipped outside. She swung the steel door shut as the sound of gunfire howled through the building.

11

EDEN HANDED a wad of cash through the glass divide of the taxi, thanked the driver, and climbed out of the vehicle. The journey back to her truck, hidden in a woodland about sixty miles from London, was always a long one without a vehicle of her own. On this occasion, Eden had been particularly careful, changing modes of transport often and doubling back on herself several times, just to make sure no one was following.

Her truck, an ex-army DAF T244, was her sanctuary. She had modified the vehicle herself. She made sure it always contained everything she needed to live off grid, including several weeks of food and water supplies stored in buried containers in the surrounding woodland.

Eden wasn't preparing for an apocalypse as such, but she knew that it always paid to be ahead of the game.

Throwing her rucksack over her shoulders, Eden started off down the narrow lane. The taxi turned out of sight around the corner. The truck was still two miles off, but that part of the journey she would have to take on foot.

Eden peered at the sky. Although the rain had stopped,

thick clouds now streamed overhead. Dusk was still an hour or so away, but the cloud cover smothered the evening in premature gloom.

The road curved down a hillside and then ran in beside a dense woodland. Eden strolled down the single-track lane as though she were just out for a walk, then ducked into the woodland. She wove her way through the dense foliage for about a hundred feet. She had planted much of the undergrowth herself, to ensure the woodland was as impenetrable as possible. As the tree cover thinned out, Eden propped herself up against a trunk. She took her bag off and placed it by her feet. If anyone was following her, they too would have to move through the undergrowth behind her and make a noise doing so.

Twenty minutes later, and satisfied that no one was on her tail, Eden set off towards her truck. The clouds, just visible through the trees' thinning canopy, turned slowly from grey to orange as the sun went down.

"Thanks, Atum," Eden whispered, remembering her conversation about Atum the Sun God with Beaumont a few hours ago.

Night had almost begun as Eden reached the truck. She clicked a small remote control and several lights snapped on. Eden was pleased to see the truck still had power. She pulled aside the camouflage netting, scrambled up the small ladder and let herself inside.

Light snapped on as she stepped into the vehicle's compact living area. A small kitchen, bathroom and bed occupied one end of the space, and Eden's desk occupied the other. Several large screens were mounted on the wall, and there was enough space for her to run several computers or work on something without getting in a mess.

It was a world away from Beaumont's cluttered office, but she loved it.

Eden took her laptop from her bag and connected it to the additional screens, the power, and the truck's secure internet connection. Routed through several servers dotted across the globe, the searches Eden performed were almost impossible to trace back to her.

Almost impossible, she thought, glancing at the surrounding woodland in infrared displayed on a screen above her. All was quiet, just the way she liked it.

Her hands darting over the keys, Eden set her search programs running. First, she input the translated text which Beaumont had given her, then she selected some relevant keywords and added them too. She struck the enter key and search progress begun.

Finally conceding to her rumbling stomach, Eden padded across the truck and pulled a couple of dehydrated meals from the cupboard. While the supplies she had in the truck were far from exciting, they did the job. Eden started up the stove, poured the strange goo from the packets into a saucepan and added some water.

Behind her, the computer dinged several times, indicating it had results for her to analyze.

Eden waited another two minutes for her food to heat through. She grabbed a fork, turned off the stove and carried her saucepan over to the desk. Sitting back at the computer she ate while scrolling through the results.

There were several results from all corners of the internet. She discounted several older articles which looked to be the work of conspiracy theorists. She could circle back across them later if needed. The tenth result was an article from a news service based in the city of Aswan, Egypt. Eden checked the date. The article had only gone live yesterday. Eden tapped on the link and the article filled the screen.

Ruins beneath the waters of Lake Nasser thought to be lost Sun Temple.

The fork slipped from Eden's hand and clattered into the pan. Eden, frantically reading the text, didn't even notice.

The article detailed how the waters of Lake Nasser in Southern Egypt and Northern Sudan had dropped to record lows over the last few months, revealing several buildings. Most of these buildings were known about, having been there when the lake was flooded in the 1960s. One however, perhaps due to currents beneath the lake moving sand and earth around, had been uncovered anew. Still mostly submerged, expert divers had taken photographs, and experts had thought it to be one of the lost temples built in dedication to Atum, God of the Sun.

Eden sat back in her chair, staring at the screen for almost a minute. Thoughts spun through her mind. If this was one of the lost Sun Temples, then what was written there, inscribed on the walls, could help them make sense of the tablets.

Eden snagged up her phone and dialed Beaumont's number. She clicked on the speakerphone as the ringing tone began.

Eden scrolled through the photos included in the article. One was taken from a distance, showing just the tops of walls jutting above the waters of the lake. Another showed a team of divers heading across the water in a small boat. None of the pictures taken by the divers were included in the article.

Eden tapped her chin. The fact they hadn't shared the pictures spoke volumes. But then again, the Egyptian authorities were known to be tight lipped about their discoveries.

The ringing tone cut to silence. That was strange, Beaumont normally answered Eden's calls immediately.

Eden saved the link of the article and then turned her attention back to the search engine. She changed her search terms to just bring up details about the appearance of the Sun Temple. Several similar articles appeared from other news outlets. Eden scanned a few of them but found no further information.

She then asked the search program just to show her images taken in that geographical area, during the time of the discovery. The program thought about it, running through social media uploads, YouTube, and internet blogs. For several seconds the loading bar flickered across the screen, before returning with nothing.

"Now that's really strange," Eden whispered, leaning forwards. With users on social media uploading millions of images a day, the fact that no one had photographed the discovery of a never-before-seen building was just plain suspicious. Alarm bells were ringing loud and clear in Eden's mind.

Eden sat back and steepled her fingers. Someone had brought in this organization to investigate the temple and consciously blocked all other information. This was a cover up—that Eden knew for sure.

A harsh beeping noise strained from Eden's computer and a dialogue box appeared in the middle of the screen.

Trace detected.

Someone had noticed Eden's search requests. Fortunately, her sophisticated masking software would lead them down several rabbit holes. Eden cut the connection and ran a program to cover her tracks.

Eden sat back and folded her arms. This was a cover up and someone with a lot of resources was paying big bucks to keep it that way.

Eden glanced at her phone. Her conversation with Beaumont just became urgent.

~

Cairo International Airport, Cairo, Egypt.

Alexander Winslow, Eden's father, strode through the umbilical corridor connecting his Bombardier Global 6000 private jet with Cairo International Airport. He quickened his pace along the empty corridor, his shoes clicking on the linoleum floor.

He tugged back the sleeve of his jacket and checked his watch. While the plane had made good time, he still felt as though it was running late.

In truth, he'd been feeling as though he had been playing catch up since this thing had started several months ago. Although he'd planned so much, the world moved in unpredictable ways. It seemed that for long periods of time, nothing happened, then everything happened all at once.

Winslow pushed through the door and darted into the terminal. Other travelers, either wearily returning home, or excitably arriving in Egypt for the first time, bustled past him towards passport control.

Winslow followed the crowd through the terminal, his mind focused on his mission.

Reaching the queue for passport control, Winslow paused. He peered around the person in front of him and scrutinized the desk twenty feet ahead. The border officer passed a passport back beneath the glass and signaled for the traveler at the front of the line to pass. The line shuffled forwards.

Reaching the front of the queue, Winslow prepared himself. He drew his passport from a pocket, then slid a finger inside his shirt collar.

The border officer waved him forward. Winslow stepped up to the glass and handed his passport beneath the glass. The officer accepted the passport, flipped it open, then tapped at his computer.

Winslow looked at the security camera on the wall behind the officer, right where he knew it would be. Then, slowly, carefully, Winslow slid his finger from his collar, bringing with it the thin chain on which hung The Key to the Nile.

12

"OIL BILLIONAIRE RAYMOND KING was found dead in his New York penthouse today." The news presenter strained through the radio in Beaumont's 1964 Jaguar E type. "King, the owner of the largest oil and gas company in the world, was a long-term climate change denier and never far from controversy. Rumors abound as to whether the killing was at the hands of activists, or a robbery gone wrong..."

Beaumont clicked the radio off and slipped the car into gear. He glanced in the rear-view mirror and pulled out into the traffic. He had enough on his mind without worrying about the death of a billionaire thousands of miles away.

For several seconds, the road behind was empty, and then a Range Rover pulled out of a parking bay. Beaumont thought nothing of it. The fuel guzzling urban tractors were relatively common on the roads of Middle-England. Not that Beaumont's machine was any more practical, he thought ruefully, tapping the elm veneered dashboard. Beaumont felt an affinity with the machine. He and this beautiful car were made in the same decade and just 100 miles apart. In this era of mass-produced, soulless commodities, connections like he had with the Jag was a thing to be cherished.

The sound of a trilling phone dragged Beaumont back from his thoughts. The traffic lights ahead clicked from green to red. Beaumont used the opportunity to rummage through his jacket pockets. Removing a board marker, a shard of rock which he really should have left in the office, and three discolored Fox's Glacier Mints, he finally found the phone. Beaumont glanced at the screen a moment before the lights turned to green. He scowled, not recognizing the number. His finger hovered over the cancel button, but then something made him change his mind. He poked the answer button.

"Richard." The voice down the line was surprisingly crisp, almost as though the speaker was in the same room.

Within one word Beaumont recognized the voice. He took a sharp intake of breath. It was the voice of Helios, the mysterious leader of The Council of Selene. For once, Beaumont was lost for words.

"I'm sorry to have to contact you like this," Helios said. "It really is most unusual, but things are moving forward rather more quickly than we'd like."

Beaumont clicked on the indicator, intending to stop the Jaguar in a nearby vacant parking space.

"Don't stop the car," Helios said, urgently. "It's important you continue exactly as you were."

Beaumont shot up in the seat, a feeling akin to déjà vu moving through him. He knew Helios and The Council were powerful, but he didn't realize they would be watching him right now. Beaumont canceled the indicator and continued towards the next junction, gripping the wheel with his free hand.

"I expect you still don't have hands free in that antique

Jaguar of yours," Helios sounded more jovial now. "Put your phone on speaker and place it on the dashboard. It's important you listen very closely to what I'm about to say."

Beaumont did as he was instructed and slid to a stop at the next set of lights.

"As we expected, your research has gained a lot of interest in the international community."

"The tablets, they're, they're...." Beaumont stuttered.

"They're getting a lot of attention, yes. We always knew that would be the case, and were ready for it, but a new faction has just entered the arena."

"I'm sorry, what do you mean?"

"Someone unexpected has just become interested in what you're looking at. Have you heard of an organization called The Alternative Power Project?"

"A.P.P. Yes, I have. Run by the daughter of that billionaire..."

"Lulu King, that's right."

Suddenly two facts lined up in Beaumont's mind. "King was murdered last night, wasn't he?"

"That's right," Helios said, his tone flat, as though they were discussing the mundane. "On the outside, A.P.P. appears to be an organization for positive change. They've spent billions on researching non-carbon power sources and have made some progress. In the background, however, they have been putting a lot of time into researching the pre-diluvian period."

"The time before The Great Flood." The lights turned green, and Beaumont set off. Approaching the center of the city, the traffic became heavier.

"Yes. King seems to believe that the societies of old had access to a power source of which we're not yet aware. King believes that these societies were able to power their cities, vehicles and the like, without oil, gas, or even batteries."

The thoughts ran through Beaumont's mind. Of course, he had heard rumors of such things spouted by people in the pseudoscientific community. Never, though, from someone as important as Helios.

"I have no doubt that you will come to the same discovery in time," Helios said. "But the intentions of the A.P.P are not good. Any discoveries they make will be controlled exclusively for their benefit. Certain countries will get the benefits, others won't. We will enter another colonial period; except this time it'll be companies in charge."

"What do we need to do?" Beaumont said, struggling now to keep up.

"You see the black Range Rover in your rear-view mirror? It's six cars behind you right now."

Beaumont peered in the mirror. Sure enough, the vehicle was still there.

"That's just one of the team they have following you. There's another in a blue sedan. They'll switch several times to make sure you don't notice."

"What, what do they want?" Beaumont stuttered, fear rising in this throat.

"You requested some documents to be sent to you. JS12 documents, above top secret."

Beaumont glanced at his bag on the passenger seat. He had requested the documents from a contact a week ago, they arrived at his office today.

"What do I need to do?"

"I'll get you through this," Helios said, "But you must do exactly what I say."

Beaumont nodded. The waiting traffic shuffled forwards

again. Beaumont gripped the wheel with both hands, his heart pounded an aggressive beat inside his chest.

Ahead, the lights turned green, and the traffic moved on. As Beaumont approached the lights, the green flicked back to red.

"Accelerate now," Helios barked down the phone.

Beaumont glanced at the Range Rover, just a few cars behind. He couldn't see who was inside the vehicle and didn't like the idea of finding out. Beaumont gripped the steering wheel and stomped on the gas. The Jaguar's powerful engine roared, and the car shot through the red light and out into the junction moments before the next wave of traffic.

"Turn left," Helios shouted.

Beaumont swung the wheel into the corner, tires protesting with a shriek.

"Good," Helios said.

Beaumont accelerated down the road and away from the city, Georgian townhouses flashing past on both sides. He glanced in the rear-view mirror just in time to see the Range Rover thunder out from the junction behind them. Driving on the wrong side of the road, the SUV forced two cars to screech to a halt and narrowly missed a cyclist. The Range Rover turned and picked up speed towards him.

"We've got company," Beaumont said.

"Yes, I can see that," Helios replied, again causing Beaumont to wonder how the man knew so much.

Beaumont overtook a cyclist and then an Amazon delivery van parked half on the curb.

"Turn right in 200 feet," Helios instructed.

Beaumont slowed the Jag, then swung the wheel into the narrow street, barely big enough for one car. Terraced houses lined both sides. Beaumont accelerated, hoping he wouldn't meet anyone coming the other way.

"Left now," Helios barked.

Beaumont swung the car into the corner. He glanced down the street behind him to see the SUV barreling down, the larger vehicle barely fitting between the houses.

Beaumont hit the gas again, and the Jaguar shot forwards.

"Right, now," Helios shouted, almost immediately.

Beaumont swung the wheel a moment too late. The Jaguar skidded across the road, the rear of the car crunching into a red telephone box. Glass shattered. The shockwave moved through the vehicle. Beaumont cursed under his breath, put the Jag in first gear and pulled away. Fortunately, the collision had only shattered the glass in the phone box. The car still drove fine.

"Shame," Helios said, dryly. "I'll get that repair sorted for you. I think we probably know someone."

Beaumont smirked at the understatement. The Council of Selene was probably the most well-connected organization on the planet—they always knew someone.

Beaumont accelerated away, following Helios' directions back towards the city. He peered in the rear-view mirror. The Range Rover was still there, gaining on them.

"Take the next right," Helios said.

Beaumont glanced at the street names. They were back in the center of the city now, heading towards the university.

"Are you sure? That's St John's Street. It's full of pedestrians and narrow too. We could get stuck down there easily."

"Of course I'm sure," Helios replied, flatly.

Beaumont swung the Jaguar around a tight corner and

into the narrow street. The turreted edifice of St John's College towered over them.

"Turn right," Helios said.

"But there isn't a right turn here. Just the pedestrian entrance to the college,"

"Yes. It's plenty wide enough for the Jaguar."

Beaumont exhaled as the entrance came into view up ahead. He slowed the car, leaned on the horn, and turned.

As Helios had suggested, the Jaguar slipped beneath the grand archway with an inch to spare. Beaumont leaned on the horn, startling a group of students who jumped out of the way just in time. Beaumont picked up speed through the building and emerged amid the grand lawns.

Behind him and back through the arch, the SUV shuddered to stop. The vehicle paused there for several moments, before continuing in the direction of the city center.

"We've lost them, I think," Beaumont said.

"For now," Helios said. "Now listen carefully, this is what I need you to do."

Beaumont navigated his way slowly through the college, emerging on a street at the other side and slipping back into the anonymous traffic.

Just over forty minutes later, Beaumont pulled into his driveway and killed the Jaguar's engine. He grabbed his bag and hurried to the door, recalling the instructions which Helios had given him. Once inside, he set about creating the scene. He pushed things from their shelves and knocked pictures from the wall, leaving only one in the lounge in its correct position. Then he ran out to the back garden. He slipped the documents from his bag and hid them in the position Helios had instructed.

Once back in the kitchen, he grabbed a piece of

notepaper and scribbled a short message. He then placed the note carefully under the flap of the letterbox. His preparations complete, Beaumont slumped into the sofa, unclipped his smart watch—his *Ubeste*—and tucked it into a hidden pocket on the inside of his jacket.

The lights went out. Beaumont sat up straight and looked around. He heard a faint scratching noise from the front door. The lock clicked, and the door swung open. A cold draft whipped into the house.

Beaumont swallowed. This was the part he wasn't looking forward to. Carefully, he withdrew a tiny pendant from his pocket and glanced down at it. The Key to the Nile symbol set in silver, glimmered in some distant light. Beaumont stashed it away and steeled his reserve. He had to trust Helios's plan.

A pair of large African men walked into the front room. They looked around, clearly surprised both to see the place already ransacked and to see their quarry waiting for them on the sofa. They shone powerful flashlights down at Beaumont.

Beaumont grinned up at the men. "What took you so long?" He stood and slipped his coat back on. He pointed at the guns which the men held. "Don't be silly, you can put those away. I don't suppose you'll tell me where we're going, so we better get moving."

13

EDEN WATCHED her phone as the call to Beaumont timed out again. She'd tried calling Beaumont twice more, but again the calls hadn't connected. Her gut twisted in a growing sense of worry.

Eden knew that patience was a virtue, but she also knew that it was a virtue of which she possessed very little. Eden's impatience had got her into trouble countless times. But then again, it had saved her life occasionally, too.

If Beaumont wouldn't, or couldn't answer his phone, Eden had to go and find out why. Eden pulled on a jacket and shoved a few things into her bag. She stepped out of the truck and shimmied down the ladder. She locked the truck behind her, snapped on her flashlight, and strode through the gloomy woodland.

She reached the barn in less than ten minutes. The structure looked even more decrepit than usual in the thin beam of light. Ivy consumed the barn's walls, and moss sprawled across the roof tiles. It was all a perfectly constructed ruse to hide the barn's contents from anyone curious enough to stray this far from the path. Reaching the door, Eden opened a hidden panel and entered a 10-digit passcode. The alarm deactivated, and the reinforced door unlocked. Eden swung open the door, stepped inside and grinned. Her 1995 Land Rover Defender, painted in matte red, stood against the rear wall.

Eden scrambled into the driver's seat and fired the old girl up. The machine roared and then coughed. She clicked on the low beamed headlights. Several weeks without use wasn't ideal for these old machines. Eden never lost faith in this beauty though, the old girl would probably work to the apocalypse and beyond. In fact, Eden thought, tapping the steering wheel lovingly, she was counting on it.

Eden pulled the Landy out of the barn. After closing the barn doors she and started off down the narrow-rutted track towards the lane. Progress was slow for the first two miles as she navigated her way across the uneven soil. Several minutes later, she pulled out onto the lane. Now on the open road, she turned on the main headlights and accelerated.

Listening to the grumble of the chunky tires on the tarmac, Eden glanced down at the place where the radio would have been. On buying the vehicle, Eden had stripped out all the unnecessary electronics. First, that meant there was less to go wrong, and second, she then knew there was no programs running that she didn't control. The simplicity of the thirty-year-old vehicle was exactly what she required: Diesel, metal, and rubber that when combined would get her exactly where she needed to go.

Two hours later, Eden pulled to a stop half a mile from Beaumont's cottage. Just in case she needed to leave in a hurry, she heaved the manual gearbox into reverse and turned the Landy around.

Eden killed the engine, swung her bag over her shoulder, and headed in the direction of the cottage.

Beaumont lived two miles from the town of Ely. Just a short journey from Cambridge, it was the perfect place for someone who wanted privacy while remaining near the university.

Eden covered the distance slowly, stopping several times to listen for approaching vehicles or nearby footsteps. An owl hooted from somewhere nearby and something scurried in the undergrowth. Used to the noises of the British countryside, Eden recognized the sounds instantly. That was a good sign—no humans had recently scared off the nocturnal wildlife.

Eden reached the cottage's front fence and ducked in behind a bush. She had visited Beaumont's house several times over the years, originally with her father and more recently alone. The cottage was simple and understated, especially considering the international fame and respect Professor Beaumont commanded.

Eden pushed the branches of the overgrown bush to one side and peered at the cottage. The building was exactly what you'd expect from a British cottage. Ivy and wisteria crept across chunky, white-washed walls, several chimneys jutted above the slate roof, and the doors and windows looked as though they were made for a smaller breed of human. Eden in fact remembered her father banging his head several times after sharing a bottle of Beaumont's good red wine.

Tonight, though, Beaumont was certainly not at home. No light came from the windows and no smoke came from the chimney.

Eden watched the place for several seconds, searching for any signs of life. There were none. She glanced at her watch. It was just before midnight. She would have expected there still to be some signs of life around the place at this time.

Something here felt off. A hard knot of worry re-formed in Eden's gut.

Eden glanced around one more time. Satisfied she was alone, she pushed open the gate and walked up the front path. An owl shrieked from a nearby bush. No security lights snapped on at her movement. A pair of bats squealed past, pounding the air with short fleshy wings.

Eden reached the front door and tapped three times on the thick oak. The sound echoed mournfully through the house. Then, as though answering her call, the door creaked open. Eden took a step back, instinctively preparing herself for an unseen assailant. No one came.

The tangle of worry in Eden's stomach built to something the size of a fist. She watched the door for several seconds. Nothing moved. Eden resisted the urge to shout for the professor. There was no need to advertise her arrival. Eden stepped forwards and pushed open the door. The ancient hinges creaked. A gust of wind streamed through the house, disturbing something in one of the back rooms. Eden reached across and flicked the light switch. Nothing happened. The power was out. Eden glanced behind her. In the distance she saw the glow from one of the neighboring houses. The power to Beaumont's cottage had been cut.

Eden dug a flashlight from her bag. The thing was constructed out of thick aluminum. As well as providing a strong beam of light, it made an effective weapon. She snapped it on, half covering the beam so as to remain discreet, and started looking around. Seeing the state of the house, Eden's worry turned to all out fear. Pictures lay shattered on the floor of the hallway, rugs and wall hangings lay crumpled and torn. The destruction continued in the kitchen. A vase had been shattered against one wall, and the remains of several china plates sat against the other. The front room was the same, with a basket of logs upturned across the floor and several pictures hanging at strange angles. Eden moved from room to room taking in the damage. When she'd checked the whole house over, she returned to the front room.

Beaumont wasn't here, and it was also clear that he hadn't gone through choice.

Eden strode back into the hallway and closed the door. As the heavy wood slammed into place, something slipped out from beneath the letter box flap. The item had been jammed inside the letter box in such a way that it wasn't visible from either side.

Eden picked it up. It was a piece of paper torn carelessly from a notepad. Unfolding the paper, Eden's muscles froze in fear. Professor Beaumont's scrawled handwriting covered one side. Furthermore, the note was addressed to her.

Eden,

Please forgive this crude note, but I don't have much time. I fear I have been followed home from the university today. The intentions of my pursuers are not good. We have clearly uncovered something of incredible importance. A few days ago, I requested some top-secret documents from a contact. I shouldn't have done it as I fear that is how they've found me.

You'll find these documents in the place where Cleopatra now rests.

I know you'll find their contents illuminating.

I hope to see you soon.

May Ubaste protect us both.

GB

Eden looked up, frowning. She scrunched the paper in

the palm of her hand. The sickening worry turned into anger. This felt all too much like the events that had led her to the tomb in the mountains of Lebanon just a few weeks ago.

But what did Beaumont mean by the place where Cleopatra now rests? Queen Cleopatra was entombed somewhere in Egypt, but Beaumont surely couldn't mean that. That made no sense.

"Come on, think," Eden muttered, pacing up and down the front room. The floorboards creaked beneath her boots and the wind rattled one of the windows above. "The place where Cleopatra now rests. Think."

Eden spun around and came face to face with a large photograph on the wall. It was the only picture remaining in its rightful place. In the photograph, a younger Beaumont sat beside a tan colored springer spaniel.

Eden snapped her fingers as the memory struck her. When she'd visited this cottage as a child, the spaniel had still been alive. Eden remembered the mutt sleeping by the fire most of the day and occasionally staggering through to the kitchen for meals.

Eden grinned as she remembered her frustration that the dog wouldn't play fetch or do anything interesting.

"And what would one of the world's leading Egyptologists call his dog?" Eden said out loud.

Cleopatra, obviously.

Eden stalked through to the kitchen, unbolted the back door, and strode into the back garden. She walked down the garden, sweeping the beam of light from side to side. She took no effort to remain unseen now. Whoever had taken Beaumont and trashed the place had long since left. The garden was large and ran down a slight incline towards a small stream. She heard trickling water as she got close by.

Eden froze as the beam of light swept across something which looked like a monument. It looked more like one of the cairns she had seen on hilltops or beaches. Suitably this one was made in the shape of a pyramid. Constructed with flat grey pebbles it stood about three feet in height. Eden ran across to the tower and examined it carefully.

The uneven pile of rocks cut the beam of light into strange shadows on the lawn behind. Eden crouched down and peered closely at the stones. She moved around the pile, inspecting each side of the carefully constructed pyramid. On the farthest side of the pyramid, several stones lay out of place on the ground. As Eden examined the cairn, something glinted from deep within the rocks.

Eden leaned in close, afraid to touch or disturb the pile. An object sat between the rocks on the far side of the pyramid. It was a small parcel, about the size of a paperback book. Eden pulled it out carefully and then replaced the cairn's missing rocks.

She examined the parcel, twisting it carefully in her hands. Several strange markings covered the wrapping.

"JS12, top secret," Eden read out loud. She felt the contents through the wrapper. The parcel was thin, just containing a few pieces of paper or photographs. Whatever this was, someone wanted it badly.

Eden ran back inside, flipped open the envelope's lid and tipped the contents onto the kitchen table. Three documents slipped out, face down. Eden picked them up and laid them out on the surface of the table. She swept the light across the assembled documents. At first, they made no sense to her. Then slowly, realization dawned.

Eden exhaled and drew her hand across her face. This case was getting more difficult by the moment.

14

"WELL, if it isn't the world-famous Professor, Richard Beaumont," Lulu King said, striding into the room. "It's so nice of you to make some time in your busy schedule to join us."

Beaumont, tied securely to a chair with a black pillowcase over his head, wiggled around in a futile attempt to see the voice's owner.

"I trust the journey wasn't too rough for you. I know you're used to getting around in that snazzy Jaguar of yours. I did tell Abdul and Sharif to look after you. They have numerous talents, but I'm afraid hospitality is not one of them."

King glanced at the Angolans, standing at the door behind her. Sharif moved his weight from one foot to the other, clearly unsure whether King's comments were a compliment or a criticism.

King stepped up to Beaumont and whisked the pillowcase from his head. The professor looked around wildly, blinking several times in the bright light.

As though on cue, one of the fluorescent tubes in the far corner began to strobe and hum.

"Welcome to the Presidential Suite," King said, her arms outstretched. She looked around the bare concrete room in mock amazement. Stains covered floor and walls, some due to the natural decay of the unoccupied warehouse, others appeared to be more sinister in origin. King pointed to one such stain on the floor beneath Beaumont's chair. "I'm sorry about the mess here," she said, smiling sweetly. "Our last guest checked out in a hurry. Left their brains all over the place."

Beaumont's Adam's apple bobbed beneath his pale skin. He sat slumped with his shirt and jacket askew.

"We offer all sorts of services here, finger removal, third-degree burns. We've even been known to do an eye surgery or two. You name it and our team can oblige." King pointed at Abdul and Sharif.

"What do you want?" Beaumont said, his voice hoarse. He coughed, attempting to clear his throat.

King snapped her fingers. "Sharif, get our guest some water. He's had a long day, which I fear will soon start to get longer."

Beaumont stared up at King. He was clearly trying not to show his fear. He was doing a relatively good job, King thought. An amateur, or certainly someone with less experience, might even buy it. Not King, she could smell fear. And in this room, it hung in the air like yesterday's fish. Beaumont reeked of it.

Sharif strode back into the room and handed King a glass of water. King accepted the glass and nodded. She placed the glass on the floor a few feet from Beaumont. The Professor's eyes followed King's every move.

"You've clearly got me here for a reason," Beaumont said. "Are you going to tell me what that is?"

"Cutting straight to the chase, interesting." King extended a well-manicured finger and pointed at Beaumont. "That's very un-British of you. I know you people love a good, what is it you say, a good chit-chat."

Beaumont's eyes narrowed to slits, clearly growing tired of King's games.

King grinned, placed her hands on her hips and looked down at the professor. "Tell me, you're supposed to be a clever man. Do you know who I am?"

"Theodora, Queen of the Roman Empire?"

King tilted her head backwards and laughed. The humorless bark reverberated fitfully around the room. "I like you, Professor." King pointed at Beaumont again. "I like you. I think you can stay as long as you like. I'm afraid I am not Theodora, the Queen of the Roman Empire, although soon I will be as powerful. My name is Lulu King. I am now in charge of King Industries which is the largest power company in the..."

"Raymond King was your father," Beaumont blurted.

For a heartbeat, King's muscles froze at the mention of her father. "That's right," she said, unable to hide the icy edge from her voice. "Raymond King was my father, the CEO and Chairman of King Industries for several decades before his recent and unfortunate death."

"I'm sorry for your loss," Beaumont said insincerely. "Did you drag me here to talk about your father? I'm not sure I'd make a very good therapist."

"No, I don't need a therapist," King said, almost giggling. "For several decades, my father built King Industries' success on the back of oil and gas. In fact, he made us one of the biggest producers of fossil fuels in the world, an accolade of which he was very proud. But I know as well as you do, that the world is a different place now. Fossil fuels are not as welcome as they once were. For twenty years I tried to tell him that we should be looking for alternatives, but he didn't listen. He wouldn't listen. That forced me into action. Fifteen years ago, I started a company called the Alternative Power Provision."

"I think I've heard of you," Beaumont interjected.

"We have funded a lot of research into alternatives to oil and gas, but with our limited budgets, our success has been limited too. Now that I have merged A.P.P. with King Industries, we have almost unlimited budgets at our disposal."

"Interesting, but I don't see…"

"Professor, have you heard of Moscovium? It's also known as Element 115."

Beaumont nodded, his expression paling as things started to make sense.

"Moscovium, or element 115, is one of the synthetic super-heavy elements," King was on a roll now, and treating Beaumont to his own private lecture. "With the A.P.P. we did a lot of research into whether Element 115 could hold the secret to sustainable and abundant power. But, no matter what we tried, we couldn't figure it out. The damn thing was just far too unstable." King caught Beaumont's gaze. The professor stared intently at her now as though he knew exactly what was coming. "We were pretty much at a dead end, and then I heard something incredibly interesting indeed. I learned about you, the man in charge of translating the Diary of Aloma, which is a newly discovered haul of stone tablets thought to date from before the Great Flood, right?"

Beaumont nodded mechanically. "I don't see the relevance," Beaumont lied, of course he knew where this was going. The conversation he'd shared with Eden Black a few hours ago scrolled back through his mind. "I'm not a scientist."

King grinned at Beaumont, her mouth widening with artificial mirth.

"Some years ago, professor, I had a realization." King examined her fingernails. "I wonder if it's a point on which we may agree. I realized how arrogant we've all become in the modern world. We look at the past like some curious oddity. As though our ancestors were mere animals walking around, doing nothing of merit until we entered the modern era. I believe, in fact I know, that was not the case. The people of the past were much more advanced than we give them credit for."

Beaumont nodded slowly. "I can agree with you on that."

"Good, good, I'm so glad you can. I believe that such ancient civilizations have already solved the riddle of stable element 115. For several years I've had a team searching all the documentation on the pre-diluvian period, for any indication on the source of their power, and one object comes up time and time again. A relic so powerful that anyone who touches it dies immediately. An artifact that is reported to be able to float above the surface of the Earth, allowing men to carry it for days on end without strain.

Beaumont arched an eyebrow.

"The Ark of the Covenant," King sounded the words out individually, carefully.

Beaumont's other eyebrow joined his first. He had to admit, that in some crazy way what King was saying made sense. "The Ark of the Covenant is one of the most sought after fabled relics in history. I don't... I have no idea where you're going to find it."

King unfurled her fingers like a cat playing with its claws. "That's where you come in, professor. I learned that you requested a set of JS12 documents—documents that are so top secret most people don't even know they exist. I went on to learn that these documents contain infrared images of The Giza Plateau, showing areas of unexplained heat somewhere beneath the second and third Pyramids."

Beaumont's mouth hung open now, unable to respond.

"You see Professor Beaumont, I want to find the Ark of the Covenant, and you are going to help me." Circling him like an animal about to pounce on its prey, she tapped a finger on his shoulder "You are going to help me, whether you like it or not."

HELIOS LEANED back in his chair and closed his eyes. He let his mind rest for a few moments, searching for clarity. When he opened his eyes again, the screen of his computer and the maps and charts spread across the table, swayed before coming into focus.

Yet again, he was looking at the problem of the world's energy production and usage. Yet again, the problem seemed insurmountable. It was clear from changing temperatures across the globe that emissions needed to be cut. The evidence had been there for nearly fifty years, but the path forwards was not an easy one. Helios knew more than anyone that fossil fuels had powered every technological development of the last two hundred years. To just reject them without a clean and abundant alternative would be like going back to the dark ages.

However, there just wasn't an alternative available yet.

Or at least, Helios knew, humankind had yet to find one on their own.

Helios pulled a cigarette from the packet on the desk and lit up. He took a deep breath, watching the smoke snake up towards the ceiling.

Helios also knew there were some big players, even within The Council, whose livelihoods depended on the price of oil and gas. If new, cleaner, and more sustainable power sources were found, these people would see their business fade into irrelevance. That was one reason The Council of Selene needed to change, Helios thought, taking another puff on the cigarette. Although the councilors came from all walks of life and all corners of the globe, they had their own biases and their own agendas. These people were not incorruptible.

Fortunately, as always, Helios had a plan. A plan for both the problem of sustainable power, and The Council of Selene. Change was coming fast.

The phone on Helios' desk buzzed. Helios leaned forwards and thumbed the button. "Your next appointment is here to see you," came the voice of his secretary.

"Send him in." Helios stubbed out his cigarette and climbed to his feet.

The door's mechanism clicked as it disengaged. The door swung open.

Helios stepped out from behind his desk as a young man strode into the office. The visitor wore a light brown shirt and black trousers. Although of an average height and size, the man was trim and muscular. His movements hinted a strength, power and most importantly, dedication.

"Captain Baxter," Helios said, taking the young man's hand in a greeting. "I trust you are recovering from your last mission well. Tell me, did everything in Lebanon go as planned?"

Choosing the more informal setting of two leather tub chairs by the window, Helios sat opposite Baxter. His assistant had furnished them with a tray of drinks, which sat on the glass table between them.

Through the window, the last colors of the day were draining quickly from the sky. The waters of the Mediterranean lapped mysterious and unbroken in all directions. Far away on the horizon a heavily laden tanker slipped towards the unseen coast of Egypt. At this distance, the thousand tons of oil and steel looked no bigger than a floating bottle.

"Everything went just as you said it would," Baxter replied, leaning back in the chair, and taking a sip of the coffee. "We took that fool Godspeed for a good old ride, anyway."

Helios grinned and steepled his fingers. "You didn't like working for old Archie Godspeed?"

"Going undercover and working for him was one of the most frustrating tasks of my career so far. I would take gangsters, terrorists or drug dealers over that, any day," Baxter replied, his voice humorless.

"I always knew it was going to be a challenge, but I knew you were the man for the job. And the mission was successful, the tablets are now in the process of being translated."

Baxter nodded slowly and took another sip of the coffee.

"How was the extraction? I'm sorry it had to be so complicated. You understand we work in the shadows. It had to appear as though you'd gone down with the ship."

Baxter stared out at the waters which surrounded the Balonia, the scene spooling again through his mind. He remembered the speed boat, powering at full throttle towards the concrete harbor arm. He remembered the look of fear on Archibald Godspeed's face, and turning to see Eden bobbing in the water behind them.

"It went as smoothly as could be expected. I bailed out of the boat as late as I could. Your team of divers were in position and got me hooked up to a tank and regulator. We then made our way slowly around the harbor to a waiting ship about half a mile away. As you'd expected, everyone was too occupied with the wreckage to pay us any attention."

Helios nodded slowly. "And the injury, how is that doing now?"

Baxter cycled his shoulder forward a few times. It still twinged somewhere deep within his muscles. "It's getting better. A bit stiff now and then, but a remarkable recovery, really."

"I'm sorry about that," Helios said, leaning back in the chair. "I didn't know Godspeed had that sort of aggression in him. Where did he get the knife, anyway?"

"I think it was in the boat already. Lucky it was blunt." Baxter ran a hand down over his shoulder and felt the ridge in his skin where the scar had formed. "You can't predict everything..."

"You're right, I can't predict everything, but the safety of my team requires me to predict as much as I possibly can. And when one of you gets hurt, I can't help but take that personally."

Baxter and Helios shared a look of mutual respect. For a few seconds no one spoke.

"And how was working with Eden Black?" Helios asked.

Baxter broke Helios' gaze and stared out through the glass.

"Athena thought the pair of you were getting on well," Helios continued.

A ghost of a smile flashed across the younger man's face. "Yes. It was fine," Baxter said, finally. "She's got quite a spirit."

"I'm glad." Helios leaned forwards and knitted his fingers together. "Because you're going to be working together again. Very soon."

15

THE PHOTOGRAPHS LOOKED, as far as Eden could tell, like aerial photographs of The Giza Plateau. One of the photos showed the whole area, including the city to one side. The other two were more focused on certain areas of The Plateau. What was interesting about the photos, though, was the colored shading that covered certain parts of the images. It looked almost as though there were two images laid one on top of the other.

"They're infrared," Eden said out loud, tapping the tabletop. She looked at the most zoomed out photo and could see that parts of the nearby city were covered in a rainbow of red and orange. That would make sense, with air conditioners, cooking equipment and other electronics kicking out heat into the atmosphere. She looked at The Giza Plateau on the other side of the photo, most of which was hued in blue. Then, looking closely at The Plateau, Eden noticed something. Some areas of The Plateau were overshadowed with hues of green and yellow, meaning they were emitting heat. Eden turned her attention to one of the other photos, which focused in on the yellow and green section. In the middle of The Plateau, a long rectangular section was emitting a heat signature.

Eden grabbed her phone and searched for a map of The Giza Plateau. She aligned the map with the photograph and looked carefully from one to the other. Sure enough, the area marked in the infrared photo was supposed to be empty.

"So where is that heat coming from?" Eden let her eyes lose focus on the photos in front of her. Her father, Alexander Winslow, would be able to shed some light on this in seconds, Eden thought. It was moments like this when Eden missed him the most. A welling sense of grief moved through her. Eden pushed it aside and turned to Beaumont's note. Sure, she couldn't talk to her father, but she wasn't powerless. One of her father's oldest friends and contemporaries, Richard Beaumont knew more about the hidden secrets beneath the Egyptian sands than almost any man alive.

Taking a sip of the now cooled coffee, Eden read Beaumont's note again. The first half of it was clearly about the photographs which Eden had already discovered, but that couldn't be everything. Eden remembered the long evenings Beaumont and her father would spend debating some of history's greatest riddles. She read the note three times. The only thing which didn't relate to the photographs was the final line.

"May Ubaste protect us both," Eden read the line out loud.

Having learned a thing or two about the Egyptian deities, Eden knew that Ubaste was a gentle warrior associated with defense and protection which usually came in the form of a cat.

"Ubaste," Eden repeated the name. It sounded strangely familiar, as though she'd heard it somewhere recently.

The memory struck like a thunderbolt. Eden froze. Beaumont had referred to his smartwatch as his own little *Ubaste*. At the time Eden hadn't thought anything of it. Beaumont, much like her father, seemed to speak a language of his own, seamlessly mixing modern English with references to ancient gods, dead languages, and other archaeological terms. It was often an effort just to understand what they were talking about.

Eden darted out of the kitchen and returned a few minutes later with the box and instruction leaflet to the smart watch. As she'd expected, Beaumont had kept the thing in his office. She laid the box on the table and pulled the laptop from her bag. Navigating to the manufacturer's website, Eden was pleased to see that they had a system for recovering lost devices.

"I should hope so, at that price," she said out loud, catching a glimpse of the cost on the home page. The student who'd bought it must have really appreciated Beaumont's help.

Eden pulled open the box and took out the instructions. Seeing Beaumont's spidery handwriting on the front of the instruction leaflet, Eden grinned. True to form, he had written down his login information. Eden logged into the manufacturers website and followed the link to the *find my device* section. Within a few seconds a map filled the screen. A blue dot showed the location of the watch and with any luck, Beaumont himself.

"Gotcha," Eden said, out loud. She snatched up the photographs and headed for the door.

Nearly three hours later, Eden pulled into an industrial estate in Southeast London. She stopped the Land Rover and checked the map. The website suggested that Beaumont was 500 feet ahead.

Eden switched off the Land Rover's lights and drove on slowly by the intermittent light of the street lamps.

From what Eden could see, the estate was made up from a collection of run-down warehouses. She passed two light-less monolithic buildings. Based on the fact they had no security lights, Eden assumed the warehouses were empty. The gentle *pat pat* of the Land Rover's diesel engine rico-cheted from the bare walls. Despite the noise she was making, Eden pushed on. She didn't want to announce her arrival, but also wanted to be able to get away in a hurry, if necessary.

One more warehouse sat at the end of the road. Eden stopped the Land Rover and checked the map again. A flame of excitement moved through her when she realized that Beaumont was inside.

Eden picked up a pair of binoculars and inspected the warehouse. At a cursory glance, the vast discolored walls and broken windows made it look like many of the other buildings in the area. Eden concentrated on a small row of windows near the roof. Sure enough, there was a dull glow coming from inside. Either the lights had been left on, or the place was in use.

Eden turned the Land Rover around and pulled in behind a broken-down truck. With nowhere nearby to prop-erly hide the vehicle, the truck provided cover at least. Eden scrambled into the back of the Land Rover and snapped open the lid of the hidden storage locker. Built into the vehi-cle's chassis, the compartment was larger than it seemed. Always one to be prepared, Eden kept it stocked with every-thing she might need for an eventuality such as this.

First, she pulled on a black hat and gloves, then clipped

a four-inch blade to one ankle and a larger knife to her hip. She looked down at the Glock and several full magazines but decided against it. Guns were noisy, attracted attention, and the last thing she wanted was a unit of armed police officers turning up. Instead, she opted for three smoke grenades. Eden had used these grenades in the past and found them particularly effective. They not only filled a large area with thick smoke but also rendered anyone without a gas mask unconscious within a few seconds. She snagged up the gas mask and slipped it into her bag along with a length of rope, her climbing harness, a powerful flashlight, and the binoculars.

Finally, feeling as prepared as she could be, she stepped outside, slipped the bag onto her back, and crept towards the warehouse.

Eden ran across the yard in front of the warehouse and slipped in behind a stack of old pallets. Peering out, she assessed the scene. Several old barrels and piles of trash littered the yard. She turned and examined the warehouse's front wall. There was a closed roller shutter on one side, with a set of double doors beside. Paint flaked from the wall in great curls. A sign, which once must have advertised the occupier's name, hung by one fixing. Eden saw no security cameras, floodlights, or motion detectors. Of course, that didn't mean they weren't there, but she would have to take her chances. At the far end of the building, Eden saw what she was looking for. A thick pipe ran down from the roof, no doubt to channel rainwater into the sewers.

Eden slipped into a crouch, preparing herself to run. She checked the yard once more for signs of movement. Satisfied that no threats were coming her way, she darted across and ducked in behind the pipe. Eden stood in the shadow for several seconds, her senses on high alert. She listened closely for the sound of raised voices or running feet—anything to indicate her presence had been spotted. The distant rumble of traffic was all she heard.

Eden turned and looked up at the pipe. About six inches in diameter, it appeared to be securely fastened to the wall. Eden pulled off her gloves and stashed them in a pocket, then she reached up and gripped the first fixing. The pipe groaned but remained in place as Eden lifted her feet from the ground. Eden peered up at the forty-foot climb ahead. Moving slowly, hand over hand, she picked her way upwards. By the halfway point, the muscles in her hands and legs ached. With each movement, the pipe strained against its fixings but fortunately remained solid.

"How long is this going to take?"

Eden heard a voice drift through the cold night air. She froze, not daring to move a muscle. She intertwined her fingers together behind the pipe. The feeling from her fingers was dissipating fast.

"She's got a plan, apparently. I hope it's not like the last one. Getting rid of bodies is always a pain," another man answered.

Eden picked up the faint smell of cigarette smoke. She risked a look over her shoulder. Thirty feet below, and almost directly beneath where she hung, two men stood smoking cigarettes. With shaven heads and wearing dark clothes, Eden recognized the classic thug type.

Eden turned back towards the pipe, the strength in her fingers beginning to wane. She peered up at the rooftop, still six feet above her.

"I know. It's getting stupid now. Does she think we're magicians or something?" the first man replied, their accents exposing them as London locals. They must be the hired muscle.

Eden held her breath and clenched her hands even harder.

"We should probably go back inside. She'll be wondering where..."

The man stopped talking as a creaking sound vibrated down the pipe.

Eden froze. Right in front of her eyes the pipe's fixing inched away from the concrete.

16

"WHAT'S THAT NOISE?" One of the thugs said, exhaling a cloud of thick cigarette smoke.

Thirty feet above them, Eden's eyes bulged as the pipe's fixings disintegrated. The pipe swung slowly backwards, further into the open air.

Eden's muscles tensed against the movement.

The fixing above her had started to come loose too, but still wasn't free of the wall. As quickly as she could, without disturbing the pipe any further, Eden pulled herself upwards.

"What noise?" the other thug asked, taking a deep drag on his cigarette. "You're hearing things now."

"Nah, I definitely heard something."

Eden freed one hand and slid it up the pipe again. She was now just two feet from the roof. She wedged her hand in behind the pipe's highest fixing and gripped hard.

Another clang echoed through the metal. Eden's hand slipped past the fixing as the bolt came clear of the concrete. A shudder vibrated up and down the metal. Eden's heart thundered its way up into her throat.

"There! Surely you heard it that time?" One of the thugs said. "I think it came from up..."

The thug's voice was cut off by another deep clang, followed by a screech.

Eden heaved herself upwards, her hands moving automatically as the pipe slipped away from the wall. With one great motion she leaped from the drainpipe and clung onto the edge of the roof. As soon as her fingers curled around the edge of the concrete she flung herself up and over.

A great clattering noise echoed up from the ground beneath her. The noise rebounded for several seconds, before dying out. Eden lay on her back, frozen in position. She listened to the night air for several seconds, expecting to hear raised voices or gunshots. None came. She rolled over, enjoying the feeling of the solid roof beneath her.

"What the hell?" The voice of one of the men came from the ground beneath her.

Eden rolled to the edge of the roof and peered down into the yard. One of the thugs lay spread out on the ground, a large section of the heavy pipe twisted across his body. The other stood, looking up at the roof, his face contorted into an expression of confusion. The thug looked back down at his fallen colleague, as though trying to understand what had just happened.

It would only take him a few seconds more, Eden figured, to charge inside and alert everyone else to her presence. If that happened, she would have a full fire fight on her hands, which was exactly not what she wanted.

Eden glanced down at her weapons. She had two knives, and three smoke grenades. She considered using one of the smoke grenades now, as that would incapacitate the man in seconds, but then she wouldn't have them for later. She cursed herself for not bringing more. Eden looked around the rooftop. Just a few feet away, several large concrete blocks were stacked up as though ready for a repair job that hadn't happened.

"Perfect," Eden whispered to herself. She shuffled across the roof and picked one up.

Down below, the thug finally shook himself into action and ran in the direction of the warehouse doors. Cutting across the center of the roof, Eden reached his destination first. She placed the block on the edge of the roof and peered down.

"Sorry dude, it's you or me."

She waited until the man was two paces from the door, then shoved the block off the roof. The ensuing wet slap, followed by the crunch of the block against concrete told her she'd hit a home run. Eden peered over the roof's edge and grimaced. "Who'd have thought the old man to have so much blood in him?" she whispered, smiling wolfishly at the Shakespearian quote.

Eden waited several seconds to see if the noise had alerted anyone else from inside. When no one came, she stalked back across the roof towards a row of windows built into the apex. Eden crawled the last two paces and peered through the yellowed glass. The inside of the warehouse lay mostly in darkness. The source of the light was an office at the far end of the space. Two Range Rovers sat in the half-light below.

"I knew it," Eden said, recognizing one of them as the vehicle she'd seen lurking outside Beaumont's office earlier that day.

Eden turned her attention to the office. The office was a separate structure with windows that looked out into the warehouse, no doubt so the mangers of old could keep tabs on their workforce. Eden shrugged off her bag and fished out the binoculars. Three people sat inside the office, watching something on a large television screen. From this angle, Eden couldn't see the faces of the watchers, but she clearly saw what they were viewing. She was in the right place. The large screen showed Beaumont tied to a chair, his hair tussled and his clothes askew.

She put her ear close to the glass but couldn't hear any noise. Either the three were sitting in silence, or the office was well insulated for sound. With the clattering and banging disposing of the first two thugs had caused, Eden assumed it was the latter.

Her eyes never leaving the occupants of the office, should they move or turn her way, Eden shuffled along the roof. Reaching the final pane of glass, she paused. The office was now directly below her. The office's inner structure had its own roof, which from here Eden could see was criss-crossed with wires and vents. She doubted the structure would take her weight, which was perfect for what she had planned.

Eden dug a multi-tool from her bag. The device contained sixteen tools in one, much like a large Swiss army knife. Flipping out the largest screwdriver, Eden scraped away the moldy seal that kept the window in place. Once the seal was clear, she slid the screwdriver under the pane and pried it up. The feeling now having returned to her hands, Eden slipped her gloves back on and then lifted the glass clear of its mounting. She placed it on the roof beside her. Leaning in towards the hole, Eden heard the faint murmur of voices, although from this distance, she couldn't work out what they were saying. She fished around in her bag and pulled out the climbing rope. She lowered the rope down inside the warehouse until it neared the roof of the office, then she leaned through the gap and secured it to one of the roof's supports. Eden took out the gas mask and pulled it down around her neck, then slipped into her climbing harness. She tucked everything else back inside the bag. She attached the rope to the climbing harness and swung down into the warehouse.

Eden lowered herself slowly down the rope until she dangled a few feet above the office. She could hear the voices more clearly now.

"I just don't understand why we don't get the information we need from him now," said a man with a thick African accent. "We'll get the information you need in minutes."

"Gentlemen, there is no rush." An American female replied. "We'll loosen him up for a day or so, then he will tell us everything."

"That didn't work with..."

"Our last guest was a trained special agent. That sort of training never leaves you. This man has spent his life in libraries and lecture halls. I bet he's never even run for a bus."

The two men tittered in a humorless laugh.

Eden grinned. Sure, Beaumont was no special agent, but it just so happened she was.

Eden lowered herself another two feet. She now hung just inches above the roof of the office. As she'd expected, the roof was constructed with little more than ceiling tiles layered over with fiberglass insulation. She reached down and pushed a section of the insulation aside, then carefully lifted one of the ceiling tiles. Eden pushed the gas mask up over her nose and mouth, then unclipped one of the capsules and dropped it into the office.

"What was that?" one of the men barked as the capsule jangled to the floor.

Eden thumbed a button on her watch and the capsule dissolved into a thick cloud of smoke. Eden shoved the ceiling tile back into place to keep the smoke inside.

The occupants of the office didn't even have time to head for the door as the smoke rendered them unconscious. Three thuds vibrated through the structure as the men and woman fell.

Eden swung to the side and released the rope. She landed in a crouch on the floor beside the office. She turned and peered through the office window. Thick smoke continued to swirl around the small space. The occupants would be out of it for at least ten minutes, which Eden hoped would be enough time.

Eden searched the warehouse quickly. Another door at the back led through to some rooms, which the team was clearly using as living quarters. Two camp beds and military style packs were set up neatly in one room, as though the occupants were ready to move out at any moment. The room beyond probably belonged to the American woman, who from the overheard conversation, Eden figured was in charge. A camp bed sat against the far wall with a small desk and laptop set up beside. Eden pressed on, not wasting time searching the occupants' belongings.

Swinging open the thick steel door of the final room, Eden was hit by the most disgusting smell. Even through the gas mask, the smell felt as though it was going to choke her. It smelled as though something had been in the room for days without the use of a toilet or bathroom.

"No, don't, no! Please!"

Eden recognized Beaumont's voice. She searched the wall for a light switch. She found one and flicked it on.

Overhead fluorescents buzzed, strobed, and then popped into life.

"No! Please! I'll tell you anything!" Beaumont's wild eyes stared at Eden.

Eden realized in her combat gear, and with the gas mask over her face, he probably didn't recognize her. She slid the mask from her face and almost retched at the foul-smelling air.

Beaumont's expression melted from one of fear to relief.

"Ubaste did a good job," Eden said, answering Beaumont's unasked question. She rushed across the room and cut the ties binding him to the chair. Vast bloodstains covered the floor and walls. Eden didn't stop to look but figured that whatever happened to this room's previous guests was very unpleasant indeed.

"*You* did a good job," Beaumont said, climbing to his feet and rubbing his wrists.

Eden held out her hand. Beaumont drew the watch from the hidden inside pocket of his torn jacket. Eden examined the thing, then dropped it to the floor and crushed it beneath her boot.

Beaumont inhaled sharply. He was about to speak, but Eden silenced him with a look.

"We don't want anyone else following us." Eden led Beaumont across the warehouse. She pulled open the door, and they stepped out into the night.

Beaumont recoiled at the sight of the thug's body crumpled on the ground.

"Don't worry about him," Eden said, leading them around the pool of blood. "The trick is to keep your head when all those around you are losing theirs."

"Then yours is the earth and everything that's in it," Beaumont replied.

"What?" Eden asked.

"Rudyard Kipling," Beaumont replied.

"Yours is the earth and everything that's in it. That's got a ring to it," Eden said. "Let's get out of here."

Lulu King opened her eyes slowly. It felt as though a metro train was rumbling directly through her cranium—The Underground, as they call those things here. She blinked, willing her eyes into focus. There was a chemical taste in her mouth that she didn't like or recognize. Shapes swam in front of her vision, spinning and swirling from one side of the room to the other. There were noises too. Distant, muffled noises. She closed her eyes again and listened closely to the nearby sounds.

"Are you alright, boss?" one voice said. It was a man with an African accent.

"She's out of it," another voice replied. "She must have got a bigger dose. That was potent stuff."

The fog in King's mind began to clear. Her memories flooded back. She remembered a noise and the room filling with smoke. She remembered the thick, noxious gas filling her lungs and clawing at her throat. Then she remembered half-stumbling, half crawling over towards the door.

King opened her eyes now. She lay on the stained carpet, one arm trapped beneath her, the other outstretched towards the door. She turned slowly. The discolored criss-cross of ceiling tiles swam and twisted in front of her vision. King's stomach lurched. Bile forced its way up into her gullet. She grunted as she scrambled onto all fours and retched.

"Can I get you anything, boss?" Abdul said, after King had finished emptying her stomach onto the carpet.

She wiped her mouth on the back of her hand and turned to face two men. "I need to know what just happened. Someone came in here and…" King stopped speaking as a thought hit her head on. "Beaumont!" She growled, forcing herself to her feet. The room shook around her as she staggered towards the door.

Pushing open the door and stepping out into the warehouse, King already knew what she would find. People didn't just break into a secure warehouse for no reason. She strode as best she could across the warehouse. The steel door to the room they'd been using as a makeshift prison lay open. The lights inside blazed.

King reached the door and steadied herself on the frame. The room was empty. The chair lay on its side with the cords which had bound the professor beside it. King's confusion dissipated, and in its place, a hot fury rose.

"I need to know what happened here," she growled.

Abdul and Sharif stepped past her into the room. Sharif bent down and picked something up from the floor. It looked like a sports watch.

"Give me that." King held out her hand. She examined the device closely. Small and sleek, it was the type designed to give the wearer data about their vital signs. This one had been destroyed, though, the screen cracked in several places. "How did this get in here? Was Beaumont wearing it when he arrived?"

Abdul and Sharif exchanged a glance. "We searched him properly, boss. Nothing on his wrists or pockets."

"Clearly not properly enough." King's hand closed around the watch. For now, she would hold on to it. It may prove to be useful later. "Go find those useless guards. I'll be in the office."

King turned, the thumping in her head now almost clear, and strode back across the warehouse towards the office. A pigeon caught her attention as it fluttered amongst the rafters.

King paused, peering upwards. "How did that get in here?" She muttered to no one. She saw that one of the windowpanes had been removed, and a rope hung from a beam. Whoever had done this was a pro.

King stepped inside the office. The smell of the smoke had dissipated, but now the acidic smell of vomit hung in the air. King glanced at the mess on the floor. She would get those stupid guards to clear it up. Good for nothing idiots.

King pulled a chair up to the computer and sat down. She placed the broken watch on the desk.

"The question is," she said out loud, "who would bother rescuing our professor? He's a nobody, really."

King tapped on the keyboard and loaded the security surveillance system. King had installed the system before taking over the warehouse several months ago. If there was movement in or around the warehouse, this system recorded it. The cameras themselves were hidden, and the footage was encrypted and then stored on a cloud drive. Even if an army turned up with the intent to level the place, King would know who they were.

Her fingers flying over the keys, she scrolled back half an hour and hit play. She looked closely at the twenty camera angles on the large screen. Two minutes later someone ran towards the warehouse. King maximized that camera and replayed the footage. A figure darted across the front yard and into the shadows beside the building. For almost half a minute, nothing moved, then the guards appeared. The burly thugs sauntered around the corner as though they didn't have a care in the world. King narrowed her eyes and glowered. How could they stand next to the intruder without noticing a thing. When she caught up with the pair of idiots, they would certainly have a thing or two to worry about.

The men stopped walking, drew out cigarettes and lit up. King couldn't believe what she was seeing. "What are you doing!" She shouted at the screen.

"Boss," Abdul's voice cut through King's concentration. "It's the guards, they're..."

"Yes, bring them to me now," King barked, without turning away from the screen.

"No, I can't, they're..."

King didn't hear the end of Abdul's final sentence, as something moved on the screen. A large object flew, catching one of the men on the side of his head. The big man went down like an avalanche, his lit cigarette sparking to the ground.

King jerked backwards in her seat, then turned slowly to face Abdul.

"That's what I was trying to tell you, boss. They're dead, both of them. One hit by a pipe, and the other..."

But King wasn't listening again. She fast forwarded through the footage until she saw what she was looking for. The other guard crumpled to the ground under the weight of a concrete block. King slowed the footage and watched their intruder rappel through the roof. King paused the video as the intruder swung around, facing the camera.

King enhanced the image, then sat back in the chair and steepled her fingers.

"Boss, I've put the guards in the van. What do you want me to do with them?"

Ignoring the question, King unfurled a slender index finger and pointed at the screen. "Gentlemen, meet our uninvited guest." All traces of anger had left King's voice. If anything, she sounded exhilarated by this new turn of events.

"It's a woman," Sharif said, surprised.

King flashed him a look out the corner of her eye.

"Do you want us to find out who she is?" Abdul said. "We could bring her in."

"As always, I'm one step ahead of you," King said, fingers tapping at her chin. "This, gentlemen, is Eden Black."

King turned back to the computer and ran an internet search for 'Eden Black.'

King already knew about Eden's latest misadventures in Lebanon, and her subsequent discovery of the tablets hidden in a mausoleum in Brighton.

"Hence her link to Beaumont," she thought out loud. King tapped the third result revealing Eden's trip to Nepal, partly to help the communities of remote villages, and partly to get away from the media attention that had plagued her after the last discovery. She then called up an obituary from the year before, in which Eden had been named but only as a footnote. The obituary was for an archaeologist called Alexander Winslow who had died during a plane crash. Without looking away from the screen, King made a note to investigate the crash.

Winslow is survived by one daughter, Eden Black (née Winslow).

"Now that is interesting." King steepled her fingers again

before typing *'Alexander Winslow Plane Crash'* into the search bar. The lead article told the tragic story of the Hawker 400xp private jet which went down somewhere over the Atlantic on its way to Washington. The article detailed Alexander Winslow as the only passenger on board. The wreckage had never been discovered. Thoughts whirred through King's mind like cogs in a machine. After several seconds an idea emerged. King examined it closely for a moment before nodding her head. It all seemed to stack together.

She grabbed her phone from the table and called her top investigator. Based somewhere in Eastern Europe, there was nothing Vakoff couldn't find. He was expensive, but worth every cent.

"I need you to run a facial recognition trace on a picture I'm about to send you. I want security cameras, social media, everything. If this guy went to a Rolling Stones gig, I want to know about it."

"Sure," Vakoff replied in his languid Eastern European tones.

King smiled. This guy was always so relaxed, it was a wonder he got anything done. King imagined him in a basement out in Belarus, or some remote place, tapping away at the keys.

"I'll contact you tomorrow."

"No. I want this yesterday."

"It will cost you."

"Whatever it costs," King barked in reply, ending the call. King leaned back in her chair and locked eyes with the picture of Eden staring at her from the screen. "I think you and I, Miss Black, will be seeing each other very soon."

18

"THIS IS WHERE YOU LIVE, all the time?" Beaumont said, looking around at the interior of Eden's truck. Eden and Beaumont had been mostly silent on the hour-long drive from the South London warehouse. Eden wasn't comfortable with how close Lulu King's warehouse was to the woodland in which her truck was hidden. She wondered whether she should have used something more lethal than the gas on King and her guards but didn't like killing for no reason.

Eden studied the wall of screens, checking that all her security systems were in place. With everything operating as it should, and no unexpected visitors within the perimeter, she relaxed slightly.

"Yes, I like it here, away from the hustle and bustle."

"Well, I've heard about getting away from the hustle and bustle, but this really is off the grid. How long have you been here?"

"About three years." Eden looked at Beaumont. "Are you hungry? You should eat. Don't want any shock setting in." Other than the tearing of his clothes and a couple of slaps, Beaumont had escaped unscathed. Eden had no doubt, though, it would have been a different story if she hadn't got him out of there.

Eden dug out a few packets of dehydrated food and set about warming them on the stove. "You'll sleep in here tonight, I'll sleep in the Land Rover. There's plenty of room for me."

"Sleep! We don't need sleep, there's far too much to work out," Beaumont bellowed excitedly. It appears the harrowing ordeal fortunately hadn't affected him.

Eden grinned, stirring the food. She could see why her father liked the man.

"You got the JS12 documents, yes? I knew you'd figure it out. You're like that. Quick, sharp!" Beaumont snapped his fingers.

"Yes, they're in that bag." Eden pointed at her bag.

Beaumont slid out the folder and took out the photographs. He lay them side by side on Eden's desk and then bent down to examine them.

"Just fantastic. Incredible. Look at this! Do you have a, urrm..." Beaumont mimed the use of a magnifying glass as though he were a 1940s detective looking for clues.

Eden suppressed a giggle. Satisfied that the food was warm enough, she spooned half of it into a tin bowl.

"I can do better than that," Eden said, passing the bowl, then the spoon across to Beaumont. "You eat."

Beaumont set about chomping away. He peered at the mushy contents of the bowl. "You know what, this isn't too bad. I mean, it's not beef bourguignon, but it's not bad at all."

"It contains everything the mind and body need," Eden said, slipping past Beaumont in the confined space. "I mean, it's engineered with exactly the vitamins and minerals I need. But it'll keep you going all right too."

Eden slid a device across the table. To the untrained eye, the thing looked like a high-tech lamp. She placed the head of the machine about a foot above the photographs and then pressed a button on the base. The light came on and a magnified image of the photographs appeared on one of the large screens.

Eden pointed at the controls on the base. "Use one to zoom and this to pan. We can do image correction with these other buttons, but I don't think you'll need them."

"Fantastic." Beaumont slurped the last bit of the sauce and dropped the spoon into the bowl. He wiped his hands on his trousers and stepped forward to examine the screen.

"You see the area?" He pointed to one of the colored shapes beneath The Giza Plateau. Whatever it was, was somewhere between The Sphinx and The Great Pyramid.

Eden nodded and dug into the food.

"Well, as you may have figured out, it's showing a heat signature which is not in line with our current under-standing of what's beneath The Plateau. There's something down there that's generating independent heat. This is not caused by the warming effects of the sun, as many people would say. This is not some tectonic nonsense. This is a heat source down there, beneath the desert, that has been there for thousands of years. No one knows anything about it, let alone what's causing it."

"Why hasn't someone gone down there to find out what it is?" Eden said.

"Egyptians are pretty cagey about such things. In the last century they've only allowed very few expeditions to explore this region, and even then, they're under guard. They're worried that something might be discovered that pulls into question their ownership of the land. You must understand religious tensions in the area. The last things the Egyptians want is to find something that changes the World's under-standing of history. The other problem is the water. Everyone who has tried to get access beneath The Plateau has been unable to get through the water. Water seeps through the rocks of all the tunnels down there. Millions of gallons of it. Several times teams have tried to drain the tunnels. On one occasion they kept pumps running day and night for years, but it made no difference. The water just kept coming. They tried to figure a way through, block it up, everything they tried, it just kept coming."

"How far away is the river from there?" Eden asked, squinting at the screen.

"The Nile runs about six miles to the east of The Plateau. But here's the thing, they tested the water beneath The Plateau, and it's got a high salt content. The water running down there is not from the freshwater Nile."

"Where does it come from then?"

Beaumont shrugged. "That, my dear, is our first mystery."

Eden placed her hands on her hips and squinted at the screen. "You think that this could be the location of The Hall of Records?"

Beaumont turned and glanced at Eden, his eyes shining with excitement. "Exactly. Many have theorized that's where it lies, but without real evidence, it would be like looking for a particular grain of sand in the desert."

"Wait a second," Eden said, a thought suddenly occur-ring to her. She stepped up to the desk and flicked through the papers she'd brought back from Beaumont's office the previous day. "Here we go," she said, finding the translation of one of the tablets.

That their inventions might not be lost before they were suffi-ciently known, upon Adam's prediction that the world was to be destroyed at one time by the force of fire, and at another time by the violence and quantity of water, they made two pillars.

"Pillars mean Pyramids!" Beaumont said, almost shouting. "That could be it. Maybe they mark the spot.

"But wait, there are nine Pyramids on The Plateau?" Eden said.

"There are nine pyramids now, but there's evidence to suggest that two are older than the others. When Aloma wrote her diary, there could have just been two pyramids already on The Plateau."

These inscriptions would exhibit their discoveries to mankind, and also inform them that there was another pillar of brick erected nearby. Now this remains in the land of Siriad to this day.

Eden's finger followed the next part of the translation, sense starting to form in her mind. "That means Siriad must be Egypt."

"Exactly." Beaumont stood up and ran a hand through his thin, grey hair. "This is incredible. Just incredible. For the first time, we actually have evidence, not just the existence of, but the location of The Hall of Records. Eden, I just can't begin to explain, to tell you quite how..."

"I get this is a big thing," Eden said, interrupting Beaumont. She had come to realize that talking over the professor was the only way to keep him on topic. "But why would someone like Lulu King be interested in this? Unless the newspapers have got her very wrong, she doesn't care about archaeology?"

Beaumont extended a wagging finger, eyebrows sliding towards his hairline. "That depends on what she thinks is down there."

Eden raised her hands in a gesture that told the professor to get to the point.

"Miss King thinks that The Hall of Records contains not

only information about the previous caretakers of our planets, but technology we 'modern people'—" the professor's fingers became quote marks "—have yet to master."

"What might that be?" Eden said, quizzically.

"The Ark of the Covenant," Beaumont whispered.

Eden grinned. "Come on Professor. Isn't the Ark of the Covenant supposed to have been built by Moses on God's instructions? Doesn't the Book of Exodus say that Moses used it to talk directly to God?"

"You're exactly right," Beaumont said, concisely, clearly surprised by Eden's knowledge of scripture.

"How would that be any use to King?"

"Well, she treated me to my own private lecture on the subject. I can't say I like her style at all. It was all so..."

"What did she tell you?" Eden interjected.

Beaumont told Eden about King's predictions that the Ark could help create element 115 in stable form. "I mean, it sounds far-fetched, but from what we know about the construction of The Ark, it seemed to have some power of its own. First, anyone who touched it was struck down in a manner which now looks very much like an electric shock. Second, The Ark could be carried for days without the men growing tired. In fact, the bearers reported it feeling weightless after a short while."

"King Industries," Eden muttered, realization dawning. "King Industries is one of the largest oil and gas companies on the globe. They provide energy to billions of people. Lulu King thinks that whatever secrets are held within The Ark, she can use it to generate power."

"Endless power, emission free, on demand power. I suspect once she gets the Ark of The Covenant, it will disappear into one of the King Industries laboratories, never to be seen again."

The implications of such a discovery slowly spun through Eden's mind. "If she's correct, if she manages to create this, not only will humanity be robbed of one of the most important artifacts that ever existed, but King Industries will become the most important company in the world."

"Governments will be quickly queueing up to do business with her."

"That is, if it doesn't get bought straight up, or worse, overtaken by some military organization." Eden turned and stared out at the countryside through the window. "We need to stop her," Eden whispered, a hard edge to her voice.

"Yes, I agree, but how? I mean, it's not like…"

Eden turned around and pointed at the professor. "… I think I've found the instructions."

WITH ABDUL STATIONED OUTSIDE, should anyone else want to pay them a visit this evening, and Sharif sent to dispose of the bodies, King continued her research. She didn't have anything certain, but something about this situation nagged at her. It seemed suspicious that Winslow's plane should come down right before he was due to make this discovery. It was almost as though he knew the tablets were to be discovered but needed himself out of the way to do it. It was selfless, complicated—but King had to admit—genius. It was exactly the sort of thing she would do—make it look like an accident, divert everyone's attention elsewhere, then have someone else make the discovery on your behalf.

King sat back in her chair and thought it through. The accident itself would have been easy enough to facilitate. With a big bribe you could easily land the plane on a remote airstrip somewhere, and then have it stripped down and destroyed. But what about the pilot and crew? For the right sum you could find a pilot who wouldn't mind pretending to be dead for a few years. After all, this didn't need to be forever, just long enough to change the world. Five years, maybe ten. What would it cost to have someone live on a desert island for a decade?

The problem though, for Winslow, would be remaining "dead." If he were able to sit on the beach for ten years, that would be one thing. But King very much doubted that would be the case. He would want to see his plan through. He would want to watch progress and course correct if necessary. No, he wouldn't want to, he would need to.

That would mean contacting people back in the real world, it would mean using the internet and it may even mean international travel. All these things would be difficult, expensive, and fraught with the constant danger of discovery.

King's phone trilled from the table. She snatched it up. An international number scrolled across the screen. That was why she paid Vakoff the big bucks. "What have you got for me?"

"You're going to like this," Vakoff said after a pause so long King thought the line had been disconnected. "Security camera footage from Cairo International Airport."

The dialogue box appeared in the corner of the screen. King clicked on it and several images popped up. Screen shots from security camera footage. The images showed a man sauntering through airport crowds towards passport control. It took King less than a second to recognize him. He was so confident that he hadn't even changed his appearance. The man was, without doubt, Alexander Winslow.

"When was this taken?" King asked, noticing the images were not time stamped.

"Yesterday," Vakoff replied. The line went dead.

King shook her head slowly and tossed her phone back on the table. Not only was Alexander Winslow alive, but he was in Egypt.

All the pieces were moving into place. All she had to do was knock them down. Or better still, King thought, have Eden knock them down for her.

19

EDEN AND BEAUMONT pushed through the crowds of sweaty bodies that filled Aswan's International Airport. The airport's air conditioning was obviously not functioning—whether this was a permanent feature or not, Eden had no idea. She was just glad to be here in the evening when the temperatures were the right side of 40 Celsius. A florescent light overhead strobed relentlessly, adding to the room's sense of chaos. Eden glanced at the other passengers. A smorgasbord of humanity lounged or hustled through the terminal—a pair of European backpackers sprawled beside an Arabic family; an African businessman sipped tea with his Chinese counterpart.

Whilst airports like this could be uncomfortable, in many ways Eden enjoyed them. Travelling through places like this felt real. It felt as though she was witnessing the authentic country in transit. It felt exciting and intoxicating.

A stuffed lion fell from the stroller a few feet ahead. Eden knelt and scooped up the soft toy. The miniature lion lay in the position of rest, like a tiny sphinx. The fur on one side of the lion's head was worn, showing that he was a well-loved toy.

"You don't want to lose this," Eden said, hurrying on and passing the lion to the woman pushing the stroller. The woman nodded and smiled, tucking the lion out of sight.

The journey from London Heathrow had been a laborious one. Beaumont apologized several times that he had been unable to replicate Eden's return trip to Nepal, which involved the personal helicopter transfer and then a seat in business class back to London. Eden didn't mind at all. Travel was all about moments like this, she thought, approaching passport control. Travel, like her own life, was about the good, the bad, the ugly, and everything in between.

Eden slid her passport across to the border official sitting in his warm glass cube. Sweat ran like morning dew down the man's skin. He stamped Eden's passport and pushed it back beneath the glass without a word.

Eden stepped through into the baggage reclaim hall. Then, flying with only a carry-on bag, she sped straight for the exit, Beaumont in pursuit.

"Little Mo will meet us in arrivals," Beaumont said, finally catching up with Eden. "First, I must..." he pointed towards the bathroom.

Eden studied the professor as he scurried off, his scruffy grey hair flying out behind him like a flag.

She imagined the professor living off grid in her truck while she was away. She had tried to suggest he stay there and let her come to Egypt alone. Beaumont had taken one look at the truck's cramped interior and insisted he come too.

The sound of snarling traffic and the constant bark of car horns drifted through the open doors.

Waiting for Beaumont to re-emerge from the bathroom, Eden eyed the expectant line of taxi drivers. Each held a scruffy piece of paper containing the name of their next client. Many of the drivers spoke irritably into Bluetooth headsets.

Eden read a couple of the names—Chan, Mostafa, Taylor. She turned her attention to the men holding the papers. Surely, she could recognize a man called Little Mo just from his appearance. None fitted the bill.

"Miss Black, Miss Black!" A deep, smooth voice carried through the clamor of the terminal.

Eden spun around. A man fitting the opposite description of what Eden had expected lumbered towards her. This man certainly didn't look like a real-life Indiana Jones Beaumont had described on the flight.

The bear-like man towered well over six feet in height, with the rotund belly a laughing Buddha would be proud of. As Little Mo charged towards her, Eden thought for a moment that he would be unable to stop and knock her flying.

"Miss Black, so good I have caught you." The big man squealed to a stop just beside Eden. "I am Little Mo, a good friend of the Professor Beaumont. He told me you were coming."

Eden looked the man up and down. He wore a brightly patterned shirt over light brown trousers with a raincloud of thinning hair swirling around the top of his head.

"Your flight was okay, I trust? May I take your bag?" Mo's voice had the tone of a purring cat.

"Sure," Eden replied, shaking all expectations from her mind. If Beaumont trusted him, she would too.

Beaumont appeared from the bathroom and the two men embraced.

"Richard it's been far too long." Little Mo held Beaumont at arm's length as though welcoming a long-lost child.

"It has, It has. Life has a habit of keeping us busy."

"That it does, and in that spirit, we must go." Mo picked up Eden's bag as though it weighed nothing and led them out to the airport parking lot. "I have a top-quality ride for you," he said as they approached a dust covered Toyota Hilux pickup which must have equaled Eden in age. "This old thing will never let us down. It will drive until the end of days, that I am promising you."

Little Mo unlocked the door and climbed into the driver's seat. The suspension protested beneath his sizable weight. Beaumont slung his bag in the backseat and wedged himself in, leaving the front seat for Eden. Eden climbed in beside the Egyptian. With a squeal of rubber and the crunch of meshing parts, they pulled out of the parking lot and headed towards the city.

"So, you are here to investigate the new Sun Temple beneath Lake Nasser," Little Mo said, getting straight to the point.

"Yes, what an interesting discovery. I'm not sure what we'll find but..."

"That's right." Eden interrupted Beaumont.

"I want to get some photos of it."

"This may be a very difficult thing. The whole area has been under tight guard since it was discovered."

Eden had assumed such things. "What sort of protection are they using?"

"The nearest shore has a temporary fence and is manned by six men, day and night. Four on the ground, and two in a speedboat patrolling the temple. The shift changes at 6am and 6pm. They are armed with MP5s and a side arm and are in constant communication. I'm not sure if they have further firepower they can call on. It would be safe to assume they do."

Eden realized her mouth had dropped open. It was clear why Beaumont had recommended Mo as her man on the ground. She snapped her jaw shut.

"You know a lot about the area?"

"I have been watching it closely for the last couple of days. As soon as I heard of the discovery, I said to myself, Mo, this will be big. I thought of our Beaumont." He jerked a thumb at the professor in the back seat. "This has got him written all over it. You will be going in alone?"

Mo dropped the Toyota down a gear and overtook a tanker crawling up a hill. He leaned on the horn the entire way. The engine of the aged 4x4 rattled and roared in protest.

"Yes," Eden said. "I work best alone."

Mo nodded. He said nothing to try to dissuade Eden. Often when Eden told people that she planned to do something potentially dangerous, they would spend the next few minutes telling her why she shouldn't. Mo just grinned and nodded, making Eden's respect for him grow further still.

A few minutes later, they pulled down a narrow street between four-story concrete buildings. Mo stopped the Hilux and jumped out. The engine whirred and ticked as it idled. Mo swung open a pair of rusted metal gates to reveal an underground parking lot. He climbed back into the Toyota and drove down the ramp. Reaching the bottom, Mo stopped the 4x4 and killed the engine. The lights died, plunging them into darkness.

"One minute," Mo said, hurrying out of the truck and disappearing into the shadows. A moment later overhead lights snapped on. It took Eden a few moments to register what she saw. She swung open the door and stepped out, wide eyed.

Not much short of a warehouse, the space occupied the entire basement level of the building. Steel shelves ran down the sides containing everything necessary for a full-scale archaeological dig. From shovels, tunneling roof supports, power generation, lighting, tents, and ropes— Little Mo had thought of it all. Eden even noticed two small excavators sitting underneath tarpaulins at the far side of the space.

"This place is well stocked, as always," Beaumont said, climbing out of the Toyota and stretching. "I think you'll find what you need here, Eden."

Mo sidled back across the room. "For many generations, archaeology has been big business here in Egypt. Before me, my father worked on the digs, and before that my grandfather." Mo beckoned Eden to follow him. "My grandfather was part of the team that opened King Tut's tomb. Obviously, we, the mere diggers, don't go down in history for such things, but I know it couldn't have been done without his help."

Beaumont shuffled off in the other direction to inspect a shelf full of strange artifacts.

Mo led Eden to a section of shelving in the far corner which seemed to hold everything necessary for excavating underwater.

"You wouldn't think you'd need things like this in the desert, no?" Mo pointed at the scuba gear. "But the Nile does have a habit of giving up her secrets once in a while."

Eden and Mo selected the kit she needed, including spare oxygen tanks, an underwater propulsion device which Mo said could travel at almost three miles an hour, and at

Mo's insistence, a pair of carbon coated knives and a strange looking spear.

"I don't want to kill anyone," Eden said, looking at the weapons. "I'm going to get in there, take photos and get out. They won't even know I'm there."

"In Lake Nasser, the men are the least of your problem. These are for the crocodiles. Very big and very aggressive. Ten, twelve feet, maybe more. Move slowly and they may not notice you. If one approaches, aim for the eye with this." Mo hefted the spear. "The tip has a poison inside, enough to kill a big one."

Eden felt her mouth go dry. She was prepared to take on several men, but a twelve foot long, hungry, and merciless crocodile, that was something altogether different.

Mo smiled and shrugged. "But you'll probably be alright. They hunt at night so by the time we get there, they will already be full." Mo tapped his rotund belly.

Eden didn't feel very reassured. She gladly added the knives and spear to her pile of supplies.

In was nearly 2am by the time Eden and Mo had loaded all the gear in the truck and prepared themselves for the mission.

"Is no problem if you want to wait until tomorrow," Mo said. "We have rooms upstairs. You can get some sleep."

"No, we go tonight," Eden said, steeling her resolve despite the crocodiles. "I'm here, there's no need to waste time."

Eden thought for a moment that Mo was going to argue. The Egyptian grinned and patted his sizable stomach. "No problem, but first we will eat."

Eden's stomach rumbled involuntarily. "I won't argue with that," she said.

Mo directed Eden and Beaumont towards a sofa, then wandered into the small kitchen. For several minutes he clattered about and then emerged with numerous trays containing a veritable banquet of falafel, shawarma kebabs, fava beans, tahini, bread and a bowl of green molokhia soup.

Seeing the food, Eden's stomach grumbled again. "This is fantastic." She tore one of the fresh breads and scooped up a large helping of the tahini. "Do you eat like this all the time?"

"I have two passions in life, this..." he pointed out to the warehouse with all its archaeological equipment, then to the food displayed before them. "And this. Plus, as a good Muslim it is my duty to be ready for, and welcome guests at a moment's notice, you see. I must keep all this nice food prepared, just in case." Mo shrugged, rolled up his sleeves and metaphorically dived headfirst into the food.

"It's one of the best things about working with Little Mo," Beaumont said, digging in too. "I've tried to get him over to work in England many times."

"Far too cold," Mo said, mock-shivering. "I went once. Was the longest ten days of my life."

Eden grinned and dug, full steam ahead, into the food. For nearly twenty minutes Eden, Beaumont and Mo chatted about the world of archaeology as they ate.

When she was full, almost to bursting, Eden lay backwards into the sofa. "That was incredible," she said, exhaling.

"Just... just a bit better than that goo you served last night," Beaumont said, finishing the last bit of falafel.

"You said you liked it," Eden quipped in reply.

Mo chuckled. "Beaumont is so English he would probably say thank you for a slap in the face."

"Well, I don't see how that's a..." Eden and Mo didn't hear Beaumont's reply as they laughed out loud.

"I think I'm just going to live with you full time," Eden said when the laughter had died away.

"You would be welcome," Mo said, shrugging.

"How did you learn to cook like that?"

"My father was an excellent cook," Mo said, between mouthfuls of another piece of bread. He pointed at a photograph in a silver frame.

Eden forced herself to her feet, wandered across the room and peered at the photograph. A middle-aged man stood beside a young boy. Eden recognized the setting as The Giza Plateau, The Pyramids rising majestically in the background. The affection between father and son was obvious.

"He was a passionate archaeologist too," Mo said. "But never got the chance to do it professionally. He worked as a security guard on The Giza Plateau, but always opted to work on the dig sites whenever the option became available." Mo leaned back in the chair and rubbed a hand across his face. "He used to always complain how much corruption there was in the world of archaeology. He spoke many times of finds going missing, or the funding being cut if they didn't like what they found. That's no way to investigate. You seek to find, not find to confirm what you already know." The big man exhaled. Eden could see that although he loved talking about his father, the memories were still painful. "Anyway, he'd got involved in a self-funded off the books dig with some other enthusiasts. He knew he was getting into something dangerous but was just too passionate. One day he didn't come home. No one knows what happened. My mother always said he'd run away with another woman and abandoned us. I don't think that. I think something happened on that dig that we never found out. For many years I tried to find out what happened to him, but with it being all off the books, there's no record." Mo shrugged and shook his head as though attempting to cast away the unpleasant memories.

"I'm sure he didn't run away," Eden said, after a long moment of silence.

"Me too." Mo placed his hands on his knees. "Now, let me tell you about Egyptian coffee. Have you ever tried it?"

20

IT WAS APPROACHING 4am by the time Eden, Beaumont and Little Mo reached the shore of Lake Nasser. Having consumed two small but deliciously strong Egyptian coffees before leaving Mo's house, Eden felt ready for anything.

Eden glanced left and right. On the way down the access road, she'd seen the outline of several giant crocs sleeping on the lake's sandy banks. The fact that they were already resting off their dinner was a good sign, she supposed.

Little Mo and Beaumont unloaded the van and then respectfully turned away as Eden slipped out of her clothes and pulled on the wetsuit. Eden pulled the cord to zip up the wetsuit and felt the rubber pull tight against her skin. The suit had the bonus of being completely black. Once in the water, she would be almost invisible, Eden hoped.

"You know where you are going, yes?" Mo said, taking Eden's dry clothes and putting them on the passenger seat.

"I've got it, thanks." Eden slid her phone into a water-proof case and attached it to her left forearm. On the screen she had a map showing her current location, the location of the temple, and the rendezvous point. She reduced the screen brightness to its lowest setting.

"Good. Remember what I say about the crocs. Go slow. No sudden movements. Any problem..." Mo made a stabbing motion as though taking on the creatures himself. Somewhere across the water, an outboard motor grumbled into life. Eden, Beaumont, and Mo turned towards the lake, the noise reminding them that the temple's armed guards were on duty.

"I'd advise you to be careful out there," Beaumont said.

The boat's searchlight swept their way, glimmering over the water's surface.

"They're just bored," Mo said, shaking his head. "Imagine spending every night out there. In the dark. Is enough to drive you mad, no?"

Eden forced a smile. Right now, the guards may be chasing shadows, but in a few minutes, Eden would be in their crosshairs. She finished a bottle of water and chucked it back in the truck. Despite the drink, her throat still felt dry with anxiety.

"You get in, get what you need, and get back to shore," Mo said brightly. He picked up the scuba tank and helped Eden slide it over her shoulders. "You have a little over an hour of air here." Mo slapped the tank with an open palm.

Eden pulled the mask down over her face and put the regulator in her mouth. She held up her watch with the 60-minute timer ready to start.

"Inshallah, we will be having breakfast by sunrise," Little Mo said, stepping back towards the truck.

"Good luck," Beaumont added, nervously.

Eden faced the water and stomped into the shallows. With the sea scooter beneath her arm, the fins attached to her feet, and the large tank on her back, she felt incredibly cumbersome.

Out in the middle of the lake, the searchlight flashed on again. Too far away to see her clearly, Eden carried on. She was more worried about the crocodiles, which moved without light or sound to announce their presence. Eden tried to push the thought from her mind.

The water level climbing above her stomach, Eden slipped forwards and began to swim.

After several feet, when the lake's bottom was out of reach, she adjusted her buoyancy control, started the timer, and powered up the sea scooter. The electric motors whirred, dragging Eden smoothly through the water. Despite the small size and light weight of the device, it was very effective. After a couple of minutes, Eden had mastered the controls and was shooting towards the temple.

She glanced up at the rippling surface twenty feet above her, lit by the glow of the moon. Suddenly, just up ahead, the sweeping light of the patrol boat snapped on. The beam panned across the water, clearly searching for anything unusual.

Eden angled the sea scooter down and kicked hard, diving towards the lakebed. Reaching thirty feet in depth, she stopped. The deeper she went, the quicker she would use her air. Eden needed all the time she could get. Now stationary, she watched a stream of bubbles heading to the surface. She observed them powerlessly. Eden wished Mo had invested in the modern diving equipment used by the military that didn't send bubbles to the surface. Clearly this gear wasn't designed for clandestine dives. She watched, powerless, as the stream of bubbles popped across the surface just a few feet from the searchlight. Eden froze, not daring to breathe or move. The search light stayed frozen for a moment and then swung erratically to the location of her telltale bubbles.

Eden watched, still not moving. The boat's four-stroke outboard kicked into action. The hull sliced through the water above her. A second light snapped on and began searching the surrounding area.

Her lungs now stinging to exhale, Eden kicked backwards, maneuvering herself beneath the craft. She looked up at the boat's silhouette in the moonlight above. Eden exhaled, sending a large stream of bubbles upwards, only to be churned into the boat's wake.

The boat shifted forwards a few feet. Eden followed carefully, staying directly underneath. For nearly ten long minutes, the searchlights swung around the surface of the lake, and the boat picked its way forward. Eden stayed close, knowing that if she broke cover, her location would be immediately revealed. Eventually, the outboard thrummed, and the boat powered away. Eden breathed a sigh of relief, now unconcerned about the torrent of bubbles heading skyward. She checked the time on her watch. She had just forty minutes remaining. She checked the pressure gauge to make sure. It was still well in the green section.

Eden turned her attention to the boat, streaming away overhead. The search lights continued to slice aggressively through the water. Then, in the glow of one of these lights, Eden saw something dark and angular. The lights swept past, plunging the object into shadow. Eden stayed fixated on where she thought the object was. The searchlight swept back, revealing the shape once again.

A sheer wall towered from the lake bed, right up to the surface. Eden checked the map on her phone. That was it—the lost Sun Temple of Ra.

Eden powered on the sea scooter again and swam in the

direction of the building. The imposing wall of the temple reared upwards as Eden neared. She pulled in close to the structure, switched off the sea scooter, and dropped it to the lake bed. She would retrieve it on her way back. First checking the patrol boat was nowhere nearby, Eden unclipped her dive torch from her belt. She turned it to its lowest setting and swept the beam across the structure. Although there were no markings here, the structure was incredibly well preserved. Having spent thousands of years beneath the sand and the last sixty underwater, the ancient stones had been spared from the ravages of the elements.

Eden powered up the camera and 3D scanner mounted on top of her mask. Back on dry land she could use the data to build a three-dimensional computer model of the temple if needed.

Eden moved carefully around the structure's entire perimeter. On the opposite side, she caught sight of the patrol boat. It was nearly a hundred feet away towards the shore. Even the most attentive guard would struggle to see her light or bubbles from there. Once Eden had checked the entire outer wall of the temple, she headed for the temple's large, arched doorway. She paused and looked up at two giant carved figures, flanking the entrance. Four stone eyes stared out into the lake. Eden unclipped another camera from her belt and carefully took several photos. With the low light, the photos wouldn't be perfect, but she needed to record as much as possible.

Eden swam inside the temple. A pair of eels darted out from the shadows beneath her, their smooth skin sparkling in the torchlight.

Once inside, Eden turned the torch up to its highest setting. The strong finger of light swept through the gloom. The wide corridor led deep into the temple, lined with more stone figures, each one at least twenty feet high. The figures stood to attention, as though holding the roof in place through sheer might. Eden carefully photographed each one, excitement building in her chest. She didn't know who the figures represented, but she figured that Beaumont would. She could feel his excitement at the discovery growing too.

She turned her attention to the floor, sweeping the light systematically throughout the room. Sand had built up in great swathes, covering the figures up to the height of their knees. In several places, spine-like objects jutted out of the sand like wonky teeth. Weeds swung from them, gently swaying in the currents.

Eden swam up to the closest object and pulled away the weed. What she saw caused a frisson of fear to move through her. The bones of a large animal lay half buried in the sand. Eden moved to the next carcass, wondering whether it could be human.

Eden remembered the crocodiles. Mo had explained how the creatures would pull their catch into a safe place and then pick it clean for days. Whatever poor creature these bones belonged to, had been dinner quite a while ago.

Eden's watch vibrated. She had just twenty minutes of air remaining. She wasn't here to study or become a crocodile's evening meal. She turned her attention back to the temple.

Eden swam towards one of the small side chambers which lay off the corridor to the right. These rooms were around ten feet in length and width. Eden didn't see anything of importance in the rooms but photographed them anyway. She swam through another archway at the end of the first chamber, startling a shoal of large writhing fish.

Eden froze, her hand reaching for the knife. The fish darted upwards, clearly more scared of her than she was of them. Eden eyed the fish, noticing that each one must have been well over two feet in length. Their sinuous bodies twisted and glimmered in the dim light. Eden watched the fish stream out through a hole in the temple's roof. Forty feet above her, Eden saw the gleaming surface of the lake in the moonlight. Then something even bigger shot across the surface of the water, blocking out the moonlight altogether.

All Eden saw was its shape, its long muscular tail flicking from side to side, its snout filled with razor-sharp teeth. A chill ran down her spine, as though the water had just dropped five degrees. The Nile crocodile, a monster at over twelve feet in length, opened its jaws and seized two of the fish. The fish flipped and fought for less than a second before they were crushed between the colossal jaws. The crocodile disappeared behind the temple wall, fish blood trailing in its wake.

Eden's heart beat like an African tribal drum. For long seconds, she didn't move a single muscle. She scanned the water above her, waiting for the crocodile to return. When it didn't, and the adrenaline had started to ease from her veins, Eden turned her attention back to the walls of the temple. She had got this far and was determined that nothing would stop her now.

Devoid of any large statues, this room looked, at first glance, like the chambers Eden had already investigated. Eden swam across to the wall and scanned her light carefully over the surface. From a distance, the surface of the stone looked textured, something Eden had put down to the age of the place. From just a foot away, though, Eden could see there was more to it than that. The texture was a grouping of lines. Lines of images carved into the stone.

Although they meant nothing to her, she knew hiero-glyphics when she saw them. Eden looked closely at the wall, getting her mask just a few inches from the stone. She saw the outline of a bird, beside a human foot, next to a bladed weapon. Hidden beneath the desert for several millennia, and then beneath the waters of the lake, could this ancient code really hold the secrets to The Pyramids?

Eden looked up at the wall. She would certainly find out. Eden's watch vibrated. She had just ten minutes of air left.

"Has she gone in?" Baxter said, striding up beside Mo and Beaumont on the shore of Lake Nasser.

"Just as Helios said she would," Mo replied, drawing the younger man into a bearhug. "Good to see you. I hear this young firecracker has already got you in some trouble?"

Baxter instinctively ran his fingers across the scar on his shoulder. It didn't hurt anymore, although the damaged skin would serve as a constant reminder of their mission.

"Yes, she's very dedicated to the cause. The perfect, fully deniable operative, actually," Baxter said. He shook hands with Beaumont. "Professor, good to see you too."

"Don't you feel bad?" Mo asked, looking from the gently lapping waters to Baxter.

"For what?"

"That Eden is being lied to, that she doesn't really know who she's working for?"

"Not at all," Baxter said, feeling a stab of guilt in his stomach. "She will be brought on board when the time is right. For now, we need someone who can operate outside of The Council. Her actions are fully deniable, even if we're on the periphery to support her."

"The Council is still not supporting this?" Mo said with an edge to his voice. "Can they not see people have needed this for decades?"

"Helios is speaking with The Council now. He will have approval very soon, then we can move forward properly."

"What... what do that bunch of idiots know?" Beaumont rolled his eyes. "I'd like to see them out here, actually doing something."

"My thoughts exactly," Baxter said. "But for now, Helios is keen to keep them on our side."

"Here we go." Beaumont pointed out across the water. The patrol boat circled again, two search lights dancing across the water's surface.

"How long's she been in?" Baxter asked.

Mo checked his watch. "Just over fifty minutes."

"We should get the rescue craft prepared," Baxter pointed back at the truck he'd arrived in. "Agreed, although we don't go in until the last minute," Mo said. "She should finish it alone."

Baxter's phone vibrated. He slid it from his pocket. "We are a go," he said, paraphrasing the message from Helios. He looked at the message for another long second. In all his years working for The Council, Baxter didn't expect to read these words. The world really was changing.

Initiate the Giza Protocol.

21

EDEN WORKED QUICKLY, moving across the surface of the wall, taking photographs in sections. Even with her light on its brightest setting, photographing the hieroglyphs was difficult. Covered in centuries of dirt and grime, in places they were completely unreadable. She would be able to lighten the pictures with computer software, but if the figures were illegible, then they would get nowhere.

Eden reached the bottom row of hieroglyphs, just inches above the sand covered floor. She adjusted her buoyancy control and knelt carefully. Despite her slow movement, a cloud of slit drifted up from the temple floor, further reducing the visibility. Eden waited two long minutes for silt to sink back down and then continued to photograph the hieroglyphs.

Reaching the final pair of figures, Eden felt a strange movement behind her. Little more than a ripple in the still waters inside the temple, it made the hairs all over her body stand on end. She lay dead still. Her breath rumbled like a passing freight train inside the diving mask.

The movement came again, sending ripples through the water. Eden held her breath, conscious of the stream of bubbles an exhale would cause. She grimaced at the thought of the pressure problems caused when breathing erratically on a dive. Not breathing correctly could cause gas embolisms to form in her body tissues or veins. In extreme cases these can block veins, arteries, and lead to all sorts of problems.

Trying to put the fear aside, Eden turned as slowly as she possibly could.

Just five feet above her, a giant crocodile swam in through the temple roof. Eden looked up just in time to see its great tail flipping this way and that, sending the stringy seaweed into a frenzy. The beast was even bigger than it had appeared before. Foot after foot of hardened iron-strength skin. The prehistoric killing machine flicked its tail again and slid into the temple.

The air in Eden's lungs burned to be released. The blood in her veins ran like liquid nitrogen. She tensed every muscle, on the trigger of fight or flight.

Eden had seen these beasts in the wild before. Most of the time they moved serenely, with the confidence that being the prime predator for millions of years brings. Occasionally though, they would surge with power, leaping for their prey, biting through muscle and bone. They were the only creature, Eden remembered, to exceed humans on the food chain. Eden, to this beast, would be little more than a snack.

Eden lay dead still. Deep beneath the wetsuit, her heart beat so aggressively she was surprised the crocodile didn't feel it through the water. With the crocodile facing away from her, Eden took the risk of releasing her held breath and took another one. A stream of bubbles surged towards the surface. Eden kept her eyes fixed anxiously on the crocodile.

The reptile slowed, its giant head twisting from one side to the other. Somehow, it hadn't spotted the bubbles.

Eden took another breath, filling her lungs greedily.

The crocodile swept through the temple with the incongruous grace of a ballet dancer. There was something strangely beautiful about seeing it here, Eden realized, amid the antique wonder of the hidden temple.

The watch on Eden's wrist pulsed, sending small vibrations through the water. She glanced down at the device. Her time was up. At any second now, her oxygen tank would run dry. Moving slowly, Eden poked the watch to cancel the alarm.

Movement in the water caused her to look up. Her heart leaped into her throat. Just fifteen feet away, the crocodile had spun around and was now peering malevolently at Eden with small green eyes. Eden involuntarily slid back towards the wall. Her hand gripped the hilt of the poisoned spear strapped to her thigh. The two-foot spike was now her only chance of salvation against the beast.

Several long seconds passed. Each one felt like the gentle melting of an ice-sheet.

The croc drifted to the ground and settled amid the weeds. More seconds passed. Neither Eden nor the crocodile moved. Eden didn't stop looking at the beast for a moment. She knew that crocodiles slept on the riverbanks and could only spend limited time underwater. Maybe this guy was waiting for his next meal to come along.

Eden risked releasing her breath. The stream of bubbles fanned upwards. The crocodile didn't move. She tried taking another breath through the regulator. Only half a lungful of oxygen came forth. Slowly, she checked the pressure gauge. Sure enough, it was firmly in the red. Eden was out of air.

Eden looked slowly from the beast, lying between the weeds a few feet away, to the moonlight shining on the surface of the water twenty feet above her head. Her lungs began to sting. She would have to swim for it and hope.

Eden slipped the spear from its sheath in preparation. Watching the great beast, she kicked her legs slowly. Her long flippers swished through the water, sending a cloud of sediment up into the temple. Eden bit her lip, expecting at any moment for the croc to charge. She kicked again and rose through the temple. She was now ten feet above the resting reptile and ten feet from the open waters. Her lungs burned now, begging for oxygen. Feelings of disorientation started to swirl through her. Eden reached the roof of the temple and froze. A new vibration pounded through the water, the deep, resonant *thump thump* of the four-stroke outboard. Eden watched the patrol boat glide above her. The engine cut out, and the boat slowed to a stop about twenty feet away. The search light snapped on and circled the water.

Eden's lungs blistered with pain. She looked behind her at the shadowy interior of the temple. The crocodile still lay there, resting amid the weeds. She looked back up at the underside of the boat and imagined the men, two of them, armed with sub-machine guns.

She longed to take a breath. She needed to breathe. Her vision narrowed and her arms and legs tingled.

Then Eden heard another noise. Above her, the hull of a second boat sliced across the lake. The wake danced above her like fireworks in a stormy sky. Then she heard the distant report of gunfire. Bullets zinged into the water above her like shooting stars. Everything happened as though it was in a dream now. A nightmare in another sleeper's head. A night train rumbling by on different tracks.

A man fell into the water from the patrol boat. Then something big, something monstrous moved beside her.

Eden swayed this way and that, trying to focus. She saw the flicking tail of the crocodile, but it wasn't coming for her, it was streaming past her.

The great reptile shot towards the surface, its jaws open wide.

The guard struggled in panic, attempting to climb back into the boat. Blood streamed from a wound on his flank.

The croc shot closer and seized the guard between its jaws. Blood billowed, turning the water red, as the crocodile rolled one way and then the other.

More gunfire pounded the surface of the water. Another man fell from the patrol boat into the blood-stained waves.

Eden watched it all through half-closed eyes. Finally, her hands lost their grip on the temple roof. She groped for her buoyancy control and turned it off. She had no choice anymore. She couldn't stay underwater any longer. She would have to take her chance with the bullets and the predators. Water streamed past Eden's face as she shot up through the water. Somewhere far away, the crocodile shot away back towards the temple, a stream of blood flowing from the corpse in its jaws.

Eden broke through the surface of the water. For a moment she bobbed there, staring up at the sky. Then, strong hands grabbed at her shoulders and pulled her into a boat. Someone pulled off her diving mask. A bright light shone in her eyes. She gasped for air several times. Then

Eden took a deep, beautiful, nourishing breath. Air streamed into her lungs. She took another breath, then opened her eyes. Recognizing the face which looked down at her, Eden gasped.

"Am I dead?" she said.

22

"YOU'RE NOT DEAD, far from it," Baxter said, looking down at Eden slumped in the boat.

"I don't understand, I thought...how did you?" Eden muttered between gasps.

Above them, the sky was beginning to lighten. A large patch of blood shimmered like an oil slick, surrounding the now empty patrol boat.

"We better get out of here," another man said. "This place will be crawling with people and crocs in a few minutes."

Eden recognized his voice, too. "Mo?" she gasped, looking beyond Baxter to the Egyptian at the boat's controls.

"At your service, mam." Mo fired up the boat and leaned hard on the throttle.

The cool morning air stung Eden's face as they powered back towards the lake's far shore. Looking from one man, and back to the other, Eden tried to work out whether she was in a dream or seeing reality.

Baxter swept his hand across her face. Eden took the hand and held it tight.

"Rest now," Baxter said softly. "All the answers are coming, and soon."

Less than an hour later, Eden had warmed up in the shower, donned a fresh set of clothes, and was sitting on Mo's sofa sipping her third cup of very sweet chai. She'd experienced several bouts of dizziness after the dive, but thankfully nothing more serious.

"These pictures are quite something," Mo said, going through the photos Eden had taken.

"Very interesting indeed," Beaumont said, leaning towards the screen.

"How long will it take for you to decode them?" Although thoughts crowded her mind, the desire to unravel the mystery hidden beneath the lake's waters burned.

Baxter walked into the room and sat in the chair opposite Eden.

"You need to start talking," Eden said, struggling to sit upwards. "The last time I saw you, you were driving a speedboat into a concrete wall with a knife in your back. Then I see you months later, in another boat here in Egypt."

Mo looked across at Baxter. "It's not like you to be reckless in a vehicle, is it?"

"Hold on, and how do you guys know each other?" The questions circled Eden's mind so ferociously, she didn't know which one she wanted answered first.

"Let me start at the beginning," Baxter said. "As I said to you on the boat in Lebanon, there is a lot more going on here than you know."

Little Mo shot Baxter a warning glance.

"It's fine," Baxter said. "I've got authority to tell her."

"You've got authority to tell me what?" Eden roared, confusion bubbling over into anger. "You tell me the truth, all of it. If you don't, this is done, the lot of it."

Baxter held out his palms to placate Eden. "Absolutely, I will." He took a deep breath and cleared his throat. It looked as though he was preparing to swallow something unpleasant. Just as Eden was about to shout at him again, Baxter started talking. "I work for an organization called The Council of Selene. I'm one of their fixers, which means I go out into civilian life, report back and sometimes make things happen in the way The Council requires. For two years, I was placed with Archibald Godspeed."

"Poor you," Beaumont muttered. "That man was a stain on the profession. Sorry to speak ill of the dead."

"Quite," Baxter said, glancing at the professor. "But we knew there was a task coming up for him, something that he was uniquely placed to discover for us."

"The tablets," Eden whispered.

"That's right. The Council arranged the discovery of the tablets. It had been their plan all along that they should be found."

"But, but, I found the tablets," Eden said, pointing a finger at her chest.

Baxter raised an eyebrow.

"Okay, we found the tablets," Eden conceded.

"We only found the tablets because The Council wanted them to be found. They are very powerful people."

Eden's mind spun at a hundred miles an hour. She thought back through the events that led them to finding the tablets—the tomb, the box of matches, the Key to the Nile. Suddenly it made a strange kind of sense. "We just followed the path," Eden said, barely above a whisper.

Baxter nodded. "That's how The Council works. All the technological advances, major discoveries, and scientific breakthroughs of at least the last four thousand years have been set up by The Council of Selene."

Eden heard the words but couldn't quite understand them. "Four thousand years?"

"Yes. We don't know exactly how long The Council has been active, but it has been at least that long. It is expected that in time Beaumont will find evidence of The Council's existence in the tablets. Aloma was..."

"Aloma was in The Council?"

"Her husband Japheth was Helios for a long while. Helios is the title of The Council's leader. He, or she, oversees the running and preservation of The Council. He also decides who should take the position on his death. Traditionally it has stayed between a group of closely knit families."

"Hold on, rewind a second." Once again, things were moving too quickly for Eden. She felt the floor move around her. "Just to get this right, the speedboat crash in Lebanon was a setup?"

"That's right," Baxter nodded. "There was a team of divers waiting just beneath the water. The boat was rigged, ready to explode, and I jumped out the moment before impact. It was scary actually..."

"Alright, Action Man, but why didn't you tell me?" Eden scowled at Baxter.

"That was up to The Council. Helios only gave me the authorization to tell you a few hours ago. I came here as soon as I could, but you had already left. I suspected authorization was coming and asked Mo to try to delay you."

Eden glanced at Mo, her expression thunderous.

"Five kebabs and two Egyptian coffees," Mo said, shrugging.

"They were good kebabs," Eden muttered under her breath.

"She's a determined woman," Mo said. "You can't say no to Eden Black, right?"

"As soon as I got here, I contacted Mo and came to find you. When your hour of oxygen had run out, we figured something was up and came out to get you."

Eden looked from Mo to Baxter to Beaumont and then down at her hands. It felt as though the turbulent waters of Lake Nasser were sloshing between her ears. A shard of light cut through her thoughts.

"So, The Council wants us to find The Hall of Records and The Ark of the Covenant?" Eden asked.

Baxter nodded. "They've been planning this for centuries. It's been known as The Giza Protocol. To be honest, I didn't think it was something I'd see in my lifetime."

Mo and Beaumont nodded in agreement.

"You see, The Council loves to talk a lot, but when it comes to making decisions, they're pretty slow," Mo interjected.

"They must make decisions very carefully. They must consider and discuss all the angles and possible implications. Once something is out in the world, there's no taking it back," Beaumont said.

"The Council knows that finding the Ark of the Covenant will further the progress of science and technology more than we've seen in the last hundred years. But it will also intensify religious friction. This is both a scientific specimen and a religious relic, you see."

Eden's eyebrows rose. "But we've seen unprecedented technological progress already in the last one-hundred years."

"Exactly. That's why this decision had to be taken carefully. Although not immediate, the technology found in The

Ark and The Book of Enoch, which is also in The Hall of Records, will pave the way for vehicles that will drive, fly, or sail for centuries on a single power cell. Within a generation, every home will generate abundant power themselves, safely and for next to no cost." Baxter's expression intensified. "There are good implications here for all the world's communities, but also concerns over warring nations."

"A war plane that would never have to return to base," Eden said, considering the thoughts. "The countries that get this technology first will have an incredible advantage."

"That's right," Baxter said, nodding. "That's why it's so important that this is done carefully, at the right time. In fact, it's written in The Council's scriptures that when the time is right, the chosen person will lead us there."

Baxter, Beaumont, and Mo looked at Eden intently.

"You can't seriously think I'm some kind of chosen one. Come on, get real."

"You found the tablets, that was your first test," Baxter said.

"And you figured out that the code was in the sunken sun temple," Mo said, pointing at the images on the screen.

"And you have one of these." Baxter slid his hand down the front of his shirt and pulled out a thin sliver chain. Mo and Beaumont did the same. On the chain hung a tiny symbol, The Key to the Nile.

Slowly, Eden's hand rose to her neck and picked up the chain which had hung there since she was a child. She looked from one Key to the Nile to the other.

"My father gave me this," Eden said, holding the chain.

Baxter's eyes flicked one way, and then the other. "Your father was a very respected member of The Council."

"We all loved him," Mo added.

"His death, was it something to do with The Council?"

Baxter pulled his chair towards Eden and took her hand. "Like all organizations, there are people who rail against The Council's work. Some of them are powerful. We're not sure who, at least, I'm not sure who, but your father's death was not the work of The Council."

"That's one of the dangers of this life we choose," Mo said. "My father died on an expedition funded by The Council." The big man pinched the bridge of his nose. "Their bodies were never recovered."

Baxter nodded slowly. "Now The Council thinks it's time to try again. And we are the team to try it."

Eden looked from one man to the other.

"Why us?" Eden said. "We're hardly Navy Seals." She caught Little Mo's gaze before adding, "No offence."

"None taken," the rotund Egyptian said, cuffing his cheeks.

"It's not to do with physical power," Baxter said, placing a hand on his chest. "It's to do with what's in here."

"Oh please, come on!" Eden snarked. "This isn't King Arthur and the Sword in the Stone."

"He was in The Council too," Mo said, sagely.

"Next you're going to tell me Boris Johnson is part of this secret society," Eden quipped.

"Absolutely not," Baxter, Mo, and Beaumont said in unison.

Eden grinned.

"Say I believe you." Eden narrowed her gaze. "Say I accept that you're not just pulling all this mumbo jumbo out of thin air. What now?"

"First, we prepare and plan. We need to know as much as we can about what we'll face in there."

Eden sighed, tiredness finally overtaking her.

"If I had eight hours to cut down a tree," Beaumont said.

"I would spend the first six sharpening the axe," Baxter completed.

Eden rolled her eyes and sighed.

"Alright Abraham, wake me up when you've finished sharpening your axe." Eden climbed unsteadily to her feet and stomped through to her room for the night.

"He was in The Council too," Baxter shouted, but Eden didn't reply, having already closed the door.

23

"YOU'RE TELLING me The Council of Selene is one of the most powerful secret organizations on the planet?" Eden said, thumbing the radio of Little Mo's decrepit Toyota pickup truck. The radio, it seemed, had commitment issues, and would flit from one station to the other without warning. In the last five minutes, they'd had snippets from an Arabic talk show, a radio drama again in Arabic, a thumping dance music station, and now a station playing classic American rock from the eighties. Meatloaf's *'Bat Out of Hell'* streamed from the worst sounding speakers Eden had ever heard. She turned it up anyway.

"That's right. They're responsible for keeping the whole of humanity on the straight and narrow."

"Pretty simple task, then." Eden glanced at Baxter, who was driving. Little Mo and Beaumont followed behind in an equally decrepit seven-ton truck, fully loaded with all the gear they thought they'd need.

Eden had woken up an hour ago, feeling fresh and revitalized, to find that Baxter, Mo, and Beaumont had already loaded the trucks and were ready to set off.

They flashed past a sign pointing out that Cairo was still several hundred miles away. Eden glanced out at the desert, lying formless on both sides of the highway.

"I suppose I get all that," Eden said. On the stereo, *'Bat Out of Hell,'* faded into a growling wall of static. Eden turned the volume down and clicked to the next station. "But what I don't understand is, if they're this high and mighty organization, why are we driving such rubbish vehicles?"

Baxter barked out a laugh. Eden thought it was probably the first time she'd ever heard the guy laugh. In Lebanon he had always been so serious.

"Remember we're under the radar here. Sure, The Council of Selene is powerful and important, but there are many people who don't agree with what we're doing. Most people, including those in power, don't even know that The Council exists."

"With all these infinite funds, we could have rented a decent Land Rover or something, though." Eden tried but failed to prevent a grin from spreading across her face. "I'm not moaning," Eden said, before adding, "well I suppose I am, but I bet our man, the almighty... what's his name?"

"Helios," Baxter said.

"I bet Helios wouldn't be seen rattling around in an old bone shaker like this."

"You'd be surprised," Baxter said. Eden caught the flicker of a knowing grin pass his face. "He's more of a down-to-earth guy than you'd expect. I've known him to take a public flight or two in the past."

"Steady on," Eden said, grinning.

Baxter pulled out to overtake a truck rattling down the slow lane. They swung around a curve and the blinding Egyptian sun streamed through the glass.

"Ahh this sun!" Eden said, momentarily dazzled. She

flipped down the sun visor only for the thing to fall off in her hands, coating her in dust and sand. Eden grumbled and Baxter laughed.

Colors still dancing in her vision, Eden glanced at Baxter.

"Our friend Ra the Sun God is strong around here." Baxter grinned from behind his aviator sunglasses.

"Tell me about it." Eden reattached the sun visor and positioned it to block the rays. "Why did we have to head up to Cairo so soon, anyway?"

"From there we're in the right place to move whenever we're ready. We've got a villa in New Giza. We can be anywhere around The Plateau within an hour from there."

Baxter's phone buzzed from the dashboard. He thumbed the answer button and Little Mo's smooth voice filled the cab.

"We stop at the next services. Need fuel. Plus, old men like us need to use the bathroom."

"Who are you calling old?" Beaumont interrupted.

Eden grinned, imagining the old friends bickering the whole way. She was glad to be in a separate vehicle, though, so as not to have to hear them.

Baxter agreed and took the next turning from the highway.

The fuel stop centered around a dusty patch of concrete with two rows of pumps and a crumbling concrete kiosk that served as a small shop and housed the all-important facilities. To Eden, the place looked like those fuel stops from great American road movies. The only thing to indicate they weren't actually on Route 66 was the small town spreading out behind them, with the spires and domes of its two or three mosques.

Baxter pulled up alongside one of the pumps and cut

the engine. Three cows, standing on the flatbed of the truck in front of them eyed Eden suspiciously.

"We might as well fill up too while we're here," Baxter said, climbing out of the truck. Desert heat swarmed into the cab, instantly prickling Eden's skin. Whilst she had been bemoaning the truck's stereo, the air conditioning had been doing a good job.

Eden climbed out too. Glancing around, she noticed a small store beside the fuel stop. Colorful fruit and vegetables were piled high in baskets at the front of the store.

With the thought of food, Eden's stomach grumbled.

"I'll be back in two," she shouted behind her. "Time for snacks."

Baxter shouted something in return, but Eden didn't hear him above the whirr of the recalcitrant fuel pump. He wasn't going to leave without her, that Eden knew for sure.

She used the bathroom as quickly as she could, trying to touch as little as possible. The bathroom looked as though the last clean it enjoyed was ordered by Rameses himself.

Eden crossed the forecourt and ducked into the shop. As she'd suspected, the place was one of those wonderful food stores found across foreign lands that contained nothing she recognized. Eden picked up a basket and spent several minutes filling it with bottles of drinks in various bright colors, crisps and other baked snacks. She looked at the packets of food, each of which pictured vegetables that could have been from outer space.

When she'd got more than enough for the remaining six-or-so hours to Cairo, she took the overladen basket to the till.

A woman wearing a bright green headscarf packed Eden's stuff into a bag. The woman twittered away in Arabic far too quickly for Eden to even begin to understand. Eden thanked the woman and handed over several notes.

As Eden was turning to leave the shop, a figure pushed past her. The man moved so quickly Eden didn't even see him coming. The pair collided, Eden taking a quick step backwards to avoid falling.

Eden tried to apologize, but the man pushed on into the store. Eden shrugged and stepped out into the sunlight.

"Come on," Baxter said, already sitting in the driver's seat. "I want to get there before sundown."

"Keep ya hair on," Eden grumbled, climbing up into the passenger seat. "Don't you know that an army munches on its stomach."

"Marches on its stomach."

"What?"

"An Army marches on its stomach. Not munches," Baxter corrected, firing up the truck and pulling back out towards the highway.

"Whatever," Eden shrugged, pulling open one of the packets.

They accelerated back onto the highway, the landscape again becoming a blur of sand and blink-and-you-miss-them towns. Somewhere out of sight to the right, the Nile slithered its way towards the Mediterranean. Finishing her first packet of crisps, the actual flavor of which Eden couldn't identify, Eden peered back into the bag to select her new target. She noticed something at the bottom of the bag which she didn't recognize.

It was a business card from the Hotel Rumbold in Cairo. Eden glowered at the card, questioning why it should end up here in her bag.

She flipped the card over. A handwritten note was scrawled on the back. Eden read the note and once again felt the tectonic plates of her understanding move around her. Her mouth felt dry and for a moment her vision lost focus. She glanced at Baxter, focusing on the road ahead, he hadn't seen anything.

Eden gazed inside the bag and read the note once more.

Alexander Winslow is alive. Come to the Rumbold at 9pm.

24

THE SUN WAS STRUGGLING beneath the horizon as the shabby convoy arrived at their villa on the outskirts of New Giza. Eden looked out at the place through the truck's dirty windscreen and agreed with Baxter—no one would notice their activities here. Set in its own walled compound, the team could set up here without worry of disturbance. On the spectrum of design, the villa's strange construction of glass and steel all set at angles, was about as far removed from the heavy limestone blocks of the Pyramids as you could get.

Baxter pulled up to the front of the building, bleached gravel snapping beneath the truck's well-worn tires. Little Mo stopped the large truck behind them. Both vehicles muted into silence.

Much of the journey had passed in silence, Eden staring out of the window at the passing desert. Countless questions circled her mind, all vying for attention. One thing she knew for certain, she needed to go to the Rumbold Hotel and find out.

Eden grabbed her bag from the rear of the truck and

followed Baxter up the front stairs and into the villa. An open plan living and dining area occupied most of the ground floor. Baxter began laying things out on the large dining table.

Eden jogged upstairs and placed her bag on one of the beds. She did a quick three-sixty. The room had an ensuite, several wardrobes she would have no use for, and more importantly a fully opening window. She peered down at the ground twenty feet below. She could get out of there without being seen with no problems.

Eden then took a few minutes to arrange several items in key places around the room. It was a habit her dad had taught her many years ago, which she now completed by instinct. She also chose items a curious person would be likely to touch. A notebook was positioned next to pile of receipts, two pens laid on top of a small stack of scribbled notes. The items were arranged in such a way, that if anyone moved them, she would know.

Back downstairs, Baxter, Beaumont and Little Mo were busily removing boxes from the trucks and carefully laying things out on the dining table. It looked as though they were preparing for war, Eden thought.

"Looks like you've got things covered here. I'm going to take a quick look around the neighborhood." Eden grabbed the truck's keys from the table.

Baxter looked up, his eyes momentarily narrowing on meeting Eden's.

"You want anything picked up while I'm out?" Eden grinned.

"No thanks, we've got everything we need here," Beaumont said, struggling through the door with a crate of books. Eden wondered when the professor would realize that digital copies were so much easier. Eden turned on her heels and scurried down to the truck. Two minutes later the truck shuddered and wheezed towards Cairo.

The Rumbold Hotel was a decaying concrete structure in Cairo's Al-Helmiya district. Although the streets were dark now, the traffic still inched forward at a frustratingly slow speed. The constant bark of car horns filled the air. Fed up that the journey had taken almost an hour to cover a few short miles, Eden bumped the truck up a curb, in violation of several parking laws, and cut the engine. She climbed out and looked around. Half a mile to the south, the brightly lit minarets of the Muhammad Ali Mosque grazed the auburn sky. Eden turned and peered up at the Hotel Rumbold. The place towered above her, giant and gloomy. At a first glance, the hotel appeared as though it hadn't been open in decades. Broken glass filled several windows and closed curtains showed the stains and tears of many decades' use. A thick covering of dust lay across the hotel's sign. Looking closely, though, Eden could make out a faint light seeping from somewhere inside.

Eden glanced behind her as a truck grumbled past, belching black smoke into the air.

She took a moment to steady herself, then slid the hotel's business card from her pocket. She checked the time, it was quickly approaching 9pm.

Eden swallowed but her mouth felt dry. Steeling her resolve, Eden stepped up to the heavy wooden door and pushed. To her surprise it swung open with very little resistance.

Eden looked inside. A solitary lamp illuminated the lobby, casting long shadows across a filth strewn floor. Faded posters advertising Cairo's many tourist attractions covered the walls. Eden's heart thumped a steady beat in her chest. She felt a glimmer of reassurance that she's brought one of Mo's knives. The blade was cold against her ankle.

"Miss Black, thank you for coming." A deep, melodic voice filled the room. Eden's breath caught in her throat. She whipped around but didn't see anything. She looked back through the open door. The truck was still within darting distance.

"This way please, Miss Black. My employer would like to speak with you." A light snapped on at the far side of the lobby revealing a man standing at the top of a stairwell. The man's skin was the color and texture of mahogany. His rippling muscles looked as hard as the wood too. He spoke slowly, his voice tinged with an African accent.

The man turned and began walking down the large, curved staircase.

Eden swung the foyer door shut, paced across the lobby, and followed the man downstairs. The bare staircase hinted at what once would have been a grand building. The balustrade was constructed in ornate ironwork and patterned tiles lay beneath a thick layer of grime on each step. Two flights below, Eden's guide led them through a set of double doors.

They stepped into what would once have been a grand ballroom. A vaulted ceiling stretched high above. Crystal chandeliers hung dark and lifeless. Strings of spiders' webs streamed from one chandelier to the next like ghostly bunting, fluttering in some distant breeze. A single bulb lit the room, hanging on a wire somewhere near the center. The ineffective light left the edges of the great space in near darkness.

"Take a seat." Eden's guide pointed to a table and two chairs in the center of the large room. The man stationed himself by the door, his straight back showing off some mili-

tary bearing. There was a second man standing a few feet to
the right. Eden looked from one to the other. The two
guards could well have been brothers with the same
complexion and mountainous body shape.

Eden's mouth grew drier still.

Trying not to show her growing nervousness, Eden
padded across the room, her footsteps squeaking on the
wooden floor.

Eden took a seat and then clicked her fingers, the sound
echoing throughout the silent hall. "Garçon," she said,
mimicking a French accent. "I want your wine list immediately, and I think I'll have the lobster!"

A sharp laugh reverberated from the hall's farthest end.
The sound certainly wasn't one of the men standing like
sentries by the door. It was both coming from the wrong
direction and sounded female. Eden turned and peered into
the shadows. In the gloom, a figure moved.

"People told me you were 'spirited.'" The figure stepped
towards Eden, moving slowly toward the light. Eden recognized an American accent. The woman took another step
closer, high-heeled shoes clicking against the floor. The
woman was tall, glamorous, and walked with a hypnotic
feline gait. A bolt of recognition chimed in Eden's memory.
She glanced back at the two men, searching her memory for
the location in which she'd come across the trio before.

"I fear, though, that your bravado is merely a coping
strategy for your nervousness." The woman sauntered
towards the table, pulled out the chair and sat down. She
put an iPad on the table, its screen glowing softy and casting
a ghostly light on her face. "That seems to be something you
do quite often Miss Black. You don't like to take things seriously, do you?"

Suddenly the memory struck Eden. "It was you. The

three of you," Eden said, her gaze hard. She glanced from the woman to the men by the door. "You kidnapped Beaumont. You were watching him from the office when I..."

"When you broke in, rescued your friend, and killed two of my guards. Yes, that was us. You got in the way of my plans quite effectively that night."

Eden's eyebrows inched together. The woman's comment sounded strangely like a compliment. Eden forced herself to smile. "Well, it must be a wonderful coincidence, but then again, it is a lovely time to visit Egypt. Where is that waiter with our wine list? What museums have you been to? I have to say, though, I don't think much of your accommodation."

The woman yapped a dry and humorless laugh. "There we go again. The good old Eden Black humor. I must say, at first, I found your intrusion frustrating. But once I recovered the footage, and found out who our midnight visitor was, I was intrigued more than anything. I thought our paths would cross but..."

Eden yawned and stretched. "Sorry. It's been a long day and you're boring me. Get to the point. Who are you and what do you know about my father?"

A fission of irritation moved across the woman's face. It was quickly forced away with a smile.

"I am Lulu King. You may know me as..."

"Raymond King's daughter. The Oil Tycoon who despite having all the scientific evidence supporting climate change, continued to pollute our planet for several decades." Eden had heard about Raymond King's death just a few days ago. She scrutinized the other woman's face for an expression of loss, no matter how fleeting, but found none. Catching Lulu's gaze, Eden felt nothing but a cold, calculating woman looking back at her.

"That's right. As soon as I was old enough to disagree, I was not a supporter of my father's work. Now with him gone, I can see that he was not an evil man, just doing what he thought was right."

"In time he will be seen akin to a war criminal," Eden snapped. "But I'm sorry to hear about your father's death. Losing a parent is always hard, whether you agree with their professional decisions or not."

"Thank you," Lulu said, shrugging. "Now to talk about your father. A contact of mine recovered this footage a few days ago. It was taken from Cairo airport." Lulu's slender fingers tapped at the screen of the iPad. She spun the device around for Eden to watch and then pressed the screen once more. A video started to play.

Eden watched closely. The video was footage from a security camera. For the first few seconds, Eden just saw the tired faces of unrecognizable travelers streaming past. Then someone strode into the shot that she recognized. It was a face she'd seen each time she closed her eyes since his death a few months before. Eden's father, Alexander Winslow, walked into the shot as though he didn't have a care in the world.

Eden cupped her face in her hands, her eyes not moving from the screen.

Alexander Winslow stepped out of the shot and video changed to another angle. A couple of seconds later, Winslow appeared in this shot too. He paused, reading the overhead signs, and then headed in the direction of passport control. The third camera was positioned above the head of the border control official. Eden watched her father approach the official and hand over his passport.

King tapped the screen, and the video froze. Eden stared at the screen for a few seconds more. Eerily, it looked as though Winslow looked directly into the lens. In a way, Eden didn't understand, it felt as though he was looking directly at her. Then she saw, laying on top of his shirt, The Key to the Nile pendant. That was strange because as far as Eden remembered he always wore it beneath his clothes, directly against his chest. She had never known him to wear it like that.

"This video was taken two days ago," King repeated, making a show of pulling the iPad back across the table and snapping its cover closed. "I have a team working on this. They have already found out the name your father is using, and the hotel he is staying in."

Eden wasn't listening. She still saw in her mind's eye the Key to the Nile, sparkling above her father's shirt. The only reason he would have worn it there, Eden realized all at once, was if he wanted someone to see it. That symbol only meant something to a handful of people. It meant the most to her.

Eden looked up and King tried not to smile. Not only was her father alive, but he had sent her a coded message loud and clear. A message that effectively said: follow the white rabbit.

25

Lulu King leaned back in her chair and scrutinized Eden.

Eden concentrated on not showing the flush of excitement in her expression.

"Your father is alive and, in this city, right now," King said.

Eden didn't bother to point out the other woman's statement of the obvious.

"I suppose now, you're going to tell me I should do something for you, in exchange for you telling me where my father is?"

A smile broke out on King's face.

Eden had heard many people describing Lulu King as beautiful. To Eden, the smile looked like that of a shark ready for its dinner.

"That's what I like when dealing with intelligent people. There is no need to waste time on details. You understand me, I understand you. For once, we speak the same language."

"And I suppose what you want is access to something within The Hall of Records?"

King's smile grew further still, showing more teeth than the allocation for the average human.

"All I want is one tiny thing from The Hall of Records. My organization has been working on alternative power systems for over a decade now, and we've made some great strides forward. Each time we think we've found the answer, though, we find something's missing."

"Several brain cells?" Eden quipped, shrugging.

"Maybe that too." King laughed. "Although there really is a shortage of staff in scientific fields these days. Everyone wants to be a pop star, I suppose."

"It would beat having you for a boss."

"Have you heard of Element 115?" King said, mirth draining from her face.

Eden yawned and stretched. "Yes, of course. Stable element 115 would create enough energy to power the whole planet."

King's eyes widened. She unfurled a long finger and leveled it at Eden. "Exactly that. It's such a pleasure to talk to someone who knows about these things. But, then again, you are a friend of our esteemed professor..."

"Cut to the chase." Eden put her palms on the table as though preparing to stand. "Or I'm out of here. I want to get to the Cairo Museum before closing."

The men standing by the door took a step forward.

"There are just three things in The Hall of Records that I need," King said. "You lead me and my men there, we will take what we need, and the rest is yours."

"Then you'll tell me where my dad is?" Eden said.

"Then I'll tell you where your dad is and let you walk out of The Hall of Records with whatever else you want. Gold, jewels, more artifacts than you'll ever see in your life. You could start a little museum of your own."

"That sounds great," Eden said, sweetly. "Let me guess what you want, The Ark of the Covenant, The Book of Enoch and The Book of Giants."

"Exactly that," King said, clearly not expecting Eden to be one step ahead. "We take those three simple things, you get everything else. You'll even get to claim the find for yourselves, I've no need for the fame and glory."

Eden tapped a finger against her chin. "That sounds like a reasonable deal. A very reasonable deal." Eden pushed her chair back and went to stand up. "But I have a better one. What if I tell you to butt out, I go and find my father myself, then keep everything I want from The Hall of Records?"

King's gaze turned icy cold.

"That's such a shame. It really is." King looked down at her hands on the tabletop for several seconds. "We were having such a nice conversation, but you had to go and ruin it."

King snapped her fingers and almost immediately two strong hands slammed down over Eden's shoulders. The fingers dug into her flesh, gripping her like a boa constrictor. Eden struggled but the meaty hands held her firm. She twisted around and caught a glimpse of her assailant. He was keeping her still without even straining. Eden realized that the man must have moved up behind her in preparation. He had moved very quietly. King stood up, walked around the table, and crouched down into Eden's light of sight.

"You know one of the problems with people in the modern world?"

Eden didn't reply, her jaw set firm as she struggled again. She thought about the knife strapped to her ankle. They hadn't bothered to search her on the way in and the knife was merely inches away. Eden dropped her shoulders, feigning dejection while reaching for the blade.

"I'll tell you," King continued. "People are just far too argumentative. Far too disagreeable. You give someone an easy option, a good option, a generous option—didn't you think that was a generous offer, Abdul?" King addressed the man.

"Yes, Miss King. Very generous."

Eden strained down further, closing in on the blade.

King nodded. "You make these offers, but people in the modern world just want to do things the difficult way. As with everything in life, Eden, there is an easy way, and there is a difficult way. The difficult way, in this instance, will be painful too."

Eden's hand reached the knife's handle. In one swift movement, she pulled it out.

Her captor moved quickly too. Sensing her movement, he took a step back.

Eden swung the knife backwards, but the blade hit nothing.

The other guard lunged forward and seized Eden's wrist. He thumped her hand hard against the table, pinning it in place.

Eden tried to move, but again was powerless.

The man crushed Eden's hand against the tabletop until her grip on the knife was so weak it slipped from her fingers.

King stepped forwards and picked up the knife. She peered at the blade, turning it this way and that. The blade sparkled.

"Thank you, Sharif." King toyed with the blade. "You see how much can be achieved when people work together."

Eden struggled again, but the men held her tightly.

"Let's try that again," King said, still looking at the knife's jagged blade. "I'm going to give you an instruction. The best thing to do, for both of us, is if you just do what you're told. Don't ask questions. Don't think about it. Just do it straight away." King turned to face Eden. "You can understand that, can't you?"

"I'm really starting to dislike you," Eden spat.

In one swift movement, Lulu lunged forwards. The glittering blade swept through the air and came to rest against Eden's throat.

"Again, you're making things difficult for yourself. Take the easy path for once in your life. Give yourself a break."

Eden tried to swallow. The blade dug further into her skin. She tried to tilt her head backwards. The abdominal muscles of the man behind her felt like a plate of steel. Eden froze, unable to move either way.

As quickly as King had swung the blade at Eden, she pulled it away again. Eden's heart slammed in her chest. Adrenaline coursed through her veins. She wanted nothing more than to grab the knife back and cut these vile criminals a third eye. She attempted to suppress her anger and think rationally. Time was on her side, and in many ways, the ball was in her court. King didn't want her or her father dead, that was clear at least. Eden swallowed and took a deep breath, forcing the fear away.

"Now you have another chance to make things easy for yourself, put your hands on the table." King pointed the knife towards Eden.

Maybe King didn't want her dead but losing a finger or two was possible. Eden remembered the state of the room in which she'd found Beaumont. It was clear that this woman would use any means to get what she wanted.

Eden struggled. Again, she got nowhere.

The guard seized Eden's other wrist and slammed it to

the table beside the first. Eden lashed this way and that but got nowhere. With the bulky man now leaning in front of her, pinning her hands to the table, Eden couldn't see what was going on. She strained to look around the man's hulking figure but was held too tightly. King's shoes clicked across the floor. The chair scraped backwards, and King sat at the table. Eden felt cold carbonized steel against her fingers.

"Everyone has their limit, Eden. It's just the case of finding out where it is." King's voice was calm and quiet, barely above a whisper.

The blade moved its way from one finger to the next.

"Here's an interesting fact for you." King's voice became strangely hypnotic. Eden tried to ignore it, but with no other sound in the silent room found it incredibly difficult. She felt herself grow woozy. "Pain receptors can take several tenths of a second to communicate with the brain, meaning that often people see the injury before they feel it. Isn't that interesting?"

The cold steel moved on to the next finger.

"You may already be one finger down and just not know it yet."

Then the feeling in Eden's fingers changed. For a moment she feared that King was right. She braced herself for a wave of pain. Eden gritted her teeth. She would face the pain full on and wouldn't cry out.

Eden felt something damp beneath her fingertips. She pictured blood pooling across the tabletop.

A whimper escaped Eden's lips. She gritted her teeth more tightly. She wasn't going to give King the satisfaction.

The damp feeling moved from the little finger on her left hand, to the next finger. The sensation came again and again on each finger until it reached her thumb. Then the sensation repeated on her right hand.

"All done," King said, the chair scraping backwards on the floor. "One more thing to do."

Eden clocked movement through the corner of her eye.

King stepped around the man and closed in on Eden, the knife extended. King moved forward slowly, impassively observing Eden's pain like a master predator. King flicked the knife past Eden's left eye. Again, Eden braced herself for pain, but felt none.

"That's it," King said, stepping backwards. "Let her go."

The guards stepped backwards. Eden felt suddenly weightless. She glanced down at her hands. Both lay complete, although slightly numb, on the tabletop. There was no blood and no severed digits. Eden turned her hands over and looked at her palms. Each of her fingertips was covered in ink and there was a tiny pinprick on her thumb.

"Sorry about the mess. Feel free to clean yourself up," King said, pointing at a box of wet wipes on the table.

Eden looked up at King. King dropped a strand of Eden's hair into a plastic evidence bag along with a blood spotted cotton swab. The prints from her fingers had been placed in a similar bag. There was a logo on the bag. *DK Labs.* Eden looked at the logo for a second, committing it to memory in case it would be useful later. There was also a sample number, which Eden repeated to herself a few times, also committing to memory. As soon as she was back in the truck, she would write both down.

Trying not to show her confusion mixed with relief, Eden yanked out a wet wipe and cleaned the ink from her fingers. Then she ran a finger through her hair. She could hardly even notice where King had taken the sample.

"Get these over to the lab," King said, passing plastic bags to one of the men. "Tell them to await our instructions."

King strode back over to the table and retook her seat opposite Eden.

"I'm sorry it had to be like that. As I said, if you'd just done it willingly, it would have been so much easier for us."

"What do you want my prints and hair for?"

King grinned at Eden. "Insurance. Just in case you decide to do things in your usual difficult fashion." King dug out the iPad again. She brought up a photo. "A few days ago, just to make a point, I had this done." King spun the tablet around and showed Eden.

Seeing the picture, Eden almost wretched. Three crumpled, bullet-ridden bodies lay on a blood-stained concrete floor. One of them was a woman, probably in her sixties, the other two Eden recognized as the guards she'd dispatched on the way into the warehouse.

"All killed by some vile predator. These people had families, don't you know?" King turned the iPad and selected another file.

Eden scowled.

"I've got a contact who's a very good video editor. They've made this for me." King tapped the screen and again held the iPad up for Eden. A video played slowing Eden rappelling into the warehouse. The shot changed and Eden ran across the warehouse, towards the room in which Beaumont was trapped.

King tapped the screen. You don't need to see the next shot. Let's just say, it relates convincingly to the photograph you just saw.

"You're trying to pin this on me? That's not enough in any court of law."

"On its own, I agree, no it's not. But when we add in this." King swung the screen around to show a small excavator digging a hole in the ground. Recognizing the surrounding woodland, Eden leaned in closely. Sure enough, in the background of the photograph, sat her truck.

Clearly losing patience, King filled in the gaps.

"In a couple of weeks three corpses will be found in the woodland near where you've been living. Your DNA and hair fibers will be found on the bodies, and just to seal the deal, your fingerprints will be discovered at the victims' houses." King placed the iPad on the table, sat back and fixed Eden with an ice-cold gaze. "Are you ready to do it my way yet, Eden?"

Eden sat up straight and folded her arms. Maybe for once it was time to play ball.

ALEXANDER WINSLOW STEPPED BACK into the doorway of a closed-up motorbike repair shop and watched Eden push out through the doors of the Hotel Rumbold. Whatever had happened inside, the scowl on Eden's face suggested it hadn't gone her way.

Winslow knew that scowl well, having been the recipient of it countless times during Eden's childhood. He smiled at the memory. It was strange to consider that the powerful and independent young woman he now watched was once small enough to sit on his knee. Eden never had been good at taking instructions. It was a trait which those in education seemed to want to condition out of her, but Winslow always encouraged. Life was too short to do things that didn't serve you, he believed.

Across the street, Eden turned back and glared at a figure at the door.

Winslow stepped forwards and crouched behind a stack of old tires to get a better look. He saw a large black man handing something across to Eden. Beneath the distant glow of a streetlight, Winslow recognized the shimmer of a knife.

He grinned to himself. Of course, Eden wasn't the type to turn up unprepared. What's more, he knew that she would use that blade with devastating precision at a moment's notice. There was no threat today, though. Right now, Lulu King needed Eden alive. And whether Lulu King knew it or not, she was doing exactly what Winslow wanted.

Eden stashed the knife away, made an obscene gesture at the man, and then stepped out into the street.

She had confidence, Winslow thought, that was good. She would need all the confidence she could get.

Eden crossed towards a rust-spattered pickup truck and climbed into the driver's seat.

As the truck grumbled to life, some of the lights working and others dull and lifeless. Winslow's heart swelled with a whole maelstrom of emotion.

Eden was his daughter. His flesh and blood. He knew that he would feel that way until the day he died. The day he really died—not just appeared to be dead.

Winslow longed more than anything to rush over and hold his daughter in his arms. He longed to tell her of everything that had and would happen and yearned to tell of her important role in it all.

As the truck banged into gear and pulled away, Winslow shook himself out of his melancholy. Having planned this for years—no, decades—Winslow knew that this was not the time for emotion. He would get his time to explain it all, once Eden was ready. Eden would learn of her rightful place, just as he had to all those years ago. Observing the correct time order was of utmost importance.

She might be one of the most important people on the

planet right now, Winslow reflected as Eden's truck sped out of sight, but she's still my little girl.

The grumbling of the truck's engine faded into the noise of the city. Winslow stared down the street for long seconds, looking into the space where Eden had been. Again, snapping out of the negative thoughts, he fished a packet of chamomile cigarettes from his pocket and started back in the opposite direction.

26

WHEN EDEN ARRIVED BACK at the villa in New Giza, Beaumont, Baxter, and Little Mo were assembled around the table studying maps and making plans. The three men spoke in whispers and the room buzzed with productive excitement.

"You guys look like you're planning a military coup," Eden said, lugging several shopping bags into the kitchen. On the way back to the villa she'd stopped off at a supermarket. Getting the shopping served two needs, first it would make her trip seem like it had a purpose to the others, and second, Eden really wanted a beer.

"That's exactly what we're doing," Baxter said, glancing up from the map. "These two are working on the translations for the hieroglyphs you found at the Sun Temple."

Eden fished a can of Sakara Beer from the bag and peered at it. The gold and blue can contained a picture of the famous Pyramid of Djoser at Saqqara, just a few miles south of Cairo. Eden snapped open the can, took a long pull and instantly felt better. She looked across the room at the men. On the way back, she'd felt angry at the possibility that these men knew her father was alive. At first, she'd planned to confront them and find out the truth as soon as she could.

"Why do these translations take so long?" Eden said, sidling across the room.

Beaumont glanced up from his notes. "I can assure you, we are working on this as quickly as humanly possible. Translating ancient texts is not as easy as you might think. You can't just..."

"I'm joking," Eden said, placing a hand on Beaumont's shoulder. "I know what it's like. My dad used to spend weeks laboring over the same old document, trying to understand what it meant."

Eden glanced from one man to the next, looking for a flicker of something that might indicate they knew he was alive. She saw nothing. If they knew, these guys were good at keeping secrets.

Beaumont nodded and turned his attention back to the computer.

Eden then remembered the way her father had looked directly into the camera at Cairo Airport. In that moment she realized that Alexander Winslow knew what he was doing. Whatever was going on here, Eden realized, he had planned it down to the finest detail. When the time was right, she would find out why.

Eden gazed out through the villa's floor to ceiling windows. Beyond the tastefully lit garden, the lights of the city smoldered. Her dad was out there, somewhere, Eden thought. He was out there somewhere close. With the thought, an unusual warmth grew inside her.

"I mean, I hope you made it a priority. I had to wrestle a giant crocodile for that," Eden added, taking another sip of beer.

"And I had to rescue you," Baxter added. "You got another one of those." He pointed at the beer.

"Knock yourself out," Eden said, waving in the direction of the bags. She peered down at Beaumont's scrawled handwriting. "What have you got for us then professor?"

"This has been a difficult one for us, I have to say Eden. It's not as straightforward as some. It seems that the temple you investigated was from an earlier epoch than a lot of the hieroglyphs we've seen before. That means, there's a fair amount of theorization that goes into creating a clear conclusion."

"Theorization!" Eden laughed out loud. "You mean you just make it up?"

Baxter dug out the pack of the beers and placed them on the table. Beaumont picked one up too.

"My dear Eden, you have such a potty mouth. One does not simply make it up. We look at the evidence, we compare with translations already existing, we consider the context of the find, and the dynasty in which the hieroglyphs were created and then we..."

"Make it up?" Eden took a sip of the beer, purposefully slurping.

"Synthesize a theory," Beaumont said, defiantly. "Fortunately, we didn't need to do that on this occasion as we have one of the word leaders in pre-dynastic hieroglyphs on hand."

"Oh fantastic, what did they make of it?"

"It's a bit of a riddle," Little Mo said, stepping forward. He dug out several printed sheets and laid them on the table. "You see here, they're taking this from later stages of hieroglyphic development and using them in ways we've not seen..."

"What a minute," Eden said. "You're one of the world experts in pre-dynastic hieroglyphs? You can read this?"

"Of course," Little Mo said, shrugging as though Eden had just asked a stupid question.

Eden studied the photographs as Mo laid them out one by one. Despite the low light and the reduced visibility under water, the pictures had come out surprisingly well.

"Quit with the science stuff, just tell me what you've come up with," Eden snapped, remembering how the dive had almost ended with her in the jaws of a Nile crocodile.

Beaumont picked up his notepad and handed it to Eden. Of several pages of writing, only two sentences remained without being crossed out.

"Don't worry about all that," Beaumont said, pointing at the mess. "This is what we've got so far."

Nun of waters primeval the amid located, Egg the of Island the on found be will this. Well the of Place the access first must seekers, soul the of underworld the enter to.

Eden raised an eyebrow. "Gentlemen, far be it for me to criticize your work, but this makes absolutely no sense whatsoever. It sounds like the ramblings of a madman."

Beaumont shrugged and took a sip of the beer.

"What can I say? Translating these ancient scripts is an art-form. You don't learn this in school," Mo said.

"If you did learn it in school, you'd still be in second grade," Eden smirked.

"Well, I don't see that that's fair," Beaumont said. "We've been working on this for hours and it's not at all..."

"Stop talking a second," Eden stepped forward, holding her palm out to Beaumont. "I think I've got something." She looked at the text again. The words seemed to move around in front of her vision, before settling in a different order. "That might just work," she said, aghast. "The underworld of the soul. The underworld of the soul!" She said again, looking up at the three men, who stared at her unblinking. "What does that phrase mean to you?"

"I think the pressure has finally got to her," Baxter said, glancing at Mo.

"Maybe it's from the dive," Mo said. "Air embolisms can cause confusion sometimes for days afterwards." Mo stepped towards Eden. "Let's get you to sit down..."

"No!" Eden shouted. "I'm fine. Just answer the question. What does the underworld of the soul mean to you?"

Beaumont, never one to miss the opportunity to give a lecture, started speaking. "The Ancient Egyptians believed that the underworld of the soul, they called it Duat, was a place that looked a lot like the earth we know, except it was the realm of the dead. Osiris was believed to be the lord there. Contrary to common..."

"Okay, but it's *a thing*, right?" Eden snapped.

"The ancient Egyptians believed it was, as you say, a *thing*, yes." Beaumont looked puzzled now. "Why do you think that?"

"Well, listen to this." Eden started to read the text Beaumont and Mo had translated, but this time backwards. "To enter the Underworld of the Soul, seekers must first access the Place of the Well. This will be found on the Island of the Egg, located amid the primeval waters of nun."

Mo and Beaumont shared a wide-eyed glance.

"I can't believe it," Mo said. "She's done it. The hieroglyphics are written backwards."

"Of course they are!" Beaumont shrieked, slapping his thigh. "That makes perfect sense. It's representative of the underworld, where things are reversed."

"As above, so below!"

Eden shrugged. "But that's it? It still doesn't really make

any sense." She read the sentences through again, hoping for the meaning to appear. "All that for two sentences."

"We're still working on it," Baxter interrupted defensively.

"Tell me, Eden," Mo said, no louder than a whisper. His Arabic inflection made the words sound even more mysterious than they already were. "Why do you need any more, if this one sentence contains all the answers you need?"

Everyone looked at Mo for several seconds. Eden turned back and focused on the two sentences. When no further meaning appeared, she looked up at the Egyptian. "Tell me then, Mo. What does all this mean?"

Mo and Beaumont grinned at each other.

Eden glanced at Baxter. He shrugged, as clueless as she was.

"Alright. Let me explain." Beaumont cleared his throat.

Eden and Baxter stood in raptured silence, waiting. Eden had to admit, Richard Beaumont had a great sense of drama. He knew when he had his audience hanging on to his every word.

"Over the last two hundred years, there have been numerous official attempts to access the cave network which we know lies beneath The Giza Plateau..."

"And hundreds of unofficial expeditions too," Mo added, no doubt thinking about the fated attempt made by his father's team.

Beaumont nodded. "Each of them, however, well, all of those we know about, have come across the same problem."

"The water," Eden said.

"The water," Beaumont repeated, clearly not liking all the interruptions to his monologue. "Many have tried to stop the water, to pump it out, or even swim through it, but the current is too strong. No one has figured out quite how to stop it. We think this is because..."

"Everyone has been trying to get in at the wrong place," Mo interrupted excitedly.

Beaumont shot a glance at the Egyptian. "Yes. We now think that is because although the subterranean caves may be below The Plateau itself, that is not the correct way to enter."

"Then where do we enter?" Baxter said, speaking for the first time in several minutes.

"That's where this gives us all the clues we need." Beaumont jabbed a finger at the notebook.

"Nun is the Egyptian god of primeval waters out of which the creation process began," Beaumont spoke more quickly now, trying to get the information out before anyone else cut him off. "He is the oldest of the gods and actually created Ra, the Sun God..."

"The guy with the bird's face?" Eden asked.

Beaumont nodded and then continued. "Nun is also associated with Giza's sacred lake which was once located towards the east of The Plateau. It is highly likely, given the topography of the area, there was a mound, or an island, created within that lake. We believe that what these hieroglyphs are saying is..."

"Through that island, you can get down into the Underworld of the Soul," Mo said, almost spitting the information out.

Eden and Baxter glanced at each other, both trying to digest the information.

"The lake isn't there anymore, though, right?" Eden said. "So, how do we know where to look?"

"Good question," Beaumont said, extending a finger. "We did this for an investigation some years ago." Beaumont searched frantically through a stack of papers. "Here we are. Here we are! This is where the technical knowledge of my contemporaries back in Cambridge always prove helpful. I'm a bit of a dinosaur when it comes to..."

"What have you got?" Baxter snapped, the man with the unshakable temperament clearly being pushed to his limits.

Beaumont slid out several large maps. "Using a computer program, my team calculated the change in the water level on The Plateau over the last few thousand years." Beaumont turned from one map to the next and showed how the Nile's span had reduced over time.

Eden looked closely at one of the maps. Sure enough, several thousand years ago, a large lake lay just to the east of The Pyramid Field.

"What's here now?" Eden said, pointing at the lake.

"Nazlet El-Samman Village," Mo said.

"Then that's where we need to go," Eden said, finishing her beer. "First thing tomorrow."

27

"IS THIS REALLY THE PLACE?" Eden furrowed her brow as Baxter slowed the truck to a crawl on the wide, dusty road. Crumbling concrete buildings lined both sides of the street. They rolled slowly past a small convenience store selling illicit booze and tobacco. Baxter swung the wheel to avoid a mound of garbage which the wind was skittering across the street.

Beaumont, sitting in the cramped back seats beside Little Mo, turned the map ninety degrees and mumbled something inaudible.

"I wonder what the pharaohs would think if they saw this place now," Eden said, thinking out loud. They passed four immaculately preened horses, usually found offering rides to tourists, eating trash from an overflowing bin. Their owner, scrolling through his phone and smoking, seemed not to care what dangerous substances his animals might be consuming.

Beaumont mumbled again from the backseat.

"Give me that," Eden snapped, turning around and grabbing the map from Beaumont. "You can read ten-thousand-

year-old hieroglyphs but can't hold a map up the right way."
She folded the map and smoothed out the section they
needed.

Baxter stopped the truck to let an old man with a cane
cross the road, his back bent, forcing his head towards the
road. The man didn't even look up at the oncoming traffic.

Scrutinizing the map, Eden saw Beaumont's problem.
"How is this supposed to help us? This is the topographical
map from two-thousand years ago. We're not going to find
anything with this. Pull over."

Baxter did as he was told. They stopped between the
grime covered windows of a small café and a closed-up shop
selling electrical appliances.

Eden dug out her laptop.

"I'll get us some coffee, and maybe a cake or two," Mo
said, his voice taking on the tone of a satisfied cat.

"Good idea," Eden said. "Make mine a large one."

Mo nodded and struggled out of the truck, much to the
relief of the aging vehicle's suspension.

Using the lines of longitude and latitude from Beaumont's map, Eden overlaid the shape of the island which
once lay in the center of the lake, onto the modern streets of
Nazlet-el-Samman.

Mo returned with a large paper bag, stuffed with various
sugary cakes and pastries. The crumbs down his shirt indicated that he had already consumed at least one while he was
waiting. He passed small cups of thick black coffee around.

Eden finished hers in one gulp, before turning back to
the map. She carefully adjusted the size to make it as accurate as possible. Satisfied, she held up the laptop.

"It looks as though our island is two streets that way."
Eden pointed to the left. "Good coffee, by the way."

"The best in the world," Little Mo purred, digging into a second sweet treat.

Baxter fired up the engine and followed Eden's directions. After a left turn, followed by a sharp right turn, Eden instructed Baxter to stop. They pulled to the side of the road, this time beside a shop called EyeFone. Eden carefully checked the map on her screen and then crosschecked it with their location, according to the sat nav.

"That, gentlemen, is our island." Eden pointed out the left side of the truck. Sure enough, the land rose slightly to the left, but the view didn't hold much promise. The place was as far from an archaeological site as Eden thought possible. It looked like any of the other dusty city blocks they'd passed. A haphazard collection of concrete buildings appeared to fill every inch of the space. In front of the buildings, an aging collection of cars were not so much parked, as totally abandoned.

"I don't see how this can be the right place," Beaumont said, sighing. The professor rubbed a hand across his face.

"This is the place your translation told us to look, and that's what we're going to do." Eden scrambled out of the car and darted across the road.

The men followed, Mo looking forlorn to have left his cakes.

"Anything here will have been destroyed decades ago. The builders of these won't have cared what they poured concrete over." Beaumont glanced up at the buildings.

Eden agreed, these were exactly the sort of quickly built utilitarian blocks that could have inadvertently concealed the find of the century.

"Beaumont, you're with me. We'll start on this side. Baxter and Mo, you start over there. Remember, we're looking for anything that could be used to access an underground passage."

The three men nodded, Beaumont reluctantly, and two by two they trudged into the tangle of buildings.

For almost half an hour, Eden and Beaumont wound their way through the block, examining each street, passage, and doorway in turn. The whole area, over four-hundred-feet in all directions, was built on or covered in concrete.

Seeing Baxter and Mo again, Eden could tell from their expressions that they'd not found anything either.

"Find anything?" Eden asked anyway.

"Nothing," Baxter replied, shaking his head.

Beaumont flicked a dismissing wrist up at the buildings. "All the buildings we saw were no older than the late twentieth century. There's no knowing what they've covered up in desperation to throw these places up."

"It's not good at all," Mo added mournfully.

Dejected, they climbed back into the truck. Baxter turned the key. The truck coughed twice before the engine caught, as though it too was reluctant to give up the search. Baxter pulled away and started back in the direction of the villa.

The four sat in silence as Baxter turned back onto the main road. Possible solutions streamed through Eden's mind. The entrance to this secret passageway could just be there, a few feet below the surface. It was tantalizingly close, but without knowing where to look, also impossibly far away.

Brake lights strobed from the vehicles ahead as they slowed to pass a group of men working on the road. A truck, overladen with crates, lumbered into the oncoming lane. Baxter took a more cautious approach, staying as close to the temporary barrier as possible. Eden peered out at the road workers. Three or four men worked in a hole, striking the ground with pickaxes, and a similar number stood idly nearby. Suddenly, a phrase which Little Mo had used the previous day bounced into her mind. She sat up straight as the idea took shape.

"As above, so below," Eden said out loud, turning and grinning at the men.

Baxter, Beaumont, and Mo looked at her, puzzled.

"What?" Baxter said, turning his attention back to the road and accelerating beyond the road works.

"As above, so below," Eden said, almost shouting now. "Just because we can't see the entrance, doesn't mean it's not there."

"Yes, obviously," Beaumont said. "We know it's there somewhere it's just—"

"There's no access to it from the street." Eden interrupted. "But what if we could get below the street?"

"I don't under—"

"The sewers!" Little Mo exclaimed from the back seat.

"Exactly," Eden said. "Cairo is a massive city, right? That means they'll be tunnels crisscrossing everywhere."

"Many of the sewers here are based around tunnels which are thousands of years old," Mo said. "Several generations have just enlarged the older system, rather than building new ones."

Baxter slammed on the brakes. A bus, forced to shudder to a stop, protested on its horn.

Eden dug out her phone and searched for local road working supply stores. She found the closest and put the sat nav to work. "Take us here," Eden said, showing Baxter the location of the store on the street.

"You got it," he said, snapping the truck into gear and pulling a one-eighty.

28

THE SUN WAS PASSING its zenith as Baxter stopped the truck in the location where the island would once have been. The abandoned cars, which this morning had sat in the shadows of the building, now baked in direct sunlight. Visible heat currents danced, rising from their rusting bodies.

Eden climbed down from the truck and paced along the road. It didn't take her long to find what she was looking for. "Pull up here," she shouted, pointing at an access cover at the side of the road.

Baxter nudged the gas, and the truck rolled forwards. Eden beckoned him closer until the truck's nose sat just over the hole.

Baxter got out of the truck and Mo scrambled into the driver's seat.

"Get out of here at any sign of trouble," Baxter said. "We will fend for ourselves if we need to."

Eden flipped down the tailgate and rummaged through the items they had just bought. First, she selected a large iron tool, which looked a bit like an oversize pry bar. She fitted it into the center of the metal cover and twisted it to the right. Reluctantly, and with a lot of effort from Eden, the heavy metal cover clunked, then screeched from its locked position.

Baxter stepped across and helped Eden heave the heavy cover out of its mounting.

Eden dug out a flashlight and peered into the gaping hole. The first thing to greet her was the cloying, nauseating odor of raw sewage.

"This is definitely a sewer," Eden said, feeling bile rise in her throat.

"No doubt about that," Baxter said, taking a step back from the stench.

Eden held her breath and sunk into a crouch. A shaft dropped about ten feet, beneath which the sewer opened into a wider tunnel. Rungs bolted to the side of the shaft oozed with sticky brown liquid.

"Lucky we've got the gear," Baxter said, pulling more items from the back of the truck. Baxter and Eden pulled on thick rubber trousers which went all the way over their shoes and were held up by straps across their shoulders. They then slipped on thick rubber gloves and head torches. Eden shoved the other things they might need into a water-proof sack and slipped it on to her back.

"I'll go first," Eden said, stepping towards the manhole.

She glanced around the street. Although cars and pedestrians continued to stream past, no one paid them any attention.

"Lower the cable," Eden shouted to Mo.

Mo flicked a switch, and the winch on the truck's front bumper buzzed. Designed to pull the two-ton truck out of sticky situations, the motor would easily handle this challenge. The steel cable slipped slowly down into the void.

Eden peered down into the hole. When the end of the

cable reached the base of the sewer, she gave Mo a thumbs up. The motor stopped. Eden dropped into a crouch and sat on the edge of the hole, her feet dangling over the putrid river below. Then, without giving herself a chance to think it through, Eden gripped the cable and slipped down into the world beneath.

If Eden thought the smell from the street was bad, down below was a different league entirely. She lowered herself hand over hand down the cable, her stomach threatening to purge her lunch at any moment.

Beyond the shaft, the sewer opened into a tunnel about ten feet in diameter. Along the base of the tunnel, a torrid stream of brown liquid ran in the direction of the river. Eden heard the scurrying and squeak of rats somewhere nearby. Eden touched down on the tunnel's slimy floor. Fortunately, the river of sewage was only a couple of inches deep, meaning she could easily walk on the drier parts of the tunnel at either side. Eden tugged the cable twice and then moved a few feet up further into the sewer.

The air in the tunnel felt at least a few degrees cooler than the outside, although the stinking humidity had increased. Eden's clothes already felt as though they were sticking to her skin. She checked the reading on her watch. It was five degrees cooler than on the street and the humidity was a touch under eighty percent.

Baxter shimmied effortlessly down the cable.

"This way," Eden said, pointing up the slight incline in the direction of the island.

Above them, the truck's engine growled. Mo rolled the vehicle forwards, covering the hole completely. The light now blocked out, the sewer darkened further. Eden glanced up at the truck's underbelly.

"The things I do for humankind," Eden muttered, picking her way forward.

Their lights sweeping through the otherwise total darkness, Eden and Baxter crept through the sewer. Hearing another squeaking, scurrying noise, Eden spun around. At the very edge of the light beam, several rats, their fur slick with excrement, scurried away. She suppressed a shudder and trudged on.

"Talk about primordial soup," Eden said, watching the liquid ooze along the center of the tunnel.

"That's a truckload of bacteria," Baxter agreed. "Maybe even a new species or two."

"That's way out of our job description," Eden muttered. She swept the beam along the tunnel wall. "It's made from concrete sections. Look."

"Yeah," Baxter mumbled in agreement. "So much for the tunnels of ancient eras that Mo thought we'd find. This can't be more than fifty years old."

They pushed on in silence for a few minutes, the only sound being the squelching of their boots against the slimy sewage.

"I think we're on the land that used to be the island now," Baxter said. The tunnel's incline had come to a stop. In front of them the sewer leveled out and behind them it ran downwards. "How big did Beaumont estimate the area was?"

"He theorized that the island was about two hundred feet across," Eden said.

Baxter laughed. "Theorization—I've never heard pulling stuff out of thin air to be described so glamorously."

"People take this seriously, though." Eden's light swept across the concrete of the sewer's interior as she looked for signs of another tunnel or opening. "Think about how many theories are now considered to be mainstream science. At one point or another, they were just pulled out of the air by people like our Beaumont."

"Like gravity," Baxter suggested.

"Yeah, I suppose. Although that's kind of hard to argue with, unless you're a bird."

Baxter turned and looked back the way they'd come. As well as climbing gently, the sewer had curved to the right, obscuring their view of the hole through which they entered. Something rumbled high above them—a bus or truck, maybe. Dust floated down through the beams of light.

"Hold on a minute, do you feel that?" Eden said, stopping. She swept her light carefully around the tunnel ahead.

Baxter turned and stepped up behind Eden. "I don't—"

"It's getting warmer." Eden glanced at the readings on her watch. "Yes, it's two degrees warmer than down there. The humidity's lower too."

Baxter shrugged. "Something to do with the incline, maybe."

They trudged on, their feet squelching through the sluggishly flowing sewage. The further along the pipe they plodded, the deeper the sewage became. To start with, they could no longer walk on the dry edges of the tunnel, then the liquid ran just across the top of their feet. Then it rose further, slopping up and around their ankles.

"I can feel that now," Baxter said, a couple of minutes later. "It's definitely got warmer."

Eden checked her watch and agreed. "It's now two degrees above the temperature outside, and the humidity has dropped by twenty percent."

"That makes no sense at all. We're underground, in a tunnel full of water—"

"And other things," Eden added, watching something gross drift past her shin.

"And all sorts of other things I don't want to think about. But it should get cooler and wetter if anything, right?"

"Agreed," Eden said, wading forwards.

The beam of Eden's light caught something in the tunnel wall fifty feet ahead. Eden froze and examined the anomaly. A flat panel jutted out from the curved wall of the tunnel. The panel ran about halfway from the floor to the roof.

"Check that out," she said to Baxter, quickening her pace.

Eden sloshed forwards, the level of the slurry increasing from her shin to above her knees as the tunnel ran slightly downhill. With the depth of the slurry and the slippery concrete beneath, Eden had to push forwards frustratingly slowly. It was like walking through two feet of custard, she thought, the image making the task of wading through human excrement slightly easier.

Strangely, either the smell in this part of the tunnel was less vile, or Eden and Baxter had become used to it.

Eden reached the panel a few moments before Baxter. She ran her finger around the panel's edge but couldn't feel anything through the thick rubber gloves. She held her watch up to the side of the panel. Slowly, the temperature reading rose, and the humidity reading fell. Eden turned to Baxter, excitement burning in her eyes. "Whatever's in here, it's not another sewer."

"Yes boss, we've followed them out to Nazlet-El-Samman," Sharif said, sitting in the passenger seat of their dusty Isuzu

Trooper. Abdul sat in the driver's seat, tapping a beat on the steering wheel.

Sharif lifted the binoculars to his eyes again. Two hundred feet away, the two older men sat in a rusting Toyota pickup. A few minutes ago, Abdul and Sharif had watched Eden and the younger man disappear down through the hole beneath the truck.

"What are they doing there?" King's brusque voice strained through the vehicle's old speakers. Sharif heard the humming of a machine in the background and assumed she was in the gym. The woman was something of a fitness fanatic.

"Will you stop that?" Sharif hissed at Abdul as his percussive tapping reached a crescendo. Abdul removed his hands from the wheel as though burned.

"What?" King said.

"No, not you, boss. Sorry. Yes, but this is interesting. The girl and the young guy have just gone down into the sewer."

"That is interesting," King replied. The humming noise stopped. Abdul heard King moving from room to room. He heard papers rustling and assumed she'd moved through to the office.

"The Island of Trampling," King said, thoughtfully.

"What's that, boss?"

"Hold on a minute, let me think."

Abdul and Sharif sat in silence, listening to King flick through papers and mutter to herself.

"That could be it," King said, excitedly. "They might be on to something. Gentlemen, you're going to have to follow them. Do not let them out of your sight."

"But boss," Sharif said. King had already hung up.

"And how exactly do you propose we follow them with

these two watching the hole?" Abdul said, pointing towards the Toyota Hilux.

"We'll get them to move on," Abdul said, glancing at a pair of police officers in his rear-view mirror.

29

EDEN WORKED QUICKLY, removing the two chunky bolts on her side of the metal panel. Despite the age of the fixings, the bolts slipped out by hand with relative ease. Years of rancid sewage clearly worked well for keeping such things lubricated. Baxter removed the two bolts on the other side of the panel. When the panel was free of its fixings, Eden and Baxter lifted it away from the wall. A gust of warm air streamed in from the tunnel behind the panel.

Eden and Baxter shone their lights into the passage. Unlike the modern concrete of the sewer, big blocks of sand colored stone made up the walls here. The passage looked dry too, sand covering the floor.

Eden scrambled through the opening and into the new tunnel. She could stand up with ease. It looked as though they were in a wide vertical shaft with a spiral staircase running around the walls. Eden swung her light around. The stairs rose to the left and fell to the right. She stepped carefully towards the center and peered downwards. Water rippled at the base of the shaft, one hundred feet below.

"I think we've found our well," Eden said, stepping

slowly away from the edge. With no railing, the drop felt perilous.

"I never doubted we would," Baxter said, scrambling out of the sewer and looking around in amazement. "It's mad that this is just beneath one of those buildings."

"Look at that," Eden said, studying how the modern sewer intersected the ancient passage. Several of the sand-colored blocks were missing and a few more lay shattered. "It looks as though they just dug straight through this when that sewer was built, then just covered it up with that plate. There's no record of this passage in the official documents, though."

"Strange. Maybe someone didn't want it to be investigated."

"A cover up, you mean?"

"Possibly," Baxter shrugged. "We should probably cover that hole again."

Eden agreed, and together they heaved the metal plate back into position. They couldn't re-secure the bolts from this side but having been cut to size, it sat securely in place.

With the sewer blocked off, Eden felt her sense of smell begin to recover.

"I say we go down," Eden said, her light pointing at the stairs curving down towards the water.

"Absolutely, but first I'm getting out of these stinking things." Baxter slipped out of his now slimy rubber trousers and pulled off his gloves. Eden did the same and felt a lot lighter for it. The sewage covered clothes deposited in a pile, the pair set off down the spiral staircase.

The air felt heavier as Eden and Baxter neared the water. Eden's senses were on full alert. She took time to try and notice everything, wondering whether their next clue would be nearby. She slid her phone from the dry bag and took pictures of everything. Just because something didn't stand out to her, didn't mean Beaumont or Little Mo wouldn't make sense of it.

First, she photographed the steps set into the floor. Despite the apparent age of the structure, they were hardly worn at all. To Eden, that indicated the well must have been scarcely used, although perhaps the experts would 'theorize' something different.

"What's that noise?" Baxter said, pausing to listen closely.

Eden had been so preoccupied photographing one of the small niches set into the walls at regular intervals that she hadn't even noticed. She turned to face the base of the well and listened closely. Sure enough, a faint bubbling sound streamed down the enclosed space.

"It sounds like we'll find out very soon," Eden said, setting off at a quickened pace.

After another minute or so of descent, all the while feeling hot air blowing towards the surface, they reached the water.

Eden swept the beam of light across the water. What surprised her, what she hadn't been able to see from above, was that the water bubbled furiously. The stairs continued to curve down beneath the crystal-clear water.

"That explains the sound," Eden said, her light sweeping across the surface.

"If this is a well, why would it be bubbling like this?" Baxter said. "It smells sulphuric."

Eden sniffed the air. She hadn't noticed the smell of the water after enduring the odor of the sewer, but Baxter was right.

Eden crouched down and tried to peer beneath the level of the water. Although the water was clear, the aggressive bubbles obscured her view beyond a few feet. Eden tentatively dipped her fingers in the water. It was warm and felt strangely soft—like the water she'd experienced bathing in the geysers of Iceland. Eden lifted her fingers to her nose and sniffed.

Satisfied it wasn't going to harm her, Eden dipped her fingers in the water again and then touched her tongue. There was no taste of salt, instead the water tasted slightly chalky.

"What are you doing!" Baxter hissed. "That could have all sorts of chemicals or dangerous substance in it."

"It's fresh water," Eden said. "I would guess it comes from the Nile. It's a bit sulfureous, but that's not harmful. Anything coming down from the surface here would have to get through several hundred feet of rock." Eden pointed her light up at the hewn walls of the shaft. "That's a pretty effective filtration system."

Baxter glanced up.

Eden stood and stripped down to her underwear.

"Now what are you doing?" Baxter said, his face turning bright red. Eden glanced at Baxter, he quickly pretended to be interested in something on the other side of the shaft. Wearing a sports bra and shorts, Eden was hardly revealing anything to him.

"It was just getting really warm down here, and I thought I'd be more comfortable this way."

Baxter mumbled a reply.

"Have you never seen..." Eden feigned taking off her bra, and Baxter's face turned from red to something nearing purple. "Just kidding. I'm going in. I suspect there's something under the water level there. Maybe it's just an airlock, meaning I can swim through and come up on the other side."

"But I, I'm not sure that's a good idea. Even if you can get through, we don't know what the air is like on the other side. There could be pathogens, or…"

Eden didn't hear the end of Baxter's sentence as she walked down into the water, took a deep breath, and submerged herself.

Holding the light in one hand, Eden kicked downwards. The beam flicked from one wall to the other, illuminating thousands of bubbles coming the other way. Eden kicked again, diving six, twelve and then fifteen feet beneath the water. She felt the pressure push against her ears as she descended. Eden kicked again, flighting her body's natural buoyancy.

She swung the light around the shaft, aware that the air in her lungs was starting to wane. Then, ten feet below her, she spotted an opening to the right. She kicked down again. About twelve feet across, the opening appeared to be the source of the bubbles.

Eden kicked and swam into the opening. Moving out of the stream of the bubbles, she was able to look down the tunnel. Twenty feet further on, the tunnel rose at a sharp angle. It looked like an airlock, just as she'd suspected.

Her lungs now screaming from the exertion, Eden kicked on. Ignoring Baxter's warnings of pathogens inside the airlock, she reached the turn in the tunnel and swam upwards as hard as she could. The water's surface shimmered above her. A few seconds later, Eden broke though the surface and gasped a lungful of air. It tasted fine and sated her burning lungs.

So far so good, she thought.

She'd emerged into another tunnel here. Again, the structure looked as though it was carefully hewn from solid rock.

Suddenly Eden felt something move beneath her. A dark shape rushed through the water, finally breaking through the surface. Baxter appeared, also gasping for breath.

"What about the dangerous pathogens?" Eden said, climbing out of the water and brushing the droplets from her skin. The air was warm and humid. A slope had been cut into the floor of the tunnel making it easy to walk out of the water.

"I thought it was worth the risk. Plus, I thought you'd need your bag." Baxter held up the dry bag which Eden had left on the floor as she'd undressed. Baxter paced out of the water.

Now it was Eden's turn to look away with something like embarrassment. Baxter had stripped down to his underwear, revealing a well-muscled body. A patchwork of scars covered his skin, hinting at previous scrapes and escapes. Eden remembered that the last time she'd seen him in Lebanon, he'd had a knife sticking out of his back.

"You see that?" Baxter said, turning his flashlight from one side of the tunnel to the other.

Eden looked at the walls, both were bare rock. "No, what?"

"The ancient Egyptians liked to write hieroglyphs on everything, didn't they? But there's none here."

Eden studied the walls again. Baxter was right.

Eden and Baxter set off at a slow jog down the tunnel. "With all those twists I've no idea in which direction we're going, but I'd put money on us now heading towards The Pyramids," Eden said, shining her light down the passage.

"Let's hope so, otherwise I've no idea what we'll find."

"What's that?" Eden said, pointing her light down the

tunnel. Fifty feet further on, it looked as though the tunnel reached a dead end.

"Maybe it just curves out of sight," Baxter said, quickening his pace.

A few seconds later, they reached a giant slab of rock which blocked the passage. Eden stepped close to the slab and panned her light from one side to the next. The slab looked as though it was constructed from a single piece of granite. Slightly different in color and texture to the walls, the slab had clearly been consciously placed there. Although who had the power to place such a giant object this far beneath the ground, Eden couldn't even begin to imagine.

"Look at that," Baxter said, his light focusing on one side of the slab.

Eden stepped across, her eyes scanning the rock's surface.

Painstakingly carved into the slab, and beautifully preserved here beneath the ground, were a neat set of hieroglyphs.

"The only ones in the tunnel. They must be important." Eden ran her light from one symbol to the next, to the next.

"Although they make no sense to me, I think we're on the right path," Baxter said. He swung the dry bag from his shoulder and dug out their camera. He photographed the hieroglyphs carefully, checking the screen to make sure he got a clear picture of each.

"What are the chances that these tell us how to get past this slab?" Eden said, looking up at the immovable rock as Baxter finished taking the photos.

"Let's get these pictures to Beaumont and Mo," Baxter said, stashing the camera away. "They'll know exactly what we need to do next."

POCKETING two thousand Egyptian pounds with a sleight of hand that David Blaine would be proud of, the pair of police officers sidled towards the pickup. The larger and senior of the two, an officer of nearly ten years named Salah, tightened his belt, and in doing so checked that his holstered side arm and handcuffs were where they needed to be. He didn't expect to need them to get a truck moved on, but on the streets of Cairo, you just never knew. The easiest jobs could sometimes turn into the most difficult—it just depended on who you came up against.

He wanted to make sure this one happened expediently, though, there was another two thousand at stake.

"Let me do the talking," he barked at Mostafa, his junior officer, as they neared the pickup. Salah directed Mostafa to the passenger side, as he sidled around towards the driver.

Leaning over slightly, Salah tapped on the glass and gave the universal sign to lower the window. At just over six feet four, Salah had to lean over, even for big vehicles like this.

The man in the driving seat wound down the window with one hand and popped the last bit of what looked like a pastry into his mouth.

Salah peered into the vehicle, narrowing his eyes. The big man in the driving seat looked like an Egyptian with olive skin and jet-black hair that was graying around the temples. Salah's beady eyes moved on to the passenger. This man was not Egyptian, English probably. His skin was the color of wet pastry and his thin grey hair looked like winter clouds.

"What are you doing here?" Salah barked.

"We're waiting for some friends. They've just gone to a shop nearby," the Egyptian replied.

Salah's gaze narrowed even further. The guy seemed nervous, almost as though he was hiding something. Salah thought about the money already burning a hole in his pocket. Whatever these guys were up to, he didn't care. He just needed to get them moved on.

"You can't wait here. I need you to move on now."

The driver looked briefly at the passenger, whose blank expression indicated that he probably didn't know what was going on. "But then they won't know where we've gone. Five minutes, officer, then we will be gone."

Salah felt the first spark of rage in his gut. His fingers tensed on his belt.

"No, you will start the truck right now, or I will drag you down to the station and give you a ticket."

"Just for parking in the wrong place?" the driver said. "A trip to the station for a parking violation is a bit extreme, no?"

Salah sensed that the man was talking now purely to waste his time. He snarled and dropped into a crouch, as though preparing to wrestle the driver from the vehicle.

"Are you being cheeky with me? That is it, I'm not being spoken to like some idiot," Salah spat out the words.

"I'm not being cheeky, officer. Just questioning the efficiency of your tactics here."

Salah rose a finger and pointed at the man. "It is not your place to question me, sir. You will move on now, or not only will I take you to the station, I'll... I'll."

"Come on, let's go," the passenger said, in flawless Arabic. Whilst not the locally spoken Egyptian dialect, Salah was still surprised. He blinked several times.

"Fine. We will move on now," the driver said angrily. He started the vehicle, revved it hard and roared off down the street.

The pickup turned a corner and disappeared out of sight ahead. Just a few seconds later, the Isuzu pulled up beside the officers.

The two large African men scrambled out. They rushed around the front of the vehicle and peered down an open access hole.

Salah hadn't seen the access hole before, as it had been beneath the pickup. He shrugged. Whatever was going on here was none of his business. He clicked his fingers and one of the men sidled across and handed him another wad of notes.

"Not a word of this," Salah said, glancing at Mostafa.

The younger officer nodded, accepting his share of the money.

If they got paid, who cared? Salah and Mostafa wandered off back towards their patrol car.

30

"I just can't believe the cheek of it," Little Mo said, spitting out the words as though they caused him great pain. "Men like that should not be allowed in the police."

"But Mo, it doesn't..." Beaumont tried to interrupt the raging Egyptian but couldn't get a word in.

"It just makes me so angry that someone should speak to us like that. And to do it in front of a foreigner too." Mo glanced at Beaumont in the passenger seat. "What sort of impression are they making of our country if a man can't even park in the street without being hassled? And one more thing..."

"Mo, it doesn't matter at all because..."

Mo glanced at Beaumont, taking his eyes off the road. "It does matter. How are we going to get Eden and..."

"Stop the truck!" Beaumont shouted, uncharacteristically.

Mo turned just in time to see two people step out in front of the vehicle, waving their arms above their heads.

He stomped on the pedal. The brakes of the aging pickup squealed. Tires skidded against the asphalt. Mo and

Beaumont shot forward in their seats, restrained by their belts. Loose objects in the back crashed and banged around.

"Are you trying to kill us!" Eden said, walking around and climbing into the truck's back seats. Baxter climbed in beside her.

"What, I don't under..."

"While you were busy arguing with the officer back there, I saw Eden and Baxter walk out of the side street here," Beaumont explained.

"We saw you had company, and thought it better to wait out of sight," Eden said, finishing off the story.

Mo looked from Eden back to Beaumont.

"You didn't come back out through the sewer?" Beaumont said, noticing the pair no longer wore the rubber protective gear.

"We found another way out. It comes out in the basement of a vacant laundromat back there. It must have just been there for years, undisturbed," Baxter said.

"You wait until you see what we've got for you," Eden said excitedly. Mo noticed her hair was slicked back in a ponytail.

"The question is," Baxter said. "Why did those officers take such an interest in where you were parking?"

Mo considered this, snapped the truck into gear and pulled a one-eighty. He drove back out to the junction and paused. The truck's occupants craned their necks to peer around the corner.

Two hundred feet down the road, a dusty Isuzu Trooper 4x4 sat in the exact position the pickup had been a few minutes before. The police officers were nowhere to be seen.

"I knew it," Mo hissed. "Those officers were as corrupt as they come. I can only apologize for the behavior of my fellow Egyptians."

Two large African men appeared from the rear of the Isuzu and gazed down into the open access hole.

Eden instantly recognized the men, as the pair she had met with Lulu King. She drew a sharp intake of breath. Again, she considered telling the others who they were. No, she decided, for now she would continue to keep that to herself.

Two hundred feet away, the men exchanged some words. One of the men pulled a rope from a duffel bag, tied one end of the rope to the Trooper's tow bar, and dropped it down into the sewer.

"They really shouldn't go down there dressed like that," Eden said, noticing the men wore black combat trousers and shirts. "Without proper waterproof gear they're going to get seriously messy."

The first man gripped hold of the rope and lowered himself down. A few seconds later, the second man followed.

"Perfect," Eden said, climbing out of the car. "Wait here a second."

Eden covered the two hundred feet quickly. She peered down the access hole. The men were already out of sight, picking their way along the tunnel. Silently, Eden untied the rope and dropped it down into the sewer. She slid the metal cover back into place. Then, with a grin on her face, she strolled back to the pickup.

"That should keep them busy for a while," Eden said, climbing in. "Back to the villa. We've got another code to solve."

31

Mo screeched to a stop outside the villa, sending a torrent of bleached gravel skittering across the driveway. During the journey, most of which had been spent in Cairo's nose-to-tail traffic, Eden and Baxter had regaled their discovery of the well, the bubbling water and the hidden passage.

"You really shouldn't have gone in the water without thorough testing," Beaumont said, climbing out of the truck and rushing towards the villa. "There could have been all sorts of things in that water, from viral parabens, an unstable PH content, there's just no knowing. You must go and have a shower immediately."

"That's what I told her," Baxter said, before adding in little more than a whisper. "But you can't tell Eden Black to do anything."

Eden turned to face the two men. "Hey, if I hadn't gone in there, then we still wouldn't know what to do, right? Plus, you followed me."

"Sure, but it's not worth risking your life for," Beaumont continued. "After all, you're important. We could always have gone back when..."

"No way, not with those guys on our tail." Eden folded her arms. "This is not some relaxing jolly-up in the country-side. We're not messing about, digging up long dead skele-tons with a paint brush here. Oh great, another Iron Age arrowhead! This is real, dangerous. We haven't got time to mess around." Eden spun on her heels and crossed to the table where Mo was switching on one of the computers.

"You know what," Beaumont said in a whisper, catching Baxter's eye. "I wouldn't want Eden Black to be any other way."

Baxter looked away almost guiltily.

"What have we got then?" Mo said, as the computer loaded up.

Eden swung the bag from her shoulder and dug out the camera. She passed it to Mo. The Egyptian selected the correct cable and connected it to the computer. Several images filled the screen. Beaumont stepped in close to study them as well.

"It certainly looks as though they're from the same period as those you recovered from Aswan." Mo pointed at one symbol which looked like a bird. "This symbol isn't used in later..."

"But what do they mean?" Eden said, impatiently.

Mo turned and glanced at Eden. "It's not that simple. There isn't an app I can use to translate them in two seconds. This is an ancient art that only a few people in the world are capable of deciphering. There are also several potential translations which I must cycle through to find..."

"Alright I get it," Eden said, slumping onto one of the high stools which surrounded the kitchen island. "How long do you think it will take?"

"Right now, I can't even tell you that. Why don't you go

and get yourself freshened up, it is smelling a bit like..." Mo drew a circle in the air while he searched for the correct word.

Baxter roared with laughter, drawing the attention of the Egyptian.

"Even with your wash in the primordial waters of Giza, you both stink," Beaumont said.

Eden grinned at Baxter like a child getting their own way. "Fine," she said, standing and lumbering towards the stairs. Baxter followed her upstairs and turned towards his bedroom, like a scorned child.

Eden padded through to her ensuite bathroom and flipped the shower on to its hottest setting. She let the water run until steam curled towards the ceiling. Examining herself in the large mirror above the sink, the water in the tunnel had left her skin covered in a white residue. Her hair had dried into a stiff wadded mess.

Eden stripped off and stepped beneath the streaming water. She rubbed soap onto her body and then let the powerful hot jets pummel her skin for a few minutes. Then she flipped the tap the other way. The cold water invigorated and enlivened her. She counted out sixty seconds, cut off the water, stepped from the shower, toweled down and headed out into her bedroom.

Looking at the items on her dressing table for the first time, Eden froze. In an old trick her father had taught her, Eden always left several items around the room in seemingly random places. Anyone entering the room, would not realize that she had painstakingly recorded the location of each.

Eden stepped towards the dressing table. The notebook, which she'd placed at the back left, was now in the center.

The pile of loose notes, instead of sitting fanned out were neatly stacked.

Eden thought about it carefully, remembering if she'd set out the items as she usually did. She remembered going through her usual process the night before. Things in this room had moved, that Eden knew for sure. Eden also knew who was behind such an intrusion: Lulu King. While her men were keeping tabs on them out in Nazlet-El-Samman, Lulu had come into their villa. Eden glanced around the room, there was only one reason King would want access to the place—to leave something behind.

They'd been bugged.

Without a word, Eden moved around the room, checking for hidden devices. First, she checked the ceiling, the television set, the smoke alarm, but everything there looked normal. Nowhere else in the room would give the viewer a decent picture, so King must just have bugged for audio. That was a smart move, Eden thought. Audio bugs were smaller, had longer battery life, and could be tucked away out of sight.

She dressed quickly and bounded down the stairs.

Baxter having already showered and changed, rummaged through the fridge.

Beaumont and Little Mo stood bent over the laptop, engrossed in the translation.

"I think we just might have something," Beaumont said, straightening up. "It's early, and we've had to send a couple of the images off to colleagues back in Cambridge, but I think we have a start."

"Great," Eden said, holding a finger to her lips and crossing to the desk. "Before we do that, let's eat. Now I've got the primordial soup out of my hair, I'm famished."

Beaumont looked at Eden quizzically. It was unlike her

to consider the needs of her stomach above their discoveries.

"Fabulous idea," Little Mo said, straightening up and patting his stomach. "My stomach is starting to think I've been beheaded."

Eden pulled a pad of paper across the desk and scribbled a note.

We've been bugged.

Two MILES away at her hotel in central Cairo, Lulu King looked from Abdul to Sharif and back again. Wet through and covered in stinking debris from the sewer, the men looked uncomfortable already. Not uncomfortable enough, King thought, not nearly uncomfortable enough.

"I just don't understand how you managed that," Lulu said, pacing across the carpet.

Through the floor to ceiling windows, the lights of inner-city Cairo had begun to twinkle in the dying daylight. The angular shapes of the Great Pyramid, bulky and muscular, crouched on the distant horizon, serving as an ever-present reminder to King about their mission here in Egypt.

"You idiots were given instructions to follow Eden and her little band of amateurs, and to tell me whatever they found. I told you, I made it explicitly clear, that we can't have them knowing anything we don't. This whole plan is based on us knowing what they know. Please tell me, you bumbling fools, what went wrong?" King pointed a perfectly manicured finger at Sharif.

The Angolan mumbled something inaudible.

"Speak up!" King roared.

"We followed them down into the sewer."

"I can see that!" King bellowed, pointing at the damp patches on the suite's luxurious carpet.

"We followed them down, but the sewer was a dead end. We tried both ways, but there was nothing."

"How did they get out then?"

Sharif shrugged.

"Because they did get out, didn't they?"

"They must have," Abdul spoke for the first time. "They must have taken all the proper gear, though. They must have had time to plan it properly. We were just there in our normal clothes. We had no tools or anything."

"You are elite soldiers. Or at least that's what I thought you were. That's what you're *supposed to* be. Are you telling me I'm wrong?"

Both men shook their heads.

"Not only did they get away from you, but they managed to trap you in the sewer. Like stinking rats. How did that happen?"

"They must have found another way out and..."

"So, there was another way out?" A vein in the side of King's head throbbed with anger. She placed her fingertips on her temples and closed her eyes. "Get out of here and get cleaned up," she whispered. "You stink."

"Yes, boss, sorry, boss," both men said, shuffling towards the doors of their adjoining rooms.

Lulu slumped into a chair and looked up at the grand ceiling. Some psychotic interior designers had thought it appropriate to have the room decorated like a renaissance painting.

"What are you looking at?" King glared at a trio of annoyingly cheerful painted cherubs, messing around with a harp. "At least one of us has been making progress," she whispered to herself, sliding her iPad from her bag. She loaded an app and saw the status of all the bugs she'd planted in Eden's villa. All were online and broadcasting as they should.

King tapped the one for the kitchen. The sound of movement came down the line followed by voices. King sat up straight and put on a pair of headphones. She checked the app to make sure the system was recording.

"What do you think about that?" one man asked. From his accent, King assumed he was local, Arabic at least.

"It could mean any number of things. It depends on the context," replied a man with an English accent.

"Richard Beaumont," King whispered to herself. "We will meet again, that I know for sure."

The Egyptian man grumbled, and King heard the striking of keys. King cursed herself for not being able to install video bugs too, but she hadn't had the time. Audio only would have to do.

Then the bug in the kitchen picked up the sound of approaching footsteps, followed by a female voice.

"Eden," King said, grinning.

"Let's eat," Eden said, cheerfully. "Now I've got the primordial soup out of my hair, I'm famished."

"Fabulous idea," replied the Egyptian. "My stomach is starting to think that I've been beheaded."

Several footsteps clicked towards the door, and a set of keys jangled. The door slammed, then, faintly, King heard the truck start up and grumbled away.

King listened to the silence for several seconds. When it was clear that the villa was empty, she set the app to notify her if any noise was detected and then slid the iPad away.

King sat back and thought through the situation. In a way, the bugs were not necessary. She had Eden over a barrel. But King knew from experience, trapped people could still be very dangerous indeed.

Often people with fewer options were even more dangerous as they were likely to take silly risks and act in unpredictable ways. That was a chance King couldn't take. This way, she was covered, whatever Eden decided to do.

32

THE BASHTAK RESTAURANT in Khan El-Kalili was exactly the sort of place Eden loved to visit while traveling. Fabrics in red and gold covered the walls and tables, and the smell of spices and incense hung thick in the air. The sound of babbled conversation in several languages drifted through the room. To Eden, it was the sort of anonymous place that made her feel instantly at home.

Eden and Baxter sat on one side of the small table with Beaumont and Mo on the other.

"Do we have any idea who would want to listen in to our conversation?" Baxter said,

Eden kept quiet. All the while Baxter, Mo and Beaumont played their cards close, she would do the same.

"There are many people whose fortunes are based on what we are set to discover," Mo said. "You saw those men today in Nazet-El-Samman. They were not there by accident. The Council of Selene is not the only powerful organization who want this for themselves. We always knew this might be an issue."

"Who, though, and how do we stop them?" Baxter pressed.

"I don't think we can. We are but four people." Mo slurped his second cup of chai.

"We can move quietly, though," Beaumont said.

"What should we do about the bugs? I say we go back there, find them, and destroy them. That will make a point that we're on to them." Baxter struck the table with his closed fist.

"Not so hasty," Mo said, dabbing his mouth with a napkin. "We know they are listening, but they don't yet know that we know, correct?"

Eden nodded. "Maybe we could use this to our advantage. Whatever we do, we don't have to decide right now. What have you both found out about the hieroglyphs?"

"Now this is very interesting," Little Mo said, his whispered voice sounding like a cat's purr. "The first part reads like instructions. It talks about the careful balance of water pressure in the cave system. The whole place is like some kind of pressure chamber. The only way to get into the vault is to stop the flow of water. That will allow that slab you discovered to be moved, I think."

"No wonder those using dynamite couldn't get anywhere," Beaumont said, referencing several so-called archaeologists of the past who had tried to blast their way into The Plateau.

"Does it tell us how to do that?" Eden pressed.

"Yes, actually, it's very specific, although you won't like it. There's a sluice gate which must be dropped down a shaft. When the slab rests at the bottom of the shaft, it works something like a dam, slowing the flow of the water. This must be done exactly as instructed. The sluice gate is designed to slow the water, not to stop it."

"Sounds simple enough," Eden quipped, receiving a glance from Mo and Beaumont. "But you haven't told me where the shaft is."

"Yes. That bit makes it rather more difficult I'm afraid."

Eden raised an eyebrow.

"The entrance to the shaft is on the back of The Sphinx."

"You're joking, right?" Eden said, laughing out loud. "We need to break into The Giza Plateau, sneak up to The Sphinx and climb into a shaft on its back?"

Little Mo nodded sagely. "That's pretty much it, yes. Only then will the tunnel from Nazlet-El-Samman be accessible. With that sluice gate open, the slab at Nazlet-El-Samman remains in place."

"You know that The Plateau is well protected? They have a security fence surrounding the whole area, armed guards, security cameras, and who knows what else."

"Eden, I'm just telling you what's written here. I've no idea how we're going to do that, but I'm sure you're capable."

"Why do we have to bother with all this?" Baxter asked, impatiently. "There must be a way we can force that slab open. A pneumatic prop or something. We've got all sorts of gear in the truck."

"The whole system is finely balanced, based on the water pressure. The doors will be impossible to open without that," Mo said. "I tell you, this is the only way it can be done."

"It *was* finely balanced," Eden said. "For hundreds of years people have been digging on The Plateau. What's to say they haven't screwed up the balance completely?"

Mo shrugged. "Of course, that's possible. But we must hope not, I suppose. There is one more line, though, right here at the bottom." Mo spun the laptop around and pointed at the final series of hieroglyphs.

Eden studied the symbols, but they made no sense to her. She nodded for Mo to continue.

"This combination I have never seen before."

"We've sent it back to a couple of colleagues of mine at the University," Beaumont said. "They should be able to help. Let me draw your attention to this line, however. This is fascinating." Beaumont pointed to a sentence before reading it out loud. "The Ennead and Almodad will show you the rest of the way."

"The Ennead clearly refers to the nine deities worshipped at Heliopolis," Mo said. "We suspect this is a representation of The Plateau with its nine pyramids."

"That makes sense," Eden said, sipping the tea.

"But I'm sure you'll agree that it's curious because they've mentioned Almodad," Beaumont said.

"I was just about to mention that," Eden quipped, shrugging.

"Almodad is a descendent of Noah, not a deity. It's unusual that they mixed-up Gods and mortals in this sentence. I suspect that's because Almodad is often credited as being the inventor of geometry. So, to find the entrance we must consider The Pyramids, and then use some geometry..."

"Why would we need to use geometry if the entrance is on the top of The Sphinx?" Eden interrupted. "It's a sixty-foot-high stone lion, which is not exactly hard to find."

"That's another mystery," Beaumont said. "I suspect all will become clear when we..."

The laptop trilled, cutting Beaumont off mid-sentence.

Mo spun the laptop around and leaned in towards the screen. His thick fingers flew dexterously across the keys. "Yes, it's from your colleague, via the secure e-mail system.

As we thought, the first line says..." Mo's voice dried up in his throat. He froze in his seat.

Beaumont leaned in and looked at the screen. Reading the words, he visibly paled. "I don't understand. I..."

"What does it say?" Baxter said, craning his neck towards the laptop.

Mo looked up at Eden, unblinking. He looked as though he were in something of a trance.

"I think you should read this for yourself." Mo spun the laptop around.

For a moment, in contrast to the dim restaurant, the bright screen danced in front of Eden's vision. She focused in on the words and read them out loud.

"You now have all you need to see through the mist of confusion. But beware, time waits for no man or woman, Eden."

The four looked at each other for several seconds.

"Time waits for no man or woman, Eden," Beaumont repeated, tapping his chin.

Mo shook his head slowly.

"Eden must be used in the biblical sense, right?" Baxter said, shaking them all out of the trance. "You know, like the garden and snake, all that."

"This form of hieroglyphs pre-date the Bible by several thousand years," Beaumont said.

"Yes, the writing of the Bible, but the stories told come from before that, right?"

"It doesn't make sense in that context," Mo interjected.

For Eden, the conversation sounded like it was happening under water. Her mind spun at double speed, considering all possible angles. Once again, she longed to speak with her father. He would be able to answer this in a few seconds. He would find order where there was chaos and bring clarity where there was presently only confusion. Suddenly, amid the incense floating through the restaurant's air, Eden smelled the scent of chamomile. She remembered the cigarettes her father used to smoke. More than remembered, the smell made her picture him sitting at his desk in the attic office of their house in Brighton. The memory floated in vivid, colorful detail for several seconds. Then the recollection that the house had now been burned to the ground hit her in the stomach and the vision faded, twisting into the picture of her father at the airport. Now she knew that he was alive. That thought burned in her veins like a powerful drug. Eden shook herself back into the present— to find out what had really happened to her father, they needed to get access to that vault. That, right now, was all that mattered.

"That is strange, certainly, but there will be some logical explanation," Eden said, taking control of the situation. "There must be. What's important now is that we get back in there and get what we came for. We're not alone in looking for this, remember. Those men have already found the sewer, and they may have found these hieroglyphs too."

"But how do we get into the shaft on the top of The Sphinx without half of The Plateau's security guards on our case?" Baxter said.

"Don't you worry about that," Mo said, picking up his phone from the table. "I have an idea. Now we go. Time or tide waits for no man or woman, Eden."

33

BEAUMONT DROVE the pickup slowly through the streets of Giza in the direction of the looming pyramids. Mo sat in the passenger seat, Eden and Baxter sat in the back. Inside the truck, all were silent. It was as though the challenges of the evening pressed an unseen weight down over the occupants, forcing them all into reflective silence.

Sliding between a pair of guesthouses, The Plateau came into view. The outlines of the three largest pyramids towered into the night sky. The lights which illuminated The Pyramids during the daily light show had long since been switched off, and the crowds had dispersed, but the monoliths were still visible just by the overflowing light pollution from the nearby city.

Eden glanced at her watch. It was just after 1am. After finishing at the restaurant, they had returned to the villa and silently loaded up the truck. Then they had paced around the villa, acting as though they were going to bed. After climbing between the sheets, each had tip-toed back out to the truck. All going well, King would think they were fast asleep by now.

Come success or failure tonight, they would be back safe and well before King even realized. Or at least, Eden thought, she hoped they would be back safe and well. This was a dangerous mission, from which many people had never returned. Throw Lulu King and her henchmen into the mix, and there was no knowing what might happen.

Beaumont slowed the truck and rolled to a stop in front of the closed security gate. Several security cameras eyed them from high poles. A pair of guards climbed dozily from chairs on the other side of the gate and sauntered up to the bars.

Eden peered through the bars. In the gloom she could just about make out the shape of The Sphinx standing enticingly close.

The guards approached the driver's window. Beaumont wound down the glass. From the passenger seat Mo entered into a quick-fire Arabic exchange with one of the men. The men peered closely at Eden and Baxter in the back of the truck. The Arabic exchange continued. Mo slipped the men a wad of notes. The men glanced at each other, then at the money, then nodded. They slid the gate open quickly and beckoned the truck inside.

Beaumont revved the engine and drove through the gate.

"Was it really that easy? What did you tell them?" Eden asked. She glanced at the guards to see they were both looking at her with something akin to awe.

"I told them that you both are American film stars, come all the way from Hollywood to see The Pyramids at the invitation of our president. You were supposed to be here a few hours ago, but your flight was delayed. Tomorrow you must start filming out in the desert so have just one night in the city."

"They really bought that?" Eden scoffed.

"Absolutely. One of them said he'd even seen one of your films. The Raider of Tombs, or something like that." Mo shrugged.

Eden laughed out loud, then waved at the guards through the glass. They looked away, suddenly bashful.

Beaumont drove the truck away from the gate and then slowed it to a crawl as they approached the back end of the Sphinx. It felt as though he was trying to extend the journey, clearly reluctant to get there.

Peering through the window, Eden was pleased to see The Plateau was deserted. The hordes of the day—the tourists, the hawkers selling knickknacks or those offering horse rides or pictures with camels—had all dispersed with the dying sun.

Beaumont slowed the Toyota further and finally crunched to a stop beneath an overhanging tree. He killed the lights.

Eden climbed out the truck and assessed the scene. Several squat buildings sat beside a rocky outcrop to the right. Ahead, the towering shape of The Pyramids reared skywards, and to their right, almost imperceptible in the gloom, lay The Sphinx.

"Get back," Baxter hissed, seizing Eden by the shoulders, and pulling her back into the shadow. Baxter pointed up the road. A hundred yards away the light from one of the patrols swept through the night. "I'm not sure our cover as film stars will hold up if we're found poking around."

Eden and Baxter crept behind the truck as the patrol neared. Beaumont and Mo slumped down in the front seats. Two men, both armed, although clearly not paying that much attention, strolled down the road. Fortunately, they paid no attention to the old Toyota pickup.

"Is that the only security they have?" Eden hissed to Baxter as they passed. "These guys look like amateurs."

Baxter nodded. "Let's hope so."

Eden watched, amazed, as the men trundled down the path and away from The Sphinx. "How often do they come around?"

"There are several teams, so I'd expect one to pass every few minutes. Remember, though, it's not just them we have to look out for."

Eden looked down the access road they'd just used. Several buildings squatted in the gloom. Nothing moved. Or at least, she couldn't see anything move. If anyone was following them, they were waiting out of sight, so far.

"We'd better get going," Eden said. "Before someone does notice we're here."

Eden and Baxter shuffled around to the rear of the truck and dropped the tail gate. All the gear they needed for the evening was strapped to the flatbed beneath a tarpaulin. There were several lengths of rope with other climbing gear, packing crates, and a first aid kit which Eden hoped they wouldn't need. With no need for digital devices of any kind, it surprised Eden how low tech the mission had become. They were going back to basics, like the early excavators of The Plateau hundreds, or even thousands, of years ago.

Eden and Baxter pulled out two lengths of rope, a small bag of other climbing gear, and a bag containing other supplies. They placed them on the ground behind the pickup.

As Baxter arranged the tarpaulin back over the rest of their supplies, Eden paced to the front of the truck. "We're ready to go," she said to Mo, before turning to Beaumont. "Stay out of sight and be ready to move as soon as we get back."

Beaumont nodded, locking eyes with Eden. "Good luck," he said. "We've got this."

"I hope…"

A pair of raised voices cut Eden off in mid-sentence. They were shouting in Arabic, although Eden's lessons were coming up short. Footsteps thundered over the asphalt in their direction.

Eden looked from Mo to Beaumont, a finger raised to her lips. The two men sunk down in the seats.

The footsteps stopped, and the voices came again.

"I'm sorry, I don't understand," Eden heard Baxter's reply. He was out of sight behind the truck. Fortunately, she was also out of sight. Eden crouched down and scurried around the front of the vehicle. She peered out from around the front fender.

Two men in sand colored khaki, stood before Baxter. They had yet to draw their weapons, but their aggressive body language suggested that they wouldn't wait much longer.

"What is this?" One of the men said, in heavily accented English. He didn't wait for a reply. "What are you doing here? This site is off limits at this time."

Eden could see that Baxter was trying to act relaxed. She hoped the guards were less observant than she was.

"Truck is broken," Baxter said finally, pointing at the vehicle. "We're on our way home and…"

"What are these things?" The guard pointed a bony finger at the bags and climbing gear clearly visible on the road.

"I'm looking for the right tool, to fix the truck. It's in here somewhere." Baxter made a show of turning back towards the truck and looking for the fictional tool.

"Do not move!" One of the guards screamed, sliding his weapon from its holster.

"Now you've done it," Eden whispered to herself. She slipped out from behind the truck. If she could take down one of the men, then Baxter could deal with the other. She didn't want to hurt the men, they were just doing their jobs after all, but tonight's task couldn't be derailed this early in the process. All going well, Eden and Baxter could tie the men up and leave them on the truck's flatbed and beneath the tarpaulin for an hour or two.

Eden charged towards the men, staying wide and out of their line of sight. Focusing on the man who was doing the talking—probably the more senior—Eden prepared herself for impact. She drew her hands back, ready. Fists clenched.

Baxter continued talking, keeping the men's attention focused on him. Eden closed the distance quickly, her feet moving silently over the uneven road.

Then another voice filled the air. Eden looked around and was shocked to see Little Mo climb from the truck. The Egyptian smiled at the men, his arms open wide. His body language was all at odds with the tension of the situation, it looked as though he was greeting a long-lost friend as he spoke in Arabic.

Eden looked from Mo to the guards and back again.

Seeing the approaching Egyptian, the guards visibly relaxed. They slid their guns away and smiled. Mo hassled across, almost pushing Baxter out of the way and embraced the men.

Eden, now confused, skidded to a stop. Her hands dropped to her sides.

"This is amazing," Mo said, switching to English. "These men used to know my father. He was one of the guards here several decades ago."

The men switched back to Arabic.

Eden looked at Baxter, the color returning slowly to his face. Baxter held out his hands in confusion and exhaled a deep breath. Like Eden, he had clearly been ready for the conflict. Little Mo removed a wad of notes from his pocket and counted out several for each of the men. Quick-fire conversation ensued. One of the men gesticulated, pointing at the notes. Finally, Mo nodded and handed over another few notes to each man. The notes tucked out of sight, Mo turned to Eden and Baxter.

"These men, very kind as they are, have offered to help us visit The Sphinx tonight." Mo smiled and made a gesture which said, *'what an amazing coincidence.'*

Eden shook her head slowly, ever more amazed by the Egyptian, his knowledge, contacts, and secret talents.

Without a break in their conversation, Mo and the guards led the way towards The Sphinx. Sidling up to a high-wire fence, one of the guards slid out a giant bunch of keys and let them through. Once inside, they crossed an open area and stood right beside The Sphinx. Eden looked up at the sculpture, cutting up to the grey night sky. From this close, the weathering on its back looked almost ghostly. The official viewing gallery was on the far side. The guards, greased with Mo's money, had brought them right into the compound surrounding The Sphinx.

Mo and the guards had another lively conversation, pointing up at The Sphinx. Finally, one of the guards drew out another key and placed it in Mo's hand. Mo handed over another few notes. Then, without another word, the guards wandered off to continue their patrol.

"They won't say anything," Mo said, clearly reading Eden's worries. "Enough money has a way of buying some-one's silence here."

"Don't they worry about what we're doing out here at night?"

Mo shook his head and pointed up at The Sphinx's back. "They have leased this beautiful creature to us for the rest of the evening. It's ours to do with what we like, as long as we're out by first light, all is good."

"I THINK WE SHOULD JUST CHECK," Abdul said, as they cut back through Giza in the direction of their hotel in central Cairo. "We'll stop at the place and look over the wall. If all's quiet, then we'll leave them to it."

"I don't know what your problem is," Sharif replied. "Boss says there's no need, there's no need."

Abdul shook his head. Through the Isuzu's dirty glass, modern buildings slid by on both sides of the road. "I've just got a feeling about this. We've met this Eden Black girl what, twice now, and each time she's outsmarted us. Always thinking..."

"The girl's a pain in the ass," Sharif snarled.

"True, but she's clever. I don't think she would get an early night before the job is done. I think they're pulling something here."

Sharif slowed the Trooper up to the front wall of the villa. "Look quickly. Then we get out of here. Boss said she wanted us straight back."

Abdul climbed out of the vehicle, paced around the back, and scrambled up on to the roof. Balancing himself on the roll bars, he peered over the wall. The villa was all dark and quiet. No one moved within the floor to ceiling windows.

"All looks quiet," he reported back to Sharif.

"They're in bed then. Let's go."

Abdul narrowed his eyes and surveyed the building again. Maybe they had just gone to bed.

"Hurry up," Sharif hissed.

Abdul prepared to climb back down when something struck him. He looked at the driveway. A seven-ton truck sat at the far end, but the pickup wasn't there. "Wait a minute," Abdul said, the realization kicking up into focus. "What vehicle were they using earlier?"

"Some rusty old pickup. A Toyota I think," Sharif replied.

"Yeah, that's right. The pickup's not here." Abdul scrambled down and got back into the passenger seat. Without a word to Sharif, he grabbed his phone from the central console and called King.

"Boss, we have a problem."

34

"THE SHAFT we need is on The Sphinx's back," Mo said, pointing up at the stone creature. "Just behind the head there."

Eden grabbed one of the lengths of rope, then took an expandable grappling hook from the bag. Eden pressed a switch on the six-inch cylinder and hooks shot out from the sides. She tied the hook to one end of the rope and then swung it high up on to The Sphinx's back.

Mo winced at the thought of the hook clunking against the ancient stone, but knew they had no other option.

On the third attempt, Eden got the hook to catch something. She pulled the rope several times to test the strength. Satisfied it would hold, she swung the bag over her back and half-scrambled, half-climbed, up the side of the creature.

She reached the top and stood. Behind her The Great Pyramid stood, giant, unyielding and ghostly against the sky.

Eden checked the grappling hook. It had fallen into a ridge on the rock on The Sphinx's back. Satisfied it would continue to hold, she signaled for Baxter to climb. When Baxter was up, they took the rope and together hauled Mo up the side.

"That was easier than I thought it would be," Mo said, brushing his hands together while taking in the view. He glanced at Eden and Baxter, panting after the exertion of pulling the large Egyptian forty feet from the ground. "You guys need to work out more," he quipped, sliding the key from his pocket.

Mo knelt and started rubbing sand from the back of The Sphinx. Within a few seconds he had exposed a panel set into a square hole in the center of The Sphinx's back. He brushed off some more sand to reveal a padlock. He unlocked the padlock and then heaved the panel upwards, metal hinges screeching. Beneath the panel, a passage led down into the rock.

Having used the sky's orange glow to see so far, Eden dug the light from her bag. She switched it on and shone the beam down into the passage. A narrow set of stairs ran down inside The Sphinx. Eden went first, awkwardly leaning forwards to fit inside the narrow passage. The staircase descended for about fifty feet before opening into a small chamber. Eden felt a flare of excitement grow. They were now beneath the level of The Plateau. She studied the walls of the chamber. It looked as though the chamber was cut directly into the rock. The work was incredibly neat, as though done with a machine, long before such machines were available. The chamber was, as far as Eden could make out, a perfect square with a vertical shaft descending in the middle. Eden crossed to the shaft and peered down into the depths. Narrow and deep, the shaft dropped over fifty feet into what looked like another chamber below.

"You're not telling me that's pre-historic," Eden said,

tracing the outline of a rickety metal ladder bolted to the wall.

"It's old enough to be dangerous," Baxter said, peering down the shaft. "We'll use the ropes just to make sure."

Baxter fished another length of climbing rope from the bag. Eden looped the rope under her arms and tied it at the front. It wasn't as good as a proper climbing harness but it would save her neck if she fell. She climbed out onto the ladder and gave it a shake. A metallic clang echoed throughout the shaft. One of the brackets crunched, loose in the wall. Eden frowned and pulled on the rope.

"I've got you," Baxter said, holding the rope in both hands. "I'll lower it down as you go."

Eden took the rungs one at a time, without looking down. Some wobbled freely, and two or three had snapped away from the vertical metal altogether. After what felt like a long time, Eden's feet hit the hard rock of the chamber below.

"Down," she shouted up, untying the rope.

Baxter pulled the rope upwards and Little Mo began his descent. The metal creaked and whined even more under his bulk. Mo grumbled and grunted several times too, but eventually reached the chamber. Eden untied the rope and sent it back up for Baxter.

Baxter tied the rope to a heavy steel beam which ran across the opening to the shaft. He carefully worked out the length so that it was short enough to prevent him smashing against the rock below, but long enough so that they could use it to climb out the shaft if necessary. Getting stuck underground at the first stage really would scuttle their plans.

As Baxter lowered himself down, Eden looked around the chamber in detail. Like the space above, it was cut from solid rock with care and precision. Eden examined the walls for tool marks but found none.

Four large niches gaped in the walls of the chamber. Eden stepped into one of them. The space was about five feet wide and eight feet long.

"Big enough for a sarcophagus," Mo said, the beam of his light dancing through the chamber. Eden checked each of the niches in turn. They were all about the same size and shape. All of them were empty. At the far end of the chamber, just one niche was cut into the wall. As Eden drew close, she noticed that this one wasn't empty. There was something large and bulky inside. Eden froze a few paces from the niche.

"Come and look at this," she whispered, her voice sounded loud against the rock walls. Mo sidled up behind her.

A large stone casket sat in the niche. The lid of the casket, placed at an angle, allowed Eden to peer inside. The casket was empty, although mysteriously the inside of the stone was a different color to the outside.

"Why are those niches empty, but this one's been left here?" Eden asked.

"There's no knowing." Mo took two steps forward and peered into the casket. "This site has been pillaged for thousands of years. Maybe what was in these caskets is now in some billionaire's antiquities collection."

"That's awful," Eden whispered, knowing that was the truth of the matter. She'd seen enough Egyptian relics around the world, and often wondered about the place they had originated. "I wonder why they left this casket."

She didn't have time to dwell on the matter as Baxter reached the bottom of the ladder, untied himself and strode to the opening of the next shaft. He shone his light down into the gloom. "There's water down there, about thirty feet below."

Eden and Mo crossed the chamber and peered down the shaft. Sure enough, water shimmered at the shaft's base.

"You smell that?" Eden said, taking a deep breath.

"Sulfur," Baxter said. "The same smell as in the tunnel. It must be from the same source."

No ladder was set into this shaft, indicating there was little to see down below. Eden's curiosity rose all the same.

"Grab another rope." She pointed at the duffel bag. "I've got to see what's down there."

Baxter fished out another length of rope. Eden looped it around under her arms and Baxter wound it around his waist and held on tight.

Eden leaned back over the edge, letting the rope take her weight. Slowly she lowered herself down the shaft. A few feet above the water, she tied off the rope and did a three-sixty within the shaft. Almost perfectly circular, the shaft continued far beneath the water line. Even though the water was incredibly clear, the beam of Eden's light would only penetrate a few feet below the surface. Eden was certain of one thing, this shaft, and the chambers above were not naturally occurring. They had been built by some-one, or something.

Eden scrambled back up the rope and hauled herself into the chamber. Her chest heaving from the exertion, she told the others what she'd seen.

"This needs a full and proper investigation," Eden said. "There are so many unanswered questions about this small cave alone."

"So many unanswered questions," Mo said, his voice serious. Mo shone his light on a set of hieroglyphs, etched into the far wall.

"We need to move." Baxter checked his watch. "We've found the water, but where's this sluice gate? The last set of hieroglyphs said it would be here." Baxter moved the beam of his light systematically around the chamber. There was nothing that could pass as a sluice gate. Certainly nothing to block the water beneath.

Mo turned to face Eden and Baxter. One look at Mo's expression told Eden that something was wrong.

"What is it?" she said, stepping towards the Egyptian.

"We're in the wrong place." Mo pointed at a set of hieroglyphs on the far wall. "They say that this is a burial chamber. They're from a completely different era than those you discovered in the passage earlier."

"No," Eden said, anger rising. "We're in the right place, we must be. We've followed the instructions you translated perfectly. What was it you said? Let's go through them again. It must be here somewhere..."

"No, Eden," Mo stepped forwards and put his hand on Eden's shoulder. "We always knew our translation was a long shot. One word wrong, and the whole meaning changes, that's the way with these ancient texts."

"What do we do now then?" Eden said. "Just go back to the villa and forget all about it?"

"That's what we'll have to do," Mo said. "We've still got people working on the translations of the hieroglyphs you found. Maybe there'll find something that makes sense in a day or so."

Baxter sighed and started back up the ladder. Mo followed, and Eden went last. In silent frustration, they climbed back to the surface.

On the back of The Sphinx, Baxter looped up the ropes, while Mo closed and locked the grill.

Eden scrambled down onto The Sphinx's paws and

looked up at the giant stone head. Still frustrated, she clambered along the large stone paws, then turned and looked back at the creature. There was something especially majestic about The Sphinx in the half-light. Enraptured by the view, Eden took two more steps backwards.

Eden didn't realize she was falling until the world whirled around her. She swung her arms this way and that, reaching for something to steady herself. Her fingers swung through the air. For several seconds she felt like she was inside a washing machine on a spin cycle. Eden tried to call for help, but her voice got caught in her throat. The ground roared up behind her. She hit the stone hard, knocking the air from her lungs.

Eden lay on her back for several seconds, wheezing. Although she didn't lose consciousness, everything spun around her for a few moments. Finally, she sat up.

Baxter and Mo, having heard Eden's cry, came tearing around the paws. When they arrived Eden was sitting up, grinning from ear to ear.

"We've been looking in the wrong place," Eden said, pointing at something between the paws. "I know exactly where we need to go."

35

"WHAT DO YOU MEAN, there's a second sphinx?" Baxter said as they hurried back towards the truck.

After a couple of shaky paces, Eden was now steady on her feet again, and seeing more clearly than usual. "There's a tablet between the paws of The Sphinx, and on it there are two sphinxes. I saw it, clear as day."

Mo pulled ahead, running at a surprising speed. "You're right," he said, excitedly. "I don't know why I didn't think of that. It makes perfect sense now. As above, so below. Almodad will show us the way!"

Eden and Baxter glanced at each other and quickened their pace.

They reached the truck and slung their bags in the back. Mo yanked open one of the back doors, startling Beaumont, and retrieved a map.

Beaumont climbed out of the driver's seat and joined the others.

Mo unfolded a map on the tailgate and shone a light on it. "For many centuries there has been talk of a second sphinx. In fact, it's mentioned in several ancient texts, including the Book of Enoch."

"It's out there, just lying beneath the sand?" Eden said, pointing back towards The Plateau. "Why hasn't it been excavated?"

"There are many reasons why people don't poke around on The Plateau," Mo said. "The bottom line is the authorities are afraid that any discoveries will undermine their authority. So, they are very careful with what they authorize."

"Okay, okay." Baxter poked at the map. "The politics of archaeology aside, if it is there, how would we even know where to start looking? Without any scanning equipment, we could walk on top of the thing and not even know it."

"As above, so below," Mo repeated, sliding his hand down the center of the map.

"What do you..." Eden tried to ask.

"We use Almodad's geometry," Beaumont hissed. "The clue was there all along, why didn't I see this?" He elbowed his way past the others and looked intently at the map. "You must remember that everything in ancient Egypt was built to represent something else. Nothing is random. It's all very, very carefully considered."

"If there is another sphinx, I know exactly where it will be," Mo said, grinning. "There," his finger jabbed at the map.

"Why?" Eden asked, her gaze narrowing. "How can you be so sure?"

"Over the last twenty years I've been working on a theory that The Giza Plateau is a representation of The Solar System. All the objects revolve around this point here." Mo pointed at a place at the bottom center, almost in line with the three largest pyramids. "This point would represent Ra, the Sun God. Moving out we then have the fourth Pyramid, which represents Mercury. The fifth representing Venus, and the sixth representing Earth. Right up until the first and second representing Jupiter and Saturn, hence their increased sizes."

"Alright, alright." Eden placed her fingers on her temples, afraid that they were getting off track. "That's all very clever and well thought out, but how does it relate to the second sphinx?"

"Ah, well, The Sphinx is a little different."

Eden rolled her eyes and felt the buoyancy of their discovery draining away.

"The Sphinx is representative, in my belief, of Sekhmet."

"The Mother Goddess of the Old Kingdom," Beaumont interjected.

Eden swallowed the urge to bang the two older men's heads together as that might help free a logical answer.

"Sekhmet is a fascinating character. Known as the 'Powerful One,' she's often depicted as a lion headed woman."

"Hence, The Sphinx," Mo manhandled a word into Beaumont's dialogue. He pointed at The Sphinx behind them.

Eden drew a deep breath and suppressed the urge to scream. "Okay," she said as calmly as she was able. "But how do we find the second sphinx?"

"Easy," Mo said, glancing at Beaumont as though the pair were sharing a private joke. "You follow the line of orbit." Mo dug a pencil from his pocket, then snagged a bit of cotton from the hem of his shirt. "If this point is the sun, or Ra." He held the string with his thumb at the point which he thought represented Ra. "Then the planets move around in an orbit." He traced a line from the back of The Sphinx, all the way around the map.

"That makes sense," Baxter said, nodding.

"I suppose," Eden agreed. "But if it's somewhere on that line, that's still an impossibly big area to search."

"Ahh but wait." Mo held up a finger and pointed it at Eden. "As above so below."

"That's really starting to get annoying," Eden muttered.

Mo passed the light to Beaumont and then dexterously folded the map in half. The fold perfectly intersected the point which he had said represented the sun, or Ra, the God of the Sun. He then flipped the map over, so they were just looking at the half with The Pyramids and Sphinx on. With surprising aggression and speed, Mo stabbed the pencil into The Sphinx. The sharp lead pierced straight through the map and shattered on the tailgate. Mo shook out the map and laid it flat again.

There were now two identical holes in the map. One was at the position of the first Sphinx. A few thousand feet to the west, and perfectly intersecting the orbital path, was the second.

"As above, so below," Eden whispered quietly.

Eden slid out her phone and cross-checked Mo's paper map with her digital one. She carefully selected the point Mo had pierced, checked it again, and then placed a pin on her digital map.

Climbing back into the truck, Eden took the front seat and instructed Beaumont to head further up the road which wound through The Plateau. Keeping the lights off, they chugged up a slight incline, guided by the ambient light of the city. Reaching a dusty and deserted car park which served the tourist trade at the famous panorama point during the day, Eden instructed Beaumont to stop.

"We're close," she said, checking the map. "It's about three hundred feet that way."

Beaumont pulled the truck in close to a small concrete building. He killed the engine and snapped on the hand-brake. They all scrambled out of the truck.

"I'm not missing this," Beaumont said, swinging the door closed.

Baxter ran around to the back of the truck and heaved out the shovels Mo had insisted they'd packed as a contingency. Only by the dim light of Eden's glowing phone, they set off across the sand.

Padding across the sand, Eden studied the map on her phone. When they drew close to the estimated place, she paused and zoomed in on the map.

"Fifty feet ahead, just to right." For some reason, Eden realized, she was whispering. She glanced around. Other than the four of them, The Plateau was empty for as far as she could see. The lights of Giza glowed several hundred feet away, and over the whole scene, the great angular shapes of The Pyramids rose.

"Look at that." Baxter drew Eden's attention back in the direction of their quest. He pointed to the exact spot Eden had told them to head. In the place Mo had predicted The Sphinx to be, the level of the sand rose sharply to a crest some sixty feet above them. In the dim light, Eden hadn't even noticed the mound until they were almost upon it.

"That's it. That's got to be it!" Beaumont hissed, scrambling up the incline. He used his hands to help him up the final ten feet which were well over forty-five degrees, then turned and helped Mo up behind him. Eden reached the summit last. She turned and peered back in the direction of the first sphinx, although from this distance it was hidden below the undulating surface of The Plateau.

"This sphinx will be the exact opposite of the other," Mo said, turning from east to west. "They'll be lying tail to tail.

I'd say the head will be about here, and if the passage behind the head is in the same place, that'll be here." He took six paces back and then drew an 'X' in the sand with his toe.

"We'd better start digging," Beaumont said, quietly, clearly not able to stay completely silent on the matter.

Eden and Baxter dug first. They fell quickly into a rhythm, standing at opposite sides of the hole and heaving their shovels into the sand one after another. After what felt like hours, Eden's pace slowed. She swept a hand across her face to remove some of the pouring sweat and dropped out of the rhythm. The shovels clanged together.

"Time out," Baxter said, flinging a large shovel load of sand over his shoulder.

The hole they'd dug was already four feet deep and about five feet across.

"We'll take over," Mo said, clambering down into the hole. "We've got quite a distance still to go."

Beaumont took Eden's shovel and digging continued. For several minutes the only sound was the crunch of the shovel blades in sand and the grunt of exertion. Then, the sound changed. The blades clunked against something hard.

"I think... I think we might just have something," Beaumont panted.

Eden and Baxter rushed to the side of the hole. She flicked on her light, but kept it cautiously pointed down into the hole. After several minutes just using the ambient light of the sky, the beam was dazzling. Mo scraped his blade carefully from right to left, clearing sand from whatever they'd found. He dropped to his knees and used his hands to brush away the sand.

"There's no knowing exactly," Beaumont said, looking

down at the rock which ran in both directions. "But I think we might have ourselves a second sphinx."

Reenergized, Eden and Baxter took the shovels again. Now they dug outwards, one of them enlarging the hole in the direction of The Sphinx's head, the other towards the tail.

Eden had made progress of about a foot when she forced the shovel down towards the rock, but it didn't stop. The blade slid straight through where she expected the sphinx's back to be. She pulled the shovel out and stared at it in momentary confusion. Then the surrounding sand started to fall away, running in rivulets, disappearing down into the desert floor. At first the sand ran slowly, then it picked up speed, sliding and disappearing into the void.

"Guys," Eden whispered, as loud as she would dare. Taking a step backwards, she dropped the shovel and fumbled for the light. The dazzling beam appeared just in time to see a passage emerge in the desert floor. Sand ran down into the passage, as though the secrets of the desert were finally revealing themselves.

Baxter, Beaumont, and Mo sidled up behind Eden, each silently watching with the reverence of observing a miracle. The sand hissed, eventually settling in place, and Eden stepped forward. She shone the light down into the void. A tight staircase ran deep down into the bowels of The Plateau.

"YOU'RE DEFINITELY sure this is the place?" King snarled from the back seat of the Isuzu Trooper.

They were parked on a side street looking out at the

place where Abdul and Sharif had seen Eden and Baxter disappear down into the sewer.

"Yes boss," Abdul said, pointing out at the street. "That's the right place. They went down there, and we followed."

Sharif slurped a drink from a paper cup. The remains of takeaway food lay strewn throughout the car.

"Well, they're clearly not here now, are they?" King huffed.

"No, not yet. But they're not at the villa either. They went through that whole ruse making you think they were going to sleep for a reason."

"That's what I'm worried about," King muttered, slumping back into the seat. "Maybe they really didn't find anything here."

"What do you want to do, boss?" Sharif said, followed by a belch.

"I want to teach you some manners to begin with." King glanced around at the litter-filled car. "And I want you to tidy this car out, it's disgusting."

"What, now?" Sharif replied.

"No," King sighed. "Now we wait. This is all we've got to go on. If they come here, we'll see them."

36

EDEN PICKED her way silently down the narrow staircase. The passage was similar in appearance to the other sphinx. Carved directly through the rock, it dropped at a steep angle, with narrow and treacherous stairs.

"I can't believe this place," Beaumont muttered from somewhere behind. "I would love to get a team down here and run some proper analysis."

"That'll never happen," Mo interrupted. "This place doesn't exist, remember. The fact we're even here is a miracle."

"I know, I know. But wouldn't it be wonderful?"

Eden reached the bottom of the narrow staircase and stepped out into a chamber. Half filled with sand which had clearly fallen down the shaft, she had to walk across the space with her back hunched. She turned back and looked up the passage, trying to calculate the distance of their descent. They must now be over one-hundred feet beneath the surface of The Plateau. The chamber too, was neatly hewn from the rock. Brightly painted hieroglyphs in gold, blue and white covered every inch of the walls. Eden spun around in amazement. In this chamber, though, there were no shafts leading further downwards. Not that Eden could see, anyway. There was, however, another narrow passage which looked as though it led to another space further on.

Eden strode towards the passage. From Eden's position, it looked as though the passage ran for about forty feet before opening out. She paused and waited for the men to catch up.

"This place," Beaumont whispered, keeping his constant monologue going. "And to think that we are possibly the only people of the modern era to set foot inside here. It's nothing short of..."

"That way," Eden said, directing them on. After twenty feet she was able to stand at full height. They were now walking on solid rock, rather than the sand which had come down from The Plateau.

Eden stepped into the next chamber. Unconsciously she stared upwards. The ceiling was much higher here, at least twenty feet above her head. The far wall was at least forty feet away. Although much bigger, the construction of this chamber looked to be like that which they'd seen previously. The colorful hieroglyphs covered every inch in here too. The room was basically a square, although this one had a large column in the center.

Walking towards the column, Eden realized that it wasn't in fact a column, but a freestanding slab. Hieroglyphs covered each side.

The men bustled into the chamber behind her.

"This place, wow. Just look at it!" Beaumont's commentary echoed from the vast walls and high ceiling.

Mo sidled up to the central slab and peered myopically at the symbols. He held the light focused on each one for a few seconds, before moving on to the next.

"I don't think I've ever seen an example as well preserved as this," Mo said, running his finger across one of the symbols.

Eden wandered around to the back of the slab, her flashlight panning across the engraved surface. Two small pieces of metal stuck out from the rock on each side of the slab, like tiny antennas. Passing her light across them, Eden noticed they glimmered bronze.

"Copper, probably," Beaumont said, noticing the antennas too. "Strange. Copper is usually used for its excellent conductive properties. Could this be evidence that this facility really was used for power generation?" He took several photos of the antennas and the surrounding markings.

"You know you'll never be able to share those pictures," Baxter said. "This is totally off the books, remember."

"Of course, just for my personal collection," Beaumont said, snapping another two photographs.

Eden wandered further around the slab. She was so engrossed in the perfectly formed hieroglyphs, that she only saw the shaft opening at the last moment. For the second time in an hour, she felt the ground slip from beneath her. She froze in position just in time, her toes curling over the edge of the rock. She lurched backwards, her feet finding solid ground. Her heart now pounding in her throat, Eden looked down the shaft.

"Come look at this," she called nervously to the others. "Careful though."

The shaft was a perfectly cut square, dropping at least fifty feet beneath the chamber. Anyone would be lucky to survive a drop like that, Eden thought nervously. Kneeling next to the shaft opening, Eden heard running water somewhere below. She squinted down into the depths and could just about see water moving through the shaft's bottom.

"This is it," Mo said excitedly, working through the hieroglyphs. He pulled out a camera and took several photographs. "You see, this is the symbol for water." He pointed at three wiggly lines lying on top of one other. "We have to push this slab down the shaft, and that will block the flow. Then the water pressure in the chamber reduces, allowing you to move the slab you found earlier. It's all been worked out perfectly."

"I can see one problem in that," Baxter said, standing back with his arms folded.

Mo turned to look at the other man.

"That slab must be twenty feet high and eight feet wide. It could easily weigh a hundred tons. We'd need an army."

Mo looked up at the giant slab and exhaled. He turned and slumped against the slab, as though he now needed it for support. His shoulders drooped like a car standing on flat tires.

Beaumont nodded, pointing towards the slab. "They would have had great teams of men working in here, with ropes and all sorts. That is if we don't believe the place was built by..." Beaumont's voice dried up in his throat. For once, no one had interrupted him. He pointed up at the slab, his mouth opening and closing.

Eden and Baxter turned towards the Professor, both surprised by his inability to speak.

"What?" Mo said standing up straight.

Beaumont caught hold of the thought. He pointed violently at the slab. "It just moved. It just moved! When you leaned on it. It moved. Do it again!"

Mo turned and looked up at the imposing chunk of rock, his eyes brimming with wonder. All eyes followed the

Egyptian's every move. Slowly, carefully, he again leaned against the slab. The colossal rock slid silently another few inches towards the shaft.

"It moves silently," Baxter said. He stepped forward and studied the bottom of the slab. "It must have hidden wheels, or rollers, or something. Incredible."

Mo stood up straight again, but this time the slab didn't stop. It slid, incredibly slowly at first, but building up speed all the time, towards the shaft.

"The floor is slightly sloped there," Baxter said, pointing. "It's just using gravity now."

The slab slipped on, effortlessly skating towards the shaft.

Eden stepped back cautiously in case the thing should topple over. As great as the ancient engineers were, this machine was well out of warranty. Eden braced herself as the slab reached the edge of the shaft. The thing would surely fall fast now, crashing to the shaft bottom with a thunderous boom.

No such noise came. With a gentle whining, and then a whirring sound, the immense pillar slid gracefully downwards.

Baxter took a step backwards, astonished. "Look at that! It must be working on a counterweight and gear system. That's... well that's..."

As the slab slid further down, Eden saw what he was talking about. On top of the giant rock, a series of wheels of various sizes whirred furiously. Several cables ran from the slab and up into a shaft in the ceiling.

"That's incredible," Baxter said, craning his neck to assess the machine's workings. "To think this has been sitting here all these years, unused, and now it works perfectly."

Touching down on the shaft bottom, the giant rock slid gently to a stop with nothing more than a distant thud.

Baxter was the first to step towards the slab, which sat proud of the chamber floor by a couple of feet. The pulley assembly was still now, although the lines connecting it to its unseen counterweight remained taut.

Baxter leaned forward and examined the mechanism. Eden took a cursory glance at the system but didn't really understand Baxter's amazement. It was obviously well built —no need for all this delay.

"Let's head out," Eden said, turning back towards the passage. "We've got a lot still to do."

"WILL YOU STOP THAT," Lulu King barked at Sharif as he tapped on the Trooper's steering wheel with his fingers. The pattern was either so complex that King couldn't follow its rhythm, or just had no regularity at all. King assumed the latter.

"Sorry boss," Sharif mumbled, dropping his hands into his lap.

In the passenger seat, Abdul stuffed another cold chip in his mouth.

"How long should we give it?" Sharif said, clearly struggling to keep his hands still.

King scowled, then glanced at her watch. They'd been sitting in the stinking Isuzu Trooper for approaching two hours already staring at an empty street. Wherever Eden and her band of reprobates had gone, it wasn't here.

King thought back to the conversation she'd had with Eden at the Hotel Rumbold. Maybe, regretfully, King had underestimated the woman. Clearly a potential murder charge wasn't enough to get her to toe the line. Maybe she would have to come up with something more aggressive.

The distant thronging of a diesel engine streamed through the open windows. At first, King didn't think anything of it. Although traffic was light by Cairo's standards at this time of night, vehicles continued to grumble past.

Abdul stuffed another chip into his mouth and chewed noisily, his mouth open.

To distract herself from a full-scale rage, King turned to look at the vehicle approaching them from behind. A white pickup truck rolled into view.

"What vehicle did you say they had?" King barked.

"Toyota Hilux, white. Rusty as anything," Abdul answered, without a break in his chewing.

The truck rolled closer, and King saw a faded Toyota logo on the grill.

"I think we've got company," King said, all frustration fading away.

Abdul started the engine but kept the lights off. Abdul and Sharif slid down in their seats. King ducked out of sight.

"Be ready to move," she snarled. "We can't lose them this time."

37

"DID ANYONE SEE THAT?" Eden asked, peering through the Toyota's filthy windows as they passed a dust covered Isuzu Trooper parked at the curb.

"What's that?" Baxter asked, turning out on to the main street and then left, almost immediately.

"I don't think it was anything," Eden said, twisting back around. "I thought for a moment that 4x4 back there was the one that followed us earlier. You know, with the two men that went down into the sewer after us?"

Baxter peered into the rear-view mirror. The vehicle was now out of sight.

"Don't worry about it," Mo said, from the seat behind Eden. "Anyone listening still thinks we're asleep back at the villa, thanks to you." Mo leaned forwards and put his hand on Eden's shoulder. Eden tapped the back of the Egyptian's large, hairy hand. She had to admit she'd grown fond of Mo in the last two days. Eden remembered what he'd told her about his father, disappearing somewhere in the labyrinthine passages they were about to re-enter. Her chest tightened. The danger was present and real.

"Even if they are following us, they're too late," Baxter said, slowing the Toyota outside the disused laundromat through which they'd exited the shaft earlier that day. "Within an hour, we will have what we need and be out of there."

"The Ark of the Covenant," Eden said. "I can't believe that's what we think we're going to find in there. It's like the stuff of legend."

"Is that so hard to believe?" Beaumont interjected. "Often the truth is stranger than fiction. Think about all those authors who peddle books about hidden skulls or ancient curses, no one could think of this."

"They'd have to be mad, that's for sure," Mo added.

Baxter reverse parked between two clapped out vans. He cut the engine, and the headlights faded into nothing.

For several seconds no one inside the truck spoke. Eden looked out through the windshield, then turned and checked the road behind them. There wasn't another moving vehicle in sight. The only visible light glowed from a second-floor apartment fifty yards away and the ever-present orange sky of Cairo's light pollution.

Eden checked her watch. The time had just crawled beyond 2am. "We better get moving. I want to be well clear of this place by sunrise."

Eden, Mo, and Beaumont scrambled out of the truck in unison.

Baxter, still in the driver's seat stashed the keys beneath the sun visor. "Whoever makes it back here first, get the truck started. Give the rest of us no more than a few minutes, then get out of here."

The instruction sent a chill down Eden's spine. She looked around at the rest of her unlikely band of heroes.

"No, we go in together, we come out together," Eden said defiantly.

Clearly seeing the fire in Eden's eyes, Baxter didn't argue. He strode around to the back of the truck and hauled out the bags. He gave one to Eden and slung the other over his back.

Eden paced to the laundromat's front door and drew out her lock picking tools. She made quick work of the front door, which she'd locked a few hours ago. Unsurprisingly, it didn't look as though anyone had used the door since. A layer of filth covered the glass, obscuring the rooms inside.

The lock clicked and Eden shoved the door open.

Once inside, Eden led the men through the laundromat and into the back room. The carcasses of long-dead washing machines and tumble dryers sat against the walls. Large stains swirled across the plaster, as though they were living things themselves.

Eden and Baxter dropped their bags and pulled the discolored rug from the floor in the center of the room. There, they found the trap door through which they'd come. They lifted the panel from its housing and propped it against the far wall. The panel was certainly easier to move from this side than underneath.

Eden slung the bag back over her shoulder and together they started off down the spiral staircase. One by one, each member of the small team slid out a flashlight and turned it on. The narrow beams swept the walls hypnotically.

"Look at this place," Beaumont said, studying the walls. "It's nothing short of miraculous that it's been here all this time, undisturbed. It must have been constructed sometime in the..."

"No time for that," Eden snapped from the front of the party.

Beaumont looked down at the rest of the group who were accelerating ahead of him. He took a few steps quickly to catch up.

With each step, the air became warmer, and the humidity increased. The smell of sulfur grew too, clawing the back of Eden's throat. The temperature in the tunnel seemed to increase with each step they took. Eden glanced at her watch and confirmed that the temperature had increased several degrees from the night air at ground level.

With each step down, Eden tried to compare their elevation to that of the chamber beneath The Sphinx. If the level of the water was to be believed, then they couldn't be far away.

Reaching the bottom of the spiral staircase, they paused. Water bubbled and lapped angrily against the lowest step. Moisture hung heavily in the air. Eden wiped a hand across her face, and it came away wet.

Eden slipped the bag from her shoulders and dropped it to the ground. "The water's the same level as earlier," Eden said. "Were we expecting it to change?"

"No, as I understand it, this is from a different source. You say this water appeared to be something of an airlock?" Beaumont didn't wait for a reply. "I believe this is more symbolic than practical. You're swimming through the cleansing waters, before you're allowed to reach the chamber."

"Let's just hope this ancient construction is as solid as we think it is," Baxter said, dropping his bag to the ground. "Put everything you want to take with you in the bags. I'll swim through first with one of the ropes, then we will pull the bags through."

The four stripped down to their swimming gear, stuffing their clothes and shoes in the bag.

Baxter sealed the bag up, then laid a rope out on the floor. He looped one end around his wrist, Eden took the other. Baxter stepped down and then disappeared beneath the water. For a second, Eden saw his light beneath the waves and then that disappeared too. The rope spooled out for thirty seconds before becoming still. Eden tied the end of the rope to the bag.

"You go now," she said to Beaumont and Mo. "Follow the rope. It'll take you less than a minute."

The two older men splashed into the water. Eden watched them duck beneath the surface and then follow the rope through the passage. Eden counted out the seconds, looking up at the well shaft above her. A sharp tug came on the rope just as she'd passed forty-five seconds. Beaumont and Mo were through. Eden carried the bag down into the water, took a deep breath, then tugged on the rope. As Baxter pulled the rope in, Eden kicked, angling the bag down and through the passage. Within thirty seconds, her head broke through the surface on the other side.

Eden scrambled out of the water, untied the rope, opened the bag, and handed everyone their clothes back. They all got dressed silently. Eden slung the bag across her back, Baxter coiled up the rope and then they set off down the tunnel. Mo and Beaumont wandered ahead, the beams from their flashlights whipping excitedly from side to side.

"It's like watching kids in a toy shop," Eden whispered to Baxter, pointing at the men.

They reached the end of the tunnel and all four of them stared up at the giant slab.

"If I hadn't seen that stone moving beneath the second sphinx, I'd have said that this was impossible," Baxter said.

Eden moved to one side and studied the corner where the slab connected with the tunnel's side wall. The monolith was so well fitted that the gap between the two stones was only a hair's breadth. Eden looked back behind them. The whole tunnel was sealed with no way through.

"Nothing has changed since we were here earlier," Eden said. "How are we supposed to get through?" She turned and shoved the rock. It didn't move.

"These ancient builders did a pretty good job, right?" Baxter said, pacing back and forth along the tunnel.

Beaumont stepped towards the slab and looked up at the hieroglyphs. He spoke as though he was studying an artifact in a museum, not in a dangerous situation several hundred feet beneath the ground. "These really are a great example." He stepped towards the slab and ran his fingers across the first pair of symbols. "The Ennead and..."

A great rumble followed by a crash cut the professor off in mid-sentence. The sound shook the tunnel, sending clouds of dust floating down from the ceiling.

Eden whipped around, looking for the source of the noise. The tunnel behind them looked as it had several moments ago, except Baxter wasn't there.

"I'm down here. Some help please!" Baxter's voice sounded urgent and pained. Eden rushed forward.

"Careful! Slowly!" Baxter shouted.

Eden froze in her tracks. Just two feet ahead of her, part of the tunnel's floor had disappeared. She moved slowly up to the edge and peered over. Three feet below, Baxter clung on to a tiny ledge. He hung, just with his fingertips above a shaft which was so deep Eden's light didn't reach the bottom. Eden rushed across to the rope which Baxter had fortunately placed on the floor. She wrapped one end around her wrist several times and dropped the rope down to Baxter. Eden tensed as Baxter climbed the rope and heaved himself back out onto the passage.

"The floor just dropped beneath me. All I heard was Beaumont reading the hieroglyphs and then I was falling through the air," Baxter said, dusting himself down.

Beaumont whipped around, the color draining from his face.

"You don't think it's got something to do with my reading this," Beaumont hissed in a near silent whisper. He pointed up at the hieroglyphs.

The four exchanged glances.

Mo was the first to speak. "There's one way to find out," he said. "Pass that rope around. Then stand still."

Eden did as Mo suggested. Everyone held on to the rope like mountain climbers on the slopes of Everest.

"The Ennead and Almodad will show you the rest of the way," Mo said slowly, his voice loud and clear.

Something grumbled and cracked around the tunnel. All eyes whipped around, searching for movement. Everyone's muscles tensed ready to move. Rocks thumped to the ground, throwing dust and debris up into the air.

"Keep going," Eden shouted, gripping the rope.

"You now have all you need to see through the mist of confusion," Mo roared as more rocks fell and more dust filled the air, perhaps symbolic of the confusing mists. "But beware, time waits for no man or woman, Eden."

Mo's voice trailed off to silence. The sound of falling rocks continued for a few seconds and then fell silent too, reverberations pounded through the tunnel before dying out.

"Everyone still alright?" Eden said, the dust clawing her throat.

Three voices came in reply.

Slowly the dust cleared. Eden looked around the tunnel. The whole wall to the side of the tunnel had slid downwards, exposing a space behind. Now, just visible through the swirling mists, nine giant figures stared out into the tunnel.

Eden felt a flurry of fear, her body preparing to run. Realizing they were stone carvings, she relaxed slightly, but only slightly. The dust cleared further.

Eden checked that the surrounding floor was still in place and stepped towards the figures. She looked up at stone edifices, towering over her at almost twice the height of modern-day humans.

After checking the surrounding floor was still in place, Eden stepped forwards again and looked up at the figures.

"I know who they are," Mo said, rushing forwards and looking up at the figures. "By any calculation, they are the creators of all modern humanity."

"Japheth, Aloma and their sons," Beaumont said in wonder. "These men are thought to have restarted civilization after The Great Flood."

"Look, up there." Baxter pointed up at the ceiling. A shaft had opened above them, rising over a hundred feet directly upwards.

"If I'm not mistaken, that'll be the Osiris shaft," Mo said.

"That would make sense," Beaumont interrupted, peering up the shaft. "Osiris was believed to be the Lord of the Underworld. We are well and truly in his domain now. We are in his clutches, so to speak."

Mo turned his attention towards the statues. He shuffled from left to right, reading off the names. "Gomer, Magog, Tires, Javan, Meshech, Tubal, and Madai, they're the sons." He pointed at the final two figures. "Japheth and Aloma."

Another rumble trembled through the tunnel. Eden felt the floor shake beneath her feet. She gripped on to the rope and ducked into a crouch. The groaning noise rose further.

Eden spun around to face the noise. It sounded as though it was coming from the slab which blocked the tunnel. The sound of a seal being broken cut through the melee.

Eden looked around frantically, trying to work out where the noise was coming from. Water gushed into the tunnel, pounding over Eden's feet. She grabbed the bag and swung it on to her back.

"Look, there!" Baxter said, pointing at the tunnel through which they'd come. The roof of the tunnel behind them descended, closing their passage back to the surface.

"The tunnel's closing," Baxter shouted, his voice hoarse against the noise. "If that gets any lower, we'll be trapped."

"But wait, look." Eden pointed back towards the slab in front of them. Two inches of space had appeared at the bottom of the monolithic rock. As though weightless, the thing was sliding upwards.

Water streamed beneath the rock, but instead of filling the tunnel, Eden noticed it ran down the shaft into which Baxter had almost fallen.

"It's working like a counterweight," Eden said, shouting over the sound of grinding rock. Beaumont and Mo spun around, looking from one side of the tunnel to the other in amazement.

"It must be an airlock too," Beaumont said. "Sealing one side off when the other's empty. That must be how they keep the air and water pressure stable."

Eden rushed over to the slab and peered through the gap. With the water pounding through, she couldn't see anything. The noise of the groaning, crunching rock intensified. The slab juddered upwards another inch, then another, then once more.

Eden glanced back at Baxter, excitement buzzing through her veins.

The slab rose another couple of inches and the pressure of the water reduced to a trickle.

Eden shone her light through the gap, all danger forgotten. "There's a chamber on the other side," she said, peering through. "I can't see in clearly yet but, almost."

The slab groaned again and shuddered upwards another inch. Tiny shards of rock and dust floated down through the air. With an almighty tremble, the slab shuddered upwards yet another inch.

"That'll do it," Eden said, pushing herself through and into the void.

38

Eden's hands snaked across the wet stone, searching for something, anything to help pull her beneath the great stone. The slab above her moaned, shuddered, but relentlessly continued to climb.

Eden glanced upwards. The rock was now three or four inches above her head. For a moment, she thought about the possibility that the ancient system could fail and send the monolith crashing down on top of her. She would be crushed instantly, her bones ground to dust beneath the stone. With that thought, Eden kicked more furiously. Her feet scrabbled across the wet stone, moving her forward an inch at a time. She dug her nails into the floor, ignoring the pain of the rough surface against her fingertips.

Glancing ahead, Eden focused on the chamber beyond the slab. She could see it clearly now. Warm, bright light, streamed under the rising slab, as though she was emerging into daylight. Eden remembered what time of day it was outside and narrowed her eyes in confusion. It must be some trick of the light.

The rock grumbled again and climbed a couple of

inches more. Eden felt the vibration of the ancient mechanism through the floor, shaking the discs in her spine. She peered over her shoulder. She was now completely beneath the rising slab and had over ten feet to go, meaning the rock must be at least twenty feet in length. Of course, Eden had been impressed by the work of the ancient civilizations that built The Pyramids above, but this was something else. For a single rock of this size not only to be positioned this far beneath the surface of the earth, but to be constructed in such a way that it was able to rise was nothing short of a miracle. Eden glanced up at the shuddering megalith. It was now over a foot above her head. She rose into a crawling position and scampered beneath the rock and out into the light.

Eden blinked several times in the dazzling white light. Over the last half an hour, her eyes had grown used to exploring the tunnel by torchlight. Now, patterns danced across her vision. For several seconds nothing came into focus as her eyes struggled to adjust. Eden climbed laboriously to her feet and rubbed the moisture from her hands. Behind her, the giant slab ground its way further towards a distant ceiling.

Eden blinked again, closing her eyes for a couple of seconds each time. Eventually her eyes caught up, bringing her surroundings into focus.

Ahead of her, a set of stairs ran up onto a giant stone block. Eden scurried up the stairs and then froze, looking around in wonder. Eden's arms dropped lifelessly to her sides. She turned one way, and then the other, at first unable to make sense of what she saw.

Eden stood in the biggest underground chamber she had ever seen. In fact, it looked more like one of the many large religious buildings she had visited the world over. A forest of columns almost the width and height of Canada's great redwoods stretched towards the distant ceiling. Peering up, her neck aching at the uncomfortable angle, Eden saw that the bright light came from several orbs hanging motionless near the ceiling.

Eden turned her attention to the chamber itself. The entrance she'd crawled through emerged at the chamber's floor level. Multiple large stone blocks about thirty-foot square were arranged throughout the chamber. All the blocks were interconnected with stone walkways. She was standing on one such stone block at the very end of the chamber. She crossed to the edge of the block and peered down. Water lapped thirty feet below. She looked closely at the side of the rock. A line about half way up the block suggested that the water had recently receded.

Then she noticed what was on each of the other blocks. Some contained large stacks of tablets, others contained what appeared to be primitive books, several had figures of animals and people gilded in various precious metals. Right at the end, on a higher block than the others, sat the object of an Archaeologist's dreams. The Ark of the Covenant.

"I think we've found it," Baxter said, running up the steps behind Eden.

Eden nodded, not having the words to describe what they saw.

The slab shuddered further skywards, and Little Mo hustled in behind them.

"Allah Akbar," Mo whispered, turning one way and then the next. Then the Egyptian beamed from ear to ear. "I knew it!" he screamed, his voice echoing several times from the distant walls and ceiling. "My father was correct! He knew this place existed. So many people doubted him, but I never doubted him for a moment. Thank you, Allah, Allah Akbar, thank you, thank you!"

The big man collapsed into Islamic prayer, touching his forehead to the stone floor.

Eden and Baxter set off at a jog towards The Ark of the Covenant. Using the interconnecting walkways, they crossed several blocks, each containing tablets, large primitive books with thick yellowed pages, and carved golden figures.

Reaching the block on which the Ark was placed, Eden and Baxter slowed. They approached carefully, as though in the presence of royalty. About four feet in length, The Ark of the Covenant was constructed out of the brightest gold Eden had ever seen. A pair of cherubim, their wings extended, crouched on the top as though in prayer. Looking at the object, Eden had the feeling that it glimmered of its own accord. She struggled to pull her gaze away. She took another step forward.

"Don't touch it," Beaumont hissed, running towards them.

Eden froze in her tracks.

"My gosh," the professor whispered. "Never in my life did I think I would see this. You mustn't touch the Ark itself, only the handles." Beaumont pointed at two horizontal bars which ran through loops on the side of the ark. The bars appeared also to be covered in gold.

Eden walked around to the back of the Ark. She could just about hold both bars on her own, although it would certainly be easier to carry with four of them.

Baxter wandered on to the next plinth. Several tablets lay across the floor, next to animals which looked as though they were constructed from solid gold.

"Look," Baxter said, pointing at a tiny vial which each animal wore on a chain around its neck.

Eden followed him and stepped towards a tiger, carved in exquisite detail. She drew her hand across the back of the animal, feeling the curvature of its muscles. She crouched down and peered into the vial. The tiny tube contained several silver hairs.

"Do you think it's the tiger's DNA?" Eden said, looking up at Baxter.

"This isn't any old tiger," Mo said, walking up behind them. "This is what we now call the Caspian Tiger, notice how its legs are longer than a normal African or Asian tiger. It was declared extinct in 2003."

Eden stepped back and examined the statue. Mo was right, the tiger had large and incredibly powerful looking long, back legs.

"This is like the ark. It's a record of life on Earth," Eden said, aghast. She suddenly noticed how many animals there were. Innumerable animals, birds, and fish, all set in gold for eternity.

"Eden!" Baxter's voice echoed urgently through the chamber.

In her amazement, Eden hadn't even realized that he'd wandered further down the causeway to the next block. Eden turned and darted off after him.

Baxter stood face to face with the statue of a woman, constructed in incredible detail. Walking towards the woman, Eden felt her knees go weak. The room swam in front of her vision. The tectonic plates of her understanding again realigned somewhere in her mind. It was a sensation Eden had experienced several times in the last few months but was becoming no less uncomfortable.

"This woman," Baxter said, pointing at the statue. Baxter turned to look at Eden. "She really does look like you."

Eden stepped closer to the statue. Baxter was right. The

height, body shape, and facial features, did share something with Eden. Eden ran a finger down the woman's golden cheek. She had the same high cheekbones, full lips, and long slender nose. Eden moved her hand down over the woman's bare shoulder, to the vial that hung from her neck. Eden slid the vial over the golden woman's head and peered into the tiny glass tube. Several black hairs floated in a viscous liquid.

A report of gunfire thundered through the chamber, echoing several times before fading to nothing.

A bolt of electricity moved through Eden's body. She closed her fingers around the golden vial.

Eden, Baxter, and Mo spun around to face the entrance. There, by the door, a gun in her hand, stood Lulu King.

The two men Eden had seen at the Hotel Rumbold and again in the sewer, flanked King. Eden was getting sick at the sight of them.

King smiled, her expression that of a cobra studying its next meal.

"Thank you for leading us down here. For what it's worth, I had every faith in you."

39

"And what an exciting place we have here," King said, crossing the causeway towards Eden, Mo, and Baxter. "You know, I've been hearing rumors about this place for years. I always thought, wouldn't it be great if it did exist? I have to say, I'm very pleased to be here." King turned momentarily to examine a group of the golden animals. "What are these here?" The guards kept their guns and eyes trained on Eden, Beaumont, Baxter, and Mo the whole time.

"This is all very cute," King said, turning away from the animals. "But I'm not interested in this. Let's be fair, although my organization claims to be in it for the environment, profit comes first. I've known for decades, a realization my poor father never had, our planet needs a fuel that's more efficient than gas, oil, or even electricity. I also realized the lucky person who first discovers this fuel will be able to set his, or her, own price. This is a new era for King Industries. We will patent the process, we will develop the technology, and we will become, the biggest company on the planet." King took another step towards Eden.

Eden's hand closed more tightly around the vial she'd taken from the golden woman's neck.

It was too late. King had already seen the thin golden chain hanging from between Eden's fingers.

"What do you have there?" King said, stepping towards Eden.

Eden scowled at the other woman. King raised her gun and clicked off the safety.

"Nothing," Eden barked. "Now get that gun out of my face before I do something you'll regret."

King laughed, a humorless wail of a laugh. "Oh, it's easy to be tough now in front of your friends," she said, extending a palm toward Eden "Give me what you've got there."

Anger boiled over in Eden's body. She leaped at the woman, grabbing King's gun hand beneath her left arm, and forcing it towards the floor. Eden felt the gun discharge several times and hoped it hadn't hit anything. Eden sent two powerful fists into King's stomach.

King coughed and wheezed for breath.

Eden then swung an elbow, hitting King square on the cheek.

Seeing this movement, Baxter charged towards one of the guards. Weaving beneath a large golden horse, he stayed out of sight until he was within striking distance. The guards, both distracted by the attack on their boss, hadn't even noticed him.

Baxter leaped from behind the animal and struck out at the nearest guard. He knocked the gun from the man's hand. It went skittering down across the rock, almost falling into the water. Baxter sent three good punches, one after another, into the man's face. The man staggered backwards, his hands raised in defense.

Eden twisted, bending King's arm out of shape until she dropped the gun. Then she sent two more heavy jabs into the woman's face.

"Stop right now, or I will shoot you," a deep voice came from just inches behind Eden's ear. She felt the cold jab of a pistol against her neck.

Eden glanced behind her. The other of King's security guards stood poised, his finger on the trigger ready to fire. From this range, he could fire with no risk of hitting his boss.

It didn't mean she couldn't cause a little more pain, though. Eden snarled, grabbed a handful of King's hair, and tore it out by the roots.

King wailed in pain. Eden stepped away with her hands raised, the clump of King's hair twisted between her fingers.

King stared at Eden, fire burning in her eyes. She rubbed her hand across her face and then sniffed.

The guard turned his attention to his partner. Baxter stepped away, his hands raised too.

The disorientated guard, blood now oozing from his nose, picked up his gun and leveled it at Baxter.

Eden slipped the handful of hair into her pocket. If they got out of here alive, she figured it may come in useful.

"And to think I was seriously considering letting you live." King spat a globule of phlegm and blood to the floor. "Not anymore. Now give me that."

Knowing she was beaten, Eden handed over the vial. King held it up to the light, then slipped it into her pocket.

"Any more of that, and you'll get a bullet for breakfast. No questions asked." King pointed at Baxter. "He's a cutie. He must really care about you. If you don't want him to get hurt, I suggest you keep your dog on a leash. Now Miss

Black, we had a deal, didn't we? You just stand aside, I'll get what I need, and you can get on your way."

Baxter, Beaumont, and Mo turned to face Eden, shock etched into their faces.

"Oh bless, you mean you didn't tell them about our little deal? Sorry gentlemen, Eden and I had a deal, isn't that right?" King took a step towards Eden. The grey eyes felt as though they were drilling into her.

Eden nodded once. "Lulu knows where my father is," Eden said.

Neither Baxter, Mo nor Beaumont spoke.

"That's not all, is it?" King said.

"No. She also has planted evidence framing me for murder, which she would release if I didn't lead her here."

"All of this was just because she was blackmailing you?" Baxter said in a violent whisper.

"No, of course not. We needed to find this place. It just happened that she needed..."

"Stop now," Lulu interjected. "You'll have all the time in the world to discuss this when I have what I need. For now, I need your help," she pointed at Little Mo. "Somewhere in this room is the Book of Enoch and the Book of Giants. I need them."

"It could take months to find that." Mo held out his palms in surrender. "This place is..."

"I don't need you to translate them for me. I have people to do that. I just need you to tell me where they are."

Mo glanced at Eden.

Eden nodded. "Show her. We have no choice."

King grinned again.

"You stay with these two. If they move, they die. Understand?" King barked.

The henchmen nodded, their bulging muscles holding the large guns as though they weighed nothing.

"That way," King pointed down the causeway. "Quickly. We don't have time for games."

As though on cue, a shudder moved through the thick rock walls around them.

Little Mo looked over his shoulder at the others and then set off down the causeway. There was a sense of calm in the Egyptian's expression, Eden thought. The look gave Eden a strange hope that Mo knew exactly what he was doing.

Another rumble echoed through the giant chamber. Several of the gold statues vibrated together with a metallic clang.

King's henchmen peered anxiously at the roof as a cloud of dust floated down.

For a moment, Eden considered using their distraction to launch an attack. Her muscles tensed just as the big men turned their attention back to her.

Mo and King were now on the next block, thirty or forty feet away. Mo had paused to look at a set of tablets. He scanned the tablets, as though searching for familiar symbols.

Bubbling water echoed through the chamber now. Eden turned and looked towards the passage they had passed through several minutes before. A slow trickle of water now flowed in from the passage.

"We don't have long. The water is coming back," Eden said, pointing. "That means the water will flow back into the tunnel. Once it does, that door will close."

"Silence!" King roared, her voice reverberating through the chamber. "Your complaints will only delay the inevitable."

"It's not here," Mo said. "I can't tell exactly, but here they're talking about the treatment of certain illnesses. There are lists of recipes and ingredients, that sort of thing." Mo walked on to the next block, on which another set of tablets were displayed.

King followed him cautiously, her gun drawn.

The trickle from the passage increased to a torrent. The white water streamed into the chamber, down onto the floor, swirling and bubbling.

Eden's head whipped from King to the thugs, then to the door and back again. Her gaze narrowed. She realized what must have caused the pressure to drop again so quickly, and how King and her rottweilers had made it inside.

"You jammed that slab open, didn't you?" Eden said. "This whole system is built on finely balanced air and water pressure, and you idiots left the door open."

The men glanced at each other anxiously.

"Right now, we have thousands of tons of water streaming this way, and you've left the door open." Eden's voice reverberated from distant stone walls.

King swung around. "I've told you to be..."

"This is it," Mo said, interrupting the women. King turned back to face him.

Mo continued speaking, as though in a trance. "For all my life, I have heard rumors of such a thing, but I never thought I would see it in all my days." Mo stepped towards a stone slab with two large, pre-historic books on it. The books looked as though they were bound in leather with thick and uneven yellowed pages inside, possibly made from papyrus. "This is it. This has got to be it. The secret that could solve all our energy needs."

"And make King Industries the most powerful organiza-tion in the world." King stepped forwards, barging Mo out of the way. Mo stumbled to the side, almost falling into the water, which now raged twenty feet below.

"You can't keep this to yourself. Humanity deserves this. It's our right…"

"There are no rights." King turned her icy gaze on the Egyptian. "Don't you get it, you fool, you have no rights, none of us do. We work, we live, we die. And even then, when you're a lifeless pile of skin and bone, even then you'll have to pay for your own hole in the ground." King snapped her fingers. The henchmen rushed towards her, forgetting about their prisoners. They slipped bags from their backs and placed them on the floor beside their boss. King and the guards slid on white gloves and manhandled the first book into one of the bags. "And with this, I will have all the money imaginable."

A slow clap reverberated through the cavern. "Bravo, well done," Eden said, stepping forwards, closing the distance between King and herself.

King looked at Eden, her head tilted curiously to one side.

"I don't understand how someone can be quite so stupid," Eden said. "This has got nothing to do with money. The potential of the information within these books and the Ark of the Covenant is so much greater than that. This is not just about having the power to run your TV or air conditioning. This could deliver affordable transport, water, food, and medicine to the world's poorest and richest people alike. This would allow all people to live in comfort, independently. How many wars are caused by gas and oil? How many corrupt governments are propped up by our need for fossil fuels? What you have here could end it all. It would start a new era where all occupants of the planet have a chance."

"It could, it could," King replied, looking genuinely thoughtful for a moment. "But what's in that for me? This isn't some utopian dream. I'm not a good Samaritan. The health of humankind does not get me up in the morning. I'm a businesswoman. I don't have time for your idealistic nonsense."

Another noise boomed through the chamber, shaking the walls.

Eden felt the stone beneath them vibrate, too. Her knees shook.

King looked back at the entrance, a flicker of concern crossing her face.

"Get this packed." King pointed at the second book. "Quickly. Now!"

King and the thugs grabbed the second book, less carefully than the first and slid it inside the bag. One of the thugs sealed up the bag tightly. It looked as though it was designed to withstand water, fortunately.

Another splintering crash boomed through the chamber. Rocks the size of fists fell from the ceiling, crashing against the priceless artifacts.

Everyone glanced fearfully at the ceiling.

The thugs heaved the bags up onto their shoulders.

King led the way down the causeway and up to the Ark of the Covenant.

"You," King pointed at Beaumont. "Here, now!" It takes four people to carry the Ark. Come with us now, and you will survive."

Beaumont swallowed, his Adam's apple bobbing. He looked guiltily from Baxter to Mo and then to Eden.

"Go," Eden whispered. "We're not dying down here. We will see you again soon."

Beaumont jogged up to the Ark and seized the front handle, beside King.

"Lift," King roared. With the guards at the back, King and Beaumont from the front, the Ark of the Covenant rose from its resting place of several thousand years. King and the guards continued to hold their weapons ready for any attack.

Another shower of rocks fell from the roof.

Eden looked at the giant slab of rock under which they'd crawled a few minutes before. The monolith was already over halfway down. The stone shuddered again as the pre-historic mechanism lowered slowly towards its resting position.

King, the guards and Beaumont shuffled towards the exit. Reaching the slab, King stopped and turned. The slab was already at the height of her shoulders. Knee high water streamed down the passage and into the chamber. King turned to face Eden, Baxter, and Mo. "If you follow us through here, you will die," King shouted over the roaring water. "You wanted to spend some time with these artifacts. I'll make that wish a reality."

40

_____

THE SLAB SHUDDERED DOWNWARDS AGAIN, now just three feet from sealing up altogether. A thunderous crack rolled through the cavern.

Eden ran down the stairs and peered through the gap. King and her men had moved to the back of the space. They would soon disappear through the airlock and into the next tunnel. White water streamed furiously through the gap, almost concealing the space on the other side.

"We need to seal this up," Mo cried, pointing towards the slab. "If this remains open, the pressure will drop and the whole place will be destroyed."

"Not yet," Eden said. "We're not dying in here."

She scanned the cavern for something they could use to hold the door open just long enough for King and her men to disappear.

To the right, just a few feet away, sat a giant golden chalice. In the excitement of entering the chamber, Eden hadn't noticed it before.

She ran across and inspected the chalice. It was about two feet in height with a sturdy stem. Set into the gold, several jewels glimmered. Eden tried to pull the chalice forwards. It was incredibly heavy and hardly moved.

Baxter ran across to help her. Together, huffing and puffing, Eden and Baxter heaved the chalice down the stairs and towards the sinking door. With each groan and shudder, the giant rock crept closer to its final, indefinite, resting place.

"Now, push it!" Eden screamed as they reached the door. Baxter shoved the chalice hard. It slid beneath the slab. The slab stuttered down, crunching against the golden rim. The chalice twisted, but miraculously, precariously, held.

An almighty groan echoed through the chamber. Numerous rocks, now the size of bricks, thudded into the water.

"Let's go," Eden said, peering through the gap. King and her men were nowhere to be seen. They would soon pick their way up the spiral staircase with the Ark of the Covenant in tow.

Baxter stepped forwards, ready to dive beneath the slab.

Eden prepared herself to go. Battling against the ferocious water, it was going to be a struggle to get out. Eden glanced around. She couldn't see Mo anywhere.

Eden stood up and turned.

Mo stood a few feet away. He stared at something where the chalice had been.

"Mo," Eden screamed, barely audible over the pounding water. "We need to go now!"

But Mo wasn't listening. He stepped, absent minded, away from the passage altogether.

Eden rushed across to the man and then saw what he was looking at.

Behind the position where the chalice had sat, there was a niche. It was a similar size and shape to those they had seen beneath The Sphinx earlier. The niche was almost filled by a large stone casket. As Eden stepped closer, she observed something else in there too.

Covered in the ragged fabric of rotting clothes, two skeletons lay side by side.

Eden stepped towards the niche. The skeletons wore green cargo pants and shirts, suggesting that these people were not from ancient times. Strands of hair and piles of dust surrounded the bodies.

Mo stepped forwards again, entranced.

A crash as loud as an exploding bomb reverberated through the chamber, but Mo didn't even turn. He was focused only on the bodies now, lying side by side in the niche.

Reaching the skeletons, Mo dropped into a crouch. To Eden, it looked as though he was in a spiritual trance.

Mo reached towards the smaller skeleton's left wrist. He lifted the skeleton's sleeve carefully. His eyes widened, and he dropped to his knees in the water.

"We need to go," Baxter roared above the sound of the hammering water. Furious foam smashed beneath the slab now, threatening to topple the chalice and seal the entrance shut.

"One minute," Eden shouted back. She rushed up to Mo's side.

Mo snapped from his trance and locked eyes with Eden. "My father was telling the truth. He discovered the chamber over thirty years ago." Mo lifted the wrist again and fiddled with something. He removed his father's watch and held it up to Eden. "As above, so below," he whispered, reading this inscription on the watch's base.

"I always believed you," Eden said, her hands closing around Mo's upper arm. "He would never have gone away and left you through choice. He's been here all along."

Another crash thundered through the chamber, shaking the rock beneath them. Water whipped around them in all directions now.

"We need to seal this chamber before it all comes crashing down," Baxter yelled.

"We need to close the door," Eden said, pulling Mo slowly away from the skeleton. "And once we do, there'll be no way to open it again. You must come with us."

Slowly, like an old man being brought to his deathbed, Mo climbed to his feet. He looked around at the chamber, holding his father's watch to his chest.

The giant slab groaned and shuddered, twisting the chalice which held it open out of shape. A splinter of gold snapped from the side and the door grunted an inch towards its base.

"We go, now!" Baxter shouted.

"Let's go," Eden said to Mo. "We're going to have to swim under."

Eden and Mo staggered towards the door, spray slamming against their shins.

"There's no time to wait now. We go together," Eden shouted when they stood beside Baxter. "Are you ready?"

Baxter nodded.

Eden looked at Little Mo, who nodded too, then slipped the watch inside his pocket.

With one more glance at Baxter, Eden took a deep breath and slid beneath the slab. She half staggered, half swam forwards.

Water rushed across her skin, tearing at her face and arms. She tried to open her eyes but saw nothing but the angry foam. She blinked, trying to clear her vision. Her eyes stung with the raging water. The water pummeled against

Eden's body like tiny fists of steel. She leaned into the torrent, her feet scrabbling against the stone beneath.

Above her, tons of rock moaned and groaned, destined to slam down at any moment.

Eden tensed every muscle in her body and pushed forwards. She dug her fingers and toes into the floor, pulling herself inch by inch towards safety.

With one final push, Eden felt the current around them reduce. She opened her eyes again and, in the gloom, saw that they had slipped from under the slab. A beam of light came from somewhere in the chamber.

Her lungs burning for air now, Eden forced herself upwards. Her arms outstretched, she kicked hard towards the surface. Water streamed across her face. Sour air burned inside her lungs.

Eventually, she felt the smooth rock of the ceiling with her hands. She kicked again and her face broke through the surface of the water. Eden gasped frantically. There was about a foot of air remaining at the top of the tunnel, but it was closing fast.

She looked across the surface of the water, swirling and bubbling angrily. A light moved somewhere deep within the water.

An explosive thud echoed through the chamber. The walls shook, and the water sloshed one way and then the other. Debris fell from the ceiling, slamming into the murky depths. The thud echoed several times and then everything went still. It felt to Eden as though she were standing in the eye of the storm. Her desperate breathing suddenly sounded loud in the enclosed space. The water around her slowed, spinning around the chamber a couple more times before coming to a rest.

Eden peered down into the depths. The light was still on

and still moving. She watched as the light turned and then powered towards the surface.

Baxter broke through the surface of the water, the light in his hand. He shook his head and then rubbed a hand across his face.

"You made it!" Eden shouted, suddenly overcome with relief and fear. She leaped forward and wrapped her arms around Baxter. He put his arms around her too. Feeling Baxter's body beside hers, Eden felt a strange sensation of comfort.

Water lapped slowly and rhythmically against the walls now.

"Where's Mo?" Eden said, little more than a whisper. "He must be down there." Eden pulled herself free from Baxter's embrace, kicked into a dive and headed down through the water. She ran her hand across the slab as she swam down. Reaching the floor, her heart sunk. She tried to force her hand between the slab and floor, but the two were so perfectly joined there was just a hairline crack. Although Eden knew her actions were futile, she pushed at the slab. With the slab back in place, the great hall on the other side was sealed to the outside world. Like it had been for thousands of years.

Her breath running out, Eden turned and kicked back to the surface.

"He didn't make it," Baxter said, when Eden broke through the water.

Eden pushed the hair from her face and looked around frantically. "We've got to find a way back through there. We can do it. I know we can. We can't leave him in there!"

Baxter shook his head once. "We need to get out of here."

"But we can't!" Eden started to argue before her voice

lost all conviction. With countless tons of rock between
them and Mo, there was nothing they could do.

LITTLE MO STOOD in the chaos, and for possibly the first
time in his life saw how simple things were. Water pounded
in from beneath the slab, flooding the chamber. He glanced
around at all the priceless artifacts which were set to be
destroyed if the water continued to flow. As though issuing
another non-subtle reminder, several clumps of rock fell
from the roof. The pressure in the chamber had already
dropped far below safe levels.

Ahead of him, Mo watched Baxter and Eden dive
beneath the slab. He stepped forward and watched them
half swim, half scramble through the gap.

He looked at the heavy golden chalice. With that in the
way, the chamber would never be properly sealed again and
all the artifacts inside would be destroyed.

Little Mo glanced over at his father's body, lying in the
niche twenty feet away. Mo put a hand to his chest and felt
the shape of his father's watch in his shirt pocket. He knew
exactly what he had to do. Like his father before him, it was
now Mo's time to be the great preserver of the vault.

Mo stepped up to the chalice and, with one mighty
sweep, pulled it from beneath the slab. The metal crunched
and groaned against the rock and then came free. With a
colossal thud, shaking the chamber from wall to wall, the
slab fell, sealing the chamber from the outside world.

The last ebbs of water ran from the causeway and
bubbled into silence. Mo exhaled, then dropped the chalice
to the ground. The clang echoed around the space for
several seconds before dying into silence.

Mo turned and looked around. The dozens of golden animals looked back at him, their secrets preserved for another generation or two.

Little Mo walked across to the niche and slumped down against the wall. He slipped the watch from his pocket again. Another boom echoed through the chamber. Mo looked up just in time to see part of the ceiling come loose and several rocks the size of cars fall towards him.

Mo closed his hand around the watch as the rocks fell.

"As above, so below," he whispered to himself.

41

Lulu King led the way out through the hatchway and into the laundromat's unassuming backroom. She and Professor Beaumont carried the front two poles, which took the weight of the Ark of the Covenant. Abdul and Sharif grumbled under the weight of the Ark at the back, and the heavy bags containing the ancient books.

Getting the Ark through the water below had been easier than King thought. Abdul had gone first, laying a rope through the water. They had tied one end to the Ark. Abdul had then pulled the thing through, while the rest of them pushed it. Although the gold was heavy and tried to sink to the bottom, the four of them managed to heave it through without too much difficulty.

"Come on," King said, swinging her light from side to side with her free hand.

They moved through the laundromat, passing the decaying machines, and the crumbling walls. There was something fitting, King thought, that a rundown place like this was quite literally the gateway to a subterranean treasure trove. It was the sort of place that no one would ever think to look.

King checked the time. Less than an hour had passed since they'd entered the laundromat. It felt like so much longer. So much had happened. She thought about the Ark now in their possession and the contents of the packs which should tell them exactly how to use it. A new future was now possible because of what was in there. A very lucrative future for King Industries.

Abdul and Sharif grunted, taking the last few steps slowly. King led them through into the laundromat's front room.

"Put it down," King barked. They lowered the Ark of the Covenant to the floor in the middle of the room. King turned and looked at the thing. It seemed to glow, as though producing a light of its own.

King slid out her phone and placed a call. "We're coming out. Be ready."

"Roger that," came the reply, before the line was cut.

King pushed open the grimy door and stepped out onto the street. Stripes of blue began to color the sky as dawn approached. King felt an uncharacteristic flare of excitement. A new dawn was coming. A dawn that was bringing with it a new era for her and King Industries.

She turned back to face Beaumont. The man took a step backwards, as though trying to shrink into the gloom.

"Thank you for your help, Professor," King said, taking a step towards the man.

Beaumont took two steps backwards and collided with Abdul's barrel chest. Beaumont turned, and the Angolan snarled.

"Not this again, Professor," Lulu crowed, watching the professor's vain attempt to escape.

Abdul grabbed Beaumont's arms behind his back.

The professor struggled for a few seconds, before accepting it was futile and becoming still.

"You know, you're lucky I'm not a sensitive person," King said, her voice oozing with sarcasm. "It seems as though you're always trying to get away from me. Was it something I said? You know, it never had to be like this. You could have been working with us. You could have had a share of the glory. Never mind. Tie him up in the truck."

King pointed towards the Toyota Hilux parked a few feet away.

"You sure, boss?" Abdul grunted. "He might become a loose end."

King thought for a moment about killing the man and dumping his body somewhere outside the city, but there really wasn't any need. She expected that in a few hours someone would find him. But then The Ark would be well away from here. She'd got what she'd come for and he'd got nothing. Of course, Beaumont might try to tell people about what she'd done—but who would believe him? The people who spouted about secret passages beneath Giza and the forgotten technologies of ancient civilizations had long been thought of as at the wrong end of the sanity spectrum.

"No. He'll be fine. Plus, we never know when we might need his knowledge again. You would be willing to help us again in the future, wouldn't you professor?"

Beaumont refused to meet the woman's gaze.

Abdul shoved Beaumont into the driver's seat of the Hilux, dug out a pair of lock ties and quickly bound Beaumont's hands. Then with a third lock tie, Abdul secured Beaumont's hands to the wheel. The Angolan pulled against the makeshift shackles, testing the strength. The man was secured, tight inside the car.

Beaumont winced as the tough plastic cut into his skin.

King stepped towards the truck. "It's such a shame. A capable man like you," King said, looking down at the professor. "Maybe I'm becoming weak, but I have respect for you and all that you've done, that's why I'm going to let you live. You'll see this through, from the side-lines at least. You'll see how it rockets my company to one of the most successful the world has ever known."

Beaumont snarled, but still refused to look at the woman attempting to rile him up.

"That's more than can be said for your idiotic friends," King continued. "They will meet their demise deep beneath The Giza Plateau tonight. In fact, they're probably already dead."

Beaumont glanced at the woman.

"Just relax, Professor. There really is nothing you can do. By the time someone finds you here, I'll have what I need, and your friends will be dead."

A black Mercedes-Benz Sprinter van sped around the corner, tires squealing across the asphalt and engine roaring. The van grunted to a stop outside the laundromat. Two men wearing tactical gear clambered out. They were the extraction team King had hired to get her prize out of Egypt and safely back to the States. Of course, she would have preferred to stay with it herself, but appearances had to be maintained. Visiting Egypt under the ruse of advising a local charity, she still had some work to do. Of course, she could wiggle her way out of it, but sometimes it paid to keep up appearances.

Still out of breath, Abdul and Sharif helped the men place the Ark of the Covenant into the back of the Sprinter. They strapped it carefully to hooks built into the van's sides.

King watched the process, hypnotized by the glow the object seemed to emit.

Abdul and Sharif placed the bags containing the complete Book of Enoch and the Book of Giants beside the Ark. Abdul slammed the doors, snapping King out of her trance.

"I want regular updates," King said to the extraction team. The men paced back to the cab.

"Of course. We'll be in the air within the hour." The engine roared again, and the van sped away.

42

THE FIRST RAYS of dawn broke over The Pyramids of Giza, as they had every morning for thousands of years. At first, tongues of purple warned of the incoming day, lighting the sky with fire. Then, the sun appeared, laboriously dragging herself from the desert sand.

One by one the lights of the nearby buildings flickered off, their work for the night complete.

In the center of it all, The Great Pyramid stood resolute, casting a bulky shadow across The Plateau.

Preparing for another day's business in the stifling heat, early merchants unpacked their loads without haste. Nearby, a pair of camels snoozed in the dust, swatting incumbent flies from each other's faces.

Suddenly, the *thump thump* of helicopter rotors cut through the still morning air. A Eurocopter AS350, flying just a hundred feet above the ground shot over the desert sand.

The resting camels peered at the incoming beast with curiosity. Having seen these machines before, they settled back into the dust. It was not yet time to get up.

The chopper powered on across The Plateau, churning dust, sand, and debris into great clouds. Tracking a line between The Pyramid of Khufu and The Sphinx, the pilot didn't even slow. This clearly wasn't a tourist trip.

After passing The Plateau, the copter circled twice over the center of Nazlet-El-Samman. Sighting its target, the machine slowed, hovered, and then dipped between the buildings. For thirty seconds, the sound of the pumping rotors muted into the murmur of the city.

"HOLD ON A MINUTE," Eden said, climbing aboard the chopper and shuffling down to make space for Baxter and Beaumont. "We had to do all of that just the four of us, and now you choose to call in the big guns."

Baxter pulled on the headset which hung from the ceiling beside him.

Eden did the same.

Beaumont shuffled into the end seat, still rubbing his wrists where Lulu King's bindings had held him captive for the last hour.

"Good to have you aboard, captain," the pilot said.

Baxter leaned over and slid the door closed with an ease that demonstrated this wasn't his first time aboard such a machine.

"Captain?" Eden said, looking at Baxter.

Baxter caught Eden's gaze. "You'll get your answers. Now it's time to get out of here." He turned to the pilot.

Eden turned and looked out through the window. Yet again she felt like the world was moving around her in a way she didn't understand. "The answers better come soon," she whispered. "I'm getting sick of this."

"When you're ready, officer," Baxter said.

The pilot turned back to the controls and the great beast shuddered upwards. Swathes of trash danced one way, and then the other in the chopper's powerful wake.

Eden looked out at the nondescript laundromat, below which the secrets to pre-historic societies lay hidden in plain sight. One small part of those secrets would soon come to light. How long the rest would lay hidden, she had no idea.

Noticing Mo's beat-up Toyota beside the laundromat, Eden felt a welling sense of sadness. For the last few months, disaster seemed to chase after her, and it was always the good guys who ended up losing out.

Baxter slipped a small device from his pocket. "Fire in the hole," he shouted, pressing the button.

A bright light flashed from the engine of the pickup below. Glass shattered as the spark became a fireball. The flames rattled from the truck, licking up into the air.

Eden pressed her nose against the window. Flames engulfed the laundromat, barely a few yards below the copter's landing gear. Within seconds, the windows shattered, and fire roared up the front of the building.

"The whole block's been evacuated," Baxter said to no one in particular. "Suspected gas leak. Our team will be in to clean it up in a few hours. They'll seal the whole place up again so that no one finds that passage."

"Unless we want them to," Eden said.

The chopper swung hard to the right, giving Eden an uninterrupted view of the destruction below.

"That's right," Baxter said. "Unless we want them to."

∽

Almost an hour later the chopper powered out of Egyptian airspace and over the Mediterranean Sea.

Eden turned and watched the land of sand and pharaohs shrink into the horizon behind them. Her mind relentlessly turned over the events of the last three days. For her, whichever way she looked at it, she couldn't help but see it as a massive failure.

Lulu King had the Ark of the Covenant, and the instructions to use it. The secret to affordable power had slipped through the fingers of the masses again, and into the undeserving clutches of the few. Punishing herself, Eden thought of all the applications for which this could be used— pumping water to remote villages, sustainably delivering food, pharmaceuticals, and other supplies, and of course, cutting the carbon emissions of the world's powerhouse nations. But that was done now. The secret was out, and all was lost, and Little Mo was dead.

Eden glanced at Beaumont. He looked exhausted, peering out of the opposite side of the chopper.

"Five minutes out," the pilot said.

"Roger," Baxter said, nodding.

Eden scrutinized the sea beneath them. If they were landing in five minutes, then their final destination would soon be revealed. Undisturbed water sparkled in all directions. She sat back and exhaled. She would find out soon enough where they were going. Frankly, if it had food and somewhere to rest, she didn't care anymore. Right now, she didn't even have the energy to ask.

A large yacht appeared, shimmering on the horizon.

The chopper slowed, and their altitude decreased.

As they drew close, Eden peered down at the craft. It had decks spread out on several levels, some clearly for relaxing with chairs tables and sun loungers, others for more functional reasons with strange apparatus, antennas, and what looked like weather measuring equipment.

Eden noticed something that caused her to sit up straight. Projecting from the front deck of the yacht was a symbol she recognized, a symbol which had been following her around through the whole sorry mess: The Key to the Nile.

The copter slowed further, descended, and then banked towards the large deck at the rear of the yacht. The railing around the deck lowered outwards, powered by hidden motors, to give the pilot more room to maneuver.

Eden peered down at the water, twenty feet below them. The spray danced in ever-increasing circles as the chopper descended. They passed over the rear deck, obscuring Eden's view of the water.

The pilot carefully touched down. The chopper bounced twice and then settled down on the gently bobbing craft. It was clear to Eden that the pilot had done this landing many times before. The pilot reached up and snapped off several switches, powering down the engine. The chopper whined and then the rotors began to slow.

Baxter took off his headset, stowed it away and slid open the door. He hopped down to the yacht's polished wooden deck.

Eden pulled off her headset and shuffled towards the door.

Baxter held out his hand to help her down.

Eden looked at the hand for a second. Then, realizing how exhausted she was, accepted the help and slipped down on to the deck. She looked up at the yacht, squinting in the bright sunlight. The location of their extraction and set down could not have been more different.

The rotors finally whined into silence. The pilot set about tethering the chopper to the deck with large straps.

Eden noticed a door at the back of the yacht slide open and several figures walked out onto the deck. Eden blinked, forcing her eyes to focus.

Three people stepped from the shadows of the yacht's interior. Two of them, Eden didn't think she'd seen before.

Setting eyes on the third person, Eden froze. She opened her mouth. The tension in her shoulders dropped. Her feelings of fatigue turned to confusion, then on to astonishment, then to elation.

Eden set off at a sprint across the deck, all tiredness forgotten.

Alexander Winslow, her father, saw her coming and opened his arms in preparation.

Father and daughter merged into a fierce hug.

Then Eden pulled away and looked at him again, still not quite believing what she was seeing.

"Welcome to the Balonia," Winslow said.

43

ONE OF WINSLOW'S ASSISTANTS, a woman named Athena, showed Eden to a cabin on the top floor of the yacht.

"I'll wait out here for you," Athena said. "Get showered and changed and I'll take you straight to your father's office. I know you'll have questions."

Eden turned and looked directly at the woman for the first time. A strange chime of recognition sounded somewhere deep within Eden's memory. She felt as though she had seen the woman before, although she couldn't place it.

"Get changed? Did you see me bring a suitcase?" Eden said, pointing down at her damp and tattered clothes.

"We've taken care of that. Our team collected a few of your possessions from the villa in New Giza." The woman pointed to a case on the side table.

Eden opened her mouth as though to say something but thought better of it. "Thank you," she snapped unconvincingly. "I won't be long."

"Take all the time you need."

Eden shut the door and stalked through the room. The cabin, like the rest of the yacht, was luxurious. One wall, made completely of glass, offered an undisturbed view of the sea. A large, incredibly comfortable looking bed sat against one wall. Eden looked at the bed longingly, suspecting she was probably tired enough to find comfort on a knife's edge.

Eden padded through into the bathroom and started the shower. She stripped off and let the hot water sooth her aching muscles for several minutes, then dumped her tattered clothes in the bin and dressed in fresh ones.

"Just so I'm clear on this," Eden said, pacing into her father's office three minutes later. "You are this Helios character I've heard so much about?"

"That's right," Winslow said. "It's a role I've had for over twenty years now. I'll explain everything to you."

"You better." Clean and changed, Eden felt better already. She was ready to find out what was so important that her father had to fake his death, even keeping his only daughter in the dark.

Eden looked briefly around the office. Set into the bow of the yacht, three sides were made from glass, affording the office a one-eighty view of the sea. Several bookshelves lined the walls that weren't made from glass and a large leather-topped desk housed a high-tech computer. Eden thought that in some ways it looked like the attic office that had been destroyed back in Brighton, just on steroids.

"Is there anything I can do, Helios?" Athena said.

"Thank you, Athena," Winslow said, turning to face the assistant who'd shown Eden back from her cabin. "Nothing now. I'll get in contact if you can help me at all."

Glancing back at the assistant, Eden was suddenly

struck by a memory. The woman looked just like someone she had met several months ago after their car had broken down in rural Lebanon. The woman had ultimately given Eden a clue that pointed them in the right direction.

Winslow shut the door, the noise raking Eden back from her thoughts. He crossed the room, folded his arms, and leaned against the desk.

"You're right, I have a lot of explaining to do. I hope that after you know everything, as well as I can explain it, you'll start to understand why I did what I did."

Eden spun around and glared at her father. "Why you made me believe you were dead for months. I attended your funeral. I watched them lower your coffin into the ground. How do you think that felt?"

Winslow held Eden's gaze. "I was there too. You didn't see me, but I was there. In fact, I've been close by these last few months making sure no harm came to you."

"Is that supposed to make it better? Was that supposed to make it easier for me? Why couldn't you just tell..."

Winslow took a step forwards, his expression grave. "There are very powerful forces at work here, Eden. Powerful organizations that have kept humankind imprisoned for thousands of years. You think people out there have freedom?" He pointed towards the sea beyond the glass wall. "If there was any suspicion that I was planning to reveal what we have, then I would have been dead in an instant. You wouldn't have been spared either. Everyone had to be totally convinced of my death. Any hint that it wasn't true and the whole thing would come tumbling down."

Thoughts churned through Eden's mind, most of which she couldn't make sense of. "But Lulu King found out you were alive. She showed me a video of you arriving at Cairo Airport in exchange for showing her into the vault. And now she has the Ark of the Covenant and Little Mo is dead, and that's on me." Eden spat the final words.

"Yes. It went exactly to plan. Almost," Winslow said, taking another step towards his daughter. "The loss of Mohammed Muhr is a hit for us all."

Eden remembered her father's knowing look in the security camera footage and the way he wore his chain with the Key to the Nile on the outside of his shirt. Eden glanced at her father's chest. The Key to the Nile was tucked out of sight, as she remembered it usually was. Her hand rose instinctively to her chest where her Key to the Nile was always placed.

She paused for a moment, events swirling through her mind. "How is that exactly to plan? When King figures out this new technology, it will make her even more rich than she already is. This was our chance to level the playing field. This was our chance to start giving people the freedom they deserve."

"And that is exactly what will happen," Winslow said, slowly. "Just because you can't see things happening in the background, doesn't mean there isn't a plan in motion" Winslow's tone softened. "We have a person inside King's organization, in fact we have several. When the time is right, the technology will be leaked to the wider world. King won't be able to stop it. She will be denied the patent and everyone else will copy the technology her team has uncovered. Of course, she will get some of the credit for discovering this, but this is too important to keep under wraps."

Slowly things started to make sense for Eden. "Why couldn't we just give this out to the people who really needed it? Wouldn't that be quicker? You've obviously got the ability to do that." Eden pointed around the yacht's opulent fixtures.

"Because," Winslow said, holding Eden's gaze. "Right now, we don't exist. This organization, this ship, everything you see here, even me, doesn't officially exist. That's the way we work. That's the way this organization has worked for thousands of years. We sit in the background, watching, controlling things, and making moves when The Council deems they are necessary."

"The Council?"

"Yes, The Council of Selene is made up of me and eight other councilors. Each of our roles have been passed down through the generations. None of us know who the other members are. They could be businesspeople, politicians, public servants, anyone—"

"Helios?" Eden said, questioning the name she'd heard the assistant call her father.

"Yes," Winslow said. "We all assume titles from the ancient gods. That ensures each council member's safety and anonymity. It's the way it has worked for generations."

Eden thought about it for a few seconds. "You needed to find the Diary of Aloma because it led us to this power source, to Seth's vault, The Hall of Records, whatever you want to call it. But isn't it a risk that it also exposes the existence of The Council of Selene?"

Winslow took another step closer to his daughter. "That is true. But it is now time for change. Over the years, The Council has monitored the progression of humankind, started conflicts, ended conflicts, elected leaders, and assassinated leaders. Our time is drawing to a close and a new era is beginning."

"Wait a minute," Eden said, not immediately understanding what her father meant. "You *want* The Council to be discovered. You are planning to bring it down from the inside."

"That's right," Winslow said. "We've had our time. It's now time for humanity to govern itself."

A beeping noise came from the phone system on the desk. Winslow turned and thumbed the button.

"Go ahead, Athena."

"Last night's disturbance around The Giza Plateau has been reported as seismic activity, just as you asked for it to be. Al-Jazeera are reporting on it now."

"Thank you." Winslow scooped up a remote control and clicked a large TV into action. A shot of a presenter standing in front of The Pyramids filled the screen.

"You've covered up the whole thing?" Eden asked, already knowing the answer.

"That's the thing about the truth," Winslow said, turning to face his daughter. "Most often, it's far too unrealistic for anyone to believe."

44

LULU KING PACED UP to the window and peered out at the streets of Cairo, baking below in the midday sun. Her gaze rose towards the horizon. There, just visible, the bulky shapes of The Pyramids danced in rising thermals.

She looked at her watch for the fifth time in as many minutes. It had been over six hours since she'd passed The Ark of the Covenant and the books to her extraction team, and she had yet to hear an update. She did some silent calculations and figured they should now be somewhere over the Atlantic. By the end of the day, they would make it to the United States, landing on a private airstrip in Texas, and then the real work would begin.

With a team of the brightest scientific minds already on the King Industries' payroll, Lulu hoped for them to turn this project around in a matter of months. Of course, that was optimistic, but paying top dollar, she also demanded the best from her team.

A ghost of a smile flashed across King's face. Very soon, if things went as she'd expected, they would be the only organization in the world to control this power. King would be able to license it for any figure she desired. She rubbed her hands together. This was indeed a new era for King Industries. The company was about to enter leagues that had been so far unimagined.

King checked her watch again. Still, she wouldn't feel comfortable until she heard that their prize was at home. Ideally, she would have liked to travel with the extraction team, but she had come into Egypt officially under the ruse of working with a local charity. Sure, she could have paid her way out of it, but sometimes it was best to play along. There was nothing she could do back in the States now, anyway. It was over to her team. She would be back there soon enough.

Even so, she was overdue an update. King strode across to the desk and picked up the bulky satellite phone. She placed the call to the leader of the extraction team. She held the phone to her ear and wandered back to the window.

The phone rang, mysterious and distant. It buzzed three times, King's anxiety rising with each tone before it was answered.

The ringing stopped. A voice strained down the line. "Yes."

"It's King. Report on your location."

The man, sounding frustrated, reported that they were, as she'd imagined, over the Atlantic. "Headwinds are slowing progress," he barked. "I'll update you when we make land."

"Sorry about that," Winslow said, putting the phone down. "Some things just can't wait." He turned away from the window, crossed the room and sat in the chair opposite his daughter.

"No bother," Eden said, shrugging. They had been talking for over two hours.

"I have some matters to catch up on this afternoon," Winslow said.

Eden's eyes welled with tears as she looked across at her father lounging in a red leather chair. She mentally pinched herself, checking she wasn't in the middle of a very realistic dream, and about to wake up.

"This all feels, sort of, unreal," Eden said, looking down at her hands. "I don't feel as though I can make sense of it right now." She wiped her cheek with the back of her hand.

"A lot has happened." Winslow climbed to his feet and walked across to Eden. He knelt and kissed her on the forehead. "Please remember this, though, I wouldn't have put you through this if I didn't know you could cope with it. I know it's been a lot, life changing even, but we are in a period of great change. In a few years, the world will be thankful for this."

"Although they won't even know what we've done," Eden said, looking up at her father. Their eyes locked and Eden felt as though her father was looking deep into her soul. Ever since she'd been a child, her father had been one step ahead. Somehow, he always knew her next move. For once, Eden wished she had the upper hand. She wished she knew what was coming next.

A typhoon of emotion twisted in Eden's guts. She was overwhelmed with relief that her father was alive and well, but betrayal bubbled deep within her, too. It felt as though her father had expected her to forget all the pain his so-called death had caused.

"I would suggest you could get some rest." Winslow

broke the stare and climbed to his feet. "But I also know you won't."

"Rest is the last thing on my mind," Eden said, glancing at the empty cup of coffee on the table.

"How about Athena gives you a tour of the Balonia? This place will be your home for a little while. That is, if you're happy to stay here."

"I think I could get used to it." Eden looked around at the yacht's opulent décor. "It's a bit like my truck, just a thousand times bigger."

"I suppose it is." Winslow smiled. "We are all very proud of her, and all she can do."

"I don't think much of the service, though," Eden said, staring at the empty cup on the table before her. "I've wanted another coffee for almost an hour."

"For you, that can be arranged."

Winslow pressed a button on the communications panel and Athena appeared at the door within an uncannily short time. Eden figured the other woman must have been waiting right outside.

"Athena, please give Eden all the coffee she requires, followed by a tour of the ship. Make sure you introduce her to the team, too."

"Great, more new people," Eden muttered inwards. For a moment, she missed her truck buried deep in the English countryside. Living there, she didn't have to see anyone, unless it suited her.

Eden climbed to her feet and followed Athena out into the corridor. At the door, Eden glanced back at her father, lowering himself into the chair. While the last two hours had been illuminating in the extreme, there was still so much she didn't understand.

"I was totally convinced by your act," Eden said, running

a few steps to catch up with Athena. The young woman paused, then glanced at Eden. Eden stared into the large, Arabic-looking eyes, which a few months ago in rural Lebanon had seemed innocent and believable. Athena's gaze was now hard, unyielding, and intelligent.

"I've had to imitate all kinds of people while working for The Council of Selene," Athena said, turning and leading them further down the corridor. Eden noticed a slight Arabic inflection to her accent. The accent matched her dark hair and olive complexion but could be just as fake as her previous persona. "Please don't take it personally. I'm something of a chameleon."

"I'm not taking it personally. Don't worry. You did what you needed to do."

Athena led Eden to a large cafeteria at the rear of the vessel and fixed them both coffees from an impressive-looking machine.

"If there is one thing I do know about my father, it's that he can't stand instant coffee," Eden said as the machine hissed with steam.

"I don't think we even allowed it on board, punishable by death," Athena said.

Eden crossed to one of the three large circular tables and sat down. The room was simply decorated and, as it seemed with every room aboard the Balonia, floor to ceiling windows led out on to one of the craft's multiple decks.

"You'll get very used to this place." Athena slid a cup of coffee across to Eden. "We can stay at sea for months on end, so when it is time to relax, this is where we do it. Not that it happens as much as it should."

Eden didn't reply.

After several seconds of silence, Athena spoke again. "It

must be quite a lot to take in." She locked eyes with Eden across the table.

Eden sipped her coffee. "That's an understatement. But yes. Yes, it is."

"Sorry. I can only imagine. It was for me when I first came on board. And I didn't have the whole your father's not dead thing to contend with."

Eden looked down at her drink.

"Sorry, that was..."

"No, not at all. Don't be. You know, thinking back to it now, there was always something about it I never believed. In a way, I had always expected him just to walk back in to my life. And on several occasions, I got the strange sense that he was nearby, almost as though I could smell..."

"Chamomile cigarettes," Athena said, a slight smile on her face.

"Yes, that's right," Eden said, looking across at Athena. "I mean, I've never known anyone else to smoke them. They're pointless. My father gave up smoking tobacco decades ago, but just couldn't kick the habit of the action, I think. He's stubborn like that."

"It was my idea, actually," Athena said, a hint of pride in her voice. "Although your father knew that you could do this, he was worried that you might lose all hope and bury yourself away in your truck. He spent months following you —he wanted to do it himself, wouldn't let anybody else— and smoking those cigarettes, just to keep it fresh in your mind."

"Clever," Eden said, taking another sip of the coffee.

"I'm glad you think so. Let's show you our floating head-quarters, then." Athena finished her coffee and got to her feet.

Eden did the same, wondering what other parts of her

life had been engineered right here. For most of the day, Eden and Athena strode through the various labs, meeting rooms, offices, and corridors of cabins. Athena even showed Eden the power plant and engine room, a large space filled with grumbling machines and hissing pipes deep in the ship's bowels.

Eden tried to keep up as she was introduced to the twenty people who worked and lived on board and was told the roles of many more who were based all over the world.

By the time Eden and Athena returned to the canteen for an evening meal with her father, it was clear that very little happened around the globe without The Council of Selene having some influence in the matter. From what movies got funded in Hollywood, to the companies that made it big, to the patent offices of all G20 countries, the reach of The Council was long, and the power it could exert, it seemed, was mighty.

After food, Eden finally retired to her cabin. Although exhausted, her mind whirled with all she'd seen and done. It felt as though the more she'd explored her father's secret organization, the more unsettled she'd become.

She understood that The Council was responsible for influencing things in the background, with all credit and blame laid at someone else's door. To Eden's mind, though, that just felt cowardly. They were playing the game from the side-lines, with no danger of getting caught in the crossfire. If she was certain of one thing, lying there in bed, Eden agreed with her father that The Council's days were numbered.

Suddenly Eden shot up in bed, a further thought darting into her mind.

"Why does it have to be like this now?" she whispered, her voice loud in the empty room. Then, slowly, in the misty badlands of her mind, an idea formed. Eden pulled it out into the light of consciousness and examined it carefully. Maybe, just maybe, all wasn't lost.

Eden leaned over and pulled her laptop from the suitcase. Fortunately, the team who'd brought her things from the villa in New Giza had thought to bring it.

Eden ran a quick internet search. The results came back in less than a second. She sat back in bed and folded her arms. Sometimes, it seemed, simple plans were the best.

45

BAXTER LAY BACK in his bed and closed his eyes. After a full day of the drawn-out debriefing and reporting process that followed any shore mobilization, he was shattered. He breathed deeply, lulled by the humming of the ship. Generally, if they rested at anchor, the only noise he heard at night was the occasional pad of footsteps on the floor above and the constant hum of the air conditioning. He'd got used to the noise over the last few months and now found it comforting. It was nice to be back on the Balonia.

Baxter was just about to slide over the precipice of sleep when another sound slipped into his consciousness. A click. Faint but sharp, like a knife thrust.

Baxter lay dead still, clawing himself back from the edge of sleep's oblivion and listened closely. He regulated his breathing, so as not to give away the change in the levels of his alertness.

The sound came again. Two clicks this time, shortly followed by a third. Then, if Baxter wasn't mistaken, the door swung gently open. A soft footstep padded into the room. Although the sound was little more than a drop of rain against a leaf, to Baxter's trained ears, it was a fanfare of impending danger.

The mystery figure took another step into the room. Baxter hadn't heard the door close again. The assailant had left it open to aid a quick retreat. With the majority of the Balonia's crew in bed, the corridor would be quiet at this time of night.

He heard another gentle footstep as the figure moved towards the bed. Whoever his midnight assailant was, Baxter realized, they had either removed their shoes or were wearing soft soled sneakers. That was a clever move, he thought. Professional.

Baxter was fully awake now. The sleep to which he had been about to surrender was a distant memory. He turned his attention to calculating the number of assailants. It sounded to him like there was just one unless they'd synchronized their movements. In which case, that would be even more impressive.

Baxter thought about the gun he kept in the top drawer of the nightstand. Although he could reach the weapon in less than a second, there was no guarantee that would be quick enough. But Baxter knew, as the footsteps pattered forward again, he had to try. He had to try before it was too late.

Baxter lay still and drew a long inhale. He pictured the movement he was about to make—roll to the side, pull open the drawer, reach for the weapon. He tried to remember which way around he had placed the weapon. It was only a small detail, but any delay here could be the difference between life and death. He pictured the gun in his mind's eye. The grip should be facing towards him, but he just couldn't be sure.

He counted down from three, slowly. Reaching one, his

muscles tensed. He threw himself into a roll, just as he'd planned. He kicked off the covers and grabbed for the nightstand.

Within a moment, there was a weight on top of him. The intruder was quicker and closer than he'd estimated.

A hand clamped down over Baxter's mouth, the other locked his arms into position. He swept his fingers through the air, as much as the hold would allow, hoping to reach the nightstand. His fingers grabbed at nothing but the empty air. He struggled again, forcing himself forwards, gaining an inch or so in the process.

Then he heard a soft voice, a woman's voice.

"Stop struggling," Eden whispered. "Don't make a noise. I don't want to wake anyone."

Recognizing the voice, the power drained from Baxter's hands. He relaxed.

Eden leaned over and clicked on the bedside light.

Adrenaline drained from Baxter's body, and embarrassment swelled.

Eden scrambled off the bed, strode across the room and pushed the door shut. The lock clicked back into place.

"What are you doing?" Baxter asked, rubbing the sleep from his eyes. He tried, and failed, to act like the whole thing hadn't spooked him out.

"I need your help with something. It's urgent."

The tone of Eden's voice told Baxter she meant what she said.

"Okay, sure, but why couldn't you just knock? You know, like a normal person?"

Baxter's eyes strained into focus. "And how did you?" Baxter pointed towards the door.

"It's amazing what you can learn on YouTube," Eden said, shrugging.

Baxter realized that Eden was already dressed in black tactical clothes, a rucksack strapped to her back.

"You going somewhere?" he asked, still sounding groggy.

"*We* are going somewhere." Eden glanced unconsciously at Baxter's torso as the cover slipped down. "I'll wait in the bathroom. Get ready. Don't be long."

As Eden padded through to the bathroom, Baxter noticed that she was wearing soft soled sneakers.

"At least I got something right," he muttered, climbing out of bed, and trying to shake off the embarrassment of being bested by someone half his size. The fact she was female didn't concern him one bit. Baxter had served alongside brave men and women. He found that when it came to the crunch, someone's gender made no difference at all. It was their spirit that counted for everything. The fact she was a civilian, though, with next to no military training— now that stung.

Baxter dressed quickly and was tying his laces as Eden came back in from the bathroom. She quickly explained her plan to him. Hearing the details, Baxter paled.

"Helios," Baxter paused, then locked eyes with Eden. "I mean, your father, won't like this. This really isn't how The Council does things. There's got to be process and deniability."

"Forget process and deniability," Eden hissed as loud as she dared. "Lulu King is still out there. She's going to use this technology to become one of the most wealthy and powerful people on the planet, while the rest of humankind suffers. On my watch, that's not okay. I'm going to put that right, tonight."

"Okay, okay," Baxter held out his hands to quiet Eden down. "What do you need me to do?"

Eden and Baxter, keeping in the shadows as much as possible, shuffled towards the Balonia's back deck. After Eden had explained her plan, Baxter admitted there was a good amount of logic to it. They had scurried down to the Balonia's arsenal on the third floor. Eden had taken a special interest in the weapons cache during her tour that afternoon, so knew exactly what she wanted.

Eden and Baxter now had both side arms and semi-automatic rifles strapped to their bodies. Turning the corner, they paused and looked up at the dormant helicopter. The machine squatted in the gloom, menacing and angular like a giant insect.

Somewhere far below them, the gentle waves of the Mediterranean lapped against the yacht. Baxter looked up at the sky. Although he'd yet to see any official weather reports, the air seemed still enough.

"You know that starting this will wake up every person on board?" Baxter said, studying the impressive machine.

Eden nodded once. "We just won't have time to hang around. How long will it take to get airborne?"

"If I can get the start-up sequence right—" Baxter calculated something on his fingers. "It can be done in as little as sixty seconds."

"Great." Eden touched Baxter on the shoulder. "I've got faith in you. What do I need to do?"

Eden listened closely to Baxter's instructions, then they both set off at a sprint towards the copter. They were out in the open now. If the security camera operator was paying attention, the Balonia's team of guards might already be on their way.

Following Baxter's instructions, Eden untethered the

chopper's blades, and then removed the straps from around the landing gear.

Baxter ran straight for the door, swung it open and leaped into the pilot's seat. He thought back to his helicopter training and tried to remember the correct startup sequence for this machine. Almost certain, he clicked several switches around the cockpit. A high-pitched whining noise echoed from the engine, slowly rising in pitch. That was a good sign.

Eden clambered into the seat beside Baxter. The rotors began to spin lazily through the air.

"Come on, come on," Eden muttered, watching the rotors complete another slow circuit.

With an audible click, lights flooded on around the Balonia, illuminating the helicopter and dazzling Baxter and Eden.

Eden looked up at the rotors. The blades swished through the air more like a rotary washing line than a flying machine. "What's going on? We won't get anywhere like this."

Baxter's training flashed through his mind again. He glanced up at the banks of switches overhead.

"Got ya!" He shouted, reaching over, and snapping another switch into the 'on' position. As though waking up from a slumber, the machine roared into action. The rotors thumped through the air, invisible now. The water around the ship whipped and danced into a milky foam.

"Almost there," Baxter shouted, tapping one of the dials. A needle slowly swept upwards, indicating the engine's revolutions.

"Come on," Eden muttered, tapping anxiously at the armrest.

The needle crept a little further towards the green area.

Then, twenty feet ahead of them, a door swung open, and a figure ran out on to the deck.

"We need to go now!" Eden shouted, pointing at the approaching person.

Baxter looked up from the dials. "We're not..."

"Now!"

Baxter grabbed hold of the flight controls and pushed. The machine grumbled, groaned and then slowly at first, rose from the deck.

Seeing the moving chopper, the figure increased speed. Silhouetted against the lights, Eden couldn't make out who it was. They were just three paces from the chopper now.

The engines growled as the copter climbed another few inches. Not yet up to full power, the ascent was slow.

Baxter toyed with the controls and the copter swung to the left, increasing the gap between them and their pursuer. The figure increased speed again, pounding across the deck, their arms hammering like pistons.

The chopper climbed another inch. Baxter used the elevation to push them back another few feet, the pursuer closed the gap in a couple of seconds.

Finally, the needle crept into the green area. The engines now settled into a primeval growl.

"Hold on!" Baxter shouted, pulling back hard on the controls. The chopper lurched forwards, almost colliding with the back of the ship. Just in time, the nose tilted towards the sky and then shot backwards, leaving the deck of the Balonia far below.

As THE CHOPPER LURCHED FORWARD, the pursuer dropped to the deck.

"That was close," she hissed, crashing hard against the

deck. A moment later and the machine would have flattened her. She rolled over and looked up at the copter's giant glinting belly, a silhoutte against the sky. The machine hovered and swayed above her, like a drunk trying to find their feet. The rotors thundered, air whipping and tearing against her skin.

In one swift move, she leaped back up to her feet and then jumped clear of the deck. Noise roared in her ears, threatening to disorientate her completely. Her hands swung out in front of her, fingers bent, ready for the catch. Like a sports champion making the catch of their career, her fingers closed around the front of the chopper's landing gear. She closed her hands tight, the muscles in her fore-arms straining.

The chopper remained still for a microsecond, as though balancing on a precipice. Then it shot backwards, clearing the deck, and gaining thirty feet in less than two seconds.

She gripped on. Her fingers felt as though they might be torn from her palms. She gritted her teeth, straining, focusing all attention on her hold.

After a few seconds, the chopper leveled out and swung around to face the distant shoreline. She swung this way and that like a rag doll. The copter's nose tilted towards the ocean, now fifty feet below them, and set off towards the coast.

She heaved herself upwards, getting first one arm, then the next across the landing gear. She swung her legs up and over. Gripping the bar with her legs, she swung upward and grabbed the door handle. She peered through the glass at Eden and Baxter, both their eyes facing forward.

"Here goes," she muttered, sliding open the chopper's rear door and launching herself inside.

Alarms shrieked through the chopper. The sound of the rotors increased to a roar. Eden spun around just in time to see a figure throw themselves through the door and into the rear of the chopper. With no lights on, the chopper's back cabin was completely dark. Eden flew into action, jumping out of her seat and scrambling into the back.

Baxter, distracted by the movement, lost control of the machine. It swung left to right several times, causing Eden to bang between the seats.

"I've got this," Eden shouted, barely audible against the engine's roar. "You fly this thing."

Baxter turned back to the controls.

Eden sprang down on the figure, determined to pin them to the floor before they had a chance to move. The figure rolled away just in time. Eden crashed hard against the floor, then scrambled up against the seats, and without pausing, pushed forward for another attack.

The figure was up now and moving quickly. Eden heard the intruder say something but couldn't make out the words against the roaring engines. She didn't give the interloper a chance to gain ground. Her hands raised in a fighting stance, Eden charged forwards. Behind the figure, the night air roared through the open door.

Eden swung a right hook, but her opponent parried just in time. Eden tried again, this time with her left. The intruder seized her arm and pulled in tight, locking them together. The interloper was a similar size to Eden and moved quickly. The two of them tumbled to the floor, rolling towards the open door. Eden struggled, trying to right herself. She looped her leg around one of the chair supports, stopping their slide towards the open door.

Eden then pushed the intruder towards the precipice. Whilst she didn't intend to kill the opponent, if the mission's only chance of success was pushing them out and into the sea, then so be it.

Eden shoved harder. The intruder scrabbled against the floor, shouting something unintelligible. The engine roared and wind howled.

Suddenly a light clicked on, bathing the cabin in a bright glow. Eden finally saw her opponent. It wasn't one of the Balonia's security team, but Athena. Fear surrounded the young woman's eyes as she neared the open door. The woman wasn't fighting back.

Eden grabbed Athena under the arms and heaved her away from the door. Her arms now free, Athena reached up and slid the door shut. The sound of the rotors sunk from a disorientating thunder to a distant growl. Eden stepped back, still unsure and scrutinized the woman. Athena took a headset from a hook and slipped it on, Eden did the same. At last, she could hear what the woman had to say.

"I know you're going after King. I'm coming with you."

THE MAN KNOWN AS HELIOS, or Alexander Winslow, stood at the railing at the rear of the Balonia and watched the helicopter pound back in the direction of Egypt. Reaching inside his jacket, he removed a packet of chamomile cigarettes.

"Eden, you're so predictable," he said to no one. He shook one of the cigarettes from the packet and placed it between his lips. "And you know what, that's just what the world needs." He lit up and drew a lungful of the sweet smoke.

46

EDEN PEERED down at the ground below as Baxter navigated the chopper around the town of El Khatatbah. Since they'd crossed the coast half an hour ago, they had avoided all population centers, in an attempt not to attract attention. Much of the land here was unpopulated, leaving great swathes of the desert beneath the chopper black and featureless.

Ahead and to the left, light pollution from Cairo radiated high into the sky.

Baxter glanced carefully down at the controls as they followed the line of a road which led like a sunbeam directly into the heart of the city. A car, sliding down the road just a few hundred feet beneath them, was the only indication there was a road there at all.

Eden glanced from the map on the chopper's central console to the land beneath them.

"Two miles ahead, on the left," Eden said, peering through the windshield. She turned and glimpsed Athena sitting silently in the back of the chopper. Although Eden hadn't decided to trust the woman yet, for now they were stuck with her. She hadn't tried to sabotage their plans so far —that was a good sign.

"There it is," Baxter said, removing one hand from the controls and pointing through the screen. Eden turned and saw a brightly lit compound a few hundred yards back from the road.

"They're not exactly subtle," Eden said, noticing the same logo she'd seen on the sample bags King had used. The sign was attached to each side of the building and illuminated with floodlights.

"I suppose King never expected you to survive," Baxter said. "I say we land and check the place out on foot?"

"No," Eden said. "We go in hot, get what we need and get out of there before they know what's happened."

"I agree," offered Athena. "Before they can call anyone to help."

Eden glanced over her shoulder and caught the woman's eye. Athena nodded once. Eden realized that Athena was willing to risk her life on an unsanctioned mission that Eden had planned. She decided in that moment she would trust Athena, for now at least.

"It's your funeral," Baxter said, circling towards the compound.

"Do a circuit. I want to see if anything looks different from the schematics I downloaded."

Baxter carefully swung the copter into a wide curve. A four-story building sat at the center, with parking lots and various smaller constructions surrounding it. A high chain-link fence, topped by swirls of razor wire and flood lights, surrounded the complex on all sides.

"It's strange that a laboratory is that well protected," Athena said.

The chopper banked hard, passing the compound's

front fence. The gate here offered the only way in or out of the site. Dull light glowed from inside a security checkpoint hut, positioned beside a red and white barrier. As the chopper thundered past, no doubt shaking the windows in their frames, a security guard stepped out of the hut. He looked up at the passing chopper and then spoke into a radio.

"It looks like we've already been spotted," Baxter said.

"We'd better give them something to gossip about. Let's get inside." Eden pointed at the laboratory building.

Baxter twisted the controls and the chopper swung hard to the left, pounding forty feet above the security guard and the fence in less than a second.

"I'll set it down on the parking lot at the far side," Baxter said.

"No, that's too far," Eden said. "We need to keep the high ground. Drop us on the roof." Eden pointed at the building. The boxy concrete construction had a flat roof with various ventilation shafts, communication dishes and ariels attached to it.

"Negative," Baxter said. "I'll never get a clean landing with all the installed apparatus."

"Who said anything about landing." Eden pulled a rope from beneath her seat and chucked it towards Athena. "All three of us don't need to go in. This way you can keep the chopper powered up too."

Baxter glanced at Eden, worry etching into the corners of his eyes. He looked as though he was about to say something, but clearly thought better of it. He adjusted the controls and the chopper hovered twenty feet above the building.

Eden unbuckled herself, pulled off the headphones, and

climbed into the back. She checked her weapons were in place, then slid a wireless comms earbud into place.

"Keep this channel open," she said, her voice already coming though the comms system.

Athena slid the door open, tied the rope to a hook mounted to the fuselage and pulled it hard to test the strength. Satisfied, she took the rope in both hands and swung free of the copter.

Eden peered down and watched the other woman descend. Cables whipped around on the rooftop below, aggravated by the downdraft.

Athena reached the rooftop. Holding the rope in one hand, she gave Eden a thumbs up with the other.

Eden held the rope with both hands and was about to drop when she heard Baxter's voice in her earpiece.

"Eden, be careful," he said.

Eden turned and looked at the man. For what felt like an unnaturally long time they locked eyes.

"Careful?" Eden said, grinning. "I'm always careful." Without a backwards glance, she stepped out of the chopper and swung down the rope.

Then, the bullets started to fly.

LULU KING SUNK deep beneath the water of the freestanding claw-footed bath in her hotel suite. She closed her eyes and slipped her head under. She rolled her shoulders gently and positioned the center of her spine over the water jets, letting them massage her muscles. There was a knot of tension she just couldn't seem to shake. It had been there ever since...

Suddenly the image of her father slammed into her mind. He squirmed backwards against the floor, begging for his life. King saw the gun in her hand, the muzzle pointed at her father's chest. She felt recoil as the gun discharged. Her father slumped to the floor, blood oozing across the tiles.

Lulu King sat up, gasping. She gripped hold of the bath sides. Water sloshed around, some splashing down to the floor.

"The old man had to die," she whispered to herself. "He was a dinosaur. A relic."

King sat back and stretched out her shoulders again. It was his own fault, really, King thought. She tried to relax and let the water massage her once again. She closed her eyes slowly and focused on her image of the future. A re-invented King Industries. A company rising like a phoenix from the ashes of the self-destructing oil and gas industry.

The anger bubbled through King's thoughts again. If only her father had been open to change, then they would be working on this together. He had forced her to act deci-sively. His stubbornness, his inability to see the changing world, to understand new opportunity, had made him obsolete. Worse than obsolete, he was a hinderance. He was a blockage to be cleared. King had only done what was right.

Another noise echoed through the bathroom.

"What now," King snarled, sitting up and sending another torrent of water cascading to the floor. She rubbed a hand across, sweeping away the wet hair, and opened her eyes. Steam curled throughout the bathroom.

The noise came again—a shrill electrical bleating. King glanced at her phone, vibrating on a table beside the bath. An unknown number scrolled across the screen.

King picked up a towel, dried her hands and then answered.

"What is it?" she snarled, greeting the unknown caller.

"Miss King, Miss King, it's Babu. Head of security at the lab. We have a problem."

King searched her memory for the name. She moved the towel and dried her face.

"From DK Labs, you had us under strict instructions to contact you if anything unusual happened."

Realization hit King like a slap around the face. "Yes, of course, Babu, what's going on?"

King listened closely as Babu explained. In the background she heard the growling motors of a helicopter, followed by the ping of gunfire.

Babu shrieked and then panted hard as though he was running.

"They're on the roof, Miss King. They're on the roof. Two of them, I think."

King's hand tightened around the phone. "Babu, can you describe them for me?"

Babu exchanged a few words in Arabic with another man. "Women, Miss King. There are two women. They're now trying to get inside."

"Eden Black," King snarled, picturing the pathetic woman she had last seen in the collapsing Hall of Records. How Eden had escaped, King couldn't fathom, but she longed to make sure it didn't happen again.

"Excellent," King said, climbing out of the bath. "Keep them inside, Babu. Don't let them escape. Kill them if you must. We'll be there soon."

King wrapped herself in a towel and rushed to the door. She ran through her bedroom and out into the suite's living area.

Abdul and Sharif looked up from the sofa, clearly surprised to see their boss draped in a towel. Water dripped to the carpet.

"Gentlemen we have a situation, roll out in two minutes."

Abdul and Sharif shot to their feet as though they'd done something wrong.

"We'll take the chopper," King said, rushing back into the bedroom and slamming the door.

King thumbed the elevator call button several times. The elevator only ran between the presidential suite in which they were staying, and the helipad on the roof. The excitable hotel manager had named several dignitaries who had used the suite over the last two decades. Behind the elevator doors, the mechanism hissed and clunked. With all that money flowing through the place, you would expect the elevator not to take years.

Eventually the doors slid open. King, Abdul, and Sharif stepped inside. The elevator car creaked under the weight of the burly Angolans.

King poked the button for the roof several times. Slowly the elevator wheezed upwards. They stepped out on to the roof as the lights snapped on automatically. Their Airbus Tiger sat on the helipad, it's four drooping rotors tethered to the roof.

Abdul and Sharif, having spent several years flying such machines for mercenary groups across Africa, leapt into action. Abdul climbed into the pilot's seat and set about the start-up sequence, while Sharif removed the machine's tethers.

Less than one minute later, the rotors now pounding, they lifted from the hotel rooftop and powered in an easterly direction.

"How long?" King said, adjusting the headset and microphone. She didn't much like being in the back seat, but

Abdul and Sharif had more experience operating one of these machines than she did.

Sharif checked the navigation. "Just under ten minutes boss. We're going as quick as we can."

Illustrating Sharif's point, the chopper accelerated hard, pinning King into her seat. King slid out her phone and called the security guard at the lab. She turned the phone to its highest volume, still struggling to even hear it ringing against the thundering of the Tiger's twin engines.

"What's happening?"

"They're heading for the roof right now."

Several gunshots came down the phone.

"Stop them," King snarled. "You need to stop them!"

King hung up the phone and glanced out of the window as they powered high above The Giza Plateau.

She smiled to herself. Did Eden Black really think she was stupid enough to keep The Ark of the Covenant in a lab protected by amateurs?

King thought of the Ark, already halfway back to The States.

"Eden, you're just too late," King whispered. "And now you'll pay."

47

EDEN DROPPED the last fifteen feet and landed in a crouch on the rooftop.

"Get down," Athena roared. Another flurry of bullets sung through the air. Fortunately, whoever was firing them was not a great shot. The round raked across the concrete but didn't hit much else.

Eden ducked in behind an air vent. Making a circular motion with her hand, she indicated to Baxter that the rope was now clear, and he should get out of there. Baxter didn't wait around. The chopper pounded away overhead.

Another barrage of bullets thundered and pinged around the rooftop.

"Two shooters, three o'clock." Athena peered over the vent, then ducked in again just in time.

Keeping low, Eden scrambled across to the edge of the roof, using the air vent as protection. When she was twenty feet from her previous position, she peered out. Two guards stood in the center parking lot beneath, guns raised up at the roof.

"They're amateurs," Eden shouted towards Athena. She swung her semi-automatic across the vent and fired a short burst down into the parking lot. The guards leapt to the ground and scurried for cover. Eden almost laughed out loud.

A car alarm wailed, adding to the mayhem.

"The labs are on the top floor, western side," Eden said, pointing across the roof. While the rent-a-cops were still scrambling for cover, Eden and Athena ran out of sight across the roof.

"That will be perfect." Athena pointed at a large aluminum vent running down into the building. About five feet in diameter, the vent extended a few feet above the roof top and then curved ninety degrees.

Eden inspected the system. A cool current of air flowed from the vent.

She pulled her laser cutter from her bag and cut the vent's wire grill.

"That's cool," Athena said, looking at the device.

"Yeah. It's my friend's design. Probably why you guys haven't locked it away."

Eden pulled the wire grill out of place and tossed it aside.

The sound of several more raised voices came from the parking lot below.

"It sounds like they've got reinforcements," Athena said.

"That's good. All the time they're in the car park, they're not going to bother us up here." Eden heaved herself up into the vent and looked down the shaft. Several feet below, the vent curved out of sight. Eden slid down inside the vent, her hands and feet scraping and clattering against the metal, despite her efforts to remain silent.

At the base of the shaft, she paused. The vent now ran horizontally in both directions. Light streamed up through grills set every few feet.

Athena slipped down the vent behind her, almost silently. Eden was impressed but didn't say anything.

Eden recalled the schematic of the buildings she'd seen earlier. She took a moment to get her bearings. "This way," she said, pointing to the left.

Together, Eden and Athena crawled along the pipe. Eden paused at the first grill and peered down inside. Getting her face close to the bars, she could just about make out the corridor below. It looked as though the larger vent followed the corridor, with smaller divisions branching off into each room.

"It looks as though we're alone," Eden said, sliding out the laser cutter again. A few seconds later the grill clanged to the floor below.

Eden swung down out of the vent and landed on the floor. The corridor was bare and colorless with doors lining both sides. The air had a strange chemical laden taste common in medical or scientific buildings.

Eden clocked a security camera mounted at each end of the corridor. Although the building was quiet right now, it wouldn't be for long.

Together Eden and Athena hurried down the corridor.

"King stole a sample of my hair and blood for DNA," Eden explained as they checked each door. "The bag she put it in had the logo of this laboratory. She planned to set me up for a couple of murders back in England,"

"Wait, what?" Athena stopped running and glared at Eden. "We came here for that? The Council can get that sort of thing forgotten in an instant."

"Here it is." Eden ran for the final door, ignoring Athena's interjection.

The two women barged through the door. The lights came on automatically. Eden looked around. Filing cabinets lined both sides of the space, and several computers sat on a table in the center. It was a large space, occupying at least a third of the building's floorspace.

"Eden," Athena said, more aggressively now. "Even if this were important, we don't even know where to start looking. The guards will be up here in seconds."

Eden turned and smiled sweetly at the other woman.

"It's just lucky I remembered the serial number of the bag she put the sample in."

"Yes, but it's just not…"

Baxter's voice coming down the in-ear comms system interrupted Athena's protest.

"We've got company. Incoming fast. Do you read me?"

Eden touched the device to activate the microphone. "Go ahead."

"It's another chopper. Still a couple of miles out, but on path for your location. I've touched down 200 feet away, engine still live. I can be with you in less than a minute."

Eden cut the communication and turned to face Athena.

The worry had melted from Athena's expression, she grinned wolfishly. "You don't care about the DNA," Athena said. "You just wanted another go at King."

"Absolutely. This part of the plan is important to her. I knew she would have eyes on this place. While we're here, though, we might as well get what we came for." Arranged in numerical order, Eden found the right cabinet and drawer quickly. She pulled out the drawer and thumbed through the plastic sample bags. Again, they were stored in numerical order, making the search very straightforward. Eden pulled out the bag which had the sample number she remembered. Sure enough, a curl of black hair and a cotton swab lay in the bottom of the bag.

The deep thundering of a chopper sounded above the silence of the building.

Athena rushed across to the window and yanked down the blinds in one aggressive move. Light strobed high in the black sky. It was difficult to tell how far away the chopper was. They were incoming fast.

"How long have we got?" Eden asked.

"One minute. Ninety seconds tops."

Eden paced over to the central table, pulled open the sample bag and tipped out her hair and the cotton swab. She made sure the bag was empty, before taking another sample bag from her rucksack. She held the bag up to the light, there were several strands of golden hair inside.

"What are you doing now?" Athena said. "We need to get out of here."

As though reinforcing the point, the grumbling and grunting of the copter engine increased. A pair of shouting voices echoed from the corridor too. Footsteps pounded across the linoleum.

"Insurance," Eden said. "Help me with this." Eden shoved three top-of-the-range computers to the floor, and then barged the heavy table towards the door. The blockade wouldn't stop the guards for long, but it may buy Eden and Athena the minute they needed.

"There's one more thing," Eden said. "I'm not totally sure it'll be here, but my hunch says it is."

Athena rolled her eyes. "You've gotta be kidding right? This isn't the time for hunches. What is it?"

Eden told Athena about the vial she had tried to take from around the neck of the golden woman in The Hall of Records. The vial that King had snatched from her before attempting to trap them inside.

"She would want to run tests on it, that I know. I don't think she would give it up to anyone else, either. She took it from me for no other reason than I wanted it. She'll be bitter about it."

Eden looked around the lab frantically, searching for any indication of where the vial might be.

Through the window, the enemy helicopter rattled closer. Another burst of voices came from the corridor. The door crashed hard against the table.

"Okay," Athena said, holding up her hands. "I can see you're not going to let this go. It'll be quicker if I just help you look. If it's in this room, we'll get it."

Eden ran over to the cabinet from which she'd got the last sample and started flicking through the drawer. Her heart sunk. With over a hundred plastic bags inside, it would take several minutes to even search one drawer.

The door thudded open again. This time the men continued pushing. The table scraped across the floor.

"This is going to take too long," Athena said. "Pass me that," she pointed at the sample bag that had once contained Eden's hair. Eden passed the bag across. "Look, as well as a sample number there's a client code. This must be a number that's unique for all the stuff King has sent in."

Athena darted across to a computer. She tapped the keyboard several times.

The door smashed against the table again. An arm snaked through the gap. Eden charged across the room and shoved the table hard. It crashed against the door, pinning the guard's arm in place. The guard struggled for several seconds, before twisting his arm back through.

"Here we go," Athena said, pointing at the screen.

"Wait a minute, how did you get through the lock screen so quickly?"

"That's easy, each computer system has a universal access code built in. They are one of the first things we learn at The Council. King has deposited two items, the one you've already tampered with and..."

"The vial. It's got to be." Eden read and memorized the serial number.

"I'm sorry to break up the party." Baxter's voice came through the earpiece. "We're going to have to get out of here soon."

Eden charged across the room to the cabinet which corresponded with the serial number. She flicked through the contents and pulled out a bag. She held the bag up to the light. The vial on the gold chain lay inside.

"Genius," Eden said, looking from the bag to Athena.

"Alright, can we go now? Or is there something else you want to do while you're here?" Athena huffed.

Eden pushed the comms device and spoke to Baxter. "Ready to give us a lift?"

"Anytime," Baxter said, anxiously. "Same place as before?"

"Negative. East side of the building. You'll see us at the window."

Eden rushed across to the window. The incoming helicopter drew closer still. The *thud thud* of its rotor blades rattled the glass. Eden stared at the menacing machine, moving like a black locust in the night.

Several more raised voices echoed from outside the lab now.

"Move aside," Athena shouted.

Eden leapt out of the way as Athena charged forwards with a heavy office chair. The metal legs crashed through the glass. Athena shoved the chair out. The chair fell four stories and crushed the roof of a car parked below. The car's alarm wailed, and its lights strobed.

"Nicely done," Eden said, raising her voice now over the noise. "That's really going to ruin someone's night."

"That's what I'm here for." Athena shrugged.

The laboratory door banged against the table again. The table moved another inch. One of the men fired his gun through the crack in the door, followed by a string of Arabic expletives.

Eden stepped towards the window. The incoming helicopter growled closer. Then another sound rose above it. The whine of a different engine. Air swirled through the broken window.

Eden snatched up the broken blind and used the fabric to smash out the remains of the glass. She then laid the material over the windowsill, the torn edge flapping frantically in the downdraft. A stack of paper streamed and swirled around the lab.

Eden leaned out and peered upwards. The belly of Baxter's Eurocopter hovered above the building, strobe lights bright against the sky.

"I see you," Baxter's voice came through the headset.

Eden saw the rope, swinging around beneath the chopper. It whipped around aggressively.

"Down a bit," Eden shouted, not sure if the comms system would even work in the noise.

It clearly did and the chopper descended again, swaying right to left, forwards and back. The rope swung closer, but then flipped ten feet in the other direction.

"Come on," Eden muttered, leaning out of the window, her fingers extended. The rope whipped several times, just inches from her grasp. She leaned further still, just her fingertips now holding on to the window's edge. The rope danced far out of her reach again.

Eden glanced back into the room. The guards hammered against the door. The gap had grown further. An arm snaked through, pointing a gun blindly into the laboratory. The gun roared several times, sending a stream of bullets zinging into the metal filing cabinets.

Athena dropped into a crouch and charged across the room, weaving this way and that to avoid further rounds. She grabbed a fire extinguisher from a hook beside the door and smashed it down over the hand. A cry of pain came through the gap in the door. The gun fell from the injured arm and clattered to the table. The arm whipped back through the gap in the door, followed by several more Arabic curse words.

Athena took the opportunity to shove the table back against the door, undoing all the progress the men had made to dislodge it.

"Move to the left," Eden shouted, the rope still dancing way out of her reach.

The chopper swung aggressively to the left. Eden glanced up at it's great shimmering belly, so close, yet so far.

She looked out at the other chopper, getting closer by the second. Something flashed from the belly of the craft. Eden's muscles froze for an instant. She knew exactly what that was. A stream of slugs slapped into the building twenty feet below the window. Fortunately, they were still too far out for an accurate shot. They wouldn't be for long.

Eden reached out, just her fingertips now holding her upright in the window.

The rope followed the chopper's movement, swinging like a snake to its charmer. It was now inches from her grip. Painfully out of reach.

From behind her, Eden heard a cry and then felt the thunder of footsteps.

Athena ran through the lab, up on to the windowsill and leapt into the void.

Eden watched the movement as though in slow motion. Athena stormed through the air, her arms flailing. She swung around, her arms in position, and grabbed the rope. At first the rope moved through her hands, slipping downwards. Athena moved hand over hand, her legs kicking, trying to loop the rope around her. She slipped further down, the end of the rope dancing perilously close beneath her.

After several long attempts Athena's grip held. She jarred to a stop and looped the rope around one wrist and ankle to lock it tight.

Eden caught the other woman's gaze, her heart recovering from several missed beats.

Athena grinned, as though such danger was the most normal thing in the world. Athena swung forwards, like a child on a swing. On the second pass, she grabbed hold of the windowsill.

A great clattering noise came from inside the room now. Eden looked behind her to see the door disintegrate under the blade of an axe. She grabbed on to the rope and the two women swung out beneath the helicopter.

"All aboard," Eden said, climbing hand over hand up the rope.

"About time," came Baxter's reply. The helicopter above them thronged as it moved away from the building.

Eden turned just in time to see the first guard reach the

laboratory window. The man pointed up at the helicopter, now speeding away, and gesticulated wildly. Eden, unable to help herself, took one hand from the rope and waved back.

Then, for the second time in ten minutes, bullets thundered through the air.

48

LULU KING SHUFFLED forwards and peered through the windshield as they approached the lab. Although they were still several hundred feet away, the lab was lit up like a beacon against the featureless desert. Another helicopter, a civilian issue by the look of it, hovered over the roof top. As King watched, two figures swung from one of the lab's windows and struggled up a rope towards the chopper.

"They're already getting away. We're too late," King barked, bouncing in the seat with anger.

The other helicopter swept away from the building, the rope rocking from side to side.

"Those idiots had one job." Lulu scowled. "Eden Black should be dead by now."

"She will be soon, boss. Don't worry about that." Sharif squeezed the trigger. The machine gun mounted beneath the Tiger's nose coughed out a storm of scorching lead.

"Get us closer," King hissed. "Don't just go shooting things up. We'll have the whole of Egyptian military down here. Get us up close to them, and end this, you hear me?"

"Yes, boss," Abdul and Sharif said in unison, the Tiger barreling to the right.

"WE'VE GOT COMPANY," Baxter's voice came through the headset. "And I don't think they're friendly."

Eden turned to see the other helicopter bank hard and give chase. A gun mounted beneath the craft flashed several times. A flurry of bullets shot like a silver shower through the night sky, sailing wide and smashing into the side of the building.

Wind, from both the chopper's downdraft and the speed of their movement, roared in Eden's ears. Eden gritted her teeth and eyed the rope above them. She was still twenty feet beneath the Eurocopter, and the speed was making it difficult to climb. She glanced down at Athena a few feet below.

"What you waiting for!" Athena shouted, looking up at the Eden.

Eden climbed the rope as fast as she could. The line bit against her skin as she pulled herself upwards, hand over hand. The rope spun with the chopper's movement, threatening to disorientate her.

Eden caught a glimpse of their pursuers. The other helicopter was still a few hundred feet behind but looked as though it was gaining. The muzzle of the nose-mounted gun flared again. A strafe of life-ending lead zinged past, dangerously close. Fortunately, they were still too far away to get an accurate shot.

The Eurocopter swung one way, then the other, as Baxter tried to evade their pursuers.

Eden pushed on, her hands burning. Her muscles felt as though they were now powered by acid. Eden hauled herself up in line with the chopper as another barrage of bullets hammered past.

Baxter pulled back on the controls, sending the chopper into a steep climb.

The force caused Eden to slip down the rope, losing two feet of progress. When Baxter levelled out, she heaved back up again. Reaching the top of the rope, Eden swung into the chopper. She let go and flopped onto the floor. Her hands tingled with exertion. She sat up, rubbed them together and then scurried across to the door.

Athena still dangled from the rope, two feet below the chopper.

"Come on," Eden shouted, reaching out and helping the other woman up.

Another onslaught of gunshots bellowed from their pursuers. A bullet ricocheted, sparks flying from the chopper's landing gear.

Athena grunted in pain and slipped several feet down the rope.

"I've been hit," Athena groaned. She continued to climb uncharacteristically slowly, gaining just an inch or two in what looked like a gargantuan effort.

Eden leaned out further and pulled on the rope, dragging Athena up. When the other woman was close enough, Eden grabbed her beneath the arms and heaved her inside. Both women collapsed to the floor, their chests heaving.

Eden scrambled up and slid the door shut. She glanced down into the formless night below. The first part of the mission had been successful, they had drawn the snake from its hole. Now they just needed to cut the damn thing's head off.

"Thanks for the ride," Eden said, pulling on a pair of headphones.

"My pleasure, ma'am," Baxter replied. "Where will it be?"

"Anywhere but the Ritz, the cocktails last time were rubbish," Eden quipped in response. "What do you think, Athena?"

"Absolutely, make mine a double." Athena struggled up onto one of the chairs, pressing her hands into the side her abdomen. Blood seeped through her fingers.

Eden grabbed the chopper's first aid kit.

"It's nothing," Athena said, groggily.

Eden pulled back Athena's top and inspected the wound. Blood bloomed across the skin from a deep graze about an inch above her hip. Eden probed the area with her hand. There was an entry and exit wound.

Athena winced, her teeth gritted.

"Yeah, it's nothing," Eden agreed. "I expect you've had worse hangovers. We do need to stop this bleeding, though. Keeping blood inside your body is kinda a big deal."

"Oh really, you should have said so, and I'd have stepped out of the way."

Eden found a large bandage and pushed it into the wound. The bandage was instantly soaked in blood. She cut one of the chopper's seat belts and tied it tightly around Athena's middle. Eden positioned Athena in one of the seats and strapped her in tight. Right now, it was the best she could do.

"Stay there. We'll stitch you up properly back at the Balonia." Eden climbed forwards into the cockpit and strapped herself in beside Baxter.

"Incoming." Baxter swung the chopper hard to the right, avoiding a hail of bullets. "What's the plan now?"

Eden paused for a moment and looked back at the other chopper. The muzzle flashed again.

"Please tell me you've got a plan," Baxter said, through gritted teeth.

"I had sort of intended to do this on the ground," Eden said. "I didn't realize they'd bring their own battleship. I presume this ride hasn't got any weapons?"

Baxter glanced at Eden. "No. This is a civilian issue chopper. No weapons."

The muzzle flashed again, and Baxter rocked the chopper to the right. He seemed to have a knack for avoiding the danger, or maybe they'd just got lucky so far.

"Unfortunate. Where are we heading anyway?" Eden peered through the windshield. Two hundred feet below, the lights of scattered buildings glinted. A street lit highway curved into view.

"We'll reach the outskirts of Cairo in a minute or two. There's no way we can lead them back to the Balonia. I think they'll be less aggressive above the city."

"I hope so," Eden said.

The following chopper's muzzle strobed again.

"Move!" Eden shouted.

Baxter heaved back on the controls and the Eurocopter shot upwards. Eden braced back into the seat. For a few seconds they saw nothing but the stars curving up ahead.

"Did you get a look at their chopper?" Eden said, when they'd levelled out. "What are we dealing with?"

"No, sorry, I didn't have the chance to…"

"Move!" Eden shouted again.

Baxter heaved the controls and the Eurocopter swung to the right. This time they weren't so lucky, several rounds thwacked into the back.

Eden and Baxter didn't speak for a moment, waiting for something to happen. No alarms shrieked and the craft didn't spiral to the ground.

"Close one," Eden said.

"Too close," Baxter agreed.

"Clearly up here in the open air, they're faster and more deadly than us. I bet we could out maneuver them, though. Take it down close to the ground, we'll give them a run around."

Baxter peered down at the land below them. They were now flying several hundred feet over suburban Cairo. Lit streets panned out in rectangles on both sides. Most of the buildings were dark. A mile or so away, The Pyramids of Giza shone against The Plateau.

"What?" Eden said, sensing Baxter's reluctance. "You not up for the challenge, Captain?"

Without another word, Baxter adjusted the controls and the chopper's nose swung towards the ground.

Eden glanced at Athena in the back. Athena gave a weak thumbs up.

Baxter levelled off the descent when they were fifty feet from the ground. Boxy concrete buildings now reached up on both sides.

Eden looked out of the side window. Their quarry was still behind but descending more slowly. Perhaps she'd been right, their craft was less maneuverable.

"Further down," Eden said.

Baxter glanced at Eden as though she was mad.

"They won't dare follow us in that." She pointed up at the other chopper which had stopped descending fifty feet above them. "I think they know it's too large to fly between the buildings."

Baxter did what he was told and lowered the chopper further. Buildings now loomed up on both sides. The sound of the Eurocopter's engines rattled from concrete and stone.

People in this neighborhood weren't going to get much sleep tonight.

Baxter adjusted the controls and the copter started down the street. Several motorists stopped their cars in the middle of the highway and gaped up at the chopper. Cables lashed hard against their fixings, as though a mini hurricane had descended.

"Fast as you can," Eden said, straining around in the seat to watch their foe. No shots had been fired, that was a good sign. Lulu and her men were clearly reluctant to fire towards the ground. They were now watching and waiting for their time to strike.

The sky above them was starting to lighten.

"It's getting light." Eden pulled out her phone. "That's good news. I think." She found the information she was looking for. "Sunrise is in thirteen minutes. That gives me an idea."

"This better be a good one, because we can't keep doing this." Baxter paused as they reached a junction. A highway ran in both directions. Ahead of them The Giza Plateau stretched out, the Pyramids floating on unlit sands.

"That way," Eden said, pointing directly across The Plateau.

Twenty feet below a police car screamed to a halt and an officer leapt out. He held on to the car door to prevent himself being blown over by the downdraft.

"We'll have the whole Air Force here in a few minutes." Baxter adjusted the controls, and they picked up speed.

"It will all be over by sunrise," Eden said, her fingers flying across her phone.

They swung across The Plateau, just twenty feet above the ground.

"How can you be so confident?" Baxter said, navigating them carefully between The Great Pyramid and the Second Pyramid. Sand billowed in great clouds all around them now.

"Because we've got Helios on our side."

They reached the other side of The Plateau and slid back in between the buildings.

"Now you're making no sense at all."

"We will use one of the oldest tactics of all time." Looking at The Pyramids now behind them, Eden was reminded of Little Mo, now lost to that subterranean world. They needed to finish this for him. "We will attack at sunrise."

49

"WHAT ARE THEY PLAYING AT?" King hissed, peering down at the helicopter flying just above a highway. Although the traffic was light at this time of day, motorists stopped and gawked up at the low flying machine. "They're causing chaos. They'll have the authorities all over the place in minutes."

"What do you want to do?" Abdul said, keeping the Tiger high and slow.

King snarled. She'd hoped for this to be over already, but then patience always paid dividends. "Keep back and watch. Don't shoot here, it'll be too messy. At some point they'll either ditch the chopper and run for it, or they'll leave the city. Either way, we'll be waiting."

BAXTER CUT the chopper carefully through the narrow streets surrounding The Plateau. Reaching a highway, they turned south and accelerated. The road was wide enough for the copter to fly down the center with ease, just making sure to stay well above the streetlights and signs. The traffic had picked up too. Some drivers slowed and gazed at the low flying chopper, others seemed to continue unaffected. Maybe seeing strange things like this was a normal occurrence on the streets of Cairo.

"We've got less than ten minutes. We need to speed up," Eden said, checking the time on her phone.

"I'm still not sure about this plan of yours," Baxter said, reluctantly pushing the chopper faster. Buildings on both sides of the road blurred past.

"You have a better one, do you?" Eden quipped.

Baxter didn't reply, focusing on the tricky job of keeping the copter steady.

Eden turned and caught a glimpse of their pursuers. King had pulled back and was now keeping her distance.

That's perfect, Eden thought.

A shot hadn't been fired in several minutes. That's the way Eden wanted it to stay. The cloudless sky blanched slowly from purple to pink. In the next few minutes, the sun would rise, and this would all be over. Or so Eden hoped.

They streamed southbound, making use of the wide roads to keep a good speed. After a few minutes, Eden saw the stepped shape of The Pyramid of Djoser off to the right. For a moment she stared at the pyramid remembering the image of it she'd seen on the can of Sakara Beer. It seems like weeks ago.

Eden turned and gazed closely into the lightening sky on the left. The four chimneys of Cairo's South Power Station stretched upwards like claws.

Eden carefully reiterated the plan to Baxter, who nodded slowly. They had one shot at this and even then, it was a very long shot.

Ninety seconds before the sun was due to peek over the

horizon, Baxter pulled back on the controls. The chopper leapt into the sky. The buildings beneath them grew small as they ascended first fifty, then one hundred, then two hundred feet.

Baxter turned his head and caught a glimpse of the other craft powering towards them. In the budding daylight he recognized it as a Tiger, the larger military cousin of their own Eurocopter. The pilot in the other chopper wasted no time. The Tiger accelerated forwards, the nose mounted gun blazing. Fortunately, they were too far for an accurate shot and bullets sailed wildly off to one side.

"It's going to work. We've got this," Eden said. Baxter hoped she was right. "Go. Now!"

Baxter hit the throttle. The Eurocopter lurched forwards, pinning them all into their seats. Their pursuers were still several hundred feet behind, but gaining all the time.

Eden gripped hold of the arm rests, her eyes focused on their target ahead. She wasn't looking at the power station itself, but the mesh of electricity wires streaming out of both sides. Strung between pylons, the high-power cables were almost invisible in the darkness.

The Eurocopter pounded forward now, reaching its top speed of nearly three-hundred kilometers an hour. The engine noise built from the whine that Eden had got used to, into an all-out howl. They screamed over a neighborhood of large villas and then out over the Nile. Eden looked down at the inky surface of the river, inching its way towards the Mediterranean.

"Twenty seconds," Eden shouted. The sun would rise in twenty seconds. Only then would they know if this mad plan would work.

"Now," King roared, forcing herself forwards in the seat. "Take them down, right now."

Abdul gunned the Tiger's twin engines. The machine roared forwards, hundreds of pounds of thrust surging through the machine.

King fought against the acceleration, trying to force her back into the seat. Like jet fuel in the engine above their heads, adrenaline pounded in her veins. She gritted her teeth and narrowed her gaze. No one stood in her way. She wanted to witness the moment they finally nailed the other helicopter and sent it spinning into the waters of the Nile.

"They'll be breakfast for the crocodiles," King muttered, reveling at the thought.

The higher-powered Tiger gained on the Eurocopter in seconds. It was like an eagle and a pigeon in a fight to the death. When they were within range, Sharif squeezed the trigger. The machine gun bellowed, spitting scorching lead at thirty rounds a second. King grinned, focused totally on the upcoming demise of the other helicopter, and along with it, Eden Black.

"Get closer to the water. Down! Down!" Eden said.

Baxter did what he was told and pulled the chopper down, increasing the speed further. Great white circles spun out across the surface of the river.

Eden peered behind them. The other helicopter was almost on top of them now. The gun blazed. Baxter lurched the chopper to the right. Eden's muscles ached from the movement.

Just a few hundred feet away the barely visible tangle of powerlines reared up like a wall of crisscrossing wires. Eden tried to calculate the distance and the time, but it didn't seem to help.

Baxter inched the chopper upwards, his hands nervously handling the controls now.

Then, all at once, it happened.

Over the horizon, which had been promising to split with sunlight, the great ball of the morning sun emerged. It shot through powerlines, through the windscreen and straight into Eden's eyes.

"Pull up, now!" Eden shouted, squinting.

As she'd expected against the dazzling African sun, the power lines were completely invisible. She had no idea how close they were, but it couldn't be far.

Baxter heaved back on the controls, forcing them into a near-vertical climb. The Eurocopter groaned and stuttered, protesting at the sudden movement. But reliably, it climbed, forcing Eden and Baxter hard into their seats. They shot upwards, missing the highest power line by twenty feet.

They spun into a turn. Everything inside the chopper shook and rattled against its tethers. An alarm sounded, warning Baxter that the move was too much for the machine. They slowed aggressively and jarred somewhere into a hovering halt, just in time to see the destruction.

HARSH SUNLIGHT STREAMED into the cab of the Tiger. King squinted, trying to block the light out, while still watching their prey. She raised her hand and tried to block out the light, but it made no difference. The scene in front of them danced and spun as her eyes struggled to adjust.

Sharif kept the trigger depressed, peppering whatever was before them with bullets. Sparks flashed as the bullets struck something. Excitement flared in King's stomach in the hope they'd hit the other craft. King blinked hard several times, unable to make sense of what she saw. When her eyes finally achieved their focus again, the blood in her veins chilled liquid nitrogen. She physically shuddered. Her hands covered her mouth. She tried to speak, but fear had swollen her tongue to the size of a dead viper. She leaned forwards and slapped Abdul on the arm, pointing uselessly through the windshield.

Looming up in front of them, crisscrossing their path like barbed wire in the Somme, countless high-power electrical cables blocked their way.

"Move!" King roared, finally gaining her ability to speak. "Move now! Up!"

She grabbed Abdul's arm and shouted again.

The Angolan, finally registering the threat for himself, heaved up on the controls. The Tiger bounced, an alarm sounded, then all too late, the machine began to climb.

FOR LONG SECONDS the Eurocopter hung in the air, as though dangling on an invisible string. Eden's heart hammered in her chest, audible even over the deafening engine of the chopper. She watched, unblinking, as pure destruction ensued.

The pursuing helicopter, travelling at several hundred miles an hour, powered on. Then all at once, the chopper climbed aggressively. Forward motion battled with the desired upwards motion. For the duration of a heart beat, the Tiger climbed. But their speed was just too great. The machine barreled on, slamming through the uppermost cables with its belly. Two of the high-voltage cables snapped. They whipped around like mad snakes, spewing lightening forks.

The chopper spun in mid-air. Its tail whipped around, catching one of the cables with its back rotor. The whole body of the chopper appeared to come alive with buzzing electricity. It shuddered and sparked.

The forward motion continued, pushing The Tiger through another line of power cables. The rotors severed two of the wires, before catching a third and snapping off, spinning like throwing knives towards the ground. The chopper jarred forwards but was lodged now. The great machine groaned and howled. Jet fuel poured from its ruptured tanks. It lurched downwards, tearing wires from their mounts for several miles in both directions. When the forward motion had all but stopped, the copter sunk towards the ground, resting like a dead fly in a spider's web.

Pouring jet fuel caught in one of the sparks and suddenly fire swept across the body of the craft. For half a second it burned on the surface and then the tank combusted. The explosion thundered through the air, shaking the Eurocopter still hovering several hundred feet away. The detonation reverberated several times. It was even audible to Eden, Baxter and Athena watching from the Eurocopter.

"Did nobody tell her power was dangerous?" Athena said weakly from the backseat.

Eden turned and looked at the other woman.

"That's totally my line," Eden said, smiling.

"Whatever, but do you think you could get us home now? I don't feel so good."

Eden turned to Baxter. "What do you say, Captain?"

50

SITTING at anchor twenty miles from the Egyptian coast, the Balonia rose and fell gently on the calm afternoon waves. Although the sun was still high in the sky, its trail danced gently across the water's surface.

Eden lay back on a sun bed, squinting into the dazzling sky. She had a pair of sunglasses on the table beside her but liked the feel of the overpowering sun. It was after all, the thing that had saved their lives, and sent Lulu King to her death. Maybe there was some truth in the old talk of the Sun God protecting them.

Three days had passed since Baxter, Athena and Eden had returned from Egypt. Stopping briefly to refuel, they had sped back to the Balonia, radioing ahead so that the yacht's small but capable medical team could prepare to immediately treat Athena's injuries.

Athena had been stretchered from the chopper and whisked to the infirmary the moment they'd landed. Eden had yet to see her but had heard encouraging news. Despite the improvement in Athena's condition, her limp body being carried away from the chopper was an image Eden couldn't seem to shake.

"I think we're about done with this," said Catherine, a research technician who doubled as one of the medical team. It seemed everyone aboard the Balonia fulfilled two or three different roles. Eden didn't yet understand what everyone did, let alone know what her place in the system might be.

"This might sting a little," Catherine said, preparing to remove the needle from the crook of Eden's arm. Athena had lost a lot of blood from her wound and was currently in need of frequent transfusions. Fortunately, both Eden and another member of the team were the same blood type, so they'd been giving blood as often as safe to do so.

Catherine unhooked the bag of blood and held it up to the light. She turned to look at Eden. "How are you feeling? You know, with everything that's going on."

Eden, still squinting against the sun, glanced up at the woman. Catherine was in early middle age with the sort of no-nonsense personality Eden instantly warmed to. She spoke with a broad northern English accent.

"Okay, I think," Eden said, shrugging. "The last few days have been a bit of a whirlwind."

Catherine nodded knowingly and pointed out towards the sea. "You see that over there?"

Eden looked but couldn't see anything beyond the glittering waves. "No?"

"That's a special place we reserve for moaners and pessimists. As far away from the rest of us as possible."

Eden barked a humorless laugh. "I just can't help but feel like I dragged Athena into this. She almost died on that chopper."

"Here we go." Catherine crouched down beside Eden.

"Athena is a very skilled operative working for The Council. She has seen more dangerous situations than you and I have had hot dinners. She will be back and fighting fit in no time."

Eden exhaled. Maybe it was the loss of blood, or the chaos of the last few days, but she just felt weak right down to her core.

"Tell you what." Catherine poked Eden's shoulder with a chubby finger. "Give me five minutes to get little missy in there hooked up with this good stuff, and you can pop in and see her. I think she'd like to see someone other than me."

A few minutes later, Eden stood outside the door of Athena's cabin.

"Just five minutes, though," Catherine said, bustling out of the room. "The woman needs her beauty sleep."

Eden knocked gently on the door. She paused for a moment, trying to force the image of Athena's pale and unconscious body from her mind's eye.

Athena was propped up in bed, watching a news report on the television. Eden was pleased to see how well she looked. The color had returned to her face and her eyes sparkled with life.

"How are you doing?" Eden said, nervously crossing the room. "Stupid question, I know. I mean, considering..."

"Apparently I'm very lucky to be alive," Athena said, muting the TV.

Eden nodded, her face serious.

"But that's nonsense, isn't it?" Athena said. "I'm lucky that I'm not a single cell organism or wasn't born as a slug."

Eden risked a smile, a weight of worry lifting from her shoulders.

Athena beckoned for Eden to sit on the edge of the bed.

"I do hate it when people say that," Eden said. "It doesn't make any sense at all."

"What makes me feel even less lucky is that I've been told when I'm finally off this, I've got to take it easy for a couple months." Athena pointed at the IV drip.

Eden made quote marks with her fingers. "Take it easy, what's that?"

"I know, right? How boring. At least we made headlines, though." Athena nodded towards the television. She picked up the remote again and turned up the sound.

"Three people died on Monday when their helicopter collided with power lines just outside Cairo. One of the dead is thought to be Lulu King, daughter of the late Raymond King and heiress to the vast King Industries empire. Authorities are investigating as to how the accident, which left half of Cairo without power, happened. Police in England have also revealed that they were looking to extradite King on suspicion of murder. They report that hair fibers matching Miss King's were found on three bodies discovered in a woodland near London."

Eden almost laughed at how well the cover up had come together. Learning of King's plans to implicate her in murder, Eden had instructed a contact to remove her truck and any evidence she'd been there at all from the woodland. The truck was now waiting in a warehouse a few hundred miles away for Eden to return to, should she want to. Then after the body was reported to the police, one of Winslow's contacts dropped King's hair fibers right into the middle of the investigation. It was a fitting end to the whole sorry mess, Eden thought.

The TV news reader went on to the next story. Athena clicked off the sound again and peered curiously at Eden.

"How did you..."

Eden smiled.

"Actually, don't tell me." Athena held up her hands in mock surrender. "Whatever you and your father have cooked up, I don't want to know about it."

"You know, if you did feel well enough to come back to work sooner, I reckon we could break into the lab and steal the doctor's notes," Eden said.

"Absolutely not. I'm not breaking into anything for at least a week." Athena folded her arms and then winced in pain. "Apparently I would have died in that helicopter if it hadn't been for your rudimentary first aid."

"Rudimentary is definitely the word. Unlike you, I can't do everything..."

"Yet," Athena interrupted with a grin. "Maybe there are a few things you can learn with us."

"I'm not sure," Eden looked through the window at the gently sparkling waters of the Mediterranean. "Living on a boat with a bunch of highly skilled secret agents sounds a bit boring."

"Maybe, but at least we don't eat rehydrated food every day."

Eden narrowed her eyes. "How did you know—ah Beaumont, the little snake! He said he liked that meal. That's my specialty."

Athena laughed out loud. "Give it a try, alright, you'll do that?"

"Sure," Eden nodded, staring once again out of the window. "I think I can give it a try."

"I've actually got a surprise for you," Athena said, her eyes now sparkling mischievously.

"What?" Eden said, narrowing her gaze.

"If you look out of the window... just about now," Athena said.

Eden walked to the window. Athena's room looked out

over the Balonia's rear deck, on which the Eurocopter was parked.

Eden watched as a team of crew untethered the chopper from its fixing.

"I don't think I ever want to go on a helicopter again," Eden said, glancing back at Athena in the bed.

"Keep watching," Athena barked.

"What! I don't get it. What am I supposed to be looking at?" Then Eden saw something that physically riveted her to the spot. Her jaw dropped open. She stuttered several inaudible words.

Down on the deck below them, several members of the Balonia's crew carried an object across the deck and loaded it carefully into the chopper. Although Eden recognized the item instantly, it took her a few seconds to make sense of what she saw.

"That's the Ark of the Covenant! Why is the Ark of the Covenant here?"

Another group of crew carried two large flight cases which no doubt contained the recovered manuscripts of the Book of Enoch and the Book of Giants.

"What's going on?" Eden said, whipping around to face Athena. "Didn't King take—"

Athena laughed out loud, real color returning to her skin now. "A bit of class deception. Simple really," Athena said, recovering enough from her laughter to explain. "King had a team all set up ready to take The Ark of the Covenant straight out of the country in a cargo jet. All we did was just step in and impersonate them."

"You did what?" Eden still didn't totally understand.

"We had some of our team turn up at the laundromat, pretending to be the extraction crew that King had arranged. She was so excited to get it back to her research facility, that she handed the thing straight over. Never even noticed. Those two men she had traipsing around after her even helped us load it into the van, apparently."

"So now we find out how it works and…"

Athena shook her head, interrupting Eden's excitement. Eden's face dropped.

"You're not going to like this bit," Athena said.

"No," Eden said, shaking head. "Tell me we're not?"

Athena nodded slowly. "Yep. We're going to give it back to the King Estate."

The color drained from Eden's face. She now looked like the one that needed the IV drip.

"But don't you worry," Athena said, grinning sweetly. "Your father has a plan."

Deep within the bowels of the ship something started to grumble. Several deep clunking noises echoed through the superstructure.

"I'm getting really sick of my father's plans," Eden said, turning away from the window and walking back into the room. "What's that noise?"

"We've started to move," Athena said.

"What? Why?" Eden turned, her brow furrowed.

"No idea. I don't know where we're going, either. That's part of the fun of this job, we don't really find out until we get there. But it looks like that's been decided for you, though, right?"

"What's that?"

"You're coming with us,"

Eden narrowed her eyes at the other woman. "I'm coming with you, for now."

51

Two floors above Athena's cabin, the man known as both Alexander Winslow and Helios, reclined behind his desk. He knitted his fingers together, placed them on top of his head and stretched.

Feeling his tired muscles tense, he closed his eyes and let the events of the past few days roll across his memory. Things had gone almost exactly the way he'd predicted. He smiled to himself.

It was a good result. The Ark of The Covenant would soon be making its way to the free market now that Lulu King wouldn't be able to control it. Soon it would be studied by scientists across the globe. Some of these scientists, of course, would use what they found for personal gain, or even for bad things, that was just part of being human. Others though, Helios knew, would put it to work for the betterment of humankind. As with any new technology, adoption and acceptance would take time. But the genie was out of the bottle now, and love, money, or wild horses wouldn't be putting it back in again.

Then, like a ghost ship in the fog, an enigma rose

through the mists of Winslow's thoughts. As though an electric current jolted through his body, Winslow jerked forwards and sat upright, placing his elbows on the green leather tabletop.

It was a mystery. To Winslow, a man who was used to having things worked out well ahead of them occurring, that felt unsettling.

He thought through the moving parts of the case again. When Beaumont had first suggested that Aloma's tablets referred to this much fabled Ark of the Covenant, Winslow had started to formulate a plan. He'd been watching Lulu King for some time and knew that she could be trusted to do whatever it took to fulfil her selfish aims—all he had to do was make sure her aims aligned with his. Then throwing Eden into the mix, as a way of bringing her into The Council, was a stroke of genius. Eden's sense of righteousness would motivate her straight into action, couple that with giving King the footage of Winslow at Cairo airport, and Eden would be in it for the long haul.

He'd even known that Eden wouldn't be unable to leave any loose ends untied. She was bound to go in for a final showdown. Winslow had instructed Baxter and Athena to help her in any way possible, which was fortunate with the way things turned out.

But still, there was something that troubled him. Something which didn't make sense. Well, Winslow corrected himself, it made perfect sense. He just couldn't understand how it made sense.

The phone on the desk buzzed, pulling Winslow out of his thoughts. He reached over and pressed the button.

"Captain Baxter to see you sir."

"Send him in, thanks." Winslow shook the troubling thoughts from his mind and stood.

"How are you feeling after your ordeal?" Winslow asked as Baxter entered the room.

"All fine. It could have ended up a lot worse. That daughter of yours is pretty good under pressure."

"Yes, that she is." Winslow lost focus for a second. "If only she'd put some of the work into planning before getting into a difficult situation to begin with."

"Maybe that's the curse of youth?"

"I suppose that's true." Winslow scowled in thought.

"I think you both complement each other rather well," Baxter said. "You're excellent at tactical forethought, and she's inspired on the ground. Do you think she'll be staying with us on the Balonia?"

Sensing an unusual warmth to the question, Winslow turned to look at Baxter. He studied the younger man for a second.

"I sense that you would like her to."

Baxter blushed.

"Of course, I would too," Winslow added quickly, curtailing Baxter's embarrassment. "She would be an asset to the organization, that I know for sure. I've asked Athena to sow that seed on our behalf. If anyone can get an idea across to Eden, it's Athena. You say they worked well together on the last deployment?"

"They did. After some initial friction, it was like they've been partners for years."

"They're like stray cats." Winslow grinned. "They've got to work out the hierarchy before anything can get done." Winslow's expression melted into one of concern. "Have you re-done the tests?"

"Yes, I've seen to them personally." Baxter opened the manilla folder he'd been carrying and drew out a plastic evidence bag. He placed the folder on the desk and passed the evidence bag to Winslow.

Winslow held the bag up to the light and examined the contents. A small golden vial on a chain sat in the bottom of the bag. Inside the vial, several strands of hair floated in a clear liquid.

"And the results?" Winslow placed the bag carefully on the table.

"The same as the previous two times we'd taken the test."

"And there's no chance?"

"That the vial had been tampered with? None. Our technicians tested part of the seal they had to take from the vial to access the contents."

"And?"

"It was at least three thousand years old."

Winslow shook his head slowly. He turned his back on Baxter and walked slowly to the window overlooking the sea. Several seconds of silence passed between the men.

"What are your thoughts?" Baxter asked.

"It's one of those things I really don't like, it's a mystery. First, we find Eden mentioned by name in a set of hieroglyphs at the entrance to The Hall. Has anyone been able to offer an interpretation as to what that could mean?"

"None at all. We've asked several experts at universities all around the world, all have come back with similar, or even identical translations."

"Now we have this vial which was taken from around the neck of a golden statue in The Hall of Records which looked a lot like Eden..."

"It was almost identical. Eerily similar. I wish I had been able to take a photo."

Winslow bit his lip in thought. "And inside that vial," he

continued, "are strands of hair, somehow preserved for several thousand years which match Eden's DNA one hundred percent."

Both men stood silently for a few seconds.

"Things are moving much more quickly than I had imagined," Winslow muttered, almost inaudibly. "But then, time is relative."

"Pardon?" Baxter asked, not understanding.

"Nothing, nothing," Winslow descended into silence again.

"Are you going to tell her about this?" Baxter asked, finally.

Winslow stood motionless, deep in thought for another few seconds.

"Not yet. Although she'll find out soon enough. I was hoping we'd have a little more time before facing our next challenge, but clearly not." Winslow turned to face Baxter. "It's time for us to move again. You prepare the crew. I'll send coordinates to the bridge within the next few minutes."

Baxter agreed and strode across the room. At the door, he turned back to face Winslow. The older man stood, staring out of the window, his eyes already glazed over in thought.

"Here we go again," Baxter muttered to himself, unable to stop a smile breaking across his face.

EPILOGUE

King Industries Headquarters, New York. Two months later.

THE GLASS and chrome of the King Industries tower, a skyscraper on the edge of Central Park, shone in the bright morning light. The tower and the businesses which occupied it, had been quiet since the murder of its charismatic owner, Raymond King, in the penthouse suite some months ago. It seemed bad luck continued as Raymond's only heir, his daughter Lulu, met her untimely end just weeks after her father.

A pair of journalists hurried across the street and up the front stairs of the tower. One of them, a woman in her twenties, paused to look up at the imposing building. Once a symbol of corporate power the world over, the tower had become something of a misnomer now that the company that owned it could barely afford to keep the lights on. A young woman, her black hair streaming around her face in New York's unforgiving breeze, hurried on inside.

"Here for the press conference," Eden Black said to the

two-person security team. She flashed her fake press card—which suggested she worked for The New York Times—dumped her bag on the belt for the x-ray machine and stepped through the security scanner. Beside Eden, Athena showed her press card too.

"Second floor," the beefy security guard barked. The man squinted lazily at the identification cards, then went back to examining Athena's legs as she trotted through the scanner.

Eden and Athena grabbed their bags from the belt and hurried up the stairs to the second floor.

A headline mainstay for decades, Raymond and Lulu had been well known to the media on both sides of the Atlantic. Often appearing at sporting events, political rallies, or celebrity fundraisers, the press lapped up their flippant comments on clearly very complex issues. Now in death, it seemed as though their notoriety had only increased.

It was fair to say that the last two months had been nothing short of disastrous for King Industries. Since the death of their chairman, and then his heir, fighting amongst the executive board and the insecure future of the company had resulted in plummeting share prices, various loans being recalled, and the company falling into dramatic liquidation. Three weeks ago, administrators had arrived at The Tower to salvage anything valuable from the sinking company, before it was too late.

Eden and Athena pushed into the hall filled with journalists from around the globe and settled into seats right at the back. Eden removed an audio recording device from her bag and pressed a few buttons. Athena dug out a pen and paper and prepared to take notes.

Aboard the Balonia, now making its way to their next position, Helios knew what was about to be announced. He had, through various streams of influence, appointed the administrators.

Two nervous men in grey pinstripe suits stepped up to the dais. One of them shuffled forward and tapped the microphone. The sound thundered through the loudspeakers, followed by a howl of feedback.

The man reeled backwards, startled. He shuffled his papers on the lectern and then began. He started by thanking the assembled crowd for their attendance and then listed some of the company's assets. Many, including the tower itself, were to be sold in auction the following month.

"As for King Industries' research and development subdivision," the administrator said, some minutes later, "which includes all research projects currently underway, and historical records of their previous work."

Eden and Athena strained forwards in their seats.

"Based on the time and money Mr. King and his daughter used to give to charities, and their unceasing work in finding affordable power solutions for all."

Eden almost laughed out loud at the platitude.

"The department itself will be dissolved, but findings and research will be placed in the public domain for the benefit of all."

Eden listened to the rest of the statement in stunned silence. Whilst her father had said this was the outcome he'd arranged, Eden had still expected something to go wrong. Sitting there, amid the noise of the press conference, Eden wondered whether it was time she trusted others just a little bit more.

When the administrator finally finished, folded over his notes, and asked if there were any questions, Athena tapped Eden on the arm. "Let's get out of here," she whispered, nodding towards the door. Around them, the assembled journalists shouted and waved to get their questions across. On the dais, the administrator held out his hands in surrender.

"One at a time please. One at a time!" His voice came all too quietly through the loudspeakers.

Eden and Athena slid unseen out of the conference hall, paced down the stairs and out through the doors.

Eden dumped her press badge in a trash can and then turned to look at Central Park across the street. Filled with people enjoying the afternoon—families, dog walkers, runners—it reflected the city's life and diversity.

"These people don't know how big a victory they've had today, do they?" Eden turned to Athena.

"Nope, and they never will." Athena took a deep breath.

Eden scowled, watching a woman with two young children wander into the park. "They should know. And for the Kings to be remembered like heroes, that's just wrong."

Athena laughed out loud. "These peoples' future is a little bit more secure now than it was yesterday. Does it really matter who gets the credit for that?"

"I suppose not," Eden huffed, although it still felt like a bitter pill to swallow.

"What time did we say we'd be back?"

Eden glanced at her watch. "About an hour from now."

Baxter was due to pick them up from a helipad on the outskirts of the city.

Athena stared out at the park. "Just because the people of the world don't know about today's victory, doesn't mean we can't celebrate."

Eden shot Athena a look. "What do you have in mind?"

"I know a place on Bleecker Street that serves the best Martinis on the planet."

"But my dad's expecting us back," Eden said

"Your dad's expecting us back!" Athena laughed out loud. "If there's one thing you need to learn about your dad, it's that he knows exactly what you're going to do, even before you do." Athena put her arm through Eden's and led her down the stairs.

"I've noticed that, but I've no idea how he does it," Eden replied. "And hold on a minute, I thought you lived on the Balonia the whole time, how do you know about this amazing place that serves Martinis on Bleecker Street?"

"Now that's a good story. I was on a case here in New York several years ago and..."

Listening to Athena's story, smiling in the cold afternoon air, for the first time in as long as she could remember, Eden let someone else lead the way.

AUTHOR'S NOTE

Thank you for reading The Giza Protocol.

I hope you've enjoyed continuing Eden's adventure, this time taking her to the land of sand and pharaohs—Egypt!

I've loved bringing Eden and her friends to life. It's been my pleasure and privilege to entertain you for a few hours.

If you read the author's note at the back of The Ark Files, I think you know what's coming next... I can tell you that there are parts of the story you've just read that could well be true.

Yet again, the idea for this story came after talking with a friend of mine, who will remain anonymous. He has spent his life researching many mysteries, including those featured in The Ark Files and The Giza Protocol. He really is the sort of friend every author needs!

It wasn't until I looked into it, though, that I realized how little evidence there is for the mainstream view of much of our history. Take the Pyramids of Giza as an example; at school we learned they were giant mausoleums built for pharaohs. That makes sense until you learn that no bodies were ever found inside. Also, a few hundred miles further south, Pharaohs were found buried in The Valley of the Kings. Their tombs are decorated in the most wonderful hieroglyphs, which somehow still retain their color today. There are no hieroglyphs inside The Pyramids of Giza. Clearly this isn't proof that The Pyramids weren't used as tombs, but it's enough doubt to make you think about it twice, right?

There are also a growing number of historians who are coming around to the idea that The Pyramids and other structures in the world are much older than commonly believed. These historians suggest that the geology does not match the established view. This not only throws into question why such structures were built, but who built them in the first place. I won't go into details here as we'll explore that in Eden's next adventure. In the meantime, should you be interested in alternative opinions, look up the works of Ian Lawton, Andrew Collins, Robert Bauval, and Graham Hancock.

The Sun Temple appearing in the receding waters of Lake Nasser is true. Unfortunately, with the changing climates of our planet, this sort of thing happens frequently. The temple isn't in the place I said it was here, and nor does it contain instructions to find the Hall of Records—or at least, I don't think it does. But who really knows?

As for The Hall of Records appearing beneath The Giza Plateau, this was originally envisioned by Edgar Cayce (1877–1945) who was an American clairvoyant. One day, during his meditations, he pictured being led into the hall and coined the phrase "Hall of Records." Although no one had called it this before, many had referred to this mythical place as "Seth's Treasure Vault." Ancient historians such as Herodotus and Flavius Josephus describe a completely different history for The Giza Plateau than modern historians do. Then there is also the Book of Enoch and now lost pages of The Book of Giants which are being translated, and some pages which are contained in the Dead Sea Scroll texts. It seems that, bit by bit, ancient historian's writings are being vindicated, yet modern historians still chose to ignore these facts and prefer to guess rather than rely on writings closer to the periods in question.

As for Little Mo's suggestion that The Giza Plateau was a representation of our Solar System, that might well be the case. Twenty years ago, Terence Maxwell proposed that The Giza Plateau was a representation of The Solar System accounting for all ten pyramids in correct order as follows, Mercury, Venus, Earth, Mars, Ceres, Jupiter, Saturn, Uranus, Neptune plus one trans-Neptunian object. We know that NASA and astronomers have been trying to locate a 10th planet for some time in the region of the constellation of Libra. Though maybe more importantly, this work also showed an 11th anti-typical pyramid that was also mentioned by ancient historians. Giorgio Tsoukalos has suggested that Teotihuacan and Stonehenge are representations of The Solar System, so why not The Giza Plateau?

What about The Ark of the Covenant and Stable Element 115? It's true that scientists are constantly searching for a stable element that can be used in power generation. Of course, for the last seventy years we've been able to split uranium atoms during a fission process to create carbon-free power—we call this nuclear power and create a good chunk of the world's electricity that way. The problem is that uranium is incredibly unstable. It is also effective for just a tiny percentage of its life span, then it has to be kept somewhere for several hundred-thousand years before it's safe again. On the side, that's an incredible thing to consider. The generally accepted age of The Pyramids is just a tiny fraction of the amount of the time it takes some nuclear waste to become safe. A stable element with a shorter half-life, is 'the holy grail' solution for this. Imagine a situation where your car didn't need fuel, or your house could run for years without connection to an energy grid. It wouldn't just be environmentally fantastic, but it would improve the lives of millions.

The cynic in me wonders, however, how long the Raymond Kings of this world will stand in the way of this change. Did Nikola Tesla find a way to produce free energy for the world, only for it to be suppressed by the powers that be because there would be no way to charge the population for it?

Linking this to The Ark of the Covenant was a stretch, but the Ark was said to have some electricity-like characteristics: people who touched it were struck down (like an electric shock), it reportedly floated above the ground like a giant electromagnet, and the construction of it was a bit like a modern-day battery. It seemed too good not to put the two of them together here.

This also plays on the idea that The Pyramids themselves were used in power generation. Christopher Dunn proposes a very intriguing theory regarding the function of the Queen's Chamber, which is buried deep within The Great Pyramid. There are two narrow shafts which lead down to this chamber. In one of these shafts, traces of hydrochloric acid (HCl) have been found and in the other, zinc chloride ($ZnCl_2$). Mixing these two substances together produces hydrogen (H_2) gas. Dunn suggests that the Queen's Chamber was the engine of a great power plant, where hydrogen was created to be turned in to piezoelectric or electromagnetic energy.

Element 115 was made infamous by Robert Lazar and his

revelations regarding Area 51. However, Moscovium is a synthetic element with the symbol Mc and atomic number 115. It was first synthesized in 2003 by a joint team of Russian and American scientists at the Joint Institute for Nuclear Research (JINR) in Dubna, Russia. In December 2015, it was recognized as one of four new elements. Michio Kaku an American theoretical physicist has produced some good podcasts and programs related to element 115, which are worth view.

Is any of it actually true? Honestly, I don't know. But it could be, and that makes a very cool story, right?

In January 2023 I took a trip to Egypt to research for this book. I had in fact written the book's first draft by then, but the trip helped me refine all of the details. My time in Egypt also helped me breathe more life into the characters here too, as they were inspired by the people I met on the way. I've put together a guide to my trip, including photos of the locations that inspired these settings and travel recommendations, should you want to make a trip there. If you are able, I would recommend it. It feels like such a shame to me that some people still believe places like Egypt are unsafe to visit. The people we met on our travels there were some of the kindest and most hospitable I've ever had the pleasure of meeting on the road.

Head here to check out my travel recommendations: www.LukeRichardsonAuthor.com/Egypt

Egypt is a wonderful and fascinating place to visit. It's full of history, stories, myths, and legends—which makes it the perfect place for a writer like me.

Back to the person who inspired this story. He prefers

his anonymity for now. He's working on something in the background, which could be very interesting.

Thank you for joining me on this adventure. I can't wait to see you again soon with Eden's next instalment, perhaps it will be Eden who unveils the physical evidence to the world...

Luke

February 2023

THE ATLANTIS AGENDA

Eden returns in THE ATLANTIS AGENDA, start reading TODAY.

DID YOU ENJOY MEETING ALLISSA?

"He won't get far," Allissa said, pointing at a stream of liquid gushing from the vehicle's rear.
"You cut the fuel line?" Eden asked, looking at the women in a different light.
"I'd say he'll get ten miles away maximum," Allissa said. "That's a week's walk to the nearest town."
"How did you know..."
Allissa turned to face Eden. "I saw you take those men on. Strange skill for an English teacher. I think it's fair to say there are things we both don't know about each other."
"Agreed," Eden said.

In the first chapters of this book, Eden had some help from another very special young woman.

Allissa Stockwell is the co-star in the first series I ever wrote. She appears alongside her anxious detective partner, Leo. In each of the books as they travel the globe in the search of missing people.

If you like the sound of thrilling mysteries set in distant and intriguing lands, then you'll love this series.

As you may be taking a chance on a new series, I would love to give you the first book for free. That way, there's no risk for you.

Tap here or copy the weblink into your browser:
https://www.lukerichardsonauthor.com/kathmandu

CAN A PRICELESS PAINTING VANISH INTO THIN AIR?

Eden Black meets Ernest Dempsey's Adriana Villa

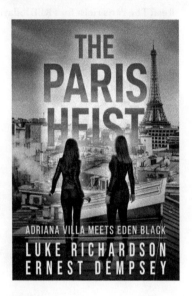

Ten years ago, Bernard Moreau baffled police by stealing a Picasso from the Modern Art Museum. He was arrested and imprisoned, but the painting was never found.

Now, back on the streets, all eyes are on Moreau. But he's a skilled thief and isn't going to make it easy.

EDEN BLACK can't stand corruption and the theft of priceless art. This case reeks of them both. Heading to Paris, she vows to return the Picasso to its rightful home as soon as possible.

ADRIANA VILLA works alone, always, that's the rule. So, when she sees another woman following her mark, things get heated.

To find the painting before a dirty police inspector with a score to settle, the pair must put their egos aside and work together. What they discover shows that nothing is as simple as it first seems.

THE PARIS HEIST is an up-tempo novella which will keep you pinned to the pages until the very end. If you like the sound of a race against the clock, action packed, adventure thriller, set amongst the blissful Parisian streets, you'll love THE PARIS HEIST.

Read The Paris Heist for FREE today!

ABOUT THE AUTHOR

First of all, thanks so much for taking an interest in my writing. My books are the culmination of years of travelling, dreaming and writing. I'm so excited to share them with you.

My journey towards writing, like most, wasn't straight-forward. I've always loved stories, but it wasn't until my thir-ties that I actually put pen to paper. I think I needed to see and experience the world a bit before writing about it.

I grew up in the South of England, near Hastings, and moved to Nottingham for university. After that I worked as a nightclub DJ for a few years - I still do from time to time.

In 2013 I trained to be an English teacher. Helping young people realize and enjoy their creativity was wonderful. But, as many teachers will testify, it's not a job that sits well with other hobbies and interests. So, in 2020 I made the decision to leave the classroom and focus on my writing, travel, and spend time with friends and family.

My stories are part adventure, part mystery, and always rely heavily on the places I go and the people I meet.

Where do you want to go now?

BOOK REVIEWS

If you've enjoyed this book I would appreciate a review.

Reviews are essential for three reasons. First, they encourage people to take a chance on an author they've never heard of. Second, bookselling websites use them to decide what books to recommend through their search engine. And third, I love to hear what you think!

Having good reviews really can make a massive difference to new authors like me.

It'll take you no longer than two minutes, and will mean the world to me.

Head to the place where you bought this book, scroll down, and click 'write a review.'

Thank you.

OTHER SERIES BY LUKE RICHARDSON

International Detectives

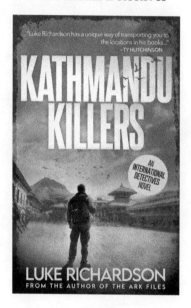

You visit a restaurant in a far-away city, only to find you're on the menu.

Leo Keane is sent abroad to track down Allissa, a politician's daughter who vanished two years ago in Kathmandu. But with a storm on the horizon and intrigue at every turn, Leo's mission may be more dangerous than he bargained for... A propulsive international thriller!

READ FREE TODAY

https://www.lukerichardsonauthor.com/kathmandu

Kickass Vigilantes

Justice is her beat

Her name is Kayla Stone

She is 'The Liberator'

The Liberator Series is a ferocious new collaboration between Luke Richardson and Steven Moore.

If you like Clive Cussler, Nick Thacker, Ernest Dempsey and Russel Blake, then you'll love this explosive series!

READ TODAY

THANK YOU!

Books are difficult to write.

Not a month goes by where I don't think it's "too hard," or "not worth it." Every time this happens — as though by magic — I get an email from a reader like you.

Some are simple messages of encouragement, others are heartfelt, each one shows me that I'm not doing this alone. Those connections have kept me going when all seemed lost, and given me purpose when I didn't see it myself.

A special heartfelt thank you to those who support me on Patreon. These people support me with a few dollars, pounds or euros a month. In exchange it's my pleasure to share my travels with them through postcards and other random gifts from the road.

Some Patreon supporters even get the opportunity to read my books early. If that resonates with you, check out my Patreon here.

Don't feel obliged, the fact you are here is more than enough.

https://www.patreon.com/lukerichardson

Thanks goes to (in alphabetical order):

Allison Valentine and The Haemocromatois Society

Anja Peerdeman

Frankie Nulph (thanks for letting me use your name!)

Fritzi Redgrave

James Colby Slater

Melody Highman

Ray Braun

Rosemary Kenny

Tim Birmingham

Valerie Richardson

Printed in the USA
CPSIA information can be obtained
at www.ICGtesting.com
LVHW041938230724
786273LV00011B/470

9 781739 352219